Picture courtesy of Les Millar

The author has been a journalist all his life – local newspapers, freelancing with British national papers, then working in film and TV publicity before returning to provincial newspapers as a military correspondent.

Forced to retire against his will twenty-one years ago, he continued with freelance and charity PR work.

Now 90, for the last eight years he has been the sole carer for a wife with Alzheimer's, but now she has moved into a care home for full-time medical care and he has resumed writing. Although he had published stories before, *The Songsters* is his first published novel.

This book is dedicated to Lorenz, Oscar, Richard, Ira, George, Cole, Jerome…and all those hundreds of other lyricists who have made me so happy over the years. And this humble dedication is also an apology to them for the dire lyrics (not theirs) that are included as part of the story…

Larry Signy

THE SONGSTERS

AUSTIN MACAULEY PUBLISHERS™

LONDON * CAMBRIDGE * NEW YORK * SHARJAH

A CIP catalogue record for this title is available from the British Library.

ISBN 9781528991131 (Paperback)
ISBN 9781528993135 (Hardback)
ISBN 9781528991148 (ePub e-book)

www.austinmacauley.com

First Published (2021)
Austin Macauley Publishers Ltd
25 Canada Square
Canary Wharf
London
E14 5LQ

With special thanks to:

- Richard Stilgoe (for his telephone interview).
- Andrew Kirk, one-time assistant curator at the Theatre Museum London (for his help on theatrical superstitions).
- And especially Scott McDaid, once a technician at the Glen Street Theatre in French's Forest, North Sydney, for taking time to show me round and explain the wonderful backstage mystic there.
- I should, perhaps, also mention Lord Lloyd Webber, who kindly agreed his staff could help – but whose people somehow continually managed to put off any meetings…and also music director, Gareth Valentine, who also promised (twice) to help, but then had trouble with his mobile phone, which always switched off whenever I consequently got through to fix a date and announced myself!

Overture

Every one of them was a stunning-looking girl or an Adonis, but as the cluster of chorus girls and boys walked calmly onto the stage behind the drawn curtain, most of them had a hard line of anxiety sketched on their beautiful features.

Opening night of a new show. Their living, their rent, their fame, their immediate future depended on how they were received.

As they slowly lined up, fiddling with shoulder straps, adjusting fishnet stocking seams, patting hair into place, wiping the odd corner of lipstick smooth, adjusting white tie and tails, and generally getting themselves prepared, they could hear the audience shuffling, coughing, and chattering softly through the closed heavy theatrical curtains.

Heavy stage lights flashed on, and as they checked their line and linked arms, some of the girls looked down and made sure their stomachs were drawn in. One or two coughed lightly showing more nervous tension, but in the main they were silent.

Front of house, the audience was almost in place. The photographers had snapped irreverently at any of the big-bosomed minor starlets who had turned up to pose, bigger name actors and actresses who had tried – not very hard – to slip by unnoticed, but turned on the smiles when the cameras focussed, and people who were famous for being famous tried to attract attention.

A new show. A big, glamorous musical.

On stage, the dulled sound of the audience as they took their seats came through the curtain, a curtain so lush and velvety from the front but with a ragged, torn lining stage-side.

On the other side, front of house, the orchestra was already in place, and as the house lights dimmed only the illuminations above the musicians' stands broke the dark around the closed stage. The audience quietened down, and as the conductor slipped onto his stand in front of them, there was a smattering of half-hearted applause. He raised his baton, and the first notes of the overture began to fill the giant auditorium. The audience quietened down.

The music the dancers had drilled to so well during rehearsals came through the curtain – soft at first, then growing loud, strident, blaring, but always tuneful. "Magic, those first notes of a new show," muttered the producer to himself.

In the wings, Danny Grover and Harry McIntyre watched and waited even more fearfully than the girls. It was their music. Their songs. Their first show.

After years of dreaming, months of working to find a way of bringing back the elegance and sounds of the great days of the big stage musical, this was their night. A packed audience was waiting with anticipation – would they like this rummage into stylish nostalgia?

Danny looked at the girls – winking at the nearest, trying not to show the tension he felt. "After the show," he mouthed at her. The girl frowned, and ignored him, turning to look the other way along the long line of other chorus girls. Danny shrugged. After a moment, the girl glanced back at him. "See you later?" he whispered again.

The girl shook her head slightly. She looked away again, down the line of other girls, still frowning but smiling inside.

There was an almost physical feeling of excitement. Tension. Edginess. Anxiety. Everyone waiting for curtain up felt they could touch it.

Danny himself picked at a loose piece of fading gilt from the side of the proscenium arch. Both he and Harry were also nervously expectant... Harry obviously edgy, but Danny trying hard to be his usual flippant self.

He carried on absent-mindedly picking at the gilt, all the time looking out almost vacantly across the stage.

The stage manager, sitting at a table just off stage in the wings on the opposite side of the stage to Danny and Harry, waited for an instruction through a set of earphones.

A props man ran across in front of the chorus line to pick up some small object he had spotted on stage, as the overture switched to the dulcet tones of the big romantic number.

The dancers settled down, the girls leaning their chins on their right shoulders as the stage manager gave the nod to get them ready to dance. With the music picking up speed again on the other side of the still-lowered drape, they got a second nod, then a thumbs up – and as they started to kick their legs up in unison, the boys behind them began swaying from side to side in rhythm.

By now, Danny was picking at a loose bit of skin on his right thumb. Then he rubbed an itch behind his left ear, wrinkling his forehead.

Then, slowly, the curtain began to rise, and the audience got its first glimpse of the dancers. A smooth, regimented, sexy, high-kicking line of girls, their traditional show costumes swirling up and gyrating sexily as they tapped and high kicked for all they were worth. The second row looking like a line of Fred Astaire's. A spontaneous burst of applause greeted the long-forgotten sight of an old-fashioned chorus line in full swing.

"Hey, they're playing OUR song," said Danny...

Act 1: Who Is Harry

It was barely dawn. The first inklings of the new day were just starting to appear in the sky, and the birds had picked up the signs and were starting to sing their beautiful melodies of welcome.

Inside the bedroom, it was dark and there were moody shadows in the corners, but as he stood by the window, the eight-year-old Harry McIntyre heard the birds and began singing inside his head along with them. It was a swaying melodic song that came easily to him, and he didn't think too much about it. Music was as easy for him as it was for the birds.

Later, as he grew into early teens then into the first faltering stages of maturity, Harry often 'heard the birds'. Music was everywhere around him – he heard music in the house all the time in the slightly upper middle-class streets of Balmain, the Sydney suburb where he grew up, in the school playground, in restaurants and in the streets. It was as much a part of him as breathing itself.

Harry McIntyre. He was son of a professional classical violinist and a mother, a retired middling successful soprano who would invariably embarrass both husband and single son by singing various arias – very loudly – at lunches or dinner parties. Neither had much compassion to give, either for each other or for a son, and neither really cared for the child – he was an irritation who just happened to be there like an itch that wouldn't go away. They were not cruel, not by any means, but there was little love between either of them and the growing Harry.

"Just go and play in your room, Harry – your father is reading a score ready for his new concert next week," his mother would say.

At first, mind, both parents quite liked the idea that the boy appreciated music and had an intrinsic understanding of its harmony and counterpoint. They liked it when he complained about modern non-melodic music, pop music, but when he later started to develop a love for jazz, then old-fashioned swing – what they regarded as 'lesser music' – the feelings of the classic-loving parents faded.

"How can you like that noise?" asked his father when he heard Harry listening to a record programme on the radio. "Just turn it off."

It was not surprising that as Harry grew, he was more often than not left alone. He was not exactly a loner, he had friends at his school, but he preferred his own company and was more a lonely young boy who – when faced with any problem – retreated into his own isolated world of song. He did not allow others into his world, and it was no surprise to either of his parents when he eventually gave up the chance of a place at a respected university to go, instead, to a college noted for producing a string of talented, but not really gifted, music teachers. No surprise, and as they did not object, they probably did not care too much either.

From his early days, Harry was a serious-minded kind of person, inwardly looking and reclusive. Even before starting his training as a musician, he had written a variety of songs in his spare time, a succession of melodies written on scraps of paper on which he had hand-drawn the five line music staves, and which he kept in a drawer in his bedroom, unseen by anyone, and especially by his parents.

He had learned to play the piano while very young, and although he didn't play all that well, he was reasonably good – or adequate if you prefer – and studied other instruments as well. At college, he soon drifted in with a like-minded group who had formed a miniature Big Band, directed by a teacher who liked to be called Dizzy something or other after his favourite jazz musician and who waved his arms around maniacally while conducting.

On top of that, Harry read everything he could find about music, either in libraries or from his father's large collection of books on the subject – but only when his father was away, because the 'study', as he called it, was sacrosanct. "You should have due respect for books," his father had once told him sternly, when he caught the young Harry in the study. "Read them in a library for knowledge – but own them for pleasure."

Because of his parental indifference and his own withdrawal into himself, Harry's shy reserve in his early teens often led to him getting on a bike and riding out to find some secluded spot on the hundreds of beaches or in the countryside around the edges of the North Shore, to sit alone watching the sea, the trees, the sky and the passing clouds – writing songs in his mind that, although he did not admit it, mainly bore a high similarity to the great songs of the 1920s and 30s. Sometimes, just sometimes, there was a new and original thought – a phrase, a hint of something good. But it had invariably vanished by the time he got home and tried to recall it to put down on paper.

There was always something else to write, though, and Harry had a huge file of basic compositions kept in an old box in a cupboard in his bedroom.

Music was a big, almost the only, part of life where Harry could be comfortable. There was always music in his head, and he dreamed continually of the miracle of making music – he didn't want big success, just one song, one major song, that he hoped would 'make it'. It was his dream – the dream of the daily musical miracle.

As he turned into his late teens, Harry, at around five feet eight inches tall, was good looking in a way, reasonably stocky, fit-looking. He had a permanently bronzed complexion, friendly brown eyes and a slightly snub nose, and his light brown hair was almost blond from constant contact with the sun, and was worn sleeked back with a slight quiff at the front.

In many ways, Harry McIntyre looked a slightly miniature, but typical, Australian from Sydney's beaches, although in manner he was far from the stereotypical Oz.

Surprisingly, as he grew older and more experienced, Harry still found it difficult to make friends despite his quiet, friendly nature and acceptable looks, and it wasn't until he began his training as a teacher that the daily contact with music helped him overcome his initial shyness, and he quickly found himself drawn to a group of like-minded individuals planning and putting on a series of amateur musical shows.

For the most part, the shows were mock Rogers and Hammerstein or Andrew Lloyd Weber – without real inspiration or that certain spark of distinctiveness that might have made them acceptable. Not that any of the proud parents or friends of those others concerned were worried about that – for them, it was an entertainment that allowed them to relax before going off to a bar (the student equivalent of the green room) for a few back-slapping pints and a laugh. Harry often felt that if his own parents would join them, they might be able to make a contribution – to help him and the other students.

Perhaps it was the lack of his parents' attending, or just basically that Harry was still inordinately reserved, but he rarely joined in the end-of-show palavers, although as he got more and more into the swing of the shows, his music became more individual and he finally started to show small signs of definite flair.

Even while the shows were being performed, he would study them, and after each performance, when the curtain fell and the carousing began, he would find his way to his bedroom and pore over the notes he had written, trying all the time to improve the music – to add that certain something he invariably felt was missing.

Eventually, Harry got his qualifications from the music school, but the thought of more years, a lifetime, following the same track of amateur shows that were, in reality, not very good dismayed him, and he cast around for something more positive that he could do.

There was teaching, of course, but outside that the whole world of music loomed large – but where to go? Harry had got over his early deep introversion about his songs at least, and without any real knowledge of what he was doing or what the outcome might be he set to work writing semi-professionally.

By now, although his songs still had a more than passing resemblance to the Big Band sounds of the 40s, they had started to develop a certain something that was beginning to make them stand out. They had a certain undeveloped raw individuality and lyrical feel that stuck in the mind of those who heard them, admittedly most of them people he had known at college.

It was then, though, that he met Lucinda Grey, a tall willowy brunette with a smiling face and an enthusiastic love of music. She was only in her mid-20s, and she had a mop of dark, curly hair above an unconventionally pretty face, but Harry got a feeling of security from the first moment he saw her.

Lucy was working at the reception desk of an office block near Central Harbour used by several publishers, and Harry was instantly infatuated when he called in unannounced one morning to try and fix up an appointment with any one of them.

"But who, exactly, do you want to see," asked Lucy. Harry noted the soft voice. He had the same feelings he had as a child when he listened to the birds at dawn.

"Well, er, I don't really know," he said, a slightly dreamy look in his eyes. "I don't know…anyone who'll take a song that captures the melody of your voice."

Lucy laughed. "I've heard it all before," she said, trying to sound prim. The forced formality did not work.

"But it's true. I had a song when I came in – but now I've got another in my mind that's just for you," said Harry, and in an uncharacteristic way began

15

humming a soft melody that immediately came into his mind, the fingers of his right hand tapping its rhythm on the desktop between him and the girl.

"OK, OK," laughed Lucy. "But there's no one available to listen to it, I'm afraid."

"You can listen."

"I'm not important enough for that. I'm just a receptionist…"

"Then at least let me finish the song and give it to you. I'm going to call it…well, let me tell you over a drink," replied Harry.

Lucy narrowed her pale green eyes, but there was something appealing about the young man and she nodded. "I finish here at five," she told him with a sudden instinctive caprice. "I'll see you at the front door."

"What, er – what's your name?" asked Harry.

"Lucinda Grey…Lucy," said the girl, her eyes smiling.

"Nice…yeah…Lucy's Song. I like that…"

He turned and left the office without looking back.

Harry spent the afternoon in a coffee bar writing the song down on a blank sheet of music paper he'd picked up from another office in the same building in which he'd met Lucy. He worked it, re-worked it, and gave it far more attention than anything he had ever done before. He was finally more or less satisfied – it was probably the first song he felt was really personal, his own song in his own style and his own way.

When he left the coffee bar, it was with a spring in his step. He looked at the blue sky and rejoiced. He could see the huge steel arch of the Harbour Bridge over the buildings, and his heart soared to the same sort of heights. He was happy with the song, and he felt Lucy would like it as well.

He was waiting outside the front door of the girl's office at least 15 minutes early, probably a few moments longer. The new song was still in his head, going round and round and round in a swaying, graceful way, as he tried to match its lyrical shape to his memory of the girl's face.

Lucy came out to join him sharp on five. Her eyes had a smile and she looked as pretty to Harry as his memory had told him, but he was too anxious to note that there was also a slight hint of apprehension about her. She was wondering what she might have let herself in for, but she was, however, smiling.

"Hello…"

"Hi there…" she said, and he noted a slight guttural twang that indicated she was not pure Australian.

"I've got it. Er, Lucy's Song," he said. "Let's go somewhere and I'll let you see it."

They took the lift to the office entrance, and Lucy suggested a bar nearby. It was a smart after-office kind of place, and Harry hoped he had enough money to cover the evening, although he didn't really mind – for the first time in his life he felt an emotion for someone else and he liked the feeling. Lucy's Song was already a love song.

In the bar, after they'd ordered drinks – he didn't like to order his normal schooner of beer, but chose a dry white Chardonnay like the girl – Harry sat facing Lucy and hummed the song to her, his right hand resting on the edge of the table with the fingers lightly waving out the rhythms as he hummed them.

"I thought of some words, but I'm not too good on lyrics right now," he told the girl. "But I'll work on them. I want to capture your looks…"

"Oh come on," said Lucy. "I don't need words as well. I've never even had a song written for me before." She smiled, and she was flattered. Harry glowed in the feeling that came across.

After a while, Lucy suggested they go on to another place she knew, and this time there was a piano in the room. When the pianist took a break, Harry jumped in and asked if he could take over. He played Lucy's Song, and the noisy crowd at the bar stopped to listen, and when he had finished, there was applause. It was the first time he had ever had recognition for anything he had written, and he made his way back to the table with Lucy while it was still going on.

"That was even better," she told him. "Hearing it actually played was something else again. It's lovely."

"It's yours," said Harry.

"Oh no," she replied. "But I'll tell you what. Give it to me, and I'll try and get someone at the office interested."

Lucy did what she had promised, but, as ever, no one seemed interested in a new song by an unknown who had not been published before. "Tell him to come back when he's got something out," they told her. It was the way of things where the arts are concerned.

Maybe it was just the rejection, maybe the song itself, but it quickly led to a feeling of affection between Harry and Lucy. As the weeks passed by, Harry grew quite serious about it all – far too serious, because on Lucy's side the relationship was purely and simply fun. But Harry was a lonely man and quickly fell deeply in love with the pretty girl he was seeing virtually every night. It was, after all, his first real personal relationship after a rather austere childhood.

The new feeling very quickly made an impression on his music, too. He churned out melody after melody, song after song, with Lucy as the main focus of his inspiration. Everyone was sweet and syrupy, because although the Glenn Miller and Les Brown Big Band influence was still there, his were romantic songs, unspoken songs without lyrics but telling of endless love, of passion, of devotion.

It was his love, his passion, his devotion, although at first, he dare not tell Lucy what the songs represented in his mind, but as their togetherness grew he began to indicate that they were his love songs to her.

Lucy was flattered. She liked the attention, and although she worked for a music publisher and heard music every day, the personalised songs flattered her self-esteem. She would listen to Harry playing them at his piano and would watch him with a warm-hearted inner sentiment as she tried to picture herself as the centre of the music.

"Is this really how you see me?" she would ask.

"Oh no, mate, my music just can't do you justice," Harry would answer. It was naïve and sincere, and Lucy always smiled.

As time went on, though, the continual 'personalised' song writing began to irritate. The continuous offerings of suffocating, sickly-sweet, saccharine music began to irk. Lucy began to get annoyed when they would go out on dates and Harry would devote too much time, virtually all his time, to writing down song ideas rather than concentrating all his attention on her. "Hello, there – I'm here," she would say, but Harry would absent-mindedly lift a forefinger to quieten her with an "OK, won't be a moment…"

It began to get out of hand. Harry thought he was being romantic as the outpouring of songs to Lucy, his Lucy, continued, but the girl was getting more and more fed up with being ignored. Yes, it was fun having songs written about you – but couldn't he compose them in his own time, at home? Unknown to Harry, she began seeing someone else from her office.

At first, Harry did not realise that she was turning down his nightly invitations more and more – the songs to the girl inside his head were coming fast and furious and he concentrated on them. Not seeing her allowed him time to work them out properly at the piano, and to get the notes down on proper stave-lined music paper rather than on table napkins or odd scraps of paper.

Things finally came to a head when Harry, on a now-rare date, took Lucy to The Jazz Club, a not so inventively named disco-style place in The Rocks area, in sight of the Opera House near the Harbour Bridge. They had a couple of drinks, but as Lucy began to relax and enjoy herself, Harry realised the pianist had left the stage to go to the toilet. He excused himself from Lucy and went to take his place, joining in with the rest of the group on a strong jazz riff and totally ignoring the girl.

Harry's piano came in solo for the old Armstrong favourite…

When the song ended, Lucy applauded along with everyone else, but by now Harry was deep into the music. As the rest of the group relaxed, he began playing again, one of his own recently written songs, and soon the other musicians joined in with him, improvising to the unknown tune he was playing.

Halfway through, Lucy finished her drink. She looked round, not really noticing anything, then stood up and left the club. Outside, the night air sobered her for a moment. "Damn him," she said aloud melodramatically and called a taxi over.

Harry did not even notice that Lucy had left, but while he played on, she was on her way to see her other boyfriend. He was excited, and welcomed her into his apartment eagerly. She made herself a coffee to clear her head, and then as she sipped it, the boy told her he was fixing up a transfer to their firm's London office. He suggested she also put in for a transfer so she could go to England with him, telling her that if she wanted, he could easily fix up the move for her.

Still annoyed by Harry's behaviour at The Jazz Club, Lucy immediately decided to go. "Great idea," she said, her words still slightly slurring. "Hell, my grandparents came from somewhere in England – it'll almost be like going home."

Back at the club, the band was still swinging noisily. The place was virtually empty, but the musicians were so wrapped up in themselves that they were not aware of it, and it wasn't until the cleaners started slopping water around the floor that they finally called it a night.

Harry was on a high. Music was bouncing round in his brain, his eyes had a wide-awake look of exhilaration, but as he stepped down from the bandstand, his face covered in a veneer of sweat, he realised for the first time that Lucy was no longer there. He was puzzled, but no one else could tell him where she was. He looked at his watch – 3.30, and he knew it was too late to call her at home.

Next morning, he rang her flat as early as he dared. There was no answer. He tried her office, but no one had seen her.

Later in the day, he went to Lucy's office, to be told that she had not been in – one of the other receptionists saying that she believed she'd heard that the girl had asked for a move to another office. She did not know where.

It was four days before Harry found out that Lucy was due to leave for London that weekend. He went to her flat, but there was no sign of her, and back at the office it was finally confirmed that she was transferring to London... 'with her boyfriend'.

Harry was distraught. He couldn't for the life of him figure out what he had done to drive Lucy away. Yeah, he had left her to play in the band at The Jazz Club but he'd often done that. What was so bad? And why London?

Over the next couple of weeks, he still couldn't figure out what had gone wrong. He didn't know what to do with himself, and it took a lot of deep thought before he eventually decided he had to follow the girl to England. He took all his money from the bank, not much admittedly, booked the air tickets before he really realised what was entailed, and within days was on board a cheap Qantas economy flight to the other side of the world, landing in London without anywhere to live, very little cash, no plans, and no real idea where he could find Lucy.

Harry took the advice of a Heathrow desk attendant to get a train link direct from the airport to Paddington, looking out of the window as the train accelerated through suburbia and soon past the grim-looking brick walls of row upon row of small, closely packed semi-detached houses. Harry, with his outdoor Australian upbringing, quickly became conscious that all had small gardens, most of them well tended and with bright-coloured flower beds, and the closer the train got to the city centre, the more he noted the long thin strips of garden – people's attempts at creating their own little bit of countryside among their drab surroundings, their own little bit of creation, independence and individuality.

Soon the train was among the age-blackened 19th-century grime of Paddington station, and as soon as it stopped Harry lifted his tightly packed backpack across one shoulder and made for the main exit.

Finding somewhere to sleep was the easy part, for in Westbourne Terrace almost immediately opposite the station he saw rooms advertised outside several rather dismal-looking bed and board houses. He booked in to the one that looked cleanest from outside, and unpacked his bag in the sparsely furnished room, looking out of the window at a view that couldn't have been more different to his hometown Sydney.

That evening, exhausted, Harry ate the cheapest hamburger and chips at a nearby McDonald's before crashing out to sleep soundly despite the noise from the street and the nearby station.

He woke early next morning, and for a few moment lay in bed listening to the not-so-dull roar from outside his window and wondering what he was doing so far from home. He had no firm ideas on how to go about finding Lucy, so he went out for a walk to see if the city would give him inspiration. It didn't.

London really scared Harry. He wandered round all morning, unsure of where he was going, and the noise, dirt and chaos of the town really upset him. From Paddington he soon found himself strolling rather aimlessly through streets swarming with people and traffic, after a while coming out into the Bayswater Road and then walking along by the side of Hyde Park to Marble Arch and then along Oxford Street and down Regent Street to the heart of the West End.

All the way through, Harry's mind was in neutral. He vaguely knew that the park and the two huge streets had some fame or notoriety, but even when he got to Piccadilly Circus and saw the theatres lining up along Shaftesbury Avenue branching off it his mind did not really click into gear.

He must have walked for five or six miles, and every sound seemed to hit a nerve – sirens, car hooters, motor bikes roaring through the traffic.

People seemed to find him invisible. He tried to step out of their way when possible, but no sooner did he move to one side than they moved with him, brushing past and almost through him as if he did not exist.

Harry's mind was racing with thoughts that were not really there. His brain was trying to think positively, but there was a vague mistiness about it all and everything seemed somehow unreal. Eventually, and without knowing how he managed it, he got back to his dingy room, and sat down to try and put it all down on paper. He tried in the only way he knew how, in song.

There was a slight theme he had carried in his mind from Australia, and as he sat on his lumpy bed that idea came back to him and seemed to fit the mood he was in. But as he tried to put it down on paper, the disconcerting noises of the city kept whirling round in his mind, and he could not concentrate. Everything became confused and even the music was, for once, not a release. It just did not happen.

Harry lay back on the bed and forced himself to try and focus on Lucy. How to find her in this dreadful, unwelcoming, stand-offish, bewildering city – a city he had read about since childhood as being great but now seemingly soiled by its growth and unruly population.

It came to him after some time, but as it was by then growing into evening he decided to wait until the next day. Then, he thought, he would try to find the firm she had worked for in Sydney, and see where that would take him. He went out to eat, another McDonald's, and went to bed troubled at what was happening to him.

Next morning he left the rooming house and walked, briskly this time, to the steely grandeur of a high-rise pile of a hotel in nearby Praed Street. In the main reception lounge he found a public telephone, and looked up the name of Lucy's firm in a telephone book left casually on a windowsill by its side. He made a note of the address, and asked the hall porter how to get there.

It took him almost an hour, once again trying to ignore the seeming hordes of people intent on walking right through him, before he got to the street, his stride getting slower the nearer he got.

It was a large, white building, with many company names listed on a metal frame by the side of the unimpressive front door. He went in, nodding to a well-built man, part hall porter, part security guard standing in the doorway, and made his way to the lift. On the third floor he found the company, and behind a plastic-looking reception desk on the inside of a double glass door was Lucy.

The girl looked up as he pushed the door open. "Harry…"

"Hello, Lucy."

"What the hell are you doing here?"

"I followed you." It was all he could say, inadequate though it was.

"Oh shit. Why? Surely you realised…" her voice tailed off. Harry just stood there. "I'm getting married on Saturday," said the girl.

"But I thought…if I came, I thought you might…"

Lucy interrupted him, "No, Harry. I'm getting married. We had some good times, but that's all over. It's finished. I'm sorry, but I've got another life now."

"I really thought you, we…" Harry did not really know what he was trying to say.

"Maybe it could have been something," said Lucy. "But you were always so wrapped up with your music, obsessed. You were always in a world of your own

– always thinking of a song, a phrase. Most of the time I felt I was never part of it, that you didn't even really know I was there."

"But there was Lucy's Song and the others. I thought…"

"No, Harry, you didn't think. It was always the music first, and that's not what I want from my life."

Lucy looked at Harry carefully. There was certain hardness in the look, but it was more pity than anything else. "I'm sorry, Harry, but I've got work to do," she said.

"Of course. I'm sorry." Harry turned slowly and walked out. By the lift he looked back, and Lucy was laughing with another girl who had joined her at the reception desk. The lift came, and Harry went down and out of the building.

Back in his bedroom, he sat on the bed for a while, then he methodically and deliberately picked up a sheet of paper and started jotting down some notes. The song he had tried to write the day before made its way easily onto the paper, and he was pleased with the result.

When the draft was finished, he sat there looking at it with a detached, professional eye. He wondered where he could find a piano to try it out.

Act 2: Who Is Danny

It was somehow appropriate that Danny Grover came into the world in the month of June – and high in the sky shone a bright full moon.

Danny was born to corny rhymes like that.

Danny – he was christened Danny NOT Daniel – grew up with rhyming words in his mind. Words seemed to go together in a logical sequence, and it seemed quite natural to him that they should be a part of the music he heard all round him. But he didn't realise someone actually wrote them.

He only found out about composers and lyricists when, as a young teenager, he began buying old vinyl records – all he could afford – and began going to libraries to look up biographies and stories about the singers and musicians he heard on them. By the time he was 14, Danny had a huge collection of discs which he kept piled up on the floor under a table in his parents' rarely used lounge – all meticulously labelled, numbered and recorded in a large book. Danny would carefully select them, dust them, and play them whenever he could, and they taught him quite a lot about music.

The family lived in a tree-lined street in a leafy suburban village near Dorchester, where Danny's father had a reasonably successful dental practise and his housewife mother spent her time dusting, cooking and attending weekly Women's Institute meetings.

Despite the ultras-suburban background, Danny grew up a middle-England mini-rebel who, virtually from birth, opposed authority. He dressed casually in jeans and sweatshirts even when supposed to be wearing school uniforms, and he had a defiant, insubordinate attitude towards anyone who tried to tell him what to do, especially his teachers.

But despite that, at most times he had quite a calm disposition, finding a sort of inner calm in his young mind by using his inherent love of words. Although he disliked regulation and was naturally untidy in almost everything, from his earliest days he began to love the tidiness in the rhymes of the childhood poetry his mother would read to him.

At school, Danny was pretty average at everything, but only because he didn't bother too much with his lessons. He had a happy knack of writing quickly and well, that got him out of scrapes, and that allowed him to pacify his teachers with the essays and stories he wrote about their subjects – often based loosely on just one small and probably inconsequential bit of information he picked up during a lesson and that others did not really think was worth mentioning.

On one memorable occasion, he entirely forgot about his homework, and when he was told about it by his friends on arriving at school the next day, he hurriedly wrote a five-page essay that won the approval of his teacher. It was so good, in fact, that next day the headmaster, Peter Greene, read it out to the entire school assembly as an example of how 'a pupil who doesn't normally bother' can succeed if he concentrates and spends time on his homework. Everyone knew it had been written in just five minutes before school began!

"Old Pea Green likes it," laughed Danny himself.

Danny was a happy-go-lucky kind of guy, and he sailed through school days without any hang-ups, with little deep learning, but with a lot of friends and some good memories. No one was surprised when he left the school before taking any major exams to take up a job as a junior trainee reporter on his local paper, the Journal. For the first time, he concentrated on learning things – about newspapers, and about writing. He began to understand how the use of words and construction of sentences or phrases can be used to reveal thoughts and ideas.

He had a natural way of interviewing people – talking to them rather than asking questions like most of his companions. And he could express the thoughts of those interviews in a simple, uncomplicated style that the paper's readers seemed to enjoy.

"The first time I met Old Joe he was wearing underpants. Y-fronts," he wrote about one former mayor of the town.

Not that it always kept him out of trouble in the office. He was frequently called in to the editor's office to be told about his casual approach, and it was still often suggested that he must dress up – wear a suit and a tie – because, it was said, it was disrespectful not to do so. But Danny always refused – casual trousers or jeans and an open-neck shirt were still good enough for him, and he always maintained it helped people to relax and get to know his personality better when they were with him.

"Anyway," he maintained, "everyone else wears a suit. People will remember me because I don't!"

Work as a local reporter, though, suited him. Although he was, in reality, a bit of a slob, he was naturally polite, and he quickly got used to watching life and writing about it; it was an easy job, and he told his friends he pitied them…because they had to go out to work.

There was, though, another advantage as far as Danny was concerned. With full time work came wages, and for the first time he was able to buy proper discs and tapes of his favourite music. He loved the Big Bands of the era just before he was born – the Harry James, Artie Shaw and Benny Goodman swinging bands – and for relaxation he would often re-write the words of their major hits.

One day, he tried to pick up a girl in a club, and she tried to put him down in front of his friends. "Grow up sunshine – you'll soon learn that girls don't like men who only think of what's inside their fly buttons," she told him with a smug look.

'Don't know why,"

he crooned, adapting a well-known lyric,

'There's no button on my fly
Use a zipper.
'cause my girl and I
Think it's quicker.'

Later, he was to crow that the re-written lyric had helped him 'pull' the girl after all.

There was an adroit, crafty slickness about Danny's re-worked lyrics – but they were not true lyrics, merely a pastiche of all the clever-clever song words he had ever heard. He did not know, at the time, about double and triple rhymes or rhythmic phrasing.

It was, though, a good time for the fast-growing Danny. By now he had blossomed into a strapping six-footer – around 6ft 1 and a bit to be exact – and he had a very pale complexion highlighted by a mop of black, flowing, unruly hair that fell into his eyes so that he continually had to push it back. By contrast, he had striking pale blue eyes wide set above a beaky nose which gave him the kind of unusual, rather aquiline, good looks that many of the girls he met adored.

Danny was more often than not seen hanging round with a large group in which pretty young girls outnumbered the boys, and he was always at the centre of things within the group. He would tell jokes, relate tales based (often slackly) on the stories he covered for the paper…and most often would reel out some bawdy song lyric based loosely on the well-known song hits of the day – more doggerel than melodic composition – which he would sing to the sycophantic, riotous laughter of his pals.

Danny was always good for a song or two, usually reeled off instantly in a mock Lorenz Hart or Ira Gershwin style. "I'll rhyme anything – a name, anything," he once boasted.

"You're on. Try Annabella," said one of the girls. "C'mon on…"

"Errr…OK…" Danny took up the challenge.

'Annabella,
Rang-a-bella me…'

was his instant reply. He shrugged his shoulders. "What d'you expect – 'Mimi' from Boheme?" he said with a cheeky grin.

Mostly, although Danny's life was largely flippant, he took his job as a reporter seriously, and he soon progressed. When he felt ready, he applied for a place with a news agency in London, and it took just five minutes of a first interview for him to be offered the job.

Much of his work with the agency involved meeting the mini celebrities of the day, and Danny slipped into the role, loving that part of it. He especially delighted in leading the various stars of stage and screen through simple PR interviews – then suddenly throwing in a difficult question about their work that showed they didn't really have much of a grasp over their jobs.

It inevitably won him a lot of enemies, and after a couple of years his status as a reputation-buster had grown quite large. A well-known film producer decided it would be better to have him on side, and when he offered him a job as a publicist Danny jumped at the chance. As he moved from poacher to gamekeeper, he began to delight in mixing with even bigger film, stage and television stars, and, in particular, he loved meeting the big-name international singers and dancers who needed his help. He delighted in seeing them rehearse and work, and would often take time out just to stand in the corner of a studio to watch them doing just that.

In turn, they delighted in his swift one-liners, and his casual, but efficient, approach – his easy manner and way of speaking to them made them feel at ease. Over lunch at a studio one day, a slightly tipsy Hollywood starlet was looking at the menu. "Try the hors d'oeuvre," said Danny seriously. Then more loudly so that others at nearby tables could hear he added: "Hors d'oeuvre. You know, like a lady of the night on petroleum." Everyone loved it.

All the time he continued to write his own perky little songlets as a diversion, often dedicating them to the particular personality he was working with – especially the more beautiful women stars and actresses with whom he was coming into more daily contact. The words were still doggerel, but the celebrities adored them and quickly included him in 'the set'. He would get invited to their parties, to clubs where they went to be seen, and to restaurants wining and dining – usually at their expense.

"I like life, it gives me something to do before death," he would often tell them.

He was always asked to make up 'a song', and he invariably provided the right kind of meal ticket to smooth talk his host.

'I'm one of those folk,
Who can't take a joke.
But when I beg...
for an egg...
The yolk's surely on me!'

...was sung to a drunken young starlet in the early hours when she suggested going for breakfast.

And when a well-known star, Wayne Devine, began upsetting his hostess, Danny chimed up in an over-loud voice –

'Wayne, Wayne, go away,
Come again another day.'

The deeper he got involved, the more Danny wrote his make-believe lyrics and words to established songs. They were still largely bad take-offs of Lorenz

Hart's clever, witty and (unlike his own) sophisticated lyrics, but they were vaguely amusing to the heavy-drinking people he hung around with.

It was all fun – and lightweight.

Danny revelled at being in the limelight, but as time went on he began mixing more with the lower dancers and musicians than with the stars – and he enjoyed that far more. Then after a while he began going to late-night clubs with them to listen to jazz.

One club, in particular, was a favourite haunt. Satch's, a jazz club in the Hampstead area just down from the underground station named after Satchmo, Louis Armstrong. He was living at the time in a one-room apartment in the decaying splendour of Randolph Crescent, quite close to the Edgware Road at Maida Vale, and someone at work told him about the club. When he went along, he found that it was a favourite with many of the West End show musicians, where they could really let their hair down and meet their friends and out-of-work instrumentalists – to play and to talk and to offer each other advice, help, or hints of possible jobs.

Danny was instantly fascinated, not only by the music being played on the small bandstand but by the whole atmosphere fashioned by the ever-changing groups of incongruent instrumentalists. He was quickly encouraged to join in their impromptu sessions, writing off-the-cuff lyrics, sometimes singing them badly, but loudly, in an attempt to impress the men of music.

He soon became a regular and would often try to talk to the bandsmen there, but they barely had time for that between their own sets on the bandstand, so he would spend most of his time between writing execrable lyrics by simply drinking to excess, throwing up, and falling over in the car park.

One night, he got drunk as usual, and staggering round the club he noticed a Chinese girl. She seemed to be having fun, and as he watched and weighed up his chances, she went to the stage carrying a violin and began playing a hot number. Danny listened, moving slowly towards the front of the stage. The girl smiled at him as she finished the number with a flourish, and Danny bowed low back to her.

He had an odd thought:

'I'd like to plant,
A kiss.
Beneath eyes that slant,

he sang.

"That's out of order – racist," said someone.

"No way. I call a spade a spade," Danny slurred and immediately a black musician who had heard him began to argue. "Shut up, man," he shouted.

In his hazy, drunken way, Danny was aggrieved. He felt wronged and he said so. "Woz wrong? 's-not racist," he bawled back. "Anyway, even if it is woz, it got to do wi' you…" The bandsman started to move forward aggressively. "'ve got a right to like or dislike anyone I want, no matter what they are," said Danny.

The musician was almost face to face with Danny. "I don't like you for instance…" The musician hit him just above the right eye, and blood began to trickle out. Another bandsman stepped forward and took him away. "Calm down…calm down…"

Danny staggered out to the car park and found his car. He got into the passenger seat, holding a handkerchief to his forehead. Suddenly he smiled. "Yeah – that's the lyric," he said out loud.

> *'Oh how I hate you.*
> *Oh how I want to see you dead…'*

He fell asleep with the car door still open.

Getting drunk was the norm. But Danny also flirted outrageously with the girls, who seemed to like him, and he had a fair bit of success with them in the car park, too!

But it was still putting words to music that appealed to him most. More and more, as he created and sang his ad-libbed lyrics off the top of his head, though, he began to wish he could do it properly and with more order. All his friends, or those who accompanied him to parties or to the late-night clubs, continued to insist he make up the doggerel that had won him quite a reputation, but Danny felt he needed more.

At one get-together he sang…

> *'You're essential.*
> *Like champagne corks,*
> *And strawberry stalks.*

And the moon on the lake,
You're essential.'

Knowing it was rubbish, he yearned to give his words a more romantic, well-written, easy-flowing panache

'Love's an emotion of the heart.
Sweet – not acid, nor tart.
You meet – and that's just the start.
You fall, and never will part...'

but he knew that though that was better, it was still amateurish. What he really wanted, deep inside his head, was to be able to write the kind of music he had heard as a child, the easy-going lilting melodies of the great age of swing and the Big Bands.

At home he would try writing what he called 'proper' song words...but they would more often than not end up as:

'I like a cracker with my tea.
A well-mixed creamy cracker; that's for me.
Not a bourbon or digestive –
I'd get suggestive with a digestive –
Or an ordinary teatime torte,
Makes me do things I didn't ought.
With a lovely, creamy daughter
Like you – the cracker sitting here with me...'

Although he once did manage to get down something he was quite proud of, a song called 'On the Loving Side of Hate'. It occurred to him when he had finished it, though, that it was the second song he had written about hatred – the other being after his altercation with the coloured musician – and he wondered if there was something wrong with his psyche.

The down moods never lasted too long, however, and Danny's natural ebullience always returned. He loved what he considered the high life he was living, surrounded by people who felt they were rich and therefore famous, some talented but mostly not, but all of them renowned for being seen in the right places and in the gossip columns. It put him at the heart of things – the country boy who'd made it in the big city.

But he wanted more, and as the months went by and lyric writing gradually took over in his mind's ambition, he had a fanciful dream that one day he would produce a big hit for one of the major stars he still worked with. It was his daily dream of a miracle.

Danny was fascinated by the sounds of the city, the noise, the bustle, the people, the hustle. They all captivated his imagination, holding him spellbound in their fly-by-night way, and the whole scene inevitably began to influence his writing. But though he tried to improve them, his flip lyrics became even more smart and began to take on an almost nasty edge.

He told one handsome actor who turned down an invitation to join a group for a drink because his partner was giving him grief.

'Soho,
Ho ho.
Wife says no no,
Can't go.
Daren't go…'

It might have gone on like that for a lot longer, but one night he was left alone at Satch's, listening to the musicians, wondering what it was like to be able to improvise like them, drinking continuously and getting maudlin.

For probably the first time in his life Danny began to look deep into his future. He knew he could produce brittle, sometimes witty, lyrics and a string of funny-at-the-time one-liners, but at the same time he knew that the instant flair he had shown many, many times to produce insubstantial words was a waste of any possible talent he might have. The band was playing an old Nat 'King' Cole number, and as the music beat insistently into his brain, he knew he had to make a decision on what direction his life could, should, go.

When he woke next morning, the mood was the same. Danny's attitude was simply down to the fact that although he still enjoyed his life, for some time he had been getting fed up deep down with the flimsy social life he was leading. Actors and celebrities bored him; the whole idea that he was some kind of pet who would make the famous laugh with his flimsy rhymes had become tedious, and now the thought had come to the fore it quickly began to irritate him immensely. He was getting sick and tired of writing what now seemed to him unfunny couplets – he wanted a more elegant style in keeping with the great song writers on whom he doted…Cole Porter, Ira Gershwin, Larry Hart.

So he asked for help.

One night when he was drinking at Satch's as usual, he got into a deep – and, at the time, meaningful – discussion with a well-known drummer, Beck Stansfield, who was in town again and wanted to meet up with some other instrumentalists so he could feel at home. Danny spoke quite seriously for once about his ability to produce frail, meaningless lyrics, and for some reason, he decided to ask the American for advice.

It was the first time he had ever consciously sought someone else's guidance, and the other man listened.

Beck, known as Drummin' Man, was well into what is known as middle age. A greying 68-year-old, he had done it, seen it, and forgotten more than most. He had been to Satch's before, and he had heard Danny. So he listened with interest as the younger man spoke to him, nodding when he told him about his 'games' writing instant lyrics purely for fun, and in turn asking questions about how serious Danny was in making a career in music.

"The trouble really," said Danny, "is that I'm bored with the people I work with. They're all lightweight, you just can't get anything back from them."

Beck nodded agreement. "Like a lot of musicians. But what you doin' about it?" he asked.

"That's just it. Nothing," said Danny. "But I've got a feeling, somehow, that I could make something more of myself if I could only find out how to write properly…"

"Hey man, if you want to write, write," said Beck. "Don't just talk about it – get on with it."

"I try, but somehow I feel there's something missing, some ingredient," said Danny.

"Know what you mean – I always wanted to be a piano player, but I was the same. Drummin' came easier so I took that line."

Beck nodded again. "You can do it – that missin' bit will come. But if you've got the talent, you gotta be sure you want to be a song writer," he added thoughtfully. Danny was pleased at the implied compliment about talent.

"But you gotta be prepared to work at it, work real hard," went on Beck. "It's a hard life writing music – you gotta remember that publishers, producers, A and

R men, all of 'em get literally dozens of songs sent in every week, every day almost. They know most of 'em are rubbish, but they want to find the one that's goin' to make it. They want your success as much as you do.

"The big thing, though, is that they'll very rarely look at words on their own. They want a song, a whole song. They want a melody – 'cause you gotta think that lyrics are only half a song, and a tune is only half a song, too. They have to go together."

Danny was listening intently. "But I only write lyrics…" he said slowly.

"Then boy, you gotta find a song writer to help you," replied Drummin' Man. "You better get yourself someone to put a tune (he pronounced it 'toon') around your words if you want to get anywhere. If you want to try and write words, you really gotta find someone you can write with as a team…unless you can do it all on your own like Porter or Berlin."

Danny pondered on this last bit. "I couldn't do that. Words I know…but writing music…" He pursed his lips. "Look, if I wanted to find a writer, where would I start?"

Drummin' Man laughed. "Just hangin' around," he finally said. "Hangin' around."

"Well, I do that already," said Danny. "Sometimes…well, sometimes I come up with some ideas for a song, but like you say, I've really got to meet a writer…" he tailed off.

"Well, I've heard your words, and boy sometimes they're goddamn awful," said Beck.

"I reckon there's enough there for you to have a real try at writin' properly. But you gotta find a notesmith to help. Now, I gotta go and play my turn…" Drummin' Man stood and made his way to the bandstand. Danny followed, and stood close by as the drummer took over the set and instantly began livening up a version of 'Sentimental Journey' that had been going nowhere.

Danny and Drummin' Man met at Satch's many times after that. They discussed music, almost as though Beck was a teacher and Danny his pupil. It was light academia, but Danny soaked up the older man's knowledge of the music business like a sponge.

They would talk ceaselessly, usually at Danny's insistence, about the great melodic songs of the 1930s, and how the music sounded with the slightly more strident sounds of the Big Bands that followed. They also spoke about the singers who could put an elegance and style to a good song. "You jus' can't ruin a good melody," said Beck.

Most of the talk was of the great song writing teams – Rodgers and Hart, the Gershwin's Gershwins – and Danny would enthuse. "That was my era," he insisted. "I love all that music, that time. It had style, classiness, it was melodic."

"Yeah," replied Beck. "But it was also commercial. Remember Mitchell Parish..."

"Who?"

"Mitchell Parish. He was jus' a hack really, simply put words to whatever music was put in front of him. Did stuff for guys like Duke Ellington and Hoagy Carmichael, and he was some writer. A real pro – but he did it for the money."

Drummin' Man lifted his shoulders and sighed, a sigh of remembered contentment. "Now that Hoagy Carmichael...there was a pianist," he said.

"I thought he wrote his own songs."

"No, Mitchell did 'Stardust' with him. Wrote the words. Then he went right the way through to a pop song called 'Volare' with all sorts of other people."

"I never heard of Parish before," said Danny. "You say he never had a regular composer?"

"Well, he wrote a lot of lyrics for a lot of people – but like you say, not too many people have heard of him. Maybe 'cause he always needed someone to write the music. Jus' like you do..."

It was the one thing Beck always insisted, that Danny find a composer with similar tastes that he could work with. "You gotta have a partner," he insisted. "Lyrics are only half the song – the music is only half the song...they need to go together to make the whole damn thing."

"Where do I find a music writer, though?" Danny always asked.

"That's up t'you, man," replied Beck. "But you gotta get yourself one."

Another time, Danny asked how two people work on one song. "Which comes first – the words or the music?" he asked with simple, almost child-like innocence.

Beck laughed. "Most people like the melody, and jus' put the words to that," he said. "But there are others, like Hammerstein, who'd always write the lyrics first and get someone to put a pretty tune around 'em.

"Generally, though, the words and the music jus' somehow come together. In my experience, the song hits you both at right about the same time. Don't ask me to explain it, it happens, and you then put your heads together and bang away until it's all put down. That's the beauty of working together..." He laughed. "...you talk, you drink, you talk some more – then suddenly it's done."

Danny nodded.

"Mind you," said Drummin' Man, "you're never satisfied. Both of you always feel the other could have done better. But then, the song is there, and you just polish it up little by little."

And it was little by little that Danny learned more about writing music. By now he was bored stupid with his jingles, and with Beck's encouragement he wanted to get down to writing some 'real' songs.

"I want to produce words like Lorenz Hart," he told the drummer one day.

"Not a bad little writer, Larry Hart," said Beck. "But you couldn't take his lyrics away from Richard Rodger's music. They went together –"

Danny interrupted. "No way, Hart was a genius in his own right..." he started to argue.

"No, no, no," came back Beck. "Great lyrics, but on their own they wouldn't mean a goddamn thing. Like if you took Rodgers music on its own, it'd be pretty but quite meaningless. But put 'em together – pow! Think of it, you can't hear the music without thinking of the words – nor can you hear a line of Hart's and not think of the tune.

"They're songs. Like I say, the two halves. You gotta get yourself a composer..."

Danny once asked Beck if he'd like to try and write the music for his songs. Beck twisted the corner of his lips and shook his head. "Not me, man. I don't like to get too formal," he said. "I just play what I want – no words, no formal song."

He seemed to go off in a bit of a daydream. "When I feel the mood, an idea jus' comes t'me and that's my song. I just let the idea take over and let it run. Off the cuff. Never last – it's free rein, an' I think having someone around making me write to a pattern would be a killer for me..."

It was all simple stuff, but all the time Danny was learning.

His lyrics were changing as well. Where, at the start of his friendship with Beck, he had written...

> *'You're essential.*
> *Like champagne corks,*

And strawberry stalks.
Like the breath that we take,
And the moon on the lake.
You're essential…'

….by the time of the last conversation he was starting to write words that had a more adult sense and feel. He was quite pleased with one song he wrote…

'There are things I shouldn't say,
Like rhyming June with moon – that way.
Or saying 'I love you'
'It makes us two'.
Or maybe 'Baby makes three'.
But I hear them al l – and pray,
Asking how my heart dare say
That the words are out-dated –
Tho' not over-rated –
But simple and few,
Saying…I really love you…'

And he was even prouder when Beck praised another lyric of his, starting…

'A house in the country
With roses round the door.'

"But you gotta have a song to go with those words," insisted Drummin' Man yet again.

It was the last thing Beck ever said to Danny. They arranged to meet again, but next morning Drummin' Man was found dead slumped over the piano in Satch's.

Act 3: How They Meet

It was three days before Danny heard that Drummin' Man had died.

He had gone to Satch's on each of those days, but although he had asked the various bandsmen who turned up where Beck was, no one told him. He never found out, in fact, what had really happened – just that his friend and mentor had died. It was a shock that he countered by drinking more and becoming even louder with his flippant joking.

It was a week or so later before Danny's feeling of loss began to cool off. And it was then that he first noticed Harry.

Harry had heard about the club when he listened to a conversation among some musicians at a table in a café where he was drinking coffee, and had asked where it was. It sounded interesting, and he had gone there a couple of times and enjoyed the atmosphere – and the music.

He was sitting in a dark corner of the club listening to some of the standards being jazzily played by the musicians during their sets – following them on a score laid out on the table in front of him. Danny sensed a bit of fun, and casually sauntered across to him, pushing his way through the dancers on the floor between them.

"Are you a musician?" he asked when the song ended.

"Yeah," replied Harry. "I write songs." He tilted his head slightly to one side and raised his eyebrows in question, and without really knowing why Danny instantly lost his predilection to torment the other man and began chatting more seriously.

"So why the score?" he asked.

"Well, I reckon you can learn a lot – y'know, following the song on a score and seeing how the bandsmen change things around," explained Harry. "It's a good way of learning."

The band started up again, and Harry looked down to see if he had the music to the new song. One of Danny's friends shouted across to him that there was another drink ready, and Danny acknowledged the call. "See ya," he said nonchalantly to Harry and returned to his pals.

A few days later, Danny again turned up at the club with some of his show biz sycophants, and while he was joking around Harry, who was once more alone, asked if he could join them. "No music score?" asked Danny, and Harry shook his head.

"Not this time."

As the evening progressed in its usual fluffy manner, Harry sat quietly on the fringes of the crowd listening to the superficial conversations. Danny was, as usual, drinking hard and smoking – something he had started because of the hectic lifestyle he was now living – and was boasting about his ability to rhyme names or words.

"How about something with 'analyse' or 'anatomy'?" asked someone,

Quick as a flash, Danny came up with an answer.

> 'My Anna lies over the ocean,
> My Anna lies over the sea.
> My Anna lies over the ocean,
> Oh bring back my An-a-to-me.'

He looked smug and the others laughed.

Harry laughed along with them, but almost instinctively noted the instant rhyming.

Later, the two men somehow found themselves together at the bar, slight adrift of the others in Danny's party, and while they waited to be served Danny took out a packet of cigarettes. He offered the pack to Harry.

"No thanks, mate," said the Australian. "Don't smoke."

Danny lit one for himself, and the two men began chatting. The conversation turned very quickly to their joint favourite subject, music, and it didn't take them too long to find that they had a lot in common in musical terms. They discovered that they were both living in a musical time-warp of the 1940s/50s, with both of them wishing fervently that so-called pop music would go back to what they agreed were 'those good old days'.

While they were talking, the musicians on the stand struck up a lively jazz version of Cole Porter's classic 'Begin the Beguine', and they paused to listen to it for a while. "Not bad, but it's still Artie Shaw's number," said Danny.

"Yeah, he did it well. But it was a show song before he recorded it," replied Harry. "Can't quite remember who sang it, but it came from a show called 'Jubilee', I believe. Quite a few years before Shaw recorded it."

"I didn't know that," said Danny. "I thought it was 'specially written for Shaw."

"Oh no. He just picked it up and arranged it – or rather, had it arranged for him. A lot of the Big Bands did that – but most, if not all, the best songs of that time came from shows. People like Porter, Irving Berlin, Jerome Kern…especially Rodgers and Hart – they all wrote their songs for the stage."

"Yeah – thinking about it, suppose you're right. Whatever, I loved the songs – to my mind, that was the best time ever for music. Mind you, I loved the way the Big Bands played as well."

"Well, I couldn't agree more, mate," said Harry with a happy look in his eye. "Shows like 'Anything Goes', 'Babes In Arms', 'On Your Toes'…oh I don't know, the list could go on and on. 'Lady Be Good', 'A Connecticut Yankee', 'Girl Crazy'. Yeah, and 'The Boys From Syracuse', now there was a show. Great stuff."

Danny raised his eyebrows at Harry's surprising familiarity with the subject. "You seem to know a lot about it," he replied. "But maybe most of those songs at the time, well even if they were written for the stage it was only when they were released on disc that people would hear them – not too many people saw the shows, remember. And surely, what made the songs so big was the fact that the big singers of the time took them up – people like Judy Garland. And the singers with the Big Bands – people like Ella, Sarah Vaughan, Billie Holliday – they took those show songs and belted 'em out so everyone got to know the words –"

Harry interrupted. "A lot maybe, and I suppose the bands did need the singers for their discs," he said. "But that's not the only reason people like Harry James, Benny Goodman and…yeah, well like Artie Shaw…why they all did so well. They had good singers – but they had good songs of their own, and good arrangements too."

Danny nodded tacit agreement. "Singing good words," he emphasised.

Harry ignored Danny's comment. "It wasn't only discs that made the Big Bands famous, ya know," he went on. "Those bands all featured in Hollywood films as well…"

"With their singers," insisted Danny. He paused for a moment, and both men contemplated the music.

"I'm surprised you know all that stuff," said Danny eventually.

"Oh God yes, I know those people," Harry replied. "Like some of the other bands – apart from James, Shaw and Goodman. People like the Dorsey Brothers…"

"Gene Krupa…"

"Stan Kenton…"

"Glenn Miller – to a lesser degree."

"Yeah, at a pinch. I didn't really rate him too high. Too schmaltzy," said Harry.

"OK, what about Bunny Berigan…?"

"Or Les Brown…"

"And his Band of Renown," laughed Danny.

They looked at each other quizzically. "Real music," said Harry.

"Real music," replied Danny.

The barman came over. "Here, let me get you that," said Danny, ordering the drinks. They waited until the two glasses were put before them, then sipped their drinks – neither moving away from the bar. For a while they drank in silence listening to the bandsmen, but there was an immediate kinship. Then suddenly they both started talking again at the same time.

"The thing about all those Big Bands and their singers was that they all played the right kind of music," said Harry.

"It was music written by the greats with great words…" said Danny.

They both laughed. "After you," said Harry.

"No, you first…"

"Well, you're right. It was great music with great lyrics," went on Harry. "But the Big Bands didn't only put those songs on the discs of the time, the old 78 vinyls, those bands often played them for dances or when they put on concerts."

Danny nodded, and took another sip of his drink. "Each number was presented just like a Broadway show," said Harry. "It was great music, and I love it." He jabbed a forefinger towards Danny to emphasise the point. "They could take a song and really turn it into something. I wish their music would come back into fashion."

Danny nodded agreement again. "Couldn't agree more. I love those old tunes – don't think today's lot can match 'em."

Both men sipped their drink. "Surprised you didn't seem to realise the difference between the shows and the Big Bands," said Harry eventually. "The songs from the great shows came a little bit earlier than the bands – when they came along, it was the sound and impression they gave that made each song seem like a show on its own."

"You're probably right. They were good songs, though. And good lyrics. They were the real good old days."

"Yep, OK – I get the message about the words. They were the days," repeated Harry.

The pair got on exceptionally well as they chatted, so much so that Danny ignored his other friends – those he had brought to the club in the first place – and stayed chatting with his new musical mate. They both found it interesting, and each listened to the others' ideas, although Danny was not too sure he wanted to hear Harry's almost professorial ideas on the mathematical and mechanical formulae of music. When he mentioned it, though, he quickly found that in actual fact, Harry, as he did himself, wrote most of his songs with a purely off-the-cuff flair.

They carried on their exchanges, and then even later in the evening, when Harry got up to walk to the bandstand to sit in with some of the musicians as most of them took a break, Danny went with him to stand by the piano humming and thinking of the occasional 'different' lyric to the old standards that Harry was playing.

As the remaining musicians stood up one by one to join their friends at the bar or outside the club for a smoking break, Harry began tinkling away at the piano on his own. He played a few more songs in traditional style, but then began playing 'Manhattan' in an unusually slow waltz-time. Danny was attracted by the novelty of it and stood there nodding approval.

When Harry moved on to another number – one of his own compositions – Danny listened for a moment, then joined in with some ad-libbed lyrics. "Was that one of yours?" he asked when the song ended.

Harry nodded. "It was good," he was told.

Between them, Harry and Danny managed three songs like that before the other musicians began drifting back to take their places on the stand.

Danny and Harry went back to the bar and carried on talking. It was about three in the morning and Danny's original party had long since left before they broke up, with Satch's virtually empty and the music over, but both agreed that they had got on so well together that they should meet again. Before leaving the club, they arranged to meet up a few days later to carry on the discussion.

***

It was about a week before they did get together, and when they did, they picked up almost exactly where they had left off in the club talking about 'the good old days' of music.

Danny had been sitting at a table outside Luigi's, a small Italian bistro in Covent Garden, waiting patiently for Harry to arrive, smoking and half-heartedly listening to some girlie group music being played over a loudspeaker as he watched the people pass. Harry was smartly dressed in a suit, but Danny wore casual clothes and looked relaxed.

"I've been listening to this rubbish, and I reckon the difference with those old songs we spoke of is that they had words that you would want to hear. Words that you could actually hear," said Danny. "I'd love to get some real lyrics published like those old ones. It would be good if I could get a break by writing something that would last."

"Jeez, yes. I wish we could get back to those good old days – good songs and musicians you could listen to," said Harry in reply replied.

"Yeah, music with a sway, a lilt. Not the modern way – the thump-thump-thump of a synthesiser."

Danny watched a fairly pretty girl walk past as he spoke. "You know, I just play at writing lyrics, but I'd give my eye teeth to really get down to doing something real – to try and get some, well some old-fashioned words out…"

"You'd never find a publisher to take that on, mate," countered Harry. "But it would be nice to get some songs you could dance to – properly dance to. All they seem to want these days is a girl waggling her bum and some backing group waving their arms around in the air and calling it dancing."

"Dancing? Fred Astaire was dancing – or Gene Kelly – or the Nicholas Brothers. Bojangles Robinson…"

Harry smiled. "You like tap?"

"Yeah – and chorus lines. Busby Berkeley's the main man."

"You betcha."

"Oh yeah – I'm sure there's a market for that sort of music again…"

"U-huh. Maybe there is, maybe not," said Harry. "I like the same kind of thing, but I reckon you'd have to be pretty lucky to get something like that going these days."

"It'd be great to get a song like…well, like those Buzz used to film – all singing and dancing. You know the sort of thing I mean – something with a real rhythm and sway to it. Something spectacular. I'd still like to give it a try sometime." Danny looked rather sad as he said it, and Harry knew he was being serious.

"Maybe you could have a go at some of my songs sometime," he said rather softly. "It might be worth a try – and it could be what we both want."

Danny looked at the other man sharply. He liked the idea, but despite the songs he had heard at the club a week or so earlier, he was not certain if Harry wrote the kind of music he wanted to be associated with. But he was interested.

"Look, I'll tell you what – why don't we get together round a piano somewhere soon and, ya know, see what kind of things we can produce?" he eventually asked, stubbing out the cigarette.

"Good idea. I'd be willing to give it a try," replied Harry, but before anything else could happen, a waitress came out to them and asked if they wanted anything. A bottle blonde with a ridge of pale, white fat stomach showing beneath her tank top.

"No, we're just sitting here waiting for the love of our lives to come and ask us what we want," joked Danny. The girl gave him a bored 'I've-heard-it-all-before' look. "Do you want a meal or a drink, or do I have to get the boss to throw you off the table?" she replied.

"I'd much rather you tried to wrestle us away," said Danny – but Harry put up his hand to stop him. "We'll just have a couple of cappuccinos," he said softly. The girl went back inside, Danny's eyes boring through the black trousers she was wearing.

The interruption had broken up the thread of the conversation, and when the coffees arrived, they drank them fairly quickly before Harry said he had an appointment. "A piano lesson," would you believe. "I've got to try and teach some grubby ten-year-old the intricacies of Mozart and Tchaikovsky!"

He finished his drink and threw some coins on the table. "That should take care of my share," he said, then he stood up and left. Before going, he suggested

44

a date when they could see each other again, and said he'd have some songs with him then. Danny waited about ten minutes for the waitress to come out again, but she didn't appear and he finally also stood and walked away.

***

They met up again frequently after that, and every time one or other would fervently wish that so-called pop music would go back to 'those good old days'. It was a never-ending mantra, but invariably the other always agreed.

Almost the only way they differed – and argued about – was about the importance of each other's job. Danny, naturally, said it was the lyricist who made the song memorable, while Harry stuck out for the need of a good song as the basis for it all. It was a discussion that was to go on, without resolve, throughout their friendship.

As was his way, Danny would often tease Harry about composing. "I was passing a cemetery on the way here when I heard this weird music coming from over the fence," he once told the other man.

"Go on then," said Harry with a resigned tone.

"It was Beethoven – de-composing!" laughed Danny.

It was stupid, but the kind of continual bad joke humour that served Danny so well. Despite himself, Harry always had to laugh.

They would meet either in a pub, or in one of the hundreds of coffee bars or snack bars that come and go around London, and most weekends at Satch's. Danny loved the café life and was always happy to arrange a meeting in one of the many places he liked to visit with the one-date-only girls and the show biz acquaintances he mixed with. Harry was not too sure about them, though, because far too often while they were talking or discussing things someone Danny knew would come up and interrupt for some frivolity or other.

It was annoying, but Harry put up with it and Danny obviously loved the attention it gave him.

Despite the seemingly constant interruptions, they still managed frequent more-or-less serious discussions, deliberations and arguments on all things to do with songs and song writing.

"I've got some words I thought you could play with," said Danny when they met up in a Soho snack bar one day. He handed over a folded sheet of paper. Harry opened it out and read:

'My life's a game of solitaire,
Alone without you.
By myself I can only dare,
To stay true
To the one I love
Who's left me playing solitaire
With life.'

Harry nodded when he had finished. "Hey, that's not bad, man," he said thoughtfully.

"Got no idea what kind of tune…" said Danny.

"That's the trouble with you writers," laughed Harry. "Proves that you need the music."

"Don't start again," said Danny. "You know what I think – it's the words that show the meaning of the song."

"Shit, mate. How many times do I have to tell you – it's the music that's all important."

Danny smiled at the instinctive move into the couple's recurring discussion. He enjoyed the banter – although he was convinced his ideas were the right ones.

"OK, then – think of some of the greatest songs ever written. I dunno, how about *'In The Still Of The Night'*? That wouldn't be anything on its own – it's just 'Da de da de da, Da de da de da da…' It's Cole Porter's lyrics that make it."

"Now don't be a wuss," replied Harry. "You can have all the words you like, but they need the music to make them into a song. Without that, what've you got?"

"I still reckon it's the words that make it what it is. And I'm not the only one – you must have heard the story about Oscar Hammerstein's wife…"

"I don't know any stories about anyone's wife," said Harry, teasing.

"Well, seems like she was at a party one day when she heard someone raving on about Jerome Kern's wonderful *'Ol' Man River'*. Mrs H apparently turned round and told the guy – 'Kern didn't write *'Ol' Man River'*. He wrote 'da da, da da…' – my husband wrote *'Ol' Man River'*." Danny looked smug. "What d'you make of that then?" he asked.

Harry laughed. "Good story," he replied. "But it doesn't alter the fact that people whistle that 'da da, da da' of Kerns'."

"Yeah, no – but the words always go through their mind when they do."

They carried on arguing like that for a while, not getting any further but enjoying the repartee.

A bit later, after they'd gone to a nearby pub for a beer, Danny carried on the theme, putting in his special argument for the importance of lyricists. "Think of the great songs," he said. "You name it, and I bet you know the words."

"Come off it, mate, don't start again," said Harry. "You've got to have a song to hang the words on…"

"Well, what if I hummed 'Da da dee da da, de da de dah, de da dee doo'…I bet you think '*We'll have Manhattan, The Bronx and Staten Island, too…*"

"True, but you'd still need the song. Like you always need Tchaikovsky – no words there, but the music tells you all you need to know."

"Don't be so bloody stupid. We're talking popular music here – take songs like '*Embraceable You*', '*Anything Goes*', '*I've Got Five Dollars*', '*It's De-Lovely*'…" They were just four songs that came instantly to Danny's mind – by chance, all of them with unusual and split rhymes.

"OK, but they're just a few songs by the oldies – Hart, Gershwin and Porter," said Harry. "You can't do that these days…"

"You forgot Irving Berlin," replied Danny. "But it's not only the oldies, the greats, I can think of dozens of other lyricists – Yip Harburg, Johnny Mercer, Dorothy Fields, Gus Kahn…yeah, Sammy Cahn too." He paused to think. "Arthur Freed, Ray Henderson…oh, dozens of them. And that's just off the top of my head. All of them great writers." He swallowed heavily.

"OK. OK," said Harry with a grin. "But what about Alan Lerner and Fritz Lowe?"

"Fritz Lowe?"

"Well, that was his name but everyone knew him as Frederick. Whatever. Think of some of the Lerner and Lowe songs – How about '*If Ever I Would Leave You*', '*On The Street Where You Live*', '*On A Clear Day*'? The words and the music are so bound together you can't tell where the seam is."

Danny flicked his hair out of his eyes, concentrating earnestly. "Suppose. The same with Hammerstein and Rodgers. Mind you, I suppose Hammerstein is a bit of an in-between, time-wise, but he's right up there with the best of them," he added, returning to his original point with a sudden flash of inspiration.

"Oscar Hammerstein? Shit – you've got a thing about him, haven't you mate? But ya got t'be joking about him being a top man," said Harry. "He's far too sickly – yuck. Like that spoonful of sugar he wrote about!"

"I'll agree with that – in some respects," said the still-intense Danny. "But he's not all schmaltz and goo like most people say. Think of '*Younger Than Springtime*' – that's beautiful. Really beautiful.

"Or what about '*We Kiss In The Shadow*'? Now that's a song – in my book it's one of the best ever. It's got some of the most beautiful words I can think of…"

He spoke the words rather than singing them.

"Beautiful. I love 'em."

Harry raised his eyebrows and shrugged. He sighed. "OK. OK," he said eventually. "It's not worth an argument."

Danny nodded, almost triumphant. He felt he had won a point over the other guy. "It doesn't alter the fact that the music and lyrics those fellas wrote was always good," he said condescendingly. "More than just good in most cases…"

"U-huh," replied Harry. "I'll go along with that. Those songs all told a story, whether it was the music or the words. But, y'know, I suppose they had to – if they were part of a show, they needed to take the story along."

"Yeah, you've said it before. But they weren't all show songs – not always. There's lots of plain, good old love songs that were written just to be sung. I like a lot of them as well, and at the moment, that's the kind I mostly write."

"Yeah, well." Harry stood up and stretched. "Gotta go now, mate. Got to see a kid about learning the piano…"

"I thought you knew how to play," quipped Danny.

"Ha, ha, ha."

Harry left the café, and Danny watched him walk down the road. Maybe he's got a point, he conceded mentally, but I like my words the way I write 'em.

For the next few weeks, despite the facts and specifics of what Harry told him during their many meetings, Danny still, for the most part, churned out the flippant, frivolous words he was used to in his own undisciplined way. Sometimes he tried to change, but the style copied, badly, from 1930s' writers of note was almost automatic.

I love she,
Her love me,
Forever we can be –
Together.
Why won't her,
Re-occur,
And make life per…
fectly grand?
She and me,
That makes we –
Forever.'

Harry would look at the more-often-than-not inconsequential words his friend provided and was usually dismissive. "Remember one thing, mate – these are just passing words, they don't mean a thing and they'll just float away into nothing," he once said. "You always say you want to be like Lorenz Hart – well, Hart did write slick words like these sometimes, to fit in with a show mood or whatever, but he usually wrote thoughts and feelings for a storyline. That's what you've got to aim at."

"U-huh," said Danny dreamily. "Yeah, I would like to be known like that."

It took several weeks, but over a period of time, Harry's insistent urging began to make an impression, a slow impression, and Danny's writing did start to change little by little. He began to put more thought into his words, and although he still liked split and unusual rhymes and jazzy interpretations of words, his lyrics gradually took on a more adult air. They were still flip, but there was enough change for Harry to notice and give his own unmentioned approval.

Harry's own contribution to their get-togethers was more conventional and predictable. He would produce dozens of themes, but there was something indefinable missing – and although many were delightfully tuneful, there was, somehow a lack of real spark about most of them.

But just as Harry's influence was starting to change Danny's lyrics, so the writer's enthusiastic stimulus slowly started to alter Harry's approach to his songs. As they started working with each other, albeit in an off-the-cuff, impromptu basis, they began to move closer to each other's way of thinking.

When Danny wasn't working, they would still get together in cafés or pubs as before, swapping song notes across the tables, but much of the time they would just talk, more and more as time went on, about how they should be doing things. And because Danny had no formal training, he had to rely on Harry to transpose his ideas to paper.

For his part, Harry was happy to explain the more technical side of things to his new colleague. "Any song can be broken down into basic parts – the idea, the melody, the structure and the style," he once said, adding, after Danny seemed about to protest, that, "Yeah, OK. The lyrics do play a good part as well."

***

Gradually, after the initial excitement of meeting up and talking in cafés, pubs or at Satch's had worn off, Harry began suggesting they get together at his flat, pointing out that as they were getting on so well with each other and he had a piano it might help them play around with their musical ideas.

By now he had left the dingy b&b in Westbourne Terrace for a larger room in Clarendon Road near Holland Park, close enough to the Australian home-from-home area around Notting Hill Gate for him to feel more relaxed about living in the big city. The main reason for his taking the apartment was that as part of an old family home, it came complete with a very ancient and battered upright piano with peeling black lacquer, which he was able to tune so that although it was not acoustically brilliant it was good enough for him to give occasional piano lessons to a series of young and unwilling young pupils.

The piano stood against one wall, sideways on to a window looking over the road, with Harry's bed – heavily disguised as a couch with thin coverlets and out-of-shape cushions when he had people visiting – in a corner on the other side, beside the door to a corridor shared with other residents of the house. It had been described as having 'fashionable minimalist furnishing' when Harry saw it advertised in a corner shop's window, and indeed it did not contain very much in the way of furniture. In actual fact, apart from the piano it was virtually bare, not even having anywhere to sit apart from the bed – although in truth it had once contained a chair, a former occupant of the room having loaned it to another resident and never having it returned.

It was, however, all that Harry could really afford, and the piano was a big plus, especially as it enabled him to earn at least a little money by giving those lessons to local children. A card had already been placed in the same corner shop window telling local parents of the facility.

When he invited Danny to come along, Danny readily accepted because quite apart from the piano, he knew it was a way they could both save money by not buying food or drinks of any kind as they talked. He knew Harry did not have much money, and although he was earning quite well – and making a fair bit extra on expenses – he was spending what he had at far too great a rate to be called wealthy.

The sessions at Harry's apartment proved to be slightly more fruitful than the airy-fairy meetings in cafés and pubs. They fooled around on the piano a lot, and Danny insisted on sticking to his flippant lyrics to many of the basic melodies Harry routinely churned out – and to be fair, few of the songs had any real trace of anything worthwhile in them anyway.

But it was not wasted time. As they messed around with music and words, they slowly began to get a feel for the others' ways of doing things, and with the relentless talk about how they were going to 'make it' in show biz prevailing they quickly picked up on moods and each other's feelings.

Apart from anything else, their two polarised feelings about the importance of the music against the words and vice versa began to draw closer to an agreed middle, and as they inevitably reiterated their love for the music of the 1940s and 50s, Danny grudgingly admitted what Beck had told him – that all good songs were 'half music and half words'.

As they assimilated each other's ideas, they began to agree that a good band or a show song was truly a cooperative affair – "Like a wedding, one no good without the other," said Harry tritely. And as they worked together, they began to get more involved in each other's lives, and a genuine feeling of friendship bonded them together quite apart from the work they were trying to set up.

Danny still spent time with any number of good-looking girls – usually met through work – and often he would not turn up as agreed. But slowly their song writing began to take on a communal shape and sound, although it was held up by the fact that Danny carried on with his job as a publicist – and the fact that when Danny was available, Harry often had to miss their joint co-operations to give a piano lesson to some scruffy youngster who did not want to know.

Danny's more forceful personality, obviously, helped develop the partnership, and his fascination for the sounds of the city began to influence Harry. At first, Harry hadn't liked London one little bit. He felt it too big, too full, and too busy-busy. But under the weight of the other man's behaviour his opinion soon began to change. Going out with Danny on his expense-driven visits to big restaurants helped; so, too, did mixing with some of Danny's show business acquaintances.

As a result, although Danny's lyrics remained largely smart-alecky as he 'gave it large' to his companions, Harry's songs gradually began to change, to become a little more strident. But as he got to quite like life in the big city and it ceased to have quite the same effect on him, he and Danny slowly settled down together to produce some songs that were an intriguing mix of both their original ideas and sounds.

By now, taking on board Danny's natural exuberance, Harry's music had become brighter, livelier, swinging – while Danny was attempting to put more thought into his words and create lyrics that were not just banal and clever-clever.

Danny was still working, but he took more and more time off to be with Harry. As they worked together, too, Harry increasingly showed a natural flair for arranging the music they were producing. "Call it 'The Sound' if you want," he would say quite frequently. "The sound of the whole piece. Y'see, by my reckoning it's not just the basic song that's important – it's the whole effect of it, y'know."

He would get an almost zealous look in his eye as he spoke. "When I write a song, I hear the trumpets coming in, the violins, saxophones – all the instruments," he would tell Danny. "I can almost hear a band playing it. It's like they were in the same room as me."

As he spoke, Danny raised his eyebrows and nodded, a slightly quizzical grin on his lips. "It's the whole arrangement, the instrumentation," went on Harry. "It's all important…"

"You haven't mentioned my lyrics," said Danny with a cheeky grin, knowing the effect it would have. The mood was broken.

It was often like that. Harry was far more intense about the songs they were jointly trying to produce, while Danny always took a more cavalier line and was facetious about almost everything in his life, not only in the lyrics he produced. He was serious about the words he wrote, but the lyrics overall still contained far too many tongue-in-cheek lines and phrases and rhymes.

And they were still very different in their approach to life in general. Harry, for instance, dressed smartly and traditionally and although he liked the nice things in life he could only eat really well when Danny's expenses paid for them both. Danny, too, liked the high living, but he still dressed badly, more often than not going out for meals in good restaurants in jeans, tee-shirts and trainers. He didn't seem to care what he looked like, and with his charming smile and twinkling eyes always seemed to get away with breaking dress codes and the other accepted social rules where they were imposed.

To begin with, Harry was not too keen on the idea of using Danny's expenses to pay for things, feeling a little formal and prudish about fleecing someone else's employer, but he soon slipped into it and quickly showed the same natural affinity for stylish elegant things as Danny. For his part, Danny could see nothing wrong with signing for meals or whatever with a company credit card.

It was a real attraction of opposites, but as their partnership progressed, it was not all work and togetherness. Danny and Harry still spent time apart, Danny with his girls and other friends (or rather work acquaintances) but Harry more often than not on his own with his piano. But as their personal friendship grew, they liked being together more and more.

Danny was still very much one for the girls – his job putting him in the ideal position to pick them up easily and giving him plenty of opportunities for one-night dates. They were usually show girls, pretty and more often than not blonde, and he refused to be serious with any of them – and the girls he chose would not have expected him to be.

Yet one night in Satch's, Harry unexpectedly saw another side to his partner. He had been playing with Danny standing beside the piano ad libbing lyrics, but during a break they had gone to the bar. Danny, as usual, looked around the room to see if there was any 'talent' he could approach.

There was no one special, but he did spot a very plain-looking girl sitting slumped in a corner, alone, and even from a distance Danny could see that there was something wrong.

He muttered an excuse to Harry and wandered over to the girl and saw she was in tears, her face puckered and her eyes puffy. When he said 'hello', she looked away and didn't want to talk, but he turned on the charm and soon managed to get her to relax.

"Don't cry – people always look better when they smile," he told her. "So come on – give us a little 'un, just a small wee smile."

The girl tried, but it hardly succeeded. "My boyfriend just dumped me," she said. "He'd been talking about getting engaged, then he just left. Just like that."

Just like that. It reminded Danny of an old comedian's punch line, but he held back. "He doesn't know what he's missing," he said instead. The girl looked at him – for some reason she felt a sympathy with him.

By now, Harry was back at the piano playing softly, and Danny suggested going to join him. The girl meekly followed him across the dance floor, and they stood by the piano. The song was smooth, and Danny started improvising words to it although he had never heard it before.

'The smile on your face, makes my clouds roll away...'

He sang as Harry looked up at him. The girl began to smile.

'But so do the wrinkles on Harry's moosh!'

She grinned again – despite her feelings, she couldn't help herself.

Harry finished the tune and there was a pause, Danny told his friend that the girl had just been given some really bad news, and Harry started up again, this time playing a lively, happy tune.

'Give me all your troubles and woe,
Be happy,'
sang Danny.
'If you're happy,
All of us can laugh.'

This time the girl managed to laugh, softly, but a definite chuckle.

"Better now?" asked Danny. "Can my pianist and I get you a drink – or take you somewhere? Home?"

"I'm OK, thanks," replied the girl. "It's a nice thought, but I've got my own car. I'll be alright now." She said her goodbyes and left.

"Hey, mate, what on earth were you doing with her? A real dog like that?" asked Harry as she disappeared across the room.

"Yeah, OK," replied Danny. "She was a dog alright. But she went home wagging her tail."

It was a surprise attitude by Danny – surprising to Harry at least.

It was an attitude, however, that manifested itself throughout their partnership. And whenever there was any kind of ill feeling, their love of music and the mutual need for the friendship of the other soon took over and healed things.

As they began to gel as a team, Danny still used his contacts and their expenses to continue treating Harry – whose sole income was from his rather too infrequent piano lessons – to the good life, and he would often arrange to meet a former comrade or a starlet for a meal or at a club, and would persuade them to pay for it all on the spurious promise of extra publicity. It was something Harry still did not fully approve of – although he went along with it, enjoying the meals and the free drinks despite those thoughts.

In any case, after several months Harry had become impressed enough to suggest that because they got on so well together and their work seemed to be tapering into a unity, he and Danny should team up and work full time to try and 'make it' in show biz.

Danny agreed instantly. "Maybe we could build up a whole folio of a few songs we could plant somewhere to give us an 'in'," he said. He had no idea what working 'full time' would mean. "Have you got any ideas where we could start?" he asked.

Harry nodded. "Yeah, I've got a few ideas, mate. I'd need a bit of time to work on 'em – perhaps we could just sit down soon and try and work things out," he said thoughtfully. "You know, a kind-a game plan…"

Danny smiled, enthusiastic. "But whatever we do, both of us have got to quite ruthless when we write something – we've both got to analyse the song as a whole. If we're going to work together, we'll both have to be ruthlessly honest about each other's work. Do your words fit the mood of my song? Is my melody singable? Does it all work together?"

Danny began to get even more keyed up. "Yeah, why don't you get some ideas we can toss around?" he replied. "You seem better at that sort of thing than me. How long d'you reckon you'd need?"

"Give me a couple of days, mate. We can meet up then."

"OK," said Danny. "I'm working a couple of evenings this week, but how about we meet up in that small coffee bar in Dean Street on Friday? What time? Seven?"

"I know the place. I'll be there," said Harry.

***

Friday was a hectic day for Danny. He was called in to several meetings he didn't want to attend, and by the time seven o'clock came round, he was hot and bothered and hadn't really had any time to think about the meeting with Harry.

He arrived at the coffee bar ten minutes late to find the other man sitting at a table with a cappuccino in front of him and a bit of a scowl on his face. "Sorry I'm late," said Danny, sitting and lighting a cigarette.

"Yeah, well it happens," replied Harry. He got out some notes, anxious to get on with the idea he had in mind. "I've worked out a rough working agreement for both of us – I don't think it gives either an advantage over the other…"

"Working agreements?" said Danny, surprised. "A handshake is enough of an agreement for me."

"Yeah, but I reckon we should make it formal. You know, just in case."

"OK," said Danny. "Not necessary, but if it's what you want, it's fine with me."

Harry handed over a copy of the proposed agreement. "Now, about the actual work," he went on. "I don't think there's any real big future, not a big future, in writing individual songs any more – but like you said the other day, I guess it's the place to start. There's all kinds of singers and bands out there just crying out for new material, if we could latch on to some of them, I reckon it would help us on our way."

Danny smiled, a huge smile. His enthusiasm was still high, and the thought of working as a 'proper' lyricist on 'proper' songs with a 'proper' song writer filled him full of fervour. "That's OK to begin with, but I think we should decide right from the start what we want to do eventually," he said. "If there were Big Bands around, that would be the answer – but as there aren't, I reckon we should aim to build up to writing musicals rather than just pop or sheet music."

"Good idea, I agree," said Harry. "But we've got to do something a little less ambitious to start with. As I said, find some bands or singers…"

Danny put a forefinger on his lips, rubbing it backwards and forwards across them. "You find the singers – I'll give 'em the words," he said.

"OK man, but you've got to be prepared to take criticism of anything you write," went on Harry. "You've got to expect me to be a bit harsh if I think you need it."

Danny nodded. "Your lyrics are getting better. They're still a bit trite, but I reckon they can be harnessed."

Danny accepted the criticism and laughed. "Hey, man, don't fence me in," he said. "Just remember, you give me some real good music to write my words to – not that tra-la-la rubbish – and the words'll get better. Then we'll have some songs!"

Act 4: They Start Working Together

It was a bright spring day, and as Danny left the stifling, depressed feeling of the Central Line underground station at Holland Park, he breathed in deeply. While the air was hardly clean and pure because of the heavy, growling, slow-moving traffic, he was still glad to be out into the fresher air.

As he strolled slowly down Holland Park Avenue towards Harry's flat, he could hear some birds sitting in the grime-blackened trees behind the houses chirruping away in useless protest at the city-haze sunshine, and he had a good feeling about the day. If he didn't exactly have a song in his heart – he had a song in his head.

He hummed it, a tuneless sort of hum even in his mind, and as he walked past the small parade of shops looking in their windows and watching the people, especially the girls, he was optimistic. As he turned into Clarendon Road, he looked over his shoulder at one particular blonde girl as they passed each other – she returned his over-the-shoulder look – and he smiled. It was going to be a high-quality, enjoyable day, of that he was sure.

The song had come to him as he dressed that morning; as always, his love for words and writing meant he had woken with a whole jumble of ideas and short sentences bursting in his mind. This time, those words had formed themselves into a decent pattern, and as he reached Harry's apartment, they were fixed in his mind. As Harry opened the door to the room, Danny blurted out the whole idea with sheer, buoyant, optimistic enthusiasm. Words and an idea of a harmony.

Harry listened, cautious, then without saying anything turned to the upright piano by the wall and started to jot down a few notes on the paper resting on the rack. He studied them for a moment, then began to play them – then he wrote down some more notes – and played them. They were slightly different to the first set, close but in a definite counterpoint, and when he was satisfied, he called

Danny over. Danny looked at the musical hieroglyphics with his words scribbled down above them and smiled.

Harry had written a melody, going back to an old three-beat rhyme rather than the more usual modern 2-4 beat. "Here, mate – I'll sing the first set – then you come in when I indicate," he said.

He began to play the first melody with his left hand, singing as he did so.

> '*The farmer in the field,*
> *The fisherman in the sea…*'

As he reached the second line, he nodded to Danny, who joined in with the same first lines as he began to play the counterpoint with his right hand, almost like a boogie player…

> '*using their age-old skills,*
> *like the hunters of the past…*'

The words were repeated between them in descant as they chanted the song like an old-fashioned rustic round, and Harry continued to play his two varying melodies.

When they finished, Danny clapped his friend on the back. "You've got it. Just as I imagined," he said, delighted. It was probably the first really good piece they had produced between them.

They walked back to Holland Park Avenue, past the station, and to the Rat and Parrot, the drab, square, brick-exteriored pub on the corner of Ladbroke Grove, to celebrate, and immediately slipped into their normal musical chit-chat.

After ordering pints of beer, Danny said he was surprised at the way the roundel had worked out. "I thought I had it – the tune as well – but you took it and right away made it into something," he told Harry. "I'm still surprised at how easy you made it all seem."

Harry shrugged, a deprecating shrug. "It all seemed to fit," he replied simply.

"Yeah, but it's just that I've always thought that the music should always come first – that I just had to fit my words round that."

"Normally true, but you've proved that it doesn't have to." He grinned. "Remember your mate Hammerstein. He always wrote the words first." He took a sip of his beer. "What I think, y'know, is that this proves we can work together.

It shows that we can be on the same wavelength – that we can work out a complete song together. It's a good feeling."

"Yeah, I agree. But I just can't get over the fact that I produced something that's turned out to be a good song. Something that you transformed – made workable. It just seems it's been the wrong way round."

"Maybe. I've got to admit that it's usually true that the tune comes first, but what this really proves is that it takes the two bits to make the whole. It has to be words and music…"

"Good title for a biography," piped in Danny.

"It's been done – Rodgers and Hart," said Harry. "But it has to be both bits. Look, you can wring the withers with your words – but if the music is wrong, it'll kill them stone dead. The words tell the story, but the music provides the mood – the music is important, very important, vital, but maybe in some cases it should just back up the lyrics."

Danny finished his beer and signalled to the barman for two refills. "People always have to be able to hear the words – they probably the most important part in a show songs," went on Harry. "You have to write something that the audience can hear – and you have to write from the point of view of the stalls… in such a way that the audience can hear the music and the words and understand what they are all about and how they fit into the story.

"But then when the audience leaves the theatre, everyone there has to be humming the music – with the words going round inside the head."

Danny was delighted that Harry seemed, at last, to be thinking as he has always said – but as they left the bar, Harry insisted that it was really just a case of the two of them working together…as HE had always insisted.

***

A few weeks later, things began to move. Danny was busy arranging a press conference at his office when he got an e-mail from Harry asking him to call round that evening – urgently. There was no reason given, nothing apart from the request, and when he called up to try and find why, he got no answer from Harry's phone.

It was about 7 o'clock that evening before Danny turned up at the Holland Park apartment.

"Where's the fire?" he asked.

"I've got some news – hey, mate, it's time to celebrate," replied Harry. "Y'see, I've been asking around, and there's a choir sings in a church near here that wants to take our piece and put it on as a kind of chorale. They want to sing it…"

"A church choir? You mad or something? We can do better…"

"It's not a church choir – they just sing in the church hall. They're willing to pay us. OK, it's only 50 quid – but it's cash in hand. I've accepted it."

Harry giggled like an excited schoolboy. "Our first payment – we're pros man, pros," he said.

Danny had never seen Harry quite as excited before – it was a very different side to the normally more sombre Australian, and he wondered if his own enthusiasm was rubbing off on the other man, having an effect on him. Whether it was or not, Harry was so ebullient about his news that this time he influenced Danny.

"They liked it so much they want to start singing it straight away," went on Harry. "They've got a concert next week or sometime soon, and they're actually going to, ya know, have a run through this evening. They said we could go along and listen – maybe make a few comments."

"Hey, like you said – real pros," said Danny, loosening up. "That'll be good."

After a while, Harry said they should go. They left his room and walked down Clarendon Road, cutting through Elgin Crescent to Ladbroke Grove and then down to a youth club behind a hospice in Lancaster Road where the choir was rehearsing. Both of them were still sniggering, slightly nervously with anticipation, as they slipped into the hall, where the choir was resting although still formed up in position. The conductor saw the two men and made some signals, waved his hands – and the first notes of Harry and Danny's chorale began softly, and then lifted high.

It was the first time either man had heard his own music played by someone else, and they both felt good about it. Good – and proud. Although they know the song would only be heard by a very limited audience in a local church hall in Notting Hill Gate, it was a first success.

Writing, they both felt, was as easy and as simple as that. Harry took a deep breath and exhaled slowly, while Danny sipped a can of beer someone had given him, desperately trying not to show his excitement. Both men felt that inner joy delight of knowing that something he had created had been accepted by others – the kind of feeling a parent feels about a child.

"Feels good, huh?" asked Danny.

Harry nodded agreement. "Hardly Broadway, but it's a start," continued Danny, "And ya gotta remember…if at first you don't succeed – lower your standards!" They both laughed and went back into the hall.

After the start with the choir, Danny and Harry began finding more work, although only on a small scale. They wrote for small local amateur pop groups, for wanna-be singers who advertised on the web – Danny picked up names from his office computer – and very occasionally through word of mouth from the musicians at Satchmo's.

As their names got round the local district, in fact, they began building up quite a bit of a business with local amateur groups and the like, and although it was hardly world-beating, they did manage a very limited success even though it hardly paid their expenses. But all the time they were learning – not only how to produce music and words for clients with specific needs but to work together. It was all good training.

Danny loved the proliferation of ethnic restaurants and tea houses in London, and even when he had nothing planned, he would often go to one of them so he could sit and watch the other customers. They would often give him ideas, and it grew to be part of his regular ritual.

Once, sitting alone with a small coffee, he noted that few of the others at nearby tables were speaking English. As usual, he had no notebook or paper with him – nor a pen. He called the waiter over, borrowed a biro, and penned some notes on a paper napkin.

'*A Frenchman eats a horse*
Of course.
A German sauerkraut.
Without a doubt.
You eat steak in a cossie,
If you're an Aussie,
And if you're from the Potomac
You'll munch a Mac
But I'm British and I like my food traditional.
So I only eat curry in a hurry,
Macaroni like bologn-ee,
And a tapas in a bite is something awful.

I like fish and chips to put bulk upon my hips…
And I always eat the beef of Good Old England.'

He went on for a few more verses in similar vein before he finally got fed up with it…then he drained his coffee cup and went for a meal. A pizza.

***

As time went by and his rapport with Harry built up, though, there was enough work for Danny to decide to pack in his public relations job so that he could concentrate more fully on the music. In spite of the fact that most of the songs he and Harry were producing for others were unpaid, he felt he could earn enough by freelancing as a journalist or occasional PR, and apart from the actual job of creating music, he was so fascinated by all that Harry was teaching him about harmony and composition and felt he would better use his time writing with him full time.

He handed in his notice, shyly telling both his boss and everyone else in the office that he wanted to return to journalism because he did not have the guts to admit he was going to try and be a professional song writer. In the main they thought he was foolish because it would mean giving up a well-paid job for just casual earnings.

"So you think I'm stupid?" he asked his colleagues (pronouncing the word 'stoopid'). "Well, you should see my grandfather – he's bent double!" Even when being serious, he could not help the flip jokey manner.

While Danny was working out his notice, he continued to meet Harry irregularly as before. They still produced songs on an ad hoc basic – one or other coming up with a melody or some lyrics, and the other matching in mainly on the spur of the moment.

Obviously, they didn't always match up. One day, for instance, Danny went to Harry's flat with some words he had produced the night before. Harry was playing about with a simple idea on the piano, trying it this way and that, and Danny suggested that the theme might be right for his new lyrics.

'To advance. Enhance.
It just needs just one glance:
To advance.
Not by chance.'

"That's quite a good start for a tune," said Harry. "I don't think they quite go with this song, but perhaps we can develop them some time."

Danny shrugged his shoulders nonchalantly. "OK," he replied. Then he laughed. "At least it shows I'm changing," he added. "In the old days I'd have written that last line as 'Then the wind turns the corner and blows up your pants'!"

Another time, Danny turned up in a café with some lyrics he had written at the office earlier that day. Harry read them carefully, then quietly went over them a second time mouthing the word silently as he did so.

He nodded when he had finished them. "Different to usual, mate," he said. "You normally stick to the rules – but this time you seem to have gone right against the 32-bar format, the natural."

"What the hell's that?" asked Danny, puzzled, and Harry had to explain.

"It's when you have a few lines rhyming, repeat the rhyme for another few lines, go away on another tack – then come back to the original rhyme," he said. "It's the way most writers normally do it – a statement, repeat the statement, throw in a contrasting melody – the release – then finish with the original statement again. They call it the AABA form."

"AABA? Isn't that a Swedish group?"

Harry laughed, a shallow laugh. "No. Most songs have two stanzas repeating the rhyme, then the release, then back to the original theme for the fourth and final stanza – AABA."

"Eh? What the hell are you talking about?"

"You must know," said Harry, suddenly annoyed. "It's the very basic of lyric writing…"

He just as quickly regained his temper and explained as he would to a young child. "Oh it's just a formal technique of writing lyrics," he said dismissively.

They paused as their coffees were served by an effeminate-looking waiter.

"You usually break the rule," went on Harry when the waiter had gone, leaving a small spill of coffee on the table. "You seem to have your own way of doing things…I suppose, it's because you're so up yourself with your split rhymes and, ya know, your weird and wonderful couplets…all Lorenz Hart'ish."

"Yeah," replied Danny. "If you say so. But you've got to admit that splitting a line can be great. Think of Hart's 'Manhattan' – that's the supreme example."

"You've got a thing about Hart, haven't you, mate?"

"Maybe…"

Harry nodded. "Yeah, OK. OK."

He thought for a moment. "If you're talking Hammerstein, it proves my point," he said eventually. "Think '*Bali Hai*' – think how the music sets the mood and the words just add to the scene. It's what I've always said, a blend."

"Yeah – a perfect blend," said Danny. He pulled a face, a wry look. "But I didn't know you cared about words."

Harry gave him an old-fashioned look. "Of course I do," he said. "Both. Words and music."

Harry would often start off their meetings by getting into some of the more technical descriptions of formal rhythms and the like, and because Danny could, or would, not be bothered would mischievously branch away quickly onto his favourite mickey-taking theme – telling Danny about writing lyrics that would go with the music he provided, about their purpose and the way they had to, must, explain or move the story he, Harry, was trying to tell forward.

He knew Danny would always bite. "It's all about story telling if you want to write good songs – good show songs," he would insist. "My music has to provide the mood – your words have to tell the listener what to think within that mood."

"Suppose so," Danny once replied dreamily.

He recalled a song he had written while they were in a café one evening. As Harry had drunk a coffee, he'd ordered a brandy and while sipping it had scribbled some words on a small cardboard table mat.

> '*Grey homes, grey streets.*
> *Grey people, No treats*
> *But you*
> *Colour my heart.*'

Danny thought of those words now. "Yep," he mused. "Lorenz Hart lyrics – and my lyrics like his. Full of passion." He laughed. "Silly bugger," he said out loud.

As they wrote, Harry's natural flair for arranging the music helped, as did the fact that because Danny had never had any formal training, he had to rely on the other man to transpose his ideas to paper. Harry had learned how to use the mechanics of music to produce a basic melody rather than just rely on inspiration, and he tried to teach Danny but to no avail. On top of that, he was able to use his own imagination, expertise and talent to create good songs. It helped him when they were working.

One day, they were getting on with one piece when Harry paused. He sat at the piano, and started 'conducting' the imaginary piece – he could hear the brass, the trumpets, trombones and saxes holding a dialogue with the piano and violins, the soothing woodwind against the strident brass, the drums interrupting both as if to show that his homily was just as important.

Danny was used to it. He quietly lit a cigarette and let his partner get on with things. He knew Harry would explain things when he'd finished the arrangement in his mind.

For his part, Harry knew it would be easier if he could explain things in technical terms. "Why didn't you ever try to learn how to read music then?" he asked Danny one day.

Danny grew defensive. "Irving Berlin couldn't either," he replied grumpily.

It was a funny thing, but knowing simple little facts like that were commonplace with both of them.

They both read a lot about music, and as a result, when they spoke, they referred to things they have read. Danny, in particular, would read about lyricists interminably. And during his nights at the club, or with other writers, he would quote chunks from the book he was currently reading.

"The book I'm reading says that while other people write lyrics, Larry Hart wrote thoughts and feelings for a storyline. I'd like to be known like that," he said simply one night.

Harry was the same, but had a wider selection of musical subjects in his reading matter. On another occasion, replying to Danny's question about how they should get started writing a song jointly, he sighed and answered as if he was talking to a young boy. "Don't you remember, you told me about it from something you read by Richard Stilgo somewhere," he said like a teacher. "When

66

you write as a team, you have to get a hook – the bit of the song that everyone is going to remember. It doesn't matter what that hook is… a bit of the tune or some of the lyrics…you've got to find it, and then both of you have to build round it…"

Danny tried to remember. "Yeah, OK," he said eventually.

Then again, as always, when Danny was reading a book, he told Harry about it. The book was about Oscar Hammerstein's partnership with Richard Rodgers. "OK," replied Harry with a smirk when he paused. "But didn't someone else once say someone like Stephen Sondheim had infinite talent but a limited soul, while Hammerstein had limited talent but an infinite soul?"

He grinned again. "Soul don't get you nowhere on Broadway baby," he said. "It's talent, pure and simple talent."

"Hammerstein didn't do too badly," countered Danny rather truculently.

They often swapped books when they had finished them, and one day Danny brought in a book by lyricist Don Black he had just finished. "You might get something from this," he said as he handed it over. "You know Don, this book of his, 'Wrestling With Elephants' – fascinating title."

Harry flipped through the book, and it fell open to a page about halfway through. Harry glanced down at it. He smiled, a wry smile, and read. "It says here that when you're writing a musical, the sheer length of writing, re-writing and changing things around, the months of deep concentration, all requires an enormous amount of emotional and mental input."

He looked up at Danny. "Do you think you're capable of that?"

Danny laughed. "Try me," he suggested.

They did not only discuss things between themselves, though. One night, Harry told a group of bored musicians about the current book he was reading. In it, he explained, several musicians spoke of 'plucking songs from the air'.

"There's this line about a guy called Bukka White, a guitarist, who said he wrote 'sky songs'," said Harry to the others around him on the band stand. "The idea was that his songs fell from the sky and onto the paper. Doesn't that sound great, just how it happens?"

Not that any of the musicians were paying any attention, at the time they were only intent on finishing the set and getting to the bar to throw more whisky down their throats before going back to pick up their own music. As so often, Harry was too sombre for their mood, too straight. But he did play pretty piano.

Not that things like that slowed down either Harry or Danny. They read about music, spoke about music, thought about music. For each of them, it was their whole life. They revelled in working together as musicians, like most songsters praying for the daily miracle of the hit song that would take the world by storm.

Danny, though, still had a job to look after, and although he now felt it got in the way of his writing with Harry, it did mean he had to reluctantly devote some of his time to his employer. But because he was working out his notice, it still took him a little by surprise when he was told he had to go to Paris for a conference. That evening, in a small club in central London, he told Harry about it.

"Lucky bugger," said Harry.

"You'll be able to get out and see the sights. The Impressionists – Monet, Cezanne, Renoir and all the others. You could even go to the Louvre and see the Mona Lisa."

"I thought Nat 'King' Cole sang that."

"Idiot."

"Yeah. It's only for one night, though," replied Danny. "And anyway, Mona's not my type – she's no oil painting. Well, she is...but..."

He turned his attention to a girl sitting close by and apparently listening to them talking. "How'd you like to come to Paris with me?" he asked in a loud voice that made others at the bar turn round and look.

"Love to," she answered. Her voice was soft and with a slight American twang. "Where are we staying?"

Danny grinned, self-confident. "Well," he told the girl as Harry listened in amazed, "I always think you get a better feel for a place if you stay in a small, cheap b&b, don't you? I know just the place..."

The girl raised her eyebrows. "Oh no," she replied. "I prefer five-star hotels – and the big boys who can afford them."

There was a hint of low laughter from around them, but Danny ignored it and turned back to Harry. "Stupid foreigner," he said grumpily.

"Hey, I'm a foreigner," replied Harry.

"Yeah," said Danny. "But you're a Colonial – that's almost human."

Harry smiled. He'd heard it all before.

About a week later, when Danny got back from the trip, Harry asked him what it was like. "Awful," said Danny. "For a start, they switched the meet from

Paris – decided Salzburg was a better place. Probably cheaper – and they flew us there on a package. No food, no drink…"

"Salzburg? Well, at least there were the dreaming spires, mate. 'The Sound of Music' and all that."

"Huh, I wish. It was getting dark when we got there, and we were picked up in the terminal building, taken straight to a hotel on the edge of the airport – and didn't get out of it until they drove us back to departures. We had no time to do anything."

"That's the way it goes," said Harry, shrugging his shoulders.

"Yeah, but what I saw of Salzburg – it looked just like Hounslow."

Harry tried not to laugh. "But there must have been something good about the trip," he said.

"I suppose," came back Danny. "There was this trolley dolly on the flight from Strasbourg – a real cracker. We were a bit late and she was busy, but I think I could have pulled her if the flight had been a little longer. Trouble is that they rushed us off at the end and I didn't get a chance. If there'd only been a bit more time, I'm sure I could have got a date. She'd been on the flight out to Paris as well, and I'm sure she recognised me. She gave me the eye all the way home even though she was busy."

Harry laughed out loud this time. "Ya stupid dingo, you couldn't pull one of those air birds even on a flight from Sydney – and that's 24 hours long."

Danny pulled a face. "Yeah, well, it's better than being you," he retorted. "Heck, most times you couldn't even pull a barrow."

About a week or so later, the two men had finished work for the day and were sitting in Harry's room talking aimlessly. They were reasonably satisfied with the outline of a song they had produced, and both were quite relaxed.

"I've been wondering about you, you mongrel. Why do you only write lyrics?" Harry asked Danny. "Why not a book, stories, something else?"

"I write press releases and news stories," said Danny defensively. "But, well, I don't know. I just feel I want to be involved in music somehow. I just like the flow, the rhythm, of songs. It's all I'm interested in."

"Yeah. Suppose I'm like that as well, mate. Always music." Harry became reflective. "Ya know, I remember, when I was a kid, I suppose I must have been about twelve, I used t'play piano in Big Bands. There were two of them, one at school, one in a youth club after school – I'd often play for both on the same day. I loved it."

Danny looked at his partner. Harry had never spoken about his childhood before. "You know, I remember I once played in both bands at the same event," went on Harry. "It was just before Christmas, and both were booked to play in a Christmas concert – Carols by Candlelight they called it. Funny, the sun was shining, temperature was up in the mid-to-late-20s, people were having picnics on the grass, sunbathing, slurping backs the beers. Now how incongruous is that? Christmas Carols by Candlelight in the summer – in the sun."

He laughed. "But that's the way music should be heard," he added. "Everyone together and enjoying it."

Danny nodded. "Yeah, funny," he said. "But somehow, music is always tied up with sunshine for me as well. I remember everything always being sunny at home – the sun was always shining when I was a kid, and as I always thought in lyrics it somehow linked the two.

"I remember there used to be a huge magnolia outside my parents' bedroom window – a huge white magnolia..." He did not notice Harry quickly look up, then reach into his pockets for a notebook and pen. "...it was tremendous in the sunshine, really beautiful. I loved that tree. Well, all of us did – and I always wanted to write a song about it.

"But I never did. I suppose I didn't do too much in those days. Too lazy, I suppose. I didn't play anything, no bands or anything like that – in fact, the only thing I remember from school was when I was about 12 or 13, one of the boys had it with a girl from the same year. I kept asking him what it was like – not because I wanted to know from any sexy point of view but because I wanted to write a song about it."

Harry stopped writing and slowly pushed the notebook across the table. Danny looked at it, and saw a collection of musical notes that didn't mean anything to him. "What's this?" he asked.

"Your song – The White Magnolia," said Harry. "You'd better let me have some words for it pdq."

The two men looked at each other, completely relaxed. It was a rare moment between them. "Hey, let's have another schooner of beer," said Harry.

***

As Danny's job notice slowly ran out, he grew more apprehensive about leaving full-time work and branching out as a freelance. He had called in favours from many of his contacts, and one or two of them had promised work when necessary (although the majority promised but had no intention of coming through).

He and Harry began to get a few extra very lowly paid writing jobs with some of the local groups that played in the clubs and especially the pubs in the Notting Hill area, but during his last weeks with the PR firm Danny seemed to work harder than ever at it. It was not only as if he was making some sort of effort to counter his growing feeling of trepidation over being without a job, he was determined to build up a financial pool from his expenses, and to date as many of the office girls as he could – and to leave behind the happy-happy regard for him he had worked so hard to build up.

What it meant, however, was that Harry was often left on his own to work on pieces that they had begun between them. He still maintained many of his New World instincts – and when he was not working (or going to music clubs like Satch's) he found he was going to long walks in the parks around London, and in the evenings would go to bed fairly early. For a while, he became something of a recluse, without friends and still rather shy in the big city.

The pair did still see each other, of course, but for a while it was less frequent than Harry would have liked, and with little to do, tried pacing the streets to keep himself busy. Harry still did not really like the frenetic pace and hustle and bustle of the town, but with nothing else to do he took the Underground to the heart of the town, the West End, and then followed his nose. He was forcing himself to like the noise, but he missed the quiet beaches and bays of his hometown Sydney.

One day, he made his way from Charing Cross down to the Embankment, this time rather enjoying the smells of the ethnic restaurants in Villiers Street, turning left by the Thames and stopping close to Cleopatra's Needle. He leaned on the wall overlooking the river, enjoying a sudden quiet.

He watched a small V-formation of geese change leadership as they navigated their way towards Docklands, thinking how strange it was to see such a marvel of nature in an overcrowded urban environment. He noticed a gull sitting on the wind low over the water, seeming to enjoy the view. A fellow gull called to him from a wooden pile projecting up from the water. A tourist boat sounded a soft hooter.

After the heavy traffic of Charing Cross and The Strand, there was a different musical resonance to the sounds of the river. He began to see a little beauty in the crowded city at last.

Finally, Danny left his job, though, and once he had things soon began to move back on course. The only thing was that with more time on his hands, Danny was now able to haunt the many pubs and clubs where small groups put on music. He went during the day to meet the musicians as they were setting up, and in the evenings would often return with Harry to sound out the chances of writing something for the performers. They were always welcomed – as long as they didn't ask for money.

"If at first you don't succeed – lower your sights," joked Danny to his partner.

Danny quickly took advantage of his new situation, with the extra spare time on his hands – and plenty of girlfriends to take out. In a bar one afternoon, skipping away from a meeting to discuss lyrics with Harry, he tried to chat up a good-looking girl and suggested she come to Satchmo's on the following Saturday.

He had arranged to meet Harry at the club, and to his surprise the girl turned up, bringing a friend along with her. Danny was delighted to see that the second girl was even more beautiful than the first, and as they crossed the floor to join the boys at the bar he thought he would go for her himself and unload the original on Harry.

The new girl had a classic beauty, and Danny was knocked out. But when she was introduced, her high-pitched, violently East Midlands twang grated. It didn't take him – or Harry – long to dump both of the girls.

"Why isn't beauty always perfect?" he asked Harry afterwards.

***

The excitement of being unemployed and with spare time to waste soon palled, and Danny now saw more and more of Harry. Since leaving his job he had begun freelancing as a journalist, but there was little work and he often felt local newspaper jobs were beneath him. What there was of that, and there was little, proved to be exceedingly easy.

By now, Harry had learned how to use the mechanics of music to produce a basic melody rather than just rely on inspiration. He had grown up with the basics all around him, but now he was able to use his own imagination, expertise and talent to create good songs on top of them. He read countless books on the subject, teaching himself more about the complicated workings of writing music, and he would often try and tell Danny about rhythm forms in songs, about the pattern of beats in a piece of music – fast or slow, with the beats arranged in groups of two, three, four or more – about words in triple time with a piano accompaniment in double time – about chromatic and pentatonic scales – about cadences that came about when switching from one chord to another at the end of a piece of music.

Harry would try to explain to his partner that scales are like a ladder of notes starting on the keynote and stepping up one note at a time. "The word scale comes from the Italian word *scala* meaning ladder," he'd explain.

Sometimes he tried simpler language, telling Danny that a sequence of notes is a small fragment of melody which a composer repeats at different pitches – he would talk of how sequences can be repeated over and over again at different pitches to create different and beautiful melodies, and he patiently repeated basic facts such as the way music is constructed from families of notes, called keys – either major or minor.

"Melodies in major keys sound happier and more upbeat; those in minor keys sound sad and wistful," he said. "But you can often switch from one to the other…and you can have a relative minor key…"

Harry spoke eagerly of harmony, playing or singing a combination of different notes simultaneously to make chords, and tried to show how adding harmony to a melody can give it depth and emotion.

Danny would inevitably look blank and turn away, disinterested in the baffling technical jargon. As he could see no real need to know such things, he let it all drift over him and simply wrote his words in the way he felt them. Without the necessity of going to work, he began to get even more haphazard in his daily life. Never the tidiest person, he started to dress down, often wearing shirts or sweaters with stains down the front, and generally forgetting to look after his appearance.

The disorderly, cluttered, chaotic frame of mind spilled over to his working habits, too. While the work itself was getting to be more than just satisfactory, getting down to it became rather hard – a chore. Dodging meetings became almost second nature – almost an art form it seemed at times. As well as taking time away from the conscientious hard work of composition, he took to frequenting bars, restaurants and clubs during the day.

He also began to spend a lot of time hanging around St. Martin's Lane and Theatreland – "Breathing in the atmosphere," he told himself – and now that he was not working in a TV or film publicity atmosphere, he got a vicarious, unnatural, enthusiastic expectation from it, especially when very occasionally he saw a big star – or more often when he spotted one of the show girls he used to work with.

When Harry asked him one day where he had been when they should have met, he mumbled and made excuses, not wanting to admit what he had really been doing.

Finally, Harry told Danny he had to be more dedicated. "According to the book I'm reading, composers write songs and stack them away. I know I did – got dozens of them, mate. But the books says lyricists have to write for an occasion. You've got t'get down to it, mate."

Danny disagreed, insisting he had a whole stack of lyrics just waiting to be put to music. He reeled off several from the top of his head to show Harry what he meant – songs he'd written like…

> *'Dandelions are a poor man's roses,*
> *The single red rose of love,*
> *Blondes can ginger up your life,*
> *You are nothing but a shadow,*
> *The sun don' shine on a broken heart.'*

"That's just a few," he snapped. "You don't have to worry about me – I've got plenty of words. And there's a lot more to come."

He paused, and then a grin took over from the start of his sudden flash of anger. He couldn't help himself.

"What about…

> *'The rainfall is tomorrow's sewage.'"*

Harry realised it was the first time Danny had been really flip for some time. Perhaps, he thought to himself, he is getting serious about our partnership after all.

And Danny was serious – when he could be made to work. He was passionate about his writing, never happier than when putting words together and using them to create a mood. As a pair, he and Harry fitted well together – they had an easy way of operating, with either one or the other providing an impetus for the other which quickly started to dovetail. No matter which came up with the basic idea, though, Harry always had to provide the music first.

Within a few months, they became not quite telepathic – but each finding himself automatically on the right wavelength with the other when they were writing their songs.

As they wrote, those songs gradually became better and better. The words and music came along in a fast succession, with Harry producing a series of tunes, some quite good, and Danny churning out words for them with an almost indecent haste.

Harry particularly liked one song, '*The Sounds Of Our Love*'. When it was completed, he played it over and over repeatedly humming the melody as Danny sang the words.

'The sigh of the wind
As it ruffles your hair.
The sound of your voice
When you say you love me.
These are the things I adore,
These are the sounds of our love.
The step of your feet
On the front garden path.
The sound of your key in the door.
These are the sounds of our love.
The sounds that I simply adore'.
There were many others.
'Words can tell you anything…
But – I love you.'

And another called '*On The Darker Side Of Midnight*', which they wrote in the hope of sending it to one of the current ballad singers they heard on the radio…

'On the darker side of midnight,
That's when I know I love you.
When the witching hour has chimed
On the darker side of midnight,

And you're not there.
Our love died away at midnight,
But my heart knows it's still there.
When the night winds blow at midnight,
And you're not there.
On the darker side of midnight,
My heart feels out to find you.
When the world is at its darkest,
And you're not there.'

The words and the harmonies were improving all the time – but really, neither Danny nor Harry had any idea of how to be commercial with them. They were still aiming at local groups and singers, and just once Harry rang a publisher to get some advice. "Get an agent," he was told curtly. He thought of it, but nothing happened.

Life, though, muddled along for the two of them. Harry still worked with little children at the keyboard, and Danny blithely sailed through things almost unaware of the need to earn money. And although they usually met in Harry's apartment, where they had the piano, he would frequently suggest a pub lunch or a local café.

One day around noon, as arranged the day before, Harry went along to the Clarenden Arms around the corner from his flat to meet Danny. Danny was talking to a stranger when he entered the bar, telling a story. "...then this bloke calls out to the ambulance man 'Help, I've lost my leg'..." he giggled, "...and the medic pointed across the road and told him, 'No you haven't. It's over there!'"

Harry walked across. "Hi, Mac," said Danny. "This is my mate...er, what's your name?"

"I'm Wayne," said the stranger, reaching out his hand and shaking Harry's hand. "Do you write West End musicals with Danny here?"

Harry shot Danny a quick look. "Well, yes. We're partners."

"What've you done...?"

Danny butted in. "Well, we did this show about a Jewish lad who goes to meet his arranged bride. She's a real dog, and when they're introduced, he bursts into song." Danny had a cheeky grin on his face as he started to sing the music from 'My Fair Lady'.

'*And this is my beloved*?'

"Come on, Danny," says Harry. "got some work to do." Wayne looked baffled as they went to a table on the other side of the pub.

Small incidents that saddened Harry somewhat. The two men couldn't have been more different if they had tried, their sense of humour, their attitude to life, their way of working, and Danny's facetious, jokey way of living somehow irritated the more strait-laced and earnest Australian. Not all the time, just occasionally.

It was not only in their approach to their work together – Harry was always meticulous, Danny a little more casual and laid-back – it was in their dress as well. Danny had by now become far more uncaring in just about everything he did away from his actual writing, and more often than not he was downright sloppy. He would often wear a sweater with a hole in the sleeve – he had several like that, and he usually wore the same one day after day – frequently one in a colour that did not match anything else he was dressed in.

Harry became determined to smarten him up as a first step to making him, as he saw it, more responsible, and persuaded his partner to go along to Marks and Spencer to buy a new sweater. "But I'm coming with you to make sure you get one," he insisted. "I don't trust you on your own."

When they got to the shop, Danny first of all chose a hideously garish yellow and blue garment, but Harry quickly put a block on that. Then after wandering around the department, he selected a suitable garment for his friend – and simply to wind up by the whole process, Danny approved it. They went to the cash point together to pay for it.

"Is it the right size?" asked Harry as they queued, waiting for their turn behind a gaggle of women shoppers. Danny checked – it was not, and he went back to replace it.

"That'll look better than those others you wear," said Harry when they left the shop.

"For Christ's sake, stop mothering me," snapped Danny.

Over the next couple of weeks, Danny always turned up to meet Harry – still wearing the old sweater and ignoring the new one! Harry mentioned it just once. "You're not my nursemaid," repeated Danny.

Act 5: Harry's Romance

Without a full-time job to go to, Danny was feeling a little lost. True, he and Harry were slowly starting to get more work, but Danny was beginning to grow more apprehensive about earning enough money until the music writing business properly recognised them.

He had called in promised favours from many of his former contacts, but there were few jobs for a freelance journalist and far too many university graduate PR people on the market. Many of the old friends or firms he went to see promised payment on results, but that was no good to Danny.

"They always used to say, in God we trust – all others pay cash," he cynically told Harry.

With the growing insecurity, Danny began to get a little edgy. His writing reverted to his old flippant way to cover his feelings, and he frequently snapped at Harry over little things. Harry somehow understood.

Harry still wanted to educate Danny in the techniques and technical parts of writing music – things like key signatures, major and minor scales and many other things he felt Danny could use in his writing – but he knew that particularly in his current mood Danny would never knuckle down to learning them. Or even listening. Danny didn't like being watched over.

As a result, the continual missed meetings, flip lyrics and lackadaisical and careless way of working began to grate with Harry. At first, he went along with things hoping Danny would settle down, but when they did not, he got ratty himself. Despite his instincts, instead of trying to nursemaid Danny, he began to look for faults in the other man.

In the few weeks since leaving his job, for instance, Danny produced several lyrics which he had quite liked. Harry had promised to run the rule over them, although for a variety of reasons, he'd never done so, but he did now, with a far more nastily critical eye than he should have done. Instead of seeing how they could be adapted or improved, he went looking for fault.

Danny did not like what was being said about his words, and finally he hit back. "Why do you always try to put me down?" he asked.

"'Cause you're still being flip," snapped back Harry. "You're trying to be too clever – why don't you try writing something serious for a change." He was sorry as soon as he said it, but it rankled with Danny and stayed in his mind.

Things were not made any better when Harry found romance.

Things were still moving along slowly when Harry went to a pub in the West End to meet a small amateur group that he'd read was interested in getting some new songs, and while they readied themselves to play, he picked up a trade magazine one of them had been reading. He got a bit of a shock when he read a headline: "Music exec marries his PA," and discovered it referred to his first girlfriend, Lucy Grey – someone he had not thought about for a long time.

Although Lucy was of no concern by now, simply a romantic event from his past, the news seemed to sadden Harry. For a while, it made him surprisingly vulnerable, and he found himself looking at girls almost in the same way as Danny – who had always insisted: "The best quality a girl can have, any girl, is availability."

The news of Lucy's marriage showed Harry his need for female companionship, because in truth, until now Danny had been his only real friend in England. He became inhibited, and his music sub-consciously started to become melancholic.

Danny struggled to write lyrics that matched his mood through the change, although he didn't like what was happening and became more angry than sympathetic towards his friend's change.

Because of that, when Danny's parents invited him to go home for a weekend, he readily accepted. He felt two days in the countryside would give him a bit of a break, a bit of peace, and would help the relationship with Harry – and their music.

He left early on the Friday evening, and after he had gone, Harry mooched around not knowing what to do with himself. Throughout the evening and most of Saturday, he felt obviously alone in a strange big city – a loner left alone when he really wanted someone to console him for something, he didn't really feel needed any consoling. The effect of the final loss of Lucy was something he couldn't comprehend.

Finally, late on Saturday night, he decided to go to Satchmo's. Once there he let the music take over, and although he didn't play with the group at first, he began to feel better.

Around midnight he noticed a girl sitting on the far side of the room, and although her back was to him, he was attracted by her long honey-blonde hair, which was pulled back tightly and held in position with an elastic band. Harry smiled to himself and thought that Danny would make a crack about her not being able to afford a proper hair tie. Danny was still in the back of his mind.

There was something about the girl, though, and he watched as she chatted to her girlfriends. When she turned round, he saw that she had a rather unusual face, with young, almost baby'ish, features that still somehow seemed to give an overall impression that she had the wisdom of a far older woman. She looked experienced. When she stood, her legs were long and she was deep waisted, and from the way she moved as she crossed to the bar where he was sitting, Harry had the feeling that she was a dancer.

She stood next to him as she unsuccessfully tried to catch the barman's attention, and Harry took a closer look. Her skin was fair and smooth, and she had incredibly blue eyes that seemed, somehow, to hide a certain sadness. But her mouth and nose wrinkled when she looked, abstractly, in his direction and smiled. She was very beautiful.

"Perhaps I can help," said Harry with a smile, clicking his fingers in the direction of the barman.

The girl smiled back. "Thanks," she said. Her voice was a trifle throaty, and still had a soft Australian twang despite the fact that it was much Anglicised. The barman came over, and she ordered a wine. "Here, let me get that," said Harry.

"Thanks," said the girl again, and when the drink was served and paid for, she raised the glass in salute to Harry. "You sound like an Oz, too," she said. "Where from?"

"Sydney," replied Harry. "You?"

"I'm from Melbourne."

"Yeah? Went there once. What's that hideous place...the Federation Square? I thought it was awful, as if someone had bought a job lot of old tin and slapped it together and called it modern design."

"You mean Foundation Square," said the girl, mock serious. "It's our city's pride and joy."

"Well, I didn't think too much of it," said Harry. The girl smiled.

"Did you like any of Melbourne?"

"Oh yeah. Around the Centenary Building – and the museum – the state capital building…"

"You mean the traditional parts?"

"Yeah. Well, I'm an old-fashioned sort of guy." He took a mouthful of his drink. "So, what are you doing over here?" he asked.

"Oh simple, really. I'm trying to be a singer or dancer, and I felt I'd get more chance over here."

"Coincidence," said Harry. "I'm sort-a trying to be a song writer – when I get a show, I'll call you."

"Is that a pitch to pick me up?" replied the girl with a cheeky smile. She had a lively, bubbly personality that Harry found intriguing.

"No, not really. Well – yes, suppose it is. But I mean it. When I get a show." She laughed out loud – but with him rather than at him.

"Can I wait that long?" she asked.

Harry nodded, and this time they both laughed, although it was more convention rather than because it was funny. They both sipped their drinks.

"So, what's your name?" asked Harry after a few moments.

"Everyone calls me Lex."

"Lex?"

"It's short for Alexis."

"But your friends call you Lex?"

"Everyone calls me Lex," she replied. "Lex Forsyth."

There was a break in the music, and some of the musicians stood down. "Look, I join in sometimes," said Harry. "Why don't you come across? You can join in."

Lex tilted her head to one side. "You don't know what my voice is like," she said.

"This is a good time to find out," replied Harry and led the way to the piano.

As he started to play, a slightly upbeat version of 'This Heart of Mine', a drummer and a bass player joining in instinctively. Lex leaned on the piano, and began to hum softly. Then she started to sing.

Her voice was clear and on pitch, and Harry was delighted. "Hey, you know it," he said, surprised.

"Harry Warren – with words by Arthur Freed." She smiled.

At the end of the song, Lex listened as Harry switched to one of his own songs. "That yours? It was beautiful," she told him when it was over. "But I'd better get back to my friends."

"OK. But let's meet again," he said.

Lex nodded.

"Lunch? Tomorrow?"

Lex reached in her bag and took out a piece of paper and a pen. When she had written her number on it, she put it down by Harry's left hand. "Call me – around 10," she told him, and she walked back across the dance floor.

Harry nodded, looked at the phone number, and switched the song to an old favourite, '*Good Night, Sweetheart*'.

They met up on the Sunday at around one o'clock, and Harry took Lex to a smart Italian bistro in Hampstead she told him about, although he knew it would stretch his finances to the limit. He didn't mind, and when they were seated, she suggested they order the house specialty – scaloppini di vitello al Marsala with asparagus on a bed of risotto verde. Harry agreed, and turned to the wine list and tried to pretend he knew more about it than he did before Lex suggested a couple of glasses of the house red. Knowing it would be cheaper, Harry agreed.

The waiter came, notebook at the ready, and Harry ordered the main course and the wine. "And let's have a bowl of chips, too," he said jokily, imitating Danny's way.

The meal arrived and the waiter brought the chips. Harry and Lex looked at each other, her lips quivering and he a little abashed – then they both started giggling.

The meal was a success after that, Harry eating with gusto and Lex eating equally heartily but with a natural gentility. When she had finished, Lex sat watching Harry still eating – occasionally reaching across and helping herself from Harry's bowl of chips. When Harry had also finished, he looked around the restaurant with a satisfied look on his face.

Later, they got the dessert menu, looking – in Lex's case – slightly apprehensive at the description of a chocolate and cream confection that sounded sinfully gorgeous. "Should we try the tiramisu?" asked Harry.

"Perhaps. We shouldn't…but what the hell…"

"Maybe we could share just one helping between us."

"Well, OK. But…"

Harry called the waiter over and ordered one portion. "But two spoons please, mate," he told the waiter, who smirked. He'd seen it all before.

The dessert had various other bits to dip into as well, and Harry fed Lex the delicacies while feasting on her face. "Just married?" asked the waiter when he passed their table carrying two huge plates for another couple.

"No," laughed Lex. Her smile softened. "Not married – just friends."

"Oh, I'm sorry – I thought…well, older married couples just gobble up their own food as fast as possible and ignore their partner."

Both Lex and Harry laughed. "One day…maybe…" said Harry and noticed a slight blush on Lex's cheek.

They carried on eating the dessert, and as they finally finished, Lex reached across and flicked a last crumb from the corner of Harry's mouth with her right forefinger. He raised his eyebrows. "Like a newly married couple…" he said with a smile.

Lex's face was enigmatic. But the blush returned.

The meal went on until almost four, and when it was over, Lex and Harry walked up Heath Street, cut round Spaniards Road, and turned onto the Heath just beyond the Vale of Health. They chatted about irrelevant matters – the meal, the look on the waiter's face when he served the chips, their flights from Australia, that kind of insignificant thing – and strolled across the grassy slopes until the traffic noise and the streets were far behind them. Then they sat at the top of a grassy bank looking across the vast panorama of London as dusk began to creep over the world. Harry loved watching the sun fade, with a mist beginning to form and layering the rows of trees with an almost ghostly white swirl between them.

Lex sat quietly, also enjoying the spectacle. She was, by nature, a quiet girl – but while she would never be the centre of attention or the automatic life and soul of a party, she had enough about her to always hold her own and not be put down in a conversation. She was educated, well raised, and polite, and although she had ambitions to stand in front of an audience to be a singer – not a star – if forced, she would have described herself as 'just an ordinary girl'.

Somehow, there was an almost inbuilt feeling between the two of them, a mutual and instant fondness that both recognised. Words were not needed, and they just sat looking at the growing darkness envelope the view.

As the sun sank further, Harry got an almost physical pleasure from watching the darkening tiered silhouettes of the bushes, and, as often happened, the narrow strips of tall trees standing like sentinels of the earth began to produce an original lyrical concerto of immense beauty in his mind, with stringed instruments soaring through his head high like the wind. It brought on feelings of nostalgia as he remembered his younger days dreaming of writing great songs on the North Shore.

Then he suddenly became absorbed watching a pair of different-type birds sitting facing each other gladiatorially on top of two tall trees quite close to them. They were taking it in turns to chirrup as loud as they could – trying to outdo each other. A song began to form in Harry's mind. "Oh God," he thought, "I really am starting to think like Danny."

"What are you smiling at?" asked Lex, and Harry explained. He told her about his partner, innocently telling of their feelings about music and what they hoped to achieve. "Trouble is, he's a mongrel," he said eventually.

Lex listened to it all sympathetically, and in her mind she hoped it would work out for them.

"If that song you played at the club last night is anything to go by, then you'll make it," she said. "Especially if your pal's words are as good as you say."

Harry looked at her and wanted to kiss her. Lex looked him in the eyes. She knew. "Go on then," she smiled.

They kissed, softly, and the two birds continued arguing in the treetops.

***

Danny came back from his weekend away late on the Monday, full of energy and enthusiasm. His prickly feelings of the previous few weeks had vanished, and he was ready to start writing again. He rang Harry from the station and was immediately invited to round to Harry's flat for a chat. Harry wanted to tell him about Lex, although he did not mention it on the phone.

Danny arrived at Clarenden Road and let himself in. He found Harry drinking tea from a huge mug with a teabag tag still hanging over the side, but he was immediately aware of something he could not quite put his finger on. There was a strange, more-than-normally pristine, slightly uncomfortable feel to the room, but Danny was in a good mood, bubbly and anxious to work, and in his usual way tried to ignore it.

"Got some great words for you," he told Harry. "While I was away, my folks took me for a long walk across the fields – I came up with a great idea…

'Fields of blue
Gentian flowers speaking softly to the wind.
And the voice of the wind answers softly,
With a sigh.'

"What d'you think of that?"

Harry walked over and put the mug down by the sink and said he liked the words. "Yeah, mate, they're great," he told Danny. But his mind was on the other issue he wanted to speak about.

Danny noted the look on his face, and for some reason he suddenly felt it to be a grey day, although outside the sun was shining brightly in a deep blue sky, and through the window he could see a small bird singing his heart out loud sitting on the chimney of a house on the other side of the road.

They began to chat – but Harry was anxious about the way his partner was going to react to the news about Lex and rattled on about irrelevant things at first. Eventually Danny cottoned on. "Are you trying to tell me something?" he asked.

"Well…look, Danny mate. There is something I want to tell you…there's this girl, Lex. I've fallen for her hard, I really think there's something between us. I mean – well, I know what you think about the lovey dovey bit, but I honestly think this could be the girl for me…"

He tailed off, knowing he was talking like a schoolboy with his first romance and uncertain how Danny was going to react. "I'd like you to meet her," he eventually said.

For some reason, Danny immediately felt an invidious resentment against the girl. "You sound like a bad love song," he jibed. "Do you really mean you feel like taking her home to your folks? Raising kids? That kind of boloney?"

Harry nodded sadly. "If you want to put it like that…" His voice tailed off again. "Look, Danny, it's not going to make any difference to the way we work together. Don't make any snap judgments – just meet her. I know you'll like her."

Danny scowled. "Yeah," he said flatly. The two men looked at each other for a moment, then Harry walked across to the piano. "I'll fix something," he said when he got there. "Meanwhile – well, let's hear those words again."

Danny followed him across the room, and they started working.

The two men continued producing words and music together, but there was something different now. Harry's head was continually full of thoughts of Lex, and although he tried not to let her appearance on the scene affect him too much his music started to alter again – it began getting more romantic.

He thought about the girl a lot. Every time they met, he discovered something new about her. She was not only good-looking, she was lively, witty and bright, and very soon she showed that she was a good foil to his music. He began to try out odd little melodies and bits and pieces on her to see her reaction, and she was an honest critic.

If she did not like something, she said so, and she usually managed a convincing argument as to why. If she liked it, however, she gave Harry encouragement to develop it – and sometimes suggested ways in which Danny could become involved in building it up. Lex realised Harry and Danny were the musicians, and as she had no hang-ups over them taking any credit for an idea, she might make she was quite willing to take a back seat in it all. She just liked the feel of being part of Harry's creative process and that was that.

At first, Harry didn't tell Danny about Lex's occasional contributions. But one day he let it slip that she had made a suggestion – and Danny didn't like it one little bit. It led to arguments between the two men, and an even bigger dislike of the girl in Danny's mind.

As time went on, it led to more frequent clashes, with Danny continually complaining about Harry's 'constantly changing' styles. "I can hardly keep up with your mood swings," he said one day. Inevitably, there was a bigger falling out, and on some days, they hardly spoke except about the songs they were writing.

Danny had an inner passion for writing, for using words, that had not always manifested itself in the past, when he had been too busy trying to create an image of himself as the permanent life and soul of the party. But he had a driving urge to create sentences, moods, feelings, and with Lex on the scene, he believed his partnership with Harry, and the outlet it gave him to use his words in a way he felt safe and happy with, was being threatened. And although it may sound a trite way to describe it, it awoke a kind of red mist, an angry passion, within him.

He definitely considered that Lex was getting in the way of the music – although in actual fact, her personality, and the way Harry reacted to her presence in his life, helped Harry's writing, in particular giving him a singer's viewpoint. His songs began to get that something extra that had possibly been missing, a touch of romance. It was the subtle missing ingredient, and the harmonies began to flow with an innovative lilt and a flow that was pleasing.

Meanwhile, despite the discord, Harry tried to arrange for Danny to meet the girl. It was hard work, because although Lex was keen on the idea, Danny continually found reasons not to make a meeting. Instead, he began to fall back into his old style of writing, producing lyrics in his former superficial, facetious way again – often aiming thoughts at Lex.

> *'Nobody ever says sorry these days, girl.*
> *So I'll just say it's been nice to know you,*
> *But I'm not sorry now that you've gone.'*

Despite that, he still wrote some good words when Harry provided a good tune. And although selling their songs was still virtually a non-existent fact, their music was getting better all the time and over-rode just about everything else. Danny felt deeply that music, any music, was the key to giving people a mood – of happiness, sadness or the like – and as he mainly liked happy music, he fell in with Harry's new lilting themes.

The two men argued, kept long silences, and both become introverted when they were together – but even though hardly speaking, their songs were finally becoming fully integrated and professional.

Both were still trying to fit in part-time work – Danny doing any freelance journalist or copywriting job that occasionally cropped up, and Harry still giving music lessons while writing away for any piano-playing jobs with music publishers. Although they had their differences, they still tried to spend as much time writing together as they could – although Harry's almost daily meetings with Lex meant he would stop early and work virtually nine-to-five office hours. Danny hated that.

Despite his insistence that Harry spend all his time working with him, though, Danny still liked to go off himself, and one evening accepted an invitation to go to a show launch organised by his old employer. Knowing that he would be away all evening, Harry arranged 'something special' for Lex – planning a surprise romantic evening together.

They had an early meal in a small Spanish restaurant in Villiers Street, just off the Strand, then walked slowly across Hungerford bridge to the Festival Hall, where Harry had booked tickets for a swing concert where they played all the old 'songs of the movies', which he knew Lex loved.

They came out of the theatre humming the songs, and went for a walk along the South Bank. The river was shimmering in the moonlight, Harry could not have planned it better. Couples wandered in both directions around them, and it was like a scene from an Astaire-Garland musical. Both of them felt that everyone round them should be singing a huge production number.

Romance was in the air, and both Harry and Lex were very relaxed in each other's company. Then as they turned a corner, they suddenly came into a blaze of light from the expensive riverside restaurants, laughing together at the people inside dining well but formally at the white cloth-covered tables inside. "I bet they're not enjoying it as much as I am," said Harry.

"And I bet it's cheaper here on the outside," laughed Lex.

They turned another corner and the lights disappeared behind them. The moon was still shining on the river, and Harry turned to Lex and kissed her.

They broke apart, Harry trying to organise his thoughts. Lex looked at him, a smile on her lips but her eyes serious.

'We kiss in a shadow,' she sang softly, almost in a whisper.

A brief, miniscule, thought of Danny talking about how much he liked the song flashed through Harry's mind, but quickly disappeared as he looked at Lex's upturned face. "Beautiful," he sighed.

"Yes, it's a lovely song."

"No, I mean you…"

He kissed her again, and this time Lex laughed, a tender laugh that showed she was happy. For some reason, Harry again felt like a schoolboy on his first date. Lex took his hand, and they walked on.

***

Harry's attempts to take charge of 'the fussy things' had always irked Danny a little, but they really began to irritate him now. He was far more laid back than the Australian, and as a natural militant against any form of authority he now rebelled against all attempts to make him conform and do things he didn't want to do – things that Harry insisted he do, such as tidying up after himself, dressing neatly, watching every word he said.

It was, probably, because he felt bitter about Lex's appearance on the scene. He resented the girl's intrusion into what had been a cosy twosome, and he begrudged the fact that she took a lot of Harry's attention away from him.

Harry, for his part, did not think he had ever been over-fussy in the way he treated Danny. Far from it. In fact, he knew that by his constant nagging and pedantic manner he had managed to get his partner to settle down to a more serious way of doing things, a more professional way of writing.

Now, though, romance hit him hard. Harry had still been something of a loner despite his growing close friendship with Danny, but he could not stop thinking about Lex, and even when he was working with Danny she was not far from his thoughts.

His music quickly began to reflect his feelings for the girl – it soon provided his songs with the missing ingredient...passion. Danny revolted, and sub-consciously he reverted to his old-fashioned flip lyrics – which did not match Harry's new mood at all, and started to cause even more friction between the two men.

Danny had thought life was becoming good, and he took exception to the girl for what it was doing to his partnership with Harry. Before she turned up, things had been starting to work out, songs were starting to be written and sold – albeit in small numbers and on a very small scale – and in Harry he had found a loyal friend and workmate. Then along came the girl, and he didn't like it one little bit.

One day, for example, the two men were working on the words to a song when Harry looked at his watch. "Got-ta go," he said.

"Hey man, c'mon. Let's get this finished while we're both in the groove..."

"No, I've got to go. You finish it – I'll check it in the morning." Harry stood up and got his coat, leaving Danny fuming. There was nothing he could do.

"How come this girl can break things up like this?" he asked.

"Look, I'll fix up something – you've got to meet her to see what she's like. You'll adore her as much as I do."

Danny hated being told how he would feel, but he let it pass. "I don't really want to meet..." But Harry was gone.

It took some time to fix up a meeting because of Danny's unyielding stubbornness, but Harry eventually managed it. He gave Danny a formal invitation to dinner at his apartment to meet Lex, and Danny agreed. "Try and make a bit of an effort, though – just for me," said Harry. "You know I like the girl. I'd like her to like you, too – so please, mate, make yourself look good, will ya?"

The day arrived, and after working on a song at Harry's flat for a while Danny went off in the early afternoon to get ready. In the evening, he returned to Holland Park, but instead of going straight to Harry's he stopped on the way at the Rat & Parrot for a couple or three drinks.

"I'm going to this poncy dinner – probably have wine, and as beer and whisky don't go with wine, you'd better give me a brandy," he told the disinterested barman.

Eventually, he turned up at the flat about twenty minutes late. Harry noted the very smart dark suit, the white shirt and tie – and also the dirty trainers.

Danny was already well on the way to being drunk, and almost immediately, before they even sat down for the meal, went to the sideboard and without offering any to the others helped himself to a glass of wine from a bottle that Harry had, ostentatiously, left 'to breathe'. Danny noticed that it was a very expensive French burgundy.

From the outset, Danny saw Lex as 'the enemy', and he was ready to do battle. Harry insisted that as Lex had cooked the meal, he would serve, and as he started handing out an hors d'oeuvre, Lex tried to open a friendly conversation with Danny by saying what a horror it had been doing the shopping for the meal. She didn't know him.

"It always is," said Danny. "Whenever you go into a big supermarket, you get women shoppers banging trolleys into you, not looking where they're going." Harry put dishes in front of him and Lex, and Danny turned the speak to him. "You've seen it too, haven't you, Harry? Woman walking round simply saying 'sorry' every two seconds without even knowing what they've done, being inconsiderate and leaving trolleys in the middle of the aisle, blocking the aisles and making it difficult for others to get at things."

It was all aimed at riling the girl, but when he paused to take a drink of wine, she simply raised her eyebrows. "I'm sure you're right," she said. "But I just went round the corner to Harts to get a small jar of paprika. No trolley…"

Harry sat down, and they began eating. Danny took one mouthful, then put his fork down.

"I don't like this foreign gear. This hot stuff," he said, deliberately rude. "I know it's un-British, but I just don't like curry."

"It's just a dash of paprika…"

"Well, it's all the same."

The meal continued, but although Danny hardly ate a thing, mainly leaving the generous portions of the excellent, delicately flavoured meal Lex had cooked on his plate, he drank a lot and got progressively more and more drunk. He continually insulted the girl and ignored Harry's attempts to placate him.

"It seems you know all about me – that I write with Harry," he said. "What about you? What do you do?"

Lex glanced at Harry. "Well, I'd like to be a singer. Or maybe a dancer," she replied. "In the meantime, I'm working for a firm of solicitors."

"A solicitor?" asked Danny.

"Don't say it," said Harry. Lex gave the two a funny look. An old-fashioned look.

"Do you do much court work?" asked Danny.

"Oh no. My boss does all that…"

"Oh, he's the criminal lawyer…"

"Shut up, Danny," said Harry.

"No, it's just that I love that phrase. Criminal lawyer – sums 'em all up."

There was a pause as Harry and Lex ate, and Danny poured himself some more wine. Then he continued with his almost constant barrage of bad taste jokes and remarks, and although Lex ignored them in the main, she was slightly amused by him.

She even laughed out loud when he asked if she had heard of the man with only one leg who took a taxi home. "When he got there, he had to crawl to the front door – he'd left his wheelchair on the back seat," said Danny.

Danny continued to be insulting all the way through, interrupting Lex and Harry's attempts to start a 'proper' conversation with his one-liners. Harry got embarrassed when his partner spilled his wine while laughing after telling Lex: "As a journalist, I go by the old motto…stop, look, listen – and fabricate," he said. And, "A woman's place is in the wrong."

Then he tried to ignore Lex completely, talking to Harry about a song they were working on. Lex didn't know anything about the tune and didn't quite know how to react to the turn in the conversation. Harry tried to keep the talk general, and tried to calm things. Eventually, he turned away from Danny to pay more attention to Lex.

"Tell me about this trip to Brussels," he said.

"Well, I hope I'll get a chance to see some of the city," said the girl.

Danny broke in. "Why bother – overseas begins at Dover, and the Middle East begins at Calais, doesn't it?" he said boorishly.

"Yes, but it's a business trip," said Lex calmly. She had started to get Danny's measure by now. "And anyway, what's wrong with...overseas? Haven't you ever travelled?"

"Yeah. Went to Paris once when I was a school kid," said Danny. "Walked everywhere to see the sights – everywhere you go overseas it's uphill...even on the way back."

"That," replied Lex, holding her ground, "is usually called old age."

Finally, the meal ended, and when Harry said there was no more booze, Danny got ready to leave. "Well, it's been...nice...meeting you at last," said Lex sweetly. "Hopefully, we'll see each other again soon. After all," she looked at Harry with a smile, "I plan to be around for a long, long time."

Danny jumped back in. "A long time? That's the trouble with the young," he said. "They think they're immortal – but really, these days they're just immoral."

For some reason, Lex bit this time. "Just what is your problem?" she asked as Harry started to look a bit apprehensive. "Why do you have to be the big guy all the time?"

"Let me explain my philosophy," slurred Danny, putting on his cherubic smile. "Same as Salvador Dali. He said that at six he wanted to be a chef, at seven Napoleon – but then his ambitions started to grow big." The cheeky grin turned to an inane smile. "Well, that's the way I feel too – and Harry's the guy I'm going to do it with."

The smile turned to a glare. "And no one's going to stop that."

Soon after the dinner, Harry moved again, this time renting a larger flat in Albert Street in Camden Town to be closer to Lex. There was bedroom, a separate cooking area – hardly a kitchen – and a fairly large living room with a better piano than Harry had had in the old place, although it was still an old upright.

Danny called there on Harry's first morning in the new apartment. As he left Camden Town underground station and walked up Parkway, grinning as he saw Palmers pet shop with its signs advertising 'Talking Parrots' and 'Monkeys', he was in a good mood. He smiled again as he passed Delancey Street.

"It's not very fancy on old Delancey Street, you know," he quipped to the tune of 'Manhattan' when he got to the new flat.

"Sometimes I don't know what you damned Poms are talking about," replied Harry, and Danny explained that it was the name of the next street along. "Oh, I never noticed that," said Harry.

Danny sat down. He ignored the fact that nothing had been unpacked or sorted out, and insisted they start work immediately. He only added to the chaos by spreading pages of half-finished lyrics across the floor by the piano.

The move meant it was easier for Lex to visit Harry, and because she was working flexible hours, she was sometimes able to visit him during the day and would occasionally sit in the flat during his working meetings with Danny. Lex loved listening to the two of them working out a song, although she refused to take part unless requested. When Harry did sometimes ask, because he wanted a singer's perspective, Danny invariably got annoyed and started messing around. He wanted Harry's full-time attention.

Harry was surprised at the ferocity of Danny's reaction, yet he knew that basically it was all down to Danny being upset over his own relationship with Lex – he realised that Danny was just taking out his frustrations and perceived grievances on everyone. After the disastrous dinner, he had spoken to Lex about it, and she had quickly worked out that Danny was disconcerted by the disruption that she was inevitably making, and told Harry that he was afraid that she was taking his place. She said they should just bide their time.

Harry agreed, but despite everything she and Danny continued in a state of almost armed neutrality. Where Harry was concerned, Danny was now beginning to buckle down and work properly, and Harry began to believe that things were starting to sort themselves out.

But with Lex he was rude and made it obvious he did not like her. She loved being with Harry, dating, watching him work, and because of that she put up with Danny's bad behaviour. Her natural niceness helped her ride above it.

Then one morning, Lex came round and was sitting in an easy chair while Harry messed around at the piano. Danny was late, and Harry began to fool around with a song they had written some week before. He played with it a little and began to like it, then turned to Lex and asked what she thought. "It's so doleful," he told him. "You've got a hint of a song there, and the words could be turned into something…but it's down beat, melancholic."

Harry immediately realised what she was getting at. She was a happy girl, she made him happy – why was his music about love not happy? "Look," she suggested, "why not put a little tra-la-la in that middle piece…" She went on to put forward a way the song could be given a whole new vibe.

It was the first time the girl had ever made any real, serious contribution to Harry's music – in the past she had only made a few minor indications of mood

– but Harry immediately set about re-working the song in a different style and different mood.

"That's better," said Lex, but before she could say anything else, she was interrupted by a ring at the front door. Lex stood. "That's probably Danny. I'll get it," she said. "I've got to go anyway."

She left, partially prompted by the fact that she didn't want any arguments from Danny, and a few moments later Danny came into the room. He was not feeling all that bright – he had a headache, and the sight of Lex had put him in a bad mood.

"What was she doing?" he asked.

"She's entitled," replied Harry blandly. "Anyway, she gave me a heads-up on a song. Here, listen." He began to play the song in its original form, then began to modify it in the more cheerful way Lex had suggested.

Danny was annoyed about Lex's involvement in its development and was not in the mood to give her any credit. "It's our song, why the hell did you have to drag her into it?" he asked.

Yet despite his protests, Danny quite liked the new version and was just as convinced as Harry that it was a vast improvement on the original. He calmed down, and decided to try and tweak up a few of the lyrics to fit the new feel of the piece.

Lex's help with the song made no difference to his overall approach to the girl, however, although Harry liked to feel things were slowly beginning to get better. By now Danny had taken over his old Clarendon Road apartment, although they still worked mainly from Harry's new place because of the piano.

Danny was there one day when Lex called round. As she didn't have a key to the new flat yet, she rang the front doorbell and Danny went out to answer it. Despite the fact that the sun was shining it was raining, and Lex stepped in shaking the damp from her hair.

"Hi, Danny, is Mac in?" she asked.

"Yeah."

"Hey, Mac, come and look at this rainbow," she called out over Danny's shoulder. They both heard Harry moving towards the door of his rooms.

"Where's this rainbow?" asked Danny. Lex pointed away to her right, and Danny stepped outside into the rain to have a look.

"I've never seen more than four colours in a rainbow," he said.

"Four? How come…?"

"I mix some of the colours up," replied Danny. "I'm not colour blind – just colour confused. I mix reds and browns – it's fairly common."

Harry joined them, and for a beat they all looked at the semi-circle of colours looping over the houses and Regents Park. "Hey, I can see five…red, orange, yellow, blue – two kinds of blue," said Danny.

He suddenly snapped his fingers. "Got it – how about a song called 'A Rainbow With Five Colours'?" he asked.

When they went indoors, Danny grabbed a piece of paper and began scribbling. Then he showed the words to Harry.

> *'Red's the colour of romance.*
> *Orange the colour of her face.*
> *Yellow's the colour of the sun,*
> *Green colour of our envy.*
> *Blue is the way you'll feel –*
> *When off she goes to the rainbow.'*

"There you are, one line for each colour in the rainbow," he said. It was crass knowing the way Harry and Lex felt about each other, but they both let it pass. It was bad taste, but eventually – months later – it sparked off a nice love song…with different lyrics.

Later, Danny went into the kitchen to make a drink and saw Lex's underwear hanging up to dry over a chair. He didn't say anything, but in the other room Lex and Harry heard banging noises before Danny came back with two steaming mugs of coffee. He handed them over, surprisingly, and then went back into the kitchen, and this time came out with another mug of coffee and a slice of white bread on which he had spread butter and a thick dollop of Heinz tomato ketchup.

"That's disgusting," said Lex.

Danny just munched on quietly.

Soon after, Lex left, and as the door closed behind her, Danny showed Harry some new lyrics he had brought with him.

> *'What do words mean?*
> *Love and romance?*
> *What do they mean…*
> *Now that you've gone?'*

95

Harry nodded. He quickly drew a five-line stave, scribbled down some notes and then went to the piano to play them. After a few moments Danny followed across the room, but instead of joining in the creation of a possible new song he began pushing the idea. "OK – what do they mean?" he asked. "Love and romance? Eh? What do they mean? You're all lovey dovey with Lex, but what the hell does it all mean?"

Danny stumbled against the side of the piano. "What the hell does it all mean then? Lovey dovey?"

Although Danny had not shown it before, Harry now realised he had been drinking again, and he was not amused. "I'm not in the mood – shut it, mate," he snapped back.

He slammed the piano lid shut but he filed the words and his song outline away for the future.

Act 6: Reunion

For a while, things plodded along. Danny and Harry would meet very day, except when one or the other was working, and would plot out harmonies and words, constantly revising them and polishing them until they were satisfied.

Soon they had quite a selection of songs they considered were quite good. They were hardly selling any of them, but they both reckoned that they would need a large stockpile when (not if) they did eventually make the breakthrough.

The trouble was that although no one else seemed interested, both were still living in that musical time warp of the 1930s and 40s – a time, they insisted, when gay meant being happy, and people adored Rogers and Hart, Cole Porter, the Gershwins and Jerome Kern because they wrote gay music that made people want to sing and dance and be happy. Harry and Danny still cherished it, indeed they had come together because of their devotion to that kind of music and because of their love for the arrangements of the old Big Bands. They continually hoped that one day they would write the same kind of foot-tapping gay music for the same kind of joyful shows.

Even now, both dreamed of the daily miracle in the same way, and normally their songs were chirpy and danceable – Fred Astaire would have loved them. Writing ordinary songs, they found, was easy, but it was harder work producing delightful melodies with that old swing and Harry had his work cut out to get Danny to knuckle down. Still, they worked well and happily together.

The one thing Danny did not like was seeing Harry and Lex cosying up together. Even when he was supposed to be working, Harry would give Lex long looks of adoration. They would hold hands, look deeply into each other's eyes, mutter words to each other that Danny couldn't hear – even when there were the three of them in a room, they were together as a pair in the deep recesses of their own togetherness. Danny thought it was a hackneyed portrayal of love – 'all old Hollywood – Gable, Vivien Leigh and Gone with the Wind' was the way he described it to himself.

Although she seemed to have quite a lot of time off so she could sit in while the writers worked, Lex herself went to the office most days, and Harry arranged to see her in the evenings. As a result, he and Danny settled into a routine of working almost nine-to-five office hours, much to Danny's disgust.

Left to his own devices in the evenings, on his own and tired – but not bored – with the constant repetition of both songs and re-writing words, Danny started to revert to his old clubbing-drinking-flirting ways. He rang girls he had once known, and they would meet in pubs or clubs…and drink until the early hours.

Harry noticed the effect it was having on his partner, because Danny would frequently turn up late next morning, and with a hangover. Whenever Lex was around, although there was never a major incident, he was invariably rude to her – or ignored her. Harry hated it, but was cautioned by Lex to bide his time.

Things came to a head a couple of weeks after Harry had broken off a get-together with Danny rather earlier than usual so he could take Lex out. Danny sulked for a while, then he rang up a rather flashy-looking dancer he had once met in a TV studio and arranged to meet her. She was very good looking, but hardly Brain of Britain.

They went for a meal, moved on to a club, then Danny became rather bored with the girl and suggested going for 'a real drink' in a bar which he and Harry had often used for their meetings in their early days together. He rather hoped he would meet up with his partner, and sure enough, as they sat at a table and ordered drinks from a rather plump waitress, Danny saw Harry drinking at the bar. Indicating the move to the waitress, Danny took the girl over.

When he got there, he started to sit at a stool next to Harry, who immediately stood and offered the girl his bar stool, and as she sat, he moved so that he and Danny were on either side of her. "What are you doing here – I thought you'd gone out with Lex," said Danny.

"She had to go home early – she's off somewhere early in the morning. What about you? What are you doing here?"

"Yeah, well we had a meal, then I thought it was time for a kind of nightcap," replied Danny.

There was a bit of a pause. "I thought of taking in a late-night movie –" he went on.

"I like pictures," interrupted the girl. Her voice was rather high and squeaky, and Harry could tell it grated on Danny.

"What sort of films?" asked Harry politely, as Danny looked round the room.

"All sorts," said the girl. "I'm well into the arts."

"Yes? What kind of art?"

"Well, I've been to that Tate Modern gallery. There was an exhibition there that was all photographs of places around the world – I loved one of the murials they'd taken in Rome. It was ever so well done."

Harry shuddered – he could not understand the banality of the girl. But Danny turned back, and seeing his friend's reaction began to smile. As usual, Harry sensed Danny was about take the mickey – whether out of him or the girl, he wasn't sure – and he didn't like it.

"Hey Marmaduke, I bet you've never seen a murial in Rome, have you?" asked Danny. He emphasised the girl's mispronunciation.

Harry was about to say something rude in reply, but the girl beat him to it. "Why did you call him Marmaduke? I thought you said his name was Harry?" she asked.

"It's because he thinks I'm a real high-falutin' Aussie," said Harry, trying to head Danny off.

Danny's face was that of a little boy around two or three, his best cherubic look. "Yeah – it's because he's so posh," he replied. "You know, you'd never believe how upmarket he can be – he's so classy he even covers his mouth when he's all alone in a car and coughs – all alone!"

The girl looked blank. "OK, OK," butted in Harry, and there was another break in the conversation, Harry and the girl looked a little uneasy but Danny turned and winked at the plump waitress as she passed.

Soon, the conversation between the two men inevitably turned to music. They chatted for a few moments, and it became obvious even to the girl that Danny wrote lyrics. She interrupted. "I'd forgotten you write songs. Were you always good at writing poems – even at school?" she asked him innocently.

"Poetry's got nothing to do with lyrics," snapped Danny, a bit cross at the question.

"But the words to a song can be poetic," said Harry.

"Yeah – but it's not poetry," replied Danny, rather nastily, and walked away from the others, who watched him cross the room and leave the club.

Harry arranged for a taxi to take the girl home, and next morning, early, he rang Danny and asked him to come over.

Harry was playing around with a song when he arrived. "Look mate," he said immediately Danny came into the room, "I don't like to say this, but what the hell are you doing? I've told you before – your behaviour's getting a bit out of hand lately. The way you acted last night – well, that was Goddam awful. It was embarrassing."

Danny tried to protest – 'she was only a bimbo' – but Harry continued. "It's not just about last night," he went on. "You've been crook for a long time. You've been narky with me, but I can take that. But you've also been out and out rude to Lex – and that's something I'm not going to take any more. It's not acceptable – not acceptable at all."

Danny looked at Harry in almost uncomprehending amazement. "Well, why shouldn't I have a dig?" he answered truculently. "It's not as if you've got someone like Lex pushing you out have you?"

"Pushing you out? Shit, you stupid dingo, no one's pushing you out," said Harry.

"Well, that's the way it looks to me…"

"Don't be so bloody stupid. Me and Lex are one thing – you and me, we're partners. We're friends. We work together, we work well together, and I've got a feeling we're going to make it. You must think that as well."

"But Lex – she's getting in the way."

"No mate. We're still writing as always – as far as I'm concerned, that's going on." He played a few bars of the song, *'Kissin' In The Moonlight'*, before going on. "This song's proof of that."

He turned away from the piano. "And there's another thing – it wasn't quite working, but Lex gave me an alternative view, and it's a bloody good view. She's helped us make something out of – well, almost nothing. So shut it. We're still a partnership."

He suddenly laughed. "In any case, you stupid wuss, I've got no wish to kiss you in the moonlight."

Danny's face also lightened into a sudden smile. "Chance would be a fine thing," he said, and both men burst out laughing.

There was a flash of warm friendship between the two men. "You really think I've been unfair to you…and Lex?" Harry nodded, and Danny pursed his lips and tried to think. "I get so confused," he said suddenly. "Away from music, I don't know what I am. Reckon I need you, not just for the music, for friendship. I just want it to stay that way…"

"OK, mate, it will," said Harry softly.

"I suppose I have been a bit rough on you and the girl…"

"Yeah, you've been a real asshole," replied Harry. They grinned at each other again. "Now, let's stop talking like a scene from a bad novel."

Danny and Harry still went to the jazz club together fairly frequently, but now Lex was usually with them. Harry would always just join in with the musicians, often improvising good songs on the piano while Lex watched adoringly, and that would leave Danny on his own. He would still drink too much and flirt outrageously with any girl who came within range, accompanied or not, but even when drunk he would frequently manage to write some kind of lyric to Harry's playing.

When he was tipsy, the words were usually way over the top, written in his old smart-alecky way as romances to the girl he was chatting up at the time.

Despite that, the two men generally worked well together, and developed an effective style of operating that meant they threw out words or song ideas to the other just to see what sparked. Sometimes Harry just played scales or arpeggios and something developed from them, and it was usually Harry's harmonies that inspired Danny the most – he wrote well to whatever the tune may be – but sometimes he had some words that produced a more than pleasant melody in Harry's mind.

What would often happen is that Harry would be idly tinkering on the piano, fingering new ideas, new melodies, when Danny would suddenly stop him. "Play that last one and the one a couple back," he'd say, and Harry, recalling the two different melodies, would play them one after the other as requested. He would never ask why – he just did it. Then as he played, Danny would jot down some lyrics for one of the melodies, and then sing them to the one melody as a counterpoint to the other piece being played on the piano.

Sometimes the songs were good – at other times less so. But they persevered, determined to build up an album covering as wide a range as possible, and the longer things went on, inevitably they got more professional. Over time they stopped being mechanical and developed a complete partnership in which they both began writing with fluency and heart, with literally dozens of ideas coming readily from them both – although they equally readily agreed that only a few were worth bothering with.

When they did have something, however, they worked hard to polish it between them – although it was invariably Harry who would eventually produce a useable orchestration. What they were seeking was to eventually have a portfolio of about twenty or thirty songs with no sameness about them, an assortment that they would be able to present to a publisher 'when they made the break-through'.

Harry was definitely the leader. He still preached constantly about the theory and history of music – how to get a harmonious blend of instruments playing in concert, each musician having to make an individual contribution to the melodic whole. "A song has to be a whole symphony of sound," he would say.

When either he or Danny put forward a useable idea, it didn't take Harry long before he could hear it playing in his mind – the huge majestic downward sweep of the brass, a pause, a further downward sweep, another pause, a final sweep even lower, then a piccolo picking up the melody. His mind was a-whirl with sounds.

Not that Danny was any slouch, either. In a music bar one night they listened as a tight group of four hacked away at a sound – neither could actually call it music – and Danny immediately picked up on something within it. There was one particular song, repeated after a desultory round of applause, which had a deep, throbbing repeated beat from the lead guitar.

"It would be better as a drumbeat," he said, to no one in particular. He started scribbling on a scrap of paper.

'Listen to the language of the drum,
Hear it beating in your heart.
Listen to the throbbing of the drum
Like love beginning – just the start...'

"Not right, but it's better," he said. In his mind, a drummer was beating out the rhythm in the background... 'boom – boom – de boom – de boom – boom – boom...'

Both of them had phrases and bars of music or lyrics running through their heads, but Harry liked the extra responsibility of producing the arrangements – "You always see the same picture when you hear a good piece of music," he would say. And he was adamant that although the hook, the introduction that had to catch the audiences' attention, was important, it was the orchestration of the release (the middle part of a song) that kept it going.

"Irving Berlin always said that every composer's only got five or six tunes to write, so it's the way they are presented that makes them stand out," he once claimed. Danny did not reply, he did not really understand, all he knew was that if a song made you want to dance, and its lyrics made you want to sing – it was a good song.

He was, though, still producing too many flip lyrics…

'Lucifer can't match love,
'cause love ignites passion.'

…although under Harry's guidance he was now making a concerted effort to change, although he still kept allowing mock-Hart or Ira Gershwin phrases to interfere. But now it was not a completely natural style anymore, and both he and Harry knew it.

The work was going well. Their reputation had grown locally, and many of the semi-pro outfits in the area took their work – quite apart from the fact that some of the songs were just what they needed, Danny's split-rhyme lyrics bestowed them with an air of superiority that made them feel better than they really were, and Harry's ability to orchestrate the songs gave their work a more professional sound.

It was not all easy going. Once they were asked to write a song for a local singer about to take part in a TV talent show, and he rejected it as completely unsuitable. Danny was angry and affected by the rebuff and for a while it changed his style completely.

Soon, though, he was back to normal. He was still one for the girls – picking them up easily and having plenty of one-night stands – and generally he refused to be serious for too long. By now he was getting on quite well with Lex, particularly after she had turned up at Harry's flat one day with a maxim, one of her girlfriends had given her. She suggested it as a lyric for Danny, and he liked the idea, worked on it – and, in turn, gave it to Harry.

'Keep your face towards the sunshine,
And the shadows will fall behind you.'

It became one of their favourites, and because of it, Lex became an 'OK girl', as Danny told Harry.

Lex had also changed. Although she had originally wanted to be a singer or dancer she was now quite happily settled in as 'the little woman' hanging on to Harry's every word and deed. She was much quieter, content to live her life through Harry.

None of them went to Satch's quite so often now – only occasionally. But one Friday evening when Lex was working, Harry did go there to get 'the feel' of a particular kind of upbeat rhythm, and after sitting in on a few sessions was leaning on the bar during a break. He soon got talking to one of the other musicians he had not met before.

"You the guy who writes those songs the others are talking about?" asked the man, a trombonist with a growing reputation.

"U-huh," replied Harry.

"I'm on the lookout." said the other man, whose name was Brent Saxon. "The others seem to rate your music – can I hear some?"

It turned out that once again he wanted some songs specifically for a TV programme, and Harry walked back to the rostrum, sat at the piano, and began tinkling away. The other man followed, listening with his head on one side to begin with but soon starting to nod appreciation. "Hey, I like that one," Brent said after hearing a few of the numbers. "Any chance you could let me look at it. Maybe a couple of others too…"

Harry agreed and took an address, and after a few minutes went outside the hall, and leaning against the wall used his mobile 'phone to try and get in touch with Danny at his office. There was no answer, and not for the first time Harry wished that Danny would get himself a mobile. It was something Danny had always rejected.

With no answer from Danny's office phone, Harry went back inside the club and finished his beer. He listened to a bit more music, especially as Brent was by now playing more and more – he was good – and after waiting for a while slowly wandered out and went home.

The next day he talked over the chance offer with Danny, and they agreed on the songs they would send – four songs arranged for a trombone and complete with words in case he had a band and a vocalist. The next day Harry posted the carefully prepared manuscripts, and a couple of days later they got a letter back asking to buy them all – and the price was right.

They all met up again at Satch's, and this time Brent told the pair that he really enjoyed their music and instantly started playing one of the numbers off the cuff, with the rest of the impromptu group joining in spontaneously although they did not know the tune. It sounded good – especially when Danny started to sing his words, badly, to the song.

It seemed to be a real break-through when they sold another song to one of the other musicians as a result. It was not much, and paid little, but the 'triumph' quickly led to more, although that was due more to luck than any planning by the two men.

Harry and Danny were delighted at the way things were turning out. Apart from the joy of the success and the money it gave them, they knew that now professionals were involved the word would spread still further. And sure enough, Brent very quickly introduced them to other full-time groups, and even more work came their way.

Things really were starting to work out, although if they were brutally honest both would have agreed that there was still something missing – that extra spark that makes for a big success. From working with small amateurs and semi-pros, Danny and Harry were now writing for serious professional musicians, and as business started to build up they were able to earn a small living from it – still not enough to give up their other jobs teaching music or writing for newspaper, but a welcome addition.

Quite by chance, it was only a few weeks after the initial meeting with Brent Saxon that the two went to Satch's again, this time with Lex, and as usual mingled with the musicians. Harry played the piano, Lex from time to time crooned softly to one of the standards, and Danny just stood there and listened – once in a while 'conducting' the impromptu session with a biro waggling in his hand.

After a while Harry wanted a break, and they all left the stand to go over to the bar. Danny ordered drinks, and as the music slipped into a slow show number Danny grabbed Lex by the hand. "Let's dance," he said, and although she looked back at Harry over her shoulder, appealing, Lex followed him onto the dance floor.

"I'll be Fred Astaire – who do you want to be?" asked Danny as they turned to face each other. "Ginger? Cyd? Or are you going to be Judy Garland in We're a Couple of Tramps?"

They started to dance, Lex well but Danny a bit clumsily. Harry watched them for a few moments then turned back to the bar and his drink, standing there half eavesdropping on the others around him. It was a trick he had learned from

Danny, and in that small half world where things don't quite seem to really exist around you, he suddenly became aware of a smart youngish-looking man standing next to him.

"The band here's good, isn't it?" said the stranger.

"It's normally better – not so good tonight, though. But it's not a regular band – just odd musicians who drop in to play."

"Well," said the stranger, "it's the first time I've heard them, and they seem to be getting it together. And I've got to say – it was going particularly well when you were up there. You play good piano."

Harry flicked his head round to look at the man. "Thanks," he said. "But it's not just down to me."

"Australian?"

"Yeah."

"What part?"

"Sydney, originally. But I live here now. In London," said Harry.

"My grandfather came from some small place near Sydney," said the stranger. "Wollongong?"

"Oh yeah, I know it."

"He left there yonks ago, and my old man was born in Milton Keynes. Milton Keynes, I ask you! Luckily, he moved out before I came along."

The stranger held out his hand. "Sean Kemp," he said by way of introduction.

"Harry McIntyre."

A trumpeter swung into a loud, slightly off-key solo. "Ouch," said Sean. "Whatever you say, it's been good until now…"

"Well," replied Harry, "it is normally very good 'cause you get some tremendous players drop in here. They usually get in late, after the West End shows. You can hear some good stuff."

"Do you come here often, as they say?" asked Sean.

"Oh yeah, I'm fairly regular. Normally meet my partner…"

"Partner?"

"U-huh, the lyricist I work with!" said Harry.

"Lyricist? So you're a writer – I thought you were just a band sidesman. What kind of thing do you do? Had much published?"

Harry resisted the impulse to boast about the chorale and the songs with Brent Saxon and just nodded. "Oh yes, we're pros," he said instead, noncommittally. "We've done a bit – all kinds. But we're really aiming to write a show."

"Well, if his lyrics are as good as those songs of yours, I've heard, you should make it," said Sean. He nodded encouragingly. "Another drink?" he asked, and when Harry accepted, he ordered the two beers.

"Look, I may be able to help," went on Sean when the glasses were served. Harry tried to feign nonchalance, but he was interested.

"I work for an ad agency, and we're looking for a song for a commercial – we've tried everywhere to get the right piece. If you're interested, why not phone my boss – he can tell you what it's all about, and maybe offer you something. Here, I'll give you his name." He wrote a name and telephone number down in a small pocket notebook, tore out the page and gave it to Harry. "Tell him I suggested you call…"

Harry took the piece of paper. "Thanks, mate. I'll certainly do that. First thing Monday morning."

"Hey look, there's my party. Got to go. Don't forget to call on Monday."

Sean went off and Harry looked at the piece of paper, then slowly and carefully folded it in half and put it in his jacket pocket. "Oh, I won't forget," he said to himself. "I sure won't forget."

Moments later, Danny and Lex came back from the dance floor, puffing slightly after the exertion – Danny put a lot of effort into his dancing. Harry told them the news, and they both seemed just as excited as he had been and – unnecessarily – urged him to make sure he did telephone on the Monday to find out what it was all about.

Harry did contact the agency, of course, and the account executive at the other end of the call told him a little more about the project. He didn't say anything because he didn't expect too much, although he was experienced enough to know that although things like that rarely worked out, he might as well give someone who was obviously a newcomer a chance – just in case.

Over the next few days, Harry came up with a few short pieces he felt might fit, and Danny created some ditties – a couple of which were adequate, but only just. Although he was enthusiastic about getting a firm commission, Danny didn't think they stood any chance of getting anywhere with the advert. "People like us just don't get things from a casual chat in a bar," he insisted.

But Harry was adamant that they should try. He was, by nature, an optimist, and he managed to persuade Danny that it was worth a little effort. They had nothing to lose, he insisted. And possibly everything to gain.

As a result, they sat down one evening with all the trivial stabs they had already rejected and between them made a concerted effort to draft out something positive between them in an attempt to impress the agency. Finally, in the early hours of the morning, they had a finished jingle.

Harry posted it recorded delivery, and a few days later got a telephone call inviting him and Danny to the agency's office. It was just off Fleet Street, a large old-fashioned-looking block from the outside, but modern and minimalist inside. There were lots of open-plan sections, a huge TV screen in the steel-and-glass reception showing banal advertisements one after the other, and with earnest young men and girls who all looked the same bustling about.

It was just like the offices in which Danny used to work, so he didn't take too much notice – but Harry thought it was all show and no talent. Nevertheless, he was polite when they were called into one of the glass partitioned executive offices. After the formalities, Harry played the ditty on a piano in the corner and it didn't take too long before the account executive rejected the offering – he turned it down, in fact, on first hearing. "It's not quite what we're looking for," he said kindly.

The look on Danny and Harry's faces told him how disappointed they were. "Look," he added, "don't get me wrong. It's not bad – just not right for this subject. But I think you've got something – perhaps if you were involved in a project right from the start it might be easier for you."

He took the pair along a corridor to meet a fellow executive and told him the circumstances. Harry and Danny were shown some blocked-out sketches for a possible commercial, and told a bit about the background. They were asked if they'd like to try and produce something for it – and Harry immediately jumped at what he regarded as a second chance.

The trouble was that the agency wanted a jingle for a butter advertisement – and after the two men had been given some clues as to what the agency wanted, it became obvious that Danny was not keen… "What you mean is…

'You need a bett-agh bit-agh butt-agh w' your bacon…'"

he suggested scornfully.

"That's it," said the ad-man happily.

When they left, Danny grumbled. "Do I really have to write that kind of shit?" he asked Harry.

"Yes, mate, if you want money."

"Money?"

"Yeah, like we both enjoy eating."

"Whatever happened to integrity?" asked Danny. "I'd rather keep that – and write shows."

"Come on man, they've just offered us £250 each. I know it's below rate, but it's cash in hand. It can't be bad," replied Harry.

Still, when they sat down to work on the ad, Danny insisted on producing unfunny lyrics – suggestive or just insulting to the ad men. It took a lot of persuading for Harry to get him to produce something good, even though the result was in his 'bad old' flip manner, and eventually the whole thing was completed. Harry sent it in full of hope.

Danny was not at all happy, and as a result, he went off on a huge bender and Harry didn't see or hear from him for a couple of days. When he came back, just walking into Harry's apartment, Harry gave him what was meant to be a stern talking to. "You have to write that kind of thing if you want to make it as a pro writer," he insisted. Danny didn't really pay much attention, but went to make cups of coffee.

Neither man ever found out if their song was used or not, but eventually they were sent a single cheque for £250, although both clearly remembered being offered £250 each. After repeated telephone calls to clear things up, most of them ignored, when it came to it a few weeks later the agency insisted that they had only agreed to pay that as a fee for the pair of them, not to each – and as there was nothing in writing, apart from a copyright clearance they had both signed, there was nothing much that Danny or Harry could do about it.

They both knew that in their unknown position there was no way they could take on the agency. Instead, they made a mental note to learn from the experience – then went away to celebrate the 'success' in what Danny instantly called 'this easy-peasy song writing business'. Over a drink, he summed up his thoughts. "I suppose it's like you said with the choir – it's something. Money for old rope."

Days later he got drunk again, and this time he ranted and raved to all around him over the way the advertisers had used them unscrupulously – "They're just on the lookout for new talent to screw," he said. "All these fat, rich, established, untalented bastards are."

Harry, however, took a more positive view. He was still trying to make contact with any music publisher who would listen to him, and now he remembered the advice he had been given by one of them some time before – advice repeated by Sean Kemp, the original advertising agent he'd met at Satch's. "Get an agent."

Talking about it with Danny, he suggested that with all his former show biz contacts Danny must, after all, know someone. Danny agreed to try and look for the right man, but in his typical offhand way did nothing about it of course.

He left it so long that eventually Harry took matters into his own hands, and started ringing round a few musical agents to see if they could help. "What have you had published?" he was asked by all – at least, in most cases by the lowly help who took the call. When he admitted there was very little actually published, none wanted to know. "How the hell do you get experience if nobody wants to know a newcomer?" he asked Danny in frustration. "They don't want to know if the stuff's any good, not even if we've sold anything…just what we've had published. It's rubbish."

Danny agreed in a kind of 'I told you so' way.

***

Days later, Harry heard that his father had died. A letter arrived from an aunt in Sydney giving him the news, and enclosing a short letter the older man had left for him in the event of his death. Harry read the covering note, then opened the letter from his father not quite knowing what to expect, but with a peculiar feeling in his mind.

The letter was full of clichés, but was basically a kind of apology from the older man that he had not been the kind of parent Harry might have wanted. Although he had never had any real emotional feelings for his father, Harry felt a surprising compassion after reading the letter – not only for what it said, but especially for the fact that the old man had even remembered him. He sat down at the piano, his refuge, and thought of his childhood.

Shortly after Danny arrived. He had walked up from Camden Town station in bright sunshine and was expecting to get a good day's work in with his partner. He smiled at people as he passed them – most of them ignoring him – and

Danny opened his mouth to speak, but once again Harry beat him to it. "I was only eight," he said this time. "But the loneliness of that no-blow-hole has stayed in my mind."

He turned back to the keyboard and started playing the song again, this time adding an eerie sub-plot to the tune. "There was all that beauty around the place," he said eventually, still playing. "The hills, the different greens of all the trees, the sun bouncing off the sea and all that. And all I had was that feeling that nothing I was ever involved in was ever right. It was like it was my fault – that the world was somehow ugly behind all that beauty."

Danny felt as if his partner was going to cry. "It's not a happy memory, but it's always been there," added Harry.

He went quiet, and his face clouded, his forehead creasing. "This song came to me that night after the blow-hole," he eventually went on. "It just came to me as I lay there – a little eight-year-old. It's always been there, like the memory of that day."

He carried on playing, and Danny stood up and went to the side of the piano. It was a sad song, with poignant undertones of gloom, and as Harry played Danny leant forward over the piano keys. He started to hum, then said rather than sang a few words, very softly, almost to himself.

'*Mem'ries of a lonely boy…*' scanned in easily, but then he stopped. For once Danny could not find the right words to fit the mood – either the mood of the song or the mood of Harry's memory.

"I dunno," said Harry. "I feel kind-a funny about it, but I never loved the old man." He looked at Danny, his eyes watery. "I feel I should at least have liked him…but…"

Danny tried once more to think of something appropriate to say, but couldn't. As Harry started to play the theme yet again, his own mind switched on to his own childhood. It occurred to him that he'd had an easy life as a youngster, a life when in his mind it never seemed to rain – when the sun always appeared to be shining and life was easy. He had wanted for nothing – it was a very happy, loving childhood.

"Funny thing is, there always seemed to be music around me," Harry's soft voice interrupted his thoughts. "Everywhere in the house – always music."

"Suppose you were lucky you had the music at home," said Danny, feeling somehow inadequate. "I had to go to the flicks – bunked in to see all the musicals – and I knew all the songs. I grew up knowing all the lyrics. I loved 'em. It wasn't 'til I grew up that I realised all the songs I liked were by the top people – Larry Hart, Porter, Ira Gershwin. I knew all their words from a kid. It's amazing, they just stuck. I still remember the words – wake up every morning with some of them on my mind."

Harry carried on playing. "My father always seemed to love the music more than me. At least he left me that," he said.

Harry was surprised when he discovered that his father had left him quite a sizeable legacy; several thousand Australian dollars in fact. After it had been transferred to his London bank, it allowed him to move again, this time with Lex back to the upper middle-class Holland Park area where he could be closer to Danny and handier for their working (and friendly) relationship.

He bought the lease of a two-room flat in Camden Hill Road, an area still run-down and past its best but slightly more upmarket than his old Clarendon Road flat. The apartment had a large window in the living room through which he could see over a garden with trees, unlike the brick walls he had become used to since moving to London. It was big enough for a larger piano, and even after paying for the new apartment he had enough cash left over to buy a grand piano as well. It was only a small grand – a second-hand Bluthner – but a grand piano never-the-less.

Harry loved the new piano and tried to 'protect' it by still using the old upright when repetitively bashing out ideas. It became a sign that he was interested in a new song when he turned to the new baby grand to complete it. Apart from just playing the grand, too, Harry often just sat on the swivel stool in front of it even when the keyboard was closed.

By now, all the troubles between Danny and Lex seemed long in the past. Although she and Harry would still frequently cuddle up and disappear into their own private world, Danny now got on reasonably well with her, and they enjoyed joking with each other without rancour.

But the old rancour cropped up again one day when Danny called at Harry's new flat and noticed a long-handled feather duster resting against a piece of furniture. He began to tease Harry about it, and told him he would 'make someone a good wife one day'.

"Oh mate, that's not mine. Lex must have left it there," said Harry. "She does all the housework – she's the one who'll make the good wife." Danny raised his eyebrows. "Y'know, I really love that girl. Reckon I'm going to ask her to marry me soon," added Harry, and the words stuck in Danny's mind.

For a while the spur-of-the-moment comment hurt Danny badly. He resented it, and the words bought back all the ill feeling towards Lex for coming between him and his partner. All the old 'gooey-lovey-dovey stuff', he thought – and for a couple of weeks it remained constantly near the forefront of his mind, even when he was working with Harry. Luckily, by now he had become more mature and sensible enough not to mention it either to his partner – or to Lex.

Then it was his own turn to find romance.

Act 7: Danny's Romance

The two men were working well together, not only producing words and music but discussing music – the theory, harmony, its history.

Harry would talk of music in grand tones, insisting it should be a harmonious blend of instruments playing in concert, each musician making an individual contribution to the melodious whole. It should, he maintained, be a symphony of sound, and he constantly had endless bars of music running through his head.

Danny, however, was only interested in the immediate production of lyrics. He had phrases and matching lines in his mind, and everything he did or saw was linked to words. He loved the lilt of a rhyme, the nuances of a verse – but it was all tied up in his own imagination with a long-gone far more romantic era.

"You always see the same picture when you hear a good piece of music," he would say.

Anything could trigger off a lyric. There was the night, for instance, when Harry and Lex came home to the Camden Hill apartment to find him sprawled in front of television – one leg draped casually over the arm of an easy chair.

"What are you doing here?" asked Harry.

"I was bored – my telly's broken, so I let myself in and I've been watching the Proms," replied Danny. "Terrific…Jerusalem." He started to hum the grand music.

Harry ostentatiously looked at his watch, but Danny ignored him and continued. "It got me thinking…this green and pleasant land. Why don't we produce a concert – a Big Band concert with music dedicated to the beauty of England."

He fumbled for a piece of paper that had fallen on the floor beside him. "Look, I've got some titles for songs…" he went on. "…'The Beauty Of A Rose', 'A New Life For Nature', 'Wild Clouds', 'The Banks Of Grass On The Hillside'."

"What the hell are you talking about? It's late, go home," said Harry, and Danny – two thirds drunk – stood and left quietly, the idea fading in his hazy mind.

Danny was often more drunk than sober these days. It was all a sign of nerves – nerves that often revealed themselves in angry outbursts against those things he perceived as ills against him or the team. He was, for instance, still upset that no agent would take them on, and on frequent occasions while drunk he would rant and rave over the difficulties facing new talent. Harry would calmly reassure him, and optimistically insists that they would be alright in the end.

Funnily enough, Lex was very much a part of the scene by now and Danny accepted her without question. Generally, life was smooth between the three of them, Danny and Harry and Lex, and Danny was writing well, although he still too often maintained his old jocular style and the words did not necessarily fit in with Harry's newfound romantic mood. After their tricky time when Lex first came on the scene, the two men were very much on side with each other again.

Although their work was taking off in a small, unglamorous way, it was still hard going, but somehow they got by, still using their other jobs – teaching and journalism – to provide the money they needed. But while Harry was starting to write really starry-eyed songs in tune with his new love, there was still that little something extra that was missing.

Both men knew what it was, but Danny was finding it hard to write words that formed a perfect romantic match to the new lyricism of Harry's songs. He tried hard to change his style, but somehow he could not happily produce tender lyrics to order. The two men spoke about it, but no matter what they discussed Danny could not provide the in-depth emotional feeling that was needed. It was a worry, and Harry even tried to alter his own 'music of love' to beat the problem.

Then one day they decided to meet on 'neutral ground' to sort things out, arranging to meet in a restaurant noted for the jazz that played over the noise of the kitchen, the waiters and the general chatter of the diners. When he got there, Danny was given a message to call Harry and did so from a phone on the bar, covering his left ear to blot out the music so he could hear.

"I'm crook, mate, I'm going to stay in bed," Harry told him.

"What is it?"

"Oh nothing, y'know, just something I ate," said Harry. "Look, I booked the table in my name – but you go ahead and I'll see you at the flat tomorrow as normal."

Danny put down the phone and went to sit on his own at a table close to the band. He ordered, and while waiting for the food looked around the restaurant at the other diners – most of them in pairs and seemingly happy in their partnerships. His own meal was soon served, and as he began eating it Danny noticed there was just one other solitary figure in the restaurant, at a table a couple along from him in the crowded restaurant.

The girl was sitting respectably and conscientiously at her table. She was all alone, and from the look of her Danny reckoned she had had a very formal, very strict upbringing. She sat bolt upright with her back ramrod straight, almost as if she had a board holding it erect, and her head was held high on a stiff neck. She looked fixedly in front of her, only lowering her eyes to look down at her food as she cut each morsel. She ate delicately with small mouthfuls, cutting the food precisely before laying down her knife and resting it accurately lined up on her plate, then holding her fork in her right hand as she replaced her left hand demurely on her lap.

Danny watched, fascinated but not wanting her to see him in case it upset her or made her feel uneasy – surprised because she was so different to all the others in the dining room lounging around at their tables. He was conscious for a moment that he was himself sprawled with his elbows on the table, back hunched, head to one side and his right forearm resting on the tablecloth with the fingers of his right hand touching his knife. His left elbow was also resting on the table, the fork held firmly in an upright grip and hovering between his mouth and chin.

He carefully moved himself into a more well-mannered position, and the words of a song to him – a song he immediately called 'Upright Lady' in his mind.

He took a pen and an old notebook from his pocket, and started jotting down the words that seemed to form themselves. For a few moments, he ignored his own meal as his musical mind switched into gear.

'Sittin' all alone,
'membering the manners,
Learned at her mother's knee.'

A waiter hovered, as if to take his still full plate, and Danny picked up his fork and began to half-heartedly play with the food.

As he ate, he continued writing, continually glancing up at the girl, Then he began to realise that both he and the girl were eating, using their forks in one hand only – and slowly, in his mind, the two forks seemed to start dancing as they built up a rhythm lifting from plate to mouth to plate to mouth. Clickety clack, clickety clack. Danny's ear picked up the tempo, and his right hand started to tap it out with the pen on the table.

Soon he had the words of '*Upright Lady*' drafted out , and the rough idea of the rhythm it would need for Harry to turn it into a song.

By now, there was a huge smile on Danny's face – he knew he had something worthwhile. But before he had a chance to go over and speak to the girl about it, she stood up and collected her things, preparing to leave. As she bent over to pick up a bag from beside her chair, her skirt got caught on the seat and Danny got a glimpse of something white she was wearing underneath it. He paused, and, in that moment, she left some money on the table and went out of the restaurant.

Danny stood, meaning to follow her into the street, but the waiter came over. "Is everything alright?" he asked, and Danny knew the moment was gone.

That night, he polished the words of '*Upright Lady*', and next day he returned to the same café to see if by any chance the girl would be there again. It was a forlorn, stupidly optimistic hope, and of course she was not there.

But although Danny was disappointed, he still took a table, and ordered a coffee – much to the annoyance of the waiter who had served him the day before, who wanted a lunch customer because the tips were better – and sat listening to the band. This time there was a small group playing, two guitars, a trumpet, and a pretty girl hitting bongos in a frenzy. Danny studied the girl for a moment, then he pulled his notebook from his pocket, turned to the page after his '*Upright Lady*' notes, and started scribbling down some words to fit the music. He knew they weren't right, that they didn't match, but he realised that Harry would easily be able to provide the song that did fit.

He read the words through two or three times, then looked up again. The waiter plonked the coffee in front of him, slopping a little in the saucer, and Danny gave him a big smile. The band ended the song, and Danny looked around him at the other customers.

On the far side of the restaurant was another girl, sitting on her own with a large black-bound book on the table in front of her. She was absorbed in the book, and was silently 'fingering' as if she was playing a violin. Danny took in the fact that she was very pretty – prettier than the bongo player – very feminine, and with eyes wide apart and covered by lightweight square-shaped glasses that gave her a sort of little-girl-lost look. Her brown hair was short and bobbed, and although she was sitting, he could see that she was tall and elegant, with a kind of trimly breasted boyish figure that was immensely attractive.

Danny looked at the girl, noting that she wore a loose blue jacket over a darker sweater – neat, smart, clothes worn well – and that she had some tasteful jewellery, a thin silver necklace and matching bracelet and a brooch worn high up on her jacket. He absent-mindedly twisted the plain gold ring of his own he wore on the fourth finger of his right hand.

Even across the restaurant, Danny could tell that she had rather bronzed-looking skin and a striking, rather than a pretty, face. Her looks, in repose, were at first glance quite ordinary, her mouth long and drooping, but the girl suddenly smiled at a secret thought, and her whole face lit up – to Danny she became quite exquisite. Her whole attitude gave him an impression of vulnerability, but he reckoned there must be more to her than frailty – As he looked at the girl, still absorbed in her book and "playing her violin", the words he was drafting to the band's song went from his mind as another idea seemed to shove it out of the way in his subconscious "Two girly songs in two days" he thought, smiling at the same time as the girl's face lit up again. He turned the page of the notebook, forgetting the words he had just jotted down while the band played, and started scribbling down new lyrics.

He finished quickly – about seven or eight lines – and went over to the girl. As he got to the table, she looked up. "Hi, what's your name?" he asked innocently.

"Who wants to know?" Her voice was well-modulated and seemed to Danny to be on the point of permanent laughter.

"Oh, I'm sorry. I've been watching you – you seem to be playing a violin or something. And I'm a musician…" He glanced down at the book on the table in front of her, and could see it contained pages of a music score.

The girl took off her glasses and laughed. "Yes, I suppose I was playing," she said. "But I'm not really a musician. I learned the violin when I was a child, and I've got to the stage where I feel it would be nice to start it up again. Just for something to do. I'm just trying to see how much I remember."

"This is a funny place for a violinist – jazzy style music and that."

"Haven't you ever heard of Django Reinhardt?" asked the girl. She looked at Danny closely. "You say you're a musician? What do you play?"

"Oh not that kind of musician," replied Danny. "I write music – well, the words."

"Oh yes? Would I have heard of you?"

"Not yet," he said. "But give it time."

Close up, Danny could see the girl had a small, very slight, scar on her top lip, right in the corner above the right side of her mouth. As far as he could see, it was the only imperfection in a face in which her attractive, almost almond-shaped green eyes sparkled and appealed.

"And your name?" she asked.

"I'm Danny. And you?"

"The name's Adela. Adela Norman."

"Adele?"

"No…Adel-ah. With an 'a' at the end. My parents were both history nuts."

Danny raised his eyebrows quizzically. "Adela was the daughter of William the Conqueror," explained the girl, emphasising the 'ah' at the end of her name. "William, the Norman king. My family name – Norman…Adela Norman." She smiled. "I'm stuck with it."

"It's an attractive name. Original, different." Danny sat down – the girl did not object – and as the waiter hovered, he began to tell her how he had returned to the café to see the 'prim and proper girl' of the day before. "I'm glad to say she's not here – but you are."

The girl pursed her lips. "Is this a pickup?" she asked, her eyes flashing with humour. "With a corny line like that…"

Danny almost blushed. He suddenly felt self-conscious. "No, well yes I suppose it is," he stumbled. "But it's these words I've written."

Adela was intrigued and asked to see them. "Well, they're not really good enough yet," said Danny, the red tinge of embarrassment now beginning to creep over his cheeks. "But if we could meet some time when I've polished them up I'd love to show them to you."

"OK, it's a date." Adela started to gather her things, putting the music score in a large leather bag. "I've got to go now, but let's fix something," she said as she stood up. Danny also rose politely, and saw that she was very slightly taller than him. "I'll call you – what's your mobile number?"

"I haven't got a mobile," said Danny. "Don't believe in 'em. Nothing is so important that it can't wait until you meet face to face – or use a proper phone."

Adela bent back over the table and wrote a number down on a paper napkin. "OK," she said, handing it to Danny, "here's my number. Call me."

She started to walk away, then stopped a few yards away. "It's a cute pick up line anyway," she said, her eyes laughing at Danny. "Don't forget to call."

Next morning, Danny rang Harry very early – very early indeed and ignoring the fact that the Australian had been ill the night before.

"What the hell time is it?" asked Harry sleepily as he answered the phone.

"Oh, I don't know. It's daylight." Harry smothered a yawn, and Danny went on. "I've got a song for you. It's the bees what-nots…"

"Don't you remember I was crook – so OK, don't ask how I am then."

"Don't be such a conformist…" Harry yawned again, a long, drawn-out obvious yawn.

"OK, how are you?"

"I'm good, thanks, mate," said Harry. "Thanks for asking."

"I'm coming right round. I've really got a song for you this time…it's a winner. I know it is…

"Give me time to get up."

Danny took no notice. He had been phoning from a public call box at Holland Park underground station, and in less than a quarter of an hour had walked round to Camden Hill Road and was letting himself into Harry's flat.

Harry was still in his pyjamas when he arrived, with Lex in the bathroom, but as soon as he arrived Danny started bubbling and babbling on about his new song, which he naturally called 'The Girl With The Silent Violin'. It didn't take Harry long to switch on to it as well, and – equally enthusiastically – he sat at the piano and let his fingers wander before a recognisable tune quickly began to emerge. After about five minutes he had struck on a suitable melody, and as Lex came into the room he began playing it with Danny talking the words through.

"Hey, that's brilliant," said Lex, but the two men were so immersed in the music that they didn't take any notice. Lex was used to that.

Soon the two partners had a fairly comprehensive outline of how the song should be. It had the sort of insidious, invasive beat that sticks in the sub-conscious for a long, long time after the music finishes – the main theme repeating itself in the mind like something you remember from childhood. The words, too, stuck because they were so unusual.

"We're going to make a pile of money out of this…it's going to be a hit, I'm sure of it," enthused Danny.

"And if it isn't – well, we'll stay poor." Harry laughed. "Poor but famous!"

"No way. We're going to hit it big with this one."

"Yeah, OK. But being poor isn't a crime – it's being found out that's the crime."

"Enough of your colonial rubbish," said Danny. "Get the kettle on."

Later that morning, Danny rang Adela's mobile and asked if they could get together for lunch – 'with my partner and his girl'. She instantly agreed, almost as if she had been waiting for the call, and they arranged to meet up in a friendly Italian restaurant near Notting Hill where Danny knew there was a piano.

Danny and Harry were the first to arrive, with Lex (who had gone to her office) turning up soon after.

Adela arrived dead on the appointed time, and as soon as they were all together Danny got Harry to go to the piano on the far side of the room to their table to play the new song, while he sat with the two girls and crooned the words. Adela loved it from the start, and was thrilled that the lyrics had been written about her.

When the song was over, they ordered food, and while waiting for the meal Harry played the melody again, then carried on playing, but now with Lex standing by his side and humming the popular songs he was playing. The restaurant was empty, and Danny asked Adela to dance – and the proprietor, an old friend and a jolly Tuscan, pulled back a couple of tables in the centre of the restaurant to make some room. He watched them dance, clapping out the rhythm of the song.

Danny couldn't help noticing that although Adela was very slightly taller than him, she had turned up wearing brand new shoes with lower heels to bring herself closer to his height.

From the outset, Danny called Adela, who normally liked to be known simply as Ady, 'Your Majesty' – joking to the others in explanation that as a many-times-removed descendent of William the Conqueror she must be a princess. Ady liked it, and throughout the meal showed she had much the same sense of humour as Danny. She was a very ebullient personality who often held centre stage in the conversation – in direct contrast to Lex, who was now content to simply bask in Harry's shadow.

Although the two girls were so completely different, they got on extremely well together, almost as well as the boys, and the lunch was a big success. "It's an omen – a first triumph for '*The Girl*'," said Danny later. "It's bought us all together – from now on it has to be a hit all the way."

And so it proved. Harry completed '*The Girl*' with an unusual but beguiling arrangement that including a central passage with notes seemingly 'plucked' from a harpsichord, and one of the musicians they knew from Satch's liked it so much he took it and promised to show it to his agent.

Soon, Danny and Harry were approached by the agent, who said he had arranged for a big-name band leader to hear it, and asked if he could sell it for them. They agreed, and soon the song could be heard occasionally on radio and TV music shows.

It was a curiously worded song with an unusual melody that might have caught the public's imagination in another age, but for some reason it didn't actually take off in a big way. It went quite well financially from the partner's point of view and it was their first big major professional hit – but it still wasn't really the big breakthrough they both wanted so desperately.

***

In the weeks leading up to the sale, Danny and Ady saw a lot of each other. She seemed to know a lot about music, and would often surprise Danny with her knowledge of older songs. Even on their first night out together, she began speaking about 'Larry' Hart.

"You know about him."

"Of course. '*Manhattan's*' the greatest…and '*There's A Small Hotel*', '*Where Or When*'. So many…," she replied emphatically.

"You do know him. Hey, great."

"You're not the only one. I love the idea of all those old musicals – Rogers and Hart, Porter, Kern and all the others, too. Sammy Cahn, Dorothy Fields, Yip Harburg – all of them. The difference between us, though, is that I reckon Johnny Mercer's the real daddy of 'em all, not Hart."

"Johnny Mercer! Now there's a name you don't hear very often these days," interrupted Danny.

"Oh, but the first song I ever learned by heart was one of his. '*How Little We Know*'." She started to sing, then Danny started to hum along with her.

"It's a great song," said Ady.

They laughed, and Danny was in raptures. A girl after his own heart.

She was indeed. Over the next few weeks Danny and Ady got to know each other well. They talked about music a lot, because she had the same affection as him – and Harry – for the Big Band sounds, although she could never quite match Danny's feelings for them with his love for show music. "Surely," she would say, "the Big Bands didn't always play show music."

"No, not always. Rarely, perhaps – but sometimes they did. Often," Danny would tell her. "What gets Harry and me is the style they played, the jazzy, swingy thing. It's ideal for shows." He recalled how Harry had described it. "You listen to a Big Band number and it's show music on its own, even if the music doesn't always come from a musical – a film or a theatre show."

"Yes, but…"

"It's just that we like the songs of the shows, and the presentation and arrangements of the bands…they connect more often than you'd think."

It was not only the Big Band sounds, though, Ady liked pretty much all the same kind of music as Danny. She was interested in the way he and Harry wrote, and would listen as Danny told her how both their styles had changed over their time together.

"We're writing any old thing at the moment," he told her. "But I'm sure we could produce a show – we will, if only we get the chance. I'm positive we could do it."

Ady listened and nodded her head, and when he had finished, she cocked her head to one side. "Does it have to be with Harry?" she asked.

Danny was surprised at the question, and tried to explain, as Harry used to argue with him, that words and music always have to go together, and theirs just did. "Somehow, our ideas link up – they just seem right," he added.

"But surely, you could put your words to any old song?"

"Oh no," said Danny. "I'm so much on the same wavelength as Harry, and things seem to work between us. These days, I can't hear something of his without thinking of the lyrics that could go with it – and I guess he's the same, he hears my words and the songs come into his mind."

"Is that important?" asked Ady.

"I didn't used to think so. But yeah, I reckon." He had a sudden flash of memory – Beck, the Drummin' Man. "Someone once told me you have to have the two writers together…"

"OK, OK," she countered, getting bored with the repeated argument. "You've convinced me. Now buy me a drink!"

Being with Ady was good for Danny. Before meeting her, he had calmed down just a little under the influence of working with Harry, and in some smaller way through the near daily connection with Lex – and now he gave up his moody binge drinking. With Ady lively, irreverent and full of beans, he seemed to perk up and would often revert to his old one-liner jokey ways.

Danny was now getting on well with Lex, and he and Ady liked going out with Harry and her for meals, drinks or to listen to music. For their part, Harry and Lex enjoyed the way Ady had come on the scene – it was not just her jolly bright and breezy personality, they also noted how it changed Danny, although he still frequently reverted to his old flippant ways.

That came out when they all went out for a posh-nosh lunchtime meal – something they could now afford thanks to the money '*The Girl With The Silent Violin*' had brought in. They were talking generally, and somehow the origin of Ady's name cropped up. Danny was proud of the girl, and he couldn't help telling the others that her name had come from Adela of Louvain.

"She was the daughter of a French count, the second queen of our very own King Henry One," he said. "When he died, she lived as a nun for a year – then one day she threw off her veil, married some duke or other, and had seven or more kids – among them were Anne Boleyn and Catherine Howard." He laughed loudly. "She went back to the nunnery – and that's the girl I've found…a nun, who married twice, had seven kids, and ended up in a convent!"

After the meal, Harry took Lex to the cinema, but Danny and Ady didn't want to go. Instead they went for a walk in Hyde Park, and as they strolled through a tree-lined section they passed a fallen tree that had not yet been cleared up, laying on its side with its roots showing. Danny didn't know what kind of tree it was, but he noted the flowers growing rounds its dead roots and was struck by the fact that nature was carving a new life out of it.

As they strolled, the harsh, jerky, staccato sounds of the City began to be replaced in Danny's mind by the smoother colours of the scenery. He started to recite some words, giving Ady lyrics about the beauty of flowers, birds and the sky. "Just look at a rose unfurling," he told the girl.

Later that night, he wrote a lyric, getting the words down first time – and next day Harry, despite the convolution of its cadences, sat down at the piano and somehow '*The Wonder Of A Baby Seeing A Rose Unfurl*' managed to immediately capture the feeling in his music. The song started almost like a nursery rhyme, then became somehow more mature as it grew, almost like a flower unfurling. It was a good first attempt by both.

Danny listened to Harry's music. "How about a second stanza – the kid seeing a bird fly for the first time?" he asked.

A few days later, Harry spent a good part of the night adapting the main theme into a near concerto, billowing out loud and like a pastoral – eventually subtly bringing in Danny's lyrics as second and third verses to be sung by a massed choir.

"Hey man, it's good. But do we want to write that kind of thing?" asked Danny when he heard it. "Let's concentrate on getting a show on the road."

Apart from the fact that it gave him a set of lyrics, Danny enjoyed that walk in the park with Ady so much that he soon began to take her off alone. Although he had never walked around London before – preferring the underground or taxis – he enjoyed strolling round London with the girl He particularly liked strolling along the South Bank – as Harry and Lex had done when they first went out – sometimes hand in hand and at other times with their arms around each other's waists.

It always amused Ady when they did that Danny still often railed against what he perceived as ills. He would, for instance, see whole streets where television aerials stood guard high over the terraced houses and tower blocks. He would stop, and stand with his hand raised to his forehead. "I salute thee, oh Gods of modernity – Gods of a modern uncultured, inelegant, dumbed down life," he would say out loud. If nothing else, it made Ady laugh.

Another day when they were out, Ady couldn't help noticing that Danny was walking with his left hand to his face. She found it difficult to hear what he was saying, and stopped, pulling the hand away to see that he had a small spot in the corner of his nose and had instinctively put his fingers up to hide it. "C'mon spotty – we all have 'em," she said, laughing.

"OK – if it's imperfections you want, what about that?" Danny pointed to the small scar above her top lip. "How did you get that?"

"It's a shaving cut!" joked Ady, then told him it was really from an accident she'd had when she was in central America on a safari holiday as a teenage student. Instinctively he leaned forward and kissed it. Then he kissed her fully on the lips.

Later that night, they sat on a couch in Danny's apartment – he with his feet up, and Ady curled into him. "What made you want to write?" she asked. "And why music?"

Danny remembered he had once told Harry he only ever wanted to write lyrics, but now he told Ady that had not been strictly accurate. "I suppose when I was young, oh I don't know, maybe ten, twelve, I used to dream of going to live in Paris. Thought maybe get a room at Shakespeare's book shop like all the wanna-be writers. I'd read all about it, and figured I'd be able to sit in the Café de la Paix surrounded by people like Hemingway and Scott Fitzgerald scribbling away at our masterpieces. I thought that would be fun – but despite it somehow, I never thought I could write a book. Too many words. And anyway, I always thought in musical terms – in lyrics. 'fraid that's my bag, whether I like it or not!"

They spoke about all kinds of things as they started to get drowsy – small talk that seemed, at that particular moment, of great importance. "You like using simple words, don't you?" said Ady.

"Yeah, but like Hemingway said – I know all the four-dollar words, but my readers don't. Well, listeners in my case."

"You know all the four-dollar words…?"

Danny grinned. "Well, a few four-letter ones maybe."

Ady smiled. "You should use them – the four-dollar ones, I mean. Do some real writing. Write a book."

"I don't think I could sustain it," replied Danny. "I couldn't come up with all the flowery phrases people seem to want in a book. I just want to stick to simple words – simple lines."

The next time they went for a walk it was along the South Bank again. After a while, they sat on a public bench watching the boats on the river. "London's a lovely place," said Danny. "With reservations."

"Have you ever been anywhere else to compare it?"

"Yeah, well," Danny replied. "I went to Paris as a boy, but I've seen pictures of all the other foreign capitals – Rome, Berlin, Prague and the like. They don't attract me – I love London and don't want to go anywhere else. It has a charm the others don't have – the only thing is that in London they just slap up gigantic tower blocks at the drop of a hat. Even St. Paul's is part-hidden by 'em – idiots with no soul put 'em up. It's got to be down to greed – greed to the detriment of good taste."

The girl started to say something, but Danny ploughed on. It was a favourite theme. "Yeah OK, I know they have tower blocks in those other places," he continued. "But from what I've seen of them they keep them away from the old sights, the heritage. Even New York doesn't have its skyscrapers willy-nilly like London – they put them all in a block on Manhattan Island. If I was in charge of London, I think I'd knock 'em all down and start to rebuild, with an artist as designer of the city not a money-machine."

Ady was smiling by now. "OK," said Danny. "Rant over."

There was a long pause. "I suppose London has got a lot going for it," Danny finally added. "You know, you're walking along and you get a sudden glimpse of an old church, an arcade or an old building – hundreds of years old – and it lightens you up. Yeah – London's lovely."

"One day I'll take you to all those other places. You can write your book on the trip – and you'll see they're quite nice, too," said Ady softly.

Lex and Harry got on well with Ady. They met her often, laughed a lot with her, talked about music a lot. She made them laugh, particularly when she tried to goad them by using Danny's old arguments that lyrics were more important than the music. Sporadically, too, she would suggest some small phrase to one of Harry's arrangements – usually with a violin solo included.

By now Danny and Harry were in full accord, they agreed that words and music were a marriage in which each played an equal part. Ady often tried to 'get them going' for fun – usually succeeding in winding up Danny – while Lex simply agreed with virtually everything Harry said.

They all had much the same tastes, even down to food. One night, Lex invited Danny and Ady to dinner in the flat she now shared with Harry, and managed a straight face when, during the meal, Danny complemented her on her cooking. "I like this," he said. "It's got a taste of…what d'you call it – paprika?"

"No," replied Lex, a demure smile on her face as she remembered her first meal with Danny. "It's curry!"

It was during that meal that Ady asked Harry if he ever planned to go 'home' to Oz. "Oh no," answered Harry. "My home's here now, y'know. I've got nothing in Australia."

"What, no family?"

"No. My old man died a while back, and I suppose my mother's still there. Dunno. But I haven't heard from her for a long, long time. Not even when Dad died. Not a word. No phone call. No letter. I suppose she's still alive – but my family's over here now." He indicated Danny and Lex. "It's all I need."

After the meal, they relaxed over a drink. "Phew, it's muggy tonight," said Ady.

"Closely followed by Tueggy, Weggy and Thurggy," sniggered Danny. He stood to pour more wine, and accidentally spilled some. "Inept as ever," said Harry.

"That's better than being ept," retorted Danny.

"You always say that."

"But it's right. How can you be inept if you can't be ept in the first place? It's like being alert...can you be lert?"

Ady laughed and egged him on. "You're incorrigible sometimes..."

"Better than being corrigible." Danny pursed his lips. "And I suppose you think hegemony is when your partner orders you to cut the hedge," he said.

Let's not get absurd about this, mate," interposed Harry.

"No – let's be surd."

"Danny, you're outrageous," threw in Ady.

"No – rageous!"

"You're a real eccentric," said Lex.

"Is that better than being centric!" came back Danny yet again.

"Now you're being nonsensical," said Lex sensibly.

"But I've never been sensincal," said Danny, pulling a funny face.

"Insensical, maybe," added Harry.

"And now you're trying to give banality a good name," countered Danny.

"That's very disingenuous of you," said Harry.

"But he's never been genuous!" piped up the girls in unison.

There was a pause. "You're so good with words," summed up Ady. "You really should write a book – what do you guys think?"

They were all laughing, because it was the kind of silly, childish, humour they all enjoyed. It was, too, the kind of game they all enjoyed, and as the evening progressed Danny tried to slip into another – his Desert Island Discs.

As always, he started off by suggesting Artie Shaw's 'Begin The Beguine', a particular favourite of his, and Ella Fitzgerald, although he said he could never make up his mind which of her songs he preferred – "Probably 'In The Still Of The Night'," he said. "It's is got to be the best disc ever issued."

130

"You always say that," put in Harry. "And I always tell you her best is '*Ev'ry Time We Say Goodbye*'…"

Danny started to interrupt, but Harry headed him off. "Let's not go there, mate," he said. "You always come up with the same songs……Nat 'King' Cole's '*Mona Lisa*'…that classical piece by Mozart – you know, the one everyone likes…"

"The Clarinet Concerto," said Lex softly.

"Yeah, that's it – the clarinet again. Then there's '*Dancing In The Dark*' – Artie Shaw again – and, and all those show songs…"

Ady started to hum '*We Kiss In A Shadow*', and the others immediately joined in 'la de da'ing' to the 'King And I' song. They all finished up laughing like children once more.

"How can you say I always come up with the same songs," asked Danny. "You know better than most, whenever I've tried to get eight songs – well, it's impossible. I think I once narrowed it down to a short list of about sixty…"

"You would go over the top, wouldn't you!" exclaimed Ady.

"Me?"

Ady held up both hands in surrender. "Do you have to argue with everything?" she asked with a laugh.

"Oh yes," said Harry. "Danny will question everything under the sun. Important things – like where's Old Malden or why did Peter Piper pick a peck of pickled peppers! He's full of questions…and you know what you can never give him an answer to any of 'em. Not one he'll accept without another argument anyway."

Danny had to smile. "Yeah, well," he said. "But why did Peter pick those pickled peppers…?"

A few days later Danny arranged to meet Ady for lunch in a restaurant in the West End. She was already there, reading a newspaper, when he arrived. She took off her reading glasses as he sat. "Listen to this, you'll like it," she said as he sat next to her. She put the glasses back on, flipped back a couple of pages and began to read. "It's in a letter, yes here it is – 'God gave us memories that we might have roses in December'. That's beautiful – any use to you?"

Danny nodded, a thoughtful smile on his face. "Yeah, I can use that," he told her. "It's nice." He made a note of the phrase on a piece of paper he took from his pocket.

They ordered, and the main course soon arrived. When they had finished it, Danny sat back contentedly watching a man on the other side of the room, sitting at a bar stool with a large pint of beer in front of him. He had a bald head and a huge walrus moustache, and as Danny watched he drew on his pint and drank deeply. When he had finished, about a third of the way through, he pushed his lower lip up to suck the excess liquid from the moustache. Then he reached in his pocket and wiped the whole of his mouth with a grubby handkerchief.

"People are fascinating!" Danny told Ady.

At the next table, a Japanese couple were sitting and eating quite formally. "Hey, that looks odd," Danny went on, his cheeky grin covering his face. "Shouldn't they use chopsticks or something?" He grinned and thought how racist that was.

"You try eating a turkey escalope with chopsticks," said Ady, looking at the menu for a dessert.

The food was excellent, and at the end of the meal, Danny expressed his delight. "I could easily live like this all the time," he told Ady. "I can resist everything but temptation. After all, the two greatest phrases in the English language are sheer greed and pure gluttony."

"You're playing with words again," smiled Ady.

"Yeah, well. It was good – I could lick the plate," said Danny.

"Then why don't you?" Ady replied with a twinkle in her eye. Danny looked round him like a naughty schoolboy, then bent over the table and lapped his tongue over the plate. He blushed brightly as he did so – but Ady just laughed.

It wasn't always posh restaurants, though. With Harry and Lex often going off on their own, Danny and Ady were frequently left to their own devices, and one day when he called on the girl Danny said he was hungry. "OK, Help yourself," she told him. Danny went to her kitchen, and as usual returned with a slice of white bread spread with margarine and with a thick dollop of Heinz tomato ketchup on it. "That looks good," said the girl when he walked out with it.

"Want one?" Ady nodded, and Danny handed the bread over and went back to the kitchen to make another for himself. They ate them together, giggling slightly at each other.

Later, Danny was looking round the flat when he noticed a postcard on the mantelpiece. Suddenly he got the feel of a song and began humming it to himself. "What's that?" asked Ady, and Danny read out the words from the card:

'Keep your face towards
The sunshine,
And the shadows will fall
Behind you.'

Ady smiled at the thought that she had possibly been able to inspire another song. She had written the card herself the night before after someone had given her the aphorism.

Although each of the couples now spent a lot of time on their own, they still met more often than not. But even when they were together as a foursome, Harry and Lex would disappear into the recesses of their togetherness, and it left the way for Danny and Ady to manage a lot of holding hands and eye gazing themselves.

Danny had really fallen for Ady hard. It was a feeling he had never experienced before, and he decided to tell her in the only way he knew how – writing some lyrics.

'I met you,
I woo'ed you,
I kissed you,
And soon I fell in love.
You flirted,
You flattered.
You dithered,
And said we shouldn't go so fast.
But now I'm getting desperate,
And you surely have to see,
I want you to consider –
Marrying me.
I'll beg you,
And plead you.
You are the meaning of my life.

Quite simply my darling –
I want you for my wife'.

He showed them to Ady next day, and she listened to them without speaking. Instead, she started to talk about their travelling together – "Let's see a bit of the world, get some experiences," she said. "I don't want to settle down yet – and you could write your book."

"I've told you, I couldn't manage that amount of words."

"You'd just have to redouble your efforts…"

"Double," snapped Danny. "Re-double means four times as many…"

Ady shrugged, but Danny was in a mood. He wanted to settle down with the girl, and his mind was a bit of a blur. He had taken the lyrics as a formal proposal of marriage, and Ady's rejection hit him hard. In the couple of weeks that followed, things didn't go too well with the romance and Danny remembered some words he had once written when Harry had girl trouble – "Love and romance? What do they mean?" They now seemed to apply to him.

Act 8: Writing the Hit

Danny and Ady continued to go out together but now there was something different about their relationship. Danny's usual blind optimism quickly returned, and he hoped, believed that Ady would simply turn up one day and say she had changed her mind about his proposal, that they would get married immediately and everything would be alright – but Ady began to bring a sharper edge to her relationship with him, Harry and Lex.

She missed no opportunity to try and talk Danny into leaving the others and travel, and she constantly urged him to write a book. But Danny steadfastly refused both ideas – he only wanted to write song lyrics, and he liked writing song lyrics to Harry's now very tuneful music.

The two men still dreamed of writing a show – an old-fashioned musical show – but Danny was drinking too much to really settle down to anything quite as solid as that. He was fine when it came to individual numbers, but Harry knew her could not sustain a whole show and backed off the subject as far as he could. It remained a dream.

By now the partners had a top portfolio of some thirty to forty songs of various sorts they really believed in – and drawers full of literally hundreds of other songs they had liked when they were written but which they had now rejected as not quite what they wanted. They had agreed they had to throw out most of their original numbers – not all of them, just those they had now outgrown – which was what they had always planned.

Harry's ability to orchestrate the songs made them instantly available to anyone, and Danny's lyrics were starting to take on their own characteristics to match Harry's now constant moods. He frequently turned his hand to romance without reverting to his old facile manner.

'There are things I'm not supposed to say,
Like rhyming June with moon in that certain way.
Say "I love you",
Or "It makes us two".
I hear them, and hope you do too.
"Will you love me?"
The words are outdated
But they're not over-rated.
They're simple, and few.
So although I shouldn't say it…
I Love You.'

The two men had, indeed, a whole series of songs that they compared with the output of any other pair of writers – of any time. *'With You', 'Our Hearts Together', 'You Make Me Human'*, and many, many more.

Both felt, too, that *'Mem'ries Of A Lonely Boy'*, the song Harry had played when he heard his father had died, could be a big success. Danny had finally managed to write a lyric that both he and Harry liked, but although both felt it was still the best thing they had written together, no one wanted to buy it.

Harry was still the driving urgency in the relationship, but although he was by far the better musician of the two he needed Danny because their music was now so interlinked that one was far less without the other. And on top of that, he was also the one who – despite Danny's previous show business experiences – heard of the opportunities.

As they began to get more and more noticed in the professional music world, it was Harry who heard that a reasonably famous singer who was preparing a new compilation disc had been let down by his team of writers, who'd gone off to the States while he was in rehearsals. One of their songs had not worked out, and he needed a replacement urgently. Harry agreed to help, and promised that he and Danny would quickly produce a couple of alternatives.

Both he and Danny were excited by the thought of working with the singer, known simply as Apache, especially as it would become their first disc if accepted. They both had ideas for Apache's style, and they immediately got down to work in Harry's flat. As Harry sat at the old upright piano, his hands sometimes danced over the piano keys and at others caressed them tenderly like a lover as various chords and tones came to him – and Danny stood by his side ad-libbing lyrics as they occurred to him.

It didn't take long for a reasonable song to emerge.

'Wait for me,
While I climb a mountain.
Wait for me,
While I swim the sea.
Wait for me,
While I cross the Arctic,
Wait for me, wait for me.'

Harry visualised a martial drumbeat behind Danny's original verse as a counterpoint, and half sang-half grunted it to his own piano playing as Danny sang the lyric and they finalised it.

"It's a good song," said Danny. "I'm sure he'll like the sound of it – good arrangement, Harry."

The next day they took it along to the recording studio together, and while they waited to play it Apache started to sing another song, this time one of his own. As Danny and Harry listened, Apache reached a crescendo and then there was a sudden lull. All that was heard was Danny passing comment, in quite a loud voice.

"He's got a God-awful song in the first place, and his lousy singing isn't helping it," said Danny. "He hasn't got a voice. Just listen to him, he's croaking."

Not surprisingly, the two of them were thrown out of the studio without even playing their song. "Sheise," said Harry as they left. "You've really bushwhacked us now."

"What the hell, it only took us one night – and it's much too good for a no-talent like him. He hasn't the voice to carry it," replied Danny nonchalantly.

Later that night, Danny apologised to Harry. "I must learn to shut my trap," he said contritely. "It's just that I can't stand these bumped up so-called stars – no-hopers."

Harry nodded, disappointed but sympathetically understanding. But Ady was furious when she heard that Danny had blown what she felt could have been a big chance.

To make it up to Ady, Harry and Danny decided to take the two girls out for a meal, but Danny objected to paying the prices at the Italian restaurant Ady suggested – his money was starting to run out. "The prices there are pasta-ronomical," he quipped to her disgust when she mentioned the name.

They went, instead, to a small, smart bar to discuss where to eat – "If only to shut him up," said Harry. Once there, Danny made a comment about how he disliked modern minimalist décor, and that started him and Harry talking, as ever, about 'the old days', a subject on which Ady usually joined in. "They were graceful times, and everything was far more romantic," said Danny, looking round him at the ugly, modern room.

"Think of the film stars – they were elegant in those days, they were really were stars. People like – well, like Bogart, William Holden, Gregory Peck, Audrey Hepburn…Kathryn Hepburn, Spencer Tracey. I grew up with them, and they were nothing like today's nobody's who all look alike. Just like modern singers…

Harry stopped him. "Now don't get started on modern singers, mate, or we'll be here all night."

"Yeah, OK," replied Danny. "But going back to those film stars – at least those old stars had a presence – and glamour. They were stars, real stars. Beautiful women, and the men had style and panache."

"They also had talent," interrupted Ady. "What do you think Lex?"

"Oh, I don't know. What do you think Harry?" replied Lex. From being quite independent when she first came on the scene, Lex had now unknowingly affected Harry's old loner attitudes and had become clinging and submissive.

"Do you have to follow his opinions on everything?" snapped Ady. "Get a life of your own."

Lex's face went a bit pale, and Danny started to come back at Ady, but Harry stopped him with a raised hand. "Let's not get into any arguments – except for where we're going to eat," he said. The moment passed, but both Ady and Danny had noted the others' anger.

The saloon had music blaring out from loudspeakers in a corner, and Danny and Harry listened, obviously, to the music for a moment – 'a cacophony of sound', Harry described it – and they both complained bitterly about modern songs. "Loud is not better," insisted Harry.

The four of them turned to a large television screen on the other side of the room instead. There was some Top Of The Pops-type show on, and this time it was Danny who grumbled. "Why can't they just learn to dance properly," he asked, looking at the apparently uncoordinated gyrations on the TV screen. "Just the usual run of hip grinders and jumpers."

"Could you do better?" asked Ady. "Can you even dance?"

"Don't be daft," replied Danny. "You know I've got three left feet."

"How can you hope to write for dancers then?"

"Well, I can't give birth – yet I like kids. I can't cook – yet I like eating. In the same way, I know I can write a song for any hoofer." He laughed, almost hysterically as he often did these days. But he still had his old exasperation for things he did not like and noticed again that Ady was continually picking him up on things.

Rather than go to find a restaurant, they stayed in the pub drinking and later that afternoon Danny took Ady back to his apartment. He started to make instant coffees, and while he was doing so, she absent-mindedly started to tidy up the inevitable mess in the room – re-arranging odd little bits of music into neat piles. For some reason, Danny didn't object, although Harry or Lex doing so would have driven him insane. But he was still very much in love with Ady despite her now almost constant carping.

Funnily enough, despite her critical nit-picking Ady could be soft and compliant when it came to doing something with Danny that she liked. She continued to try and persuade him to take an overseas trip with her so he could get material for a book – "I don't think I could come up with all the flowery phrases and long meaningless words people seem to want in a book, I just stick to simple words in a simple tune," reiterated Danny – and in an effort to get him excited about travel she took him to an exhibition showing some of the world's greatest art treasures, including several pictures of some Michelangelo statues.

"You should go to Italy to see them," she insisted.

"And be in-Continent together?" quipped Danny.

Danny, of course, knew about Michelangelo, and went into raptures over the pictures. When they came to the one showing the David in Florence, he jokily described it as 'Little Willy' – upsetting a rather elderly lady also looking at the photo. But Ady laughed and told him to shut up, this time pleased that he knew something about the giant statue.

From that, they soon discovered a mutual love in all Michelangelo's works. "And, Your Majesty, Bernini's not too bad either," insisted Danny.

"Yes, OK, I'll give you him. But Michelangelo is by far the best in my mind," said Ady. "I'd love to see them in the flesh, as it were, particularly the Rome Pieta. But I've only seen pictures."

"Well, I've got all the books about him – and I agree, they're tremendous," went on Danny. "But there's more than just the David or the Rome statues – I love the other Madonna in Bruges, that's also beautiful. I've got a book about them all at home – somewhere…"

Back at his flat, he got down on his knees and began searching on the floor for a giant 'coffee-table' book about Michelangelo. When he found it, he quickly opened the pages showing the two Madonnas – both marked with a paper clip – and showed them to Ady. "Just look at the expression he's got in the Madonna's eyes," he enthused passionately. "Look, here in Bruges, she's got the look of a mother who knows what's going to happen to her baby son…and here, well, the Pieta shows the look of a mother who's lost her child. In my mind, they're a matching pair. They're like a good song, they make you want to sing out loud."

Ady had not tied the two sculptures together in her mind before, but now she was enthralled and had to agree. "Oh, they're beautiful…" she said, looking intently at the two pictures in turn.

Then almost to herself, "…and to think that…well, that he said the Bruges statue wasn't worth seeing as it was too small!"

"Small?" exclaimed Danny, ignoring the 'he'. "It's a giant. I'll take you to see it, even if it's only a day trip to Bruges."

"You do that," smiled Ady.

Despite days like that, Danny was still generally unhappy following Ady's rejection of his proposal, and in his unhappiness, he was now sometimes starting to find it difficult to match lyrics to Harry's current romantic themes. Romance was not really in his heart at all.

One day, Ady called on him at his flat while he was alone trying to draft out some words to a song Harry had suggested, words he was having trouble organising…

'I wander the fields of lavender blue
But you are not there.
I'm all alone,
And where used to be
Loneliness is my companion.

I'm alone, wishing my life away. .
I wish I didn't love you.
Wish I could say I didn't care.
But there's something I see about you,
That says I wish to share...'

He knew they weren't right and was concentrating, but Ady got bored and began wandering round the room, finally looking over his shoulder at the words he was writing. She started to 'finger' an imaginary violin to the music – just as she had been doing when he first saw her – and it distracted him. He looked up at her with a slight appeal in his eyes, and Ady moved away and instead picked Danny's book on Michelangelo, flicking the pages noisily.

"Hey, look at this one, the Risen Christ," she said, interrupting his flow of thought again.

Danny left his writing in mid-line and stood up. "OK, I'll do this later," he said. "Want a coffee?"

"U-huh."

While he was making the drink, Ady once again started to tidy things up – wandering round the room idly re-arranging odd little bits of music, putting books into neat piles and looking with little interest at the words Danny had been trying to write. When he came back, she was looking at the Michelangelo book again, flicking backwards and forwards between the marked pages showing the two Madonna's.

"Remember, you once promised to take me to Bruges and Rome – to see these two?" she asked him.

By now, the two partners had settled down to dividing their portfolio into groups, putting some in a collection they felt were in a more popular field they felt they could sell immediately – because although they had managed to sell one or two, they were still fairly unknown and like most unknowns found most of their work hard to place. It didn't stop them continuing to work hard on more new songs, and although Lex was quite content to let Harry get on with things Ady didn't like it now when Danny tried to work when she was around.

She and Lex were both in Harry's apartment one afternoon while the two men were, as usual, trying out some fresh ideas. Lex was excited when Harry eventually came up with a nice, simple rough draft for a song, and Danny was also taken with it and quickly scribbled down some equally simple, almost old-fashioned, words to it in rustic round, similar in style to the original song they sold at the outset of their partnership to the church choir in Notting Hill.

As Harry seized on the words, grabbed a piece of scrap white paper, drew a five-line stave on it, and began to organise his theme, Ady stood and started mooching around the room. The two men were absorbed by their work.

"I think I know how to present this," said Harry as he hurriedly penned a few amended notes to fit Danny's libretto. He handed them to Danny. "You sing the first part, high like a girl," he said, and Danny did so without question, imitating a semi-high quasi-falsetto. As he ended his part, Harry played the basic theme on the piano, then picked up and repeated the words in a deep, bass, masculine voice.

"Yeah, that's good," said Danny when they had finished. "But do you think we can convince people that it's a modern piece and not stolen from some old church or something?" He giggled with excitement.

"Trust me," replied Harry, a huge smile on his face. "I'm a pianist."

Lex was still laughing at Danny's attempts to sing like a woman, but Ady ignored it all. She ambled around as usual, not quite consciously distracting them even though Danny gave her the occasional irritated glance. Eventually, as Harry was writing things down, Danny paused to light a cigarette.

"Ugh," said Lex, waving away the smoke that blew across her as Danny exhaled the first puff. "Why do you do that – haven't you any self-control?"

"It gives me a chance to collect my thoughts," replied Danny abstractly.

"You should be able to do that without upsetting everyone else's sense of smell," countered Lex.

Ady raised her eyebrows, but Danny stubbed out the just-lit cigarette. The chance comment stayed in his mind, though, and he decided to give up smoking. It was surprisingly easy for him to quit – he stopped just as fast as he had started the habit – but when Ady realised a few days later she wouldn't let it be and teased him about it. "I thought you once said smoking's for real men," she told him. "But Lex said...are you a man or a girly?" she asked in fun.

"Who rattled your cage then? Get out of my face," snapped an irritated Danny.

The outburst, although small and instant, shocked Ady, and she began to get more possessive and aggressive. Where she had been blissfully light-hearted at first, she now seemed far more pushy and intent on getting her own way. It showed particularly when she nagged him about writing a book or travelling –

two things he didn't want to do but which she, for some reason, seemed to think he should.

"You should write something meaningful," she would tell him. "A book, or at least short stories to sell."

"I couldn't."

"Why not? You can talk – tell a story."

The constant pushing started to rankle Danny, and he reverted to his old flippant mannerisms. Whenever anything even moderately serious was mentioned, he switched to his former punning ways.

"I'm reading a good book…" someone would say. "Well, Lenin was well red too," wisecracked Danny.

"I'm tired," said someone else late one night. "So were Mr Dunlop and Mr Pirelli," quipped Danny.

"I'm hungry," insisted Ady one day. "But I'm too well bred to offer you a loaf, Your Majesty," joked Danny.

The others usually ignored the puns and witticisms, just as they did on another day when they were all talking over the top of some kind of concert on television in the background. Danny stood to go to the loo – "Just going for a wee," he said, and when he got to door, he turned… "W-h-e-e-e-e."

It was his usual joke, and after he had left the room the other three sat listening to the music on TV for a little while. There was a sudden surge to the music, and Ady sat forward. "I love masses of strings like that," she said.

"Yeah, me too," countered Harry. "Y'know, whenever I can I try and fit them into an arrangement. I love seeing the look on Danny's face when I do. He loves big banks of sweeping strings as well."

Ady gave him a funny look, sensing a proprietorial hold over Danny that she didn't like. By chance, Danny came back into the room just in time to hear her reply. "Is that because you told him he does?" she asked. "He's not your servant you know – not like Lex."

Danny had already had words with Ady because of her constant insistence that they 'try to bring Lex back to life' rather than subjugate herself to Harry, and later he told her to leave the other couple alone, to back off. Harry, he said forcibly, was his friend and partner, and he wanted what was best for him – and if Lex being submissive was part of that, well that was their business.

"Why you have to get involved in the way the rest of us get on is beyond me," he told her. "There's no reason for you to interfere in the way Harry and Lex behave – why can't you just let 'em get on with things in their own way?"

The criticism hurt Ady once again, and she wanted to hit back. Over the next week or so, Danny began to notice how she increasingly took every chance she could to have a dig at him and his relationship with Harry, and it began to irk although by now he was mature enough not to say anything about it. He could not figure out what was causing it, and for some reason in his own mind figured that it was probably something to do with his giving up smoking.

Danny realised that he was now starting to get upset with Ady's comments far more often than before. It was quite noticeable and for a while his work was affected, enough for Lex to tell Harry she felt something was wrong with Danny. For his own part, Harry tried to find out what it was, but Danny simply shrugged off the questions and things seemed to settle down and continue as before.

But Ady was deep-down upset – his comments about Lex had been the first time he had spoken really harshly to her. "You were fun to begin with, but you're just a stick in the mud now," she told him one evening when they were alone. "You seem so stuck with those other two – why don't you just snap out of it? Come and see the world with me, I'll show you what fun we can have. You know, there's more to life than just writing piddling little lyrics, but all you ever want to do is hang around with your damned music. And Harry."

Danny started to protest. "Just get a life. Come and see the world," Ady repeated.

"But music's important to me..."

"But you don't need Harry to have music. In any case, you don't even understand it. Not you – not Harry – not Lex. All your rubbish about show music and Big Bands. Both of you always say how they're linked – but they're not. Big Bands are just a sound, a way of playing. In a show you get something completely different – not that listening to you two rabbiting on about it would let you know."

Danny didn't know how to answer, and soon after they said goodnight and Ady went home.

There was more friction between the two of them for a week or more after the argument. Ady still wanted to travel, and more than ever began urging Danny to join her, arguing that she wouldn't become like Lex and give up her life for him. Danny resented the inference, and snapped back whenever she made the point. It was a running sore for both, with neither willing to give way.

Ady had already had a taste of touring and wanted more. She knew there was a whole world of high adventure just waiting for her – a world that she somehow uncharacteristically pictured in her mind as being inhabited by dark sheiks with flowing robes and flashing eyes. It was a world where romance and exciting escapades lurked in waiting for her.

Danny was depressed at the thought of going on any trip abroad, though, although his disagreements and differences of opinion with the girl made him feel wretched at what was happening to the pair of them. He was extremely happy in the cosy 'family' atmosphere he had built around himself – both living and working with Harry and Lex close by – and it led to several unpleasant arguments and incidents with Ady.

Things were not made any easier by the fact that as well as continuing to urge him to go away with her, Ady was still pressing Danny to write a book. Why? Well Danny didn't ask, but he somehow felt that it was perhaps so that she could bask in his reflected glory as a 'proper' writer, although she always insisted she did not want to be subjugated to him as Lex had to Harry.

Throughout it all, Danny's work continued to suffer, and Harry in particular, became ever more concerned. He tried again to talk about it to Danny, but once more without getting any response as to what was wrong. Soon, he and Lex began making excuses not to meet up when Ady was around, and there seemed to be a bit of a rift growing between them and Danny as well. Danny did not know what to do. He was still in love with Ady, and he believed she was in love with him, but he was sad and miserable. Desolate and dejected. He determined to talk to the girl to find out what was really the matter and to try and sort things out once and for all, but as always he kept deferring the moment when he had to bring up the subject.

After a particularly nasty exchange one evening, however, they did arrange to meet the next evening, with Danny saying they should go to a restaurant or bar to talk things over. Ady knew he was serious, and agreed.

Throughout the next day, Danny was like a cat on heat. Harry hardly dare say anything while they were working in case it upset him more, and Lex sensibly made an excuse to go shopping so she could keep away from the flat all day.

The evening slowly arrived, and Danny smartened himself to meet Ady. He went to the meeting place and waited, and waited, and waited. After more than an hour he tried to call the girl on her mobile, but he couldn't get through – so he waited a little bit more before finally going home not quite sure what was happening.

The next day, too, Ady did not answer her mobile, although Danny left several messages asking her to get in touch. He still didn't know what to do, but finally that evening he went back to the meeting place and waited for a further hour or so in case he had got the wrong day – something he knew was not the case, but he felt it was a chance.

When there was still no sign of Ady, nor still any answer to her mobile phone, Danny started to wander the streets, thinking what he could do. After a while, his mind a complete mess, he decided to go to a jazz club he knew in the West End. It was closed. So, too, was another music bar he once used to visit, and finally as night began to fall he caught an underground train and made his way to Satch's. But that, too, was closed and looking forlorn – a note on the door saying it was being revamped.

By now Danny's mind was a blank, a blur of nothing, and he wandered round some more, not really knowing where he was going, until finally he found himself outside the house where Ady lived off the Brompton Road, near the Natural History Museum where she had been doing some freelance research work.

Danny had never been encouraged to visit her there because, as he believed, she was sharing a flat with three other girls – but when he got there the door was opened by a burly man wearing a dressing gown.

"Oh, I thought this was Ady's place – that she lived here with some girls…"

"No, it's my house. She and a couple of others have been sharing rooms."

"Sharing…? Is she here now?"

"No. They all left yesterday morning."

"Left?"

"Yep…going to Europe, I think. Somewhere." The man looked at Danny intently. "Are you Danny by any chance?" he asked.

"Yes."

"Well, there's a letter here for you – where'd I put it?" He turned into the flat and looked around. Finally he found the envelope and gave it to Danny. As

Danny took it, looking at the envelope with his name scrawled on it in Ady's neat, feminine handwriting, the other man shut the door with a bang.

Danny held the letter in his right hand for quite a time before he opened it carefully under a streetlamp and began to read the note inside. It told him, in simple terms, that Ady had decided to leave with her girlfriends to go on a tour of Europe. "I won't be back for a long time, but I doubt you'll be too upset," she wrote. "You seem so tied up with Harry and your music you probably won't even notice I've gone."

Danny was staggered; the news took him completely by surprise. Sure, they had been arguing – sure, they'd had their differences recently. But he loved her, and he never expected Ady to walk out like that.

He meticulously refolded the letter and put it back in the envelope. Still holding it in his right hand, he absent-mindedly tapped it against the knuckles of his other hand before wandering off to the end of the street. He got there, stood for a moment or two, then turned and went back to stand on the opposite side of the lonely street all night in a deep depression, just watching the bedroom windows of Ady's apartment.

It was still dark when, several hours later, he turned and started to walk away.

He was, he supposed, going home, and it turned out to be a slow, tortuous route. From the flat in Yeoman's Row he crossed the Brompton Road walked along to Montpelier Street, ambling wearily round Trevor Place and over Knightsbridge into Hyde Park through the Rutland Gate.

As he made his way alone through the park, Danny once again saw the fallen tree he had passed with Ady – but this time, it was like a dead log on the ground. He walked straight past, thinking of a lyric… '*There Is Death Among New Life*'.

Finally he somehow got across the park, although he was not watching where he was going, and came out into the Bayswater Road. As he walked, the music of Ella Fitzgerald singing '*Ev'ry time We Say Goodbye*' came into his mind, and he tried to think of the words. But they wouldn't all come. His thoughts turned to Porter, Hart, Gershwin, Kern, and he wished he was like them. What were those words… '*Ev'ry time we say goodbye…*'

Finally Danny reached Notting Hill Gate – where a policeman on patrol stopped to watch him, but seeing he was no trouble left him to his own devices. It was a long trudge, a very long trudge, but as he walked in a kind of dream Danny's mind began to catch a hint of a melody – a rhyme that came from somewhere deep in his psyche although he could not think what it was.

As he sauntered in the half mist of the breaking new day he felt a cold gust of wind.

Then a cold drizzle of rain fell, and through it all the cold touch of depression sat on him.

A fleeting shower dampened his hair and the shoulders of the lightweight suit he was wearing. A cold drizzle.

It stopped, and a breeze flew along the road. A chill wind which would have frozen him if he had noticed.

The moon emerged for a few moments from behind the rain clouds. A pale, cold blue moon in a still black unfriendly sky.

As he wandered, a vague recollection came into his mind – a song Harry had given him a few weeks before, and a new set of lyrics began to form alongside it. He started to hum the vague rhyme, and eventually he felt the true lyrics for the song. As he got to Holland Park he suddenly seemed to come to his senses and turned purposefully, aiming for Harry's apartment in Camden Hill Road.

Eventually he got there, and pressed his finger solidly on the bell to Harry's apartment to wake him – even though it was still only 5am. After several minutes, Harry opened the door, his hair tousled, and wearing just pyjama trousers and a watch.

"What the hell…"

"Look, I've got a song…" said Danny enthusiastically.

"Yeah mate, you woke me up to tell me that! What's the time, you stupid mongrel?" He looked at his watch. "Five o'clock? Christ man, what the hell…"

"No, no. Listen. Ady's left, but I've got this song…"

"Ady's left?" Harry yawned.

"Yeah, she's run away to Europe or somewhere. Listen…"

"Run away? What the…"

Harry yawned again, and he wiped a scab of sleep from the corner of his right eye. It lodged on the side of his nose, and he scraped it off with his forefinger.

"No, just listen to this," repeated Danny. "I think they're great words – they'll make a great song…"

"What d'you mean she's run away? Where?" Harry looked perplexed.

Danny ignored him. "It doesn't matter," he said, fluttering his hand in the air.

"Oh come on. Where is she? Has she gone for good?"

"Probably – but it doesn't matter. Just listen to me – I've got something really good…"

"No, you can't just write her off like that."

"I'm not bothered. Look…"

Danny gathered his thoughts and told Harry the full story of the past couple of days. "It was over between us. I didn't realise, but it was," he finished. "She was getting far too bossy. She was coming between us, you and me…now she's gone…"

"She's gone?" repeated Harry trying to put his brain into gear. "Oh mate, I'm so sorry."

"It doesn't matter. Just listen to the song…"

He pushed his way off the doorstep and led the way into Harry's apartment. As he did so, he started to give Harry the basic outline of the idea that had come to him while he was walking. Harry listened, and then despite the early hour sat right down at the piano in his pyjamas and started to play – Danny had reminded him of his old tune, and he instinctively caught his partner's mood. From the moment he began playing, the song was an almost a perfect whole, and Danny crooned the words with ease:

'The cold streets of London,
Are not for romance.
They're cold and unpleasant,
Don't give you a chance.
Your love's one of many,
You see her – you're proud.
But she's only one person
Among that great crowd.
It just needs one glance
To see her and fall.
But the cold streets of London
Are not made for love.
The cold streets of London
Don't give you a chance.'

As they ran through it, Lex came out of the bedroom – she was wearing Harry's pyjama top, which was far too big and too long for her. "What the…"

She realised, and listened, and when the two men had finished, she was just as enthusiastic as the pair of them.

Harry was really excited. All thoughts of sleep had vanished, he was wide awake and wanted to get down to finalising the song immediately. "I'll make some coffee," said Lex, but neither Harry nor Danny really heard her. "Even if it's only to wake myself up," she added.

Both Danny and Harry were chuckling with delight. "Just think," giggled Danny, "in the old days I'd have written that third line as: '*The wind turns the corner and blows up your pants!*'"

It didn't take them long to call the finished song '*The Cold Streets Of London*', Harry realising instinctively that in his own bitter-sweet tale of lost love he had written a melody in an old 3-beat rhythm a semi-tone apart rather than in the more usual 2-4 beat. As Lex came back with the coffee, they made a few more notes, then Harry followed Lex into the bedroom to get dressed.

When they came back, they found Danny sitting on a couch crying his eyes out. Danny looked up at them. "She's gone," was all he said.

Danny eventually fell asleep on the couch in Harry's apartment, exhausted, and he was dead to the world until waking up just after noon. Lex made him and Harry a snack, then the two men sat down together to work on '*The Cold Streets Of London*'. The work went swiftly because most of it had been done just after Danny had turned up at dawn, and between them they finalised everything and Harry even got down to working out a possible arrangement – at one point, a muted trumpet followed, as if in echo, by a mournful tuba, both backed by a huge bank of sweet violins.

With just a little bit of extra work by both men, within a couple of hours they had developed it into what they both felt was an ideal song that completely caught the spirit of Danny's original words. Harry had wrapped those words into his sweet-toned tune, giving an almost classic underlying theme behind the original bitter-sweet idea of Danny's long walk. By early evening they were satisfied, and added it to their strongest set.

Although both felt it was the best thing they had created together – the best, in fact, either of them had ever written individually – no one seemed to want it. They tried all the publishers, all the agents, they could think of, but there was a complete absence of any enthusiasm for it from any potential buyer. It was depressing, but they both felt – and said – it was probably because they were unknowns…and publishers and the music companies were not willing to take a chance on unknowns.

It was a small consolation, but it allowed them to persist, and the denials helped Danny throw himself into his work almost in frenzy as he completely wiped out the memory of Ady. After the girl's disappearance, he even made a conscious decision to give up drinking virtually completely.

Both Harry and Lex had expected at least some bitterness, but although there was sometimes an astringent edge to his lyrics, Danny now seemed to have found those vital ingredients that had been missing – dedication, passion and emotion.

He and Harry were, by now, writing in near perfect harmony, the words and the music slotting together seamlessly. '*The Cold Streets Of London*' fitted in to their compilation of collected love songs – although neither seemed to see the irony rising from the fact that it had been written because Ady had walked out on Danny.

Although 'Cold Streets' did not sell, over the next few weeks the two men managed to sell an increasing number of other songs, cheaply – and although unaccountably none of their top 'specials' seemed to attract any interest, things seemed to be working quite well. But neither could understand why the best songs were not selling.

Harry was still trying to get an agent – although with a little less enthusiasm now as they were coping moderately well without one – but the two men still took their songs and personally tramped round all the publishers, all the singers they could think of. Then one small agent, Thomas Sibley, suggested they make a demo disc. "Without one, no one's going to listen to you. They won't know what you've got to offer," he recommended kindly.

"What's a demo disc?" asked Danny innocently.

Harry started to answer, but Thomas interrupted. "Quite simply, it's a rough and ready version of your song," he said. Then, with Danny cocking his head to one side, he explained it in very plain words. "Basically, it's just a very straightforward interpretation of your song. On a piano or something," he went on. "You have to get something on disc that sounds like the song you're trying to sell, it's a good way for the likes of me to understand what it is that you're selling."

"But surely the music itself does that," said Danny.

"Maybe," smiled Thomas. "But what if I can't read music? I know the words and the music are the most important thing, but if I, or a publisher, was given a disc they'd all be there for us. Remember, the point is that you and Harry have worked very hard producing your songs – why give up on the small matter of presenting them?"

Harry butted in. "It's like a Monet painting. It would be great slapped down on a piece of paper, but mate…put it inside a good frame, give it the right lighting, and hang it in a gallery and…like wow!"

"Exactly," said Thomas. "Presentation. The song is still the most important part, but you have to present it properly."

Danny nodded. "Just remember, get your disc done, and send it round with a copy of the music and lyrics," added the agent.

"If we get a disc, will you listen to it?" asked Danny.

"I'd love to, but I think your songs are way above my lowly level," said Thomas. "From what you've shown me, you're good, very good, and you really need a top man to sell for you. Get a demo disc and I think you'll get one easily enough."

"The trouble," said Harry, ever cautious, "is that we can't really afford to get a demo done,"

"You'll find a way," said Thomas. "It doesn't matter how bad it is – but you have to have one if you want to sell your work. You don't need Hit Parade quality – it doesn't have to be brilliant as long as it shows off the song."

"And the words," said Danny softly.

"Oh yes, and the words," smiled Thomas, standing to show the interview was at an end. "Good luck."

Over the next couple of days, Danny and Harry discussed agent Thomas Sibley's advice – Danny, especially, enthusing over his comments that 'you're good, very good' – and finally they agreed they had to make a demo disc.

Harry had the idea of getting the singers from the Notting Hill choir who had been the first to buy one of their songs to tape a recording, suggesting – rightly as it turned out – that they would probably do it for nothing. When he asked them about it, they willingly agreed, and by a stroke of luck also told him that one of the singers had enough technical equipment to 'burn' the disc for them.

Harry also got a few of the musicians from Satch's – which had, by now, re-opened – to play a backing behind the enthusiastic choir, and arrangements were soon made for the recording session at the Notting Hill church hall one mid-week night.

On the evening itself, Danny was in a bit of a panic, but Harry was completely in charge and relaxed as the bandsmen and singers ran through their paces. Two trumpeters and a trombonist from Satch's turned up for the pure love of playing some new music, and with Harry himself at the piano and one of the choir singers at the drums they got down to work with a couple of microphones on flimsy booms covering them all.

They played from orchestrations painstakingly mapped out by Harry and the recording went without hitch. Well before their hire of the hall ran out, they had 'burned' several separate discs – including tracks like *'The Cold Streets Of London', 'The Girl With The Silent Violin', 'Upright Lady', and 'Mem'ries Of A Lonely Boy'.*

Next day, Harry collected the actual discs and got Lex to meticulously copy out all the lyrics and scores to go alongside them. Despite their previous sales, Danny and Harry listened to their music and finally felt proud and fully professional.

Act 9: The Song Is Recorded

With the demo discs safely in hand – several copies had been enthusiastically made by the drummer who'd played on them 'just in case' – Danny and Harry began the job of trying to sell themselves in a different way. Instead of barging in on agents or publishers, they prepared a list and prepared to send the discs around.

At the same time, they decided to get back 'in the know' with the bandsmen at Satch's, who had always been good at providing tips as to what was wanted in the music world. As Lex also wanted to see the club in its new incarnation, the partners took her there on a Saturday night. It was different – it had been given over to pop music, and although a few of the old jazz musicians still dropped in to see if they could play, it was mainly pop groups holding the roost to a crowd that seemed to Danny and Harry to be far younger than they remembered.

They stayed for a while, and while having a drink at the bar – it still sold beer and spirits, but they noticed Alco Pops were now the norm – they listened to one of the groups. Danny exploded at the grunting and emphatic bang-bang-bang of the drums which was all that was holding the song together. Harry and Lex just turned their backs.

Then a rising 'celebrity' stood up to sing his latest song. "Only three lines in the lyric – 'ooh, ah, ooh, ah, yeah, yeah, yeah' – how the hell does he manage to learn all the words?" asked Danny out loud. Harry put out a hand to calm him when a few of the younger people standing nearby turned to him with loud 'shushes'.

Danny carried on the rant. "Could you do better?" asked one youngster aggressively. Danny nodded, and sang softly:

'Red, white and sky-blue pink,
You're the colour of my love.'

The youth blushed, Danny grinned, and added another line.

'Red faced and yellow of tooth.
They say you're ugly,
And that's the truth.

You really are –
The colour of my love.'

During the immediate week that followed, Lex went out with some girlfriends and Danny also disappeared on another visit to his family. Left on his own, Harry decided to go back to Satch's to see if any of the 'real' musicians would turn up to give him the latest news. And there was some – good news, as it turned out.

While chatting to a couple of bandsmen, Harry picked up that a rising young singer, Toni Benito, who was beginning to make a name for himself on disc on and TV, was recording, and wanted a new song. Harry had briefly met Toni in passing when the singer was also trying to find an agent – they had hit the same brick wall at several offices – and he knew the style. He felt that he and Danny could certainly offer something that would be appropriate – if they could get a new introduction.

When Danny came back on the Monday morning, they discussed the news about Toni Benito, and agreed that it might well be worth trying out 'Cold Streets' on the off-chance that he might take it. Harry found the address of his recording company, and sent the rough demo disc of the song – pointing out, in the third person as though by a critic, its intriguing arrangement.

It turned out to be exactly the kind of bitter-sweet romantic song that Toni was looking for – the final song for the new album he was to record that week. Danny and Harry were asked to call in to the record company offices on the following Monday to discuss it, and when they got there immediately give permission for Toni to record it.

They shook hands on it, no more, and they were told that the Thursday of that week had been fixed for the recording. A couple of days before, Danny and

Harry helped the record company's appointed conductor, Norman Something-or-other, a nondescript man, map out the piece, imaginatively interpreting the song in a way that meant the orchestra would be able to maintain the mood of the song while allowing Toni to hold the melody in the front. It took most of a day – quick by any standards – and when it was done the conductor claimed he was exhausted and went home, but Harry carried on, using his own not-inconsiderable technical skill to get a rough plot of where all the separate instrumental parts should come in – slotting the brass with the strings, the percussion with a harp that portrayed a cold, whistling wind.

"Don't worry – I can do it all," Harry told Toni when asked whether the studio should take over. "In fact, I'd prefer to. I've helped with the arrangements –"

"And they're good," interrupted Toni…

"Well, mate, I don't see how you can write a complete song without arranging it. It's the way you see it in your mind."

Next day, Danny and Harry made their way to the recording studio again. Both were keyed up, but in different ways – Danny had seen and worked in studios before, slotted in with ease, and was raring to go; but to Harry it was all new and exciting, and although outwardly he gave the appearance of being calm, inside he was bubbling.

The studio was in the middle of an industrial estate south of the River Thames, one of a series of ugly prefab style square blocks housing an assortment of small companies. Inside it was different. There was an expensive-looking reception area, and the building had been split into three main recording areas. The two writers were shown to the relevant studio by a bored young man with long hair, and stood there waiting as nothing much seemed to be happening.

The final preparations were being made, however, and soon after Danny and Harry had entered the recording room they saw Toni. He was one of a small group of rising young singers beginning to make their mark – an Anglo-Italian, a home-loving boy who enjoyed home-loving things, and very natural in everything he did. He had a perfectly modulated, slightly too-English accent, with a laugh in his voice when he spoke. He laughed a lot, and when he did his eyes creased up at the sides, his mouth opened to reveal firm white teeth, and his scalp rode up when he started. His ears, too, twitched just once when he began to chortle.

At first meeting, Toni always struck people as being quite ordinary, there was no show-biz pretence about him. It was when he sang, though, that he became something quite out of the ordinary. The laugh in his speaking voice was replaced by romance when he crooned – and when he sang anything even the slightest bit amorous, the women in his audiences became starry-eyed and temporarily in love.

Danny and Harry spoke to him briefly about the song, then Toni went off to a small rehearsal room somewhere away from the main studio. Danny and Harry remained chatting to the musical director, Norman, who offered to show the two musicians around. As he did so, the orchestra members slowly assembled and began tuning their instruments. Danny was intrigued by one earnest-looking young girl in a sleeveless, backless dress playing a clarinet – her left elbow was held horizontally as she played, and he could see she wore no bra.

The studio itself had the most up-to-the-minute computer-based recording systems, and was geared to handle professional recording assignments from start to finish. It was able to record up to 128 audio tracks, and Harry, in particular, was enthusiastic in his questions trying to find how it all worked.

Recordings, he was told, covered everything from tracking to mixing and then to final mastering. Behind the scenes there were high quality 24-bit converters – even after a detailed explanation he didn't understand what they were – and a variety of monitors and stereo speakers for creating the final masters.

Special high-quality microphones were scattered between the rows of chairs laid out for the musicians, and individual screens isolated parts of the orchestra while glass baffles allowed for Toni, or any other soloist, to do their own thing while being able to keep an eye on both the bandsmen and the conductor. "It's to try and keep the separate bit separate," a technician told Harry. Harry didn't understand the need for that either.

In the main recording room, the dimensions had been worked out well – carefully planned to allow even the largest orchestra to sit and play and record together. Even the walls had been specially constructed and treated to eliminate unwanted harmonics and 'reflections', and while Harry and Danny watched extra baffle boards were placed seemingly haphazardly above and around the orchestra area.

Wires snaked all over the floor, and as they were shown around the two writers had to tread carefully not to step on them in case they accidentally pulled out a vital plug – although no one else seemed bothered. After a quick look round, they ended the tour back on the studio floor where Harry became engrossed talking to the director about the music sheets.

Danny just looked on as the other two went through the song – the mysterious squiggles, swirls, circular blobs and things were like hieroglyphics to him because he still couldn't read music, although when he read the lyrics below the master sheets of some of the other songs due to be recorded in that session he usually managed to work out the tune. He watched casually for a while as Harry spoke to Norman and some of the recording people, then he drifted away and began chatting to another of the pretty girl violinists. Soon after, some suited officials from both the recording company and the music publishers backing the album turned up and started laying down what they described as 'the ground rules'. Simply, that meant the recording of 'Cold Streets' had to be just as they wanted it.

Eventually Toni walked back onto the floor and joined in the conversation, which was beginning to get animated. The trouble was that the company men wanted an electronic background because they felt it would be quicker to record, saving on over-time for the expensive session musicians hired for a limited period only, but Harry didn't think that would give the song the right feel.

The album promised to be a big step forward for Danny and Harry both as individuals and as a team, and Harry didn't want anything to lessen the impact of their one song in it. The two men had been so keen to get the song recorded that they hadn't bothered arguing about fees or contracts, so Harry couldn't argue about artistic control – but Toni agreed with him that they needed the full orchestra.

Toni was also adamant about the orchestral backing because he never used electronics and only wanted 'pure music' – and insisted that as the singer he should get things the way he wanted them.

"It's my name on the cover – my name that will sell it," he said firmly.

Luckily Danny was not around to join in. Harry knew that if he did, he would get agitated and then someone would remember his offensive remark during the Apache clash. A lot of people had heard about the unpleasant incident and the story had taken on a life of its own, full of half-truths and a lot of imagination. Some people had taken offence without knowing the full facts, and some of the record company's executives might have had had certain reservations about using the lyricist.

Although Norman, as conductor, tended to agree with Harry and Toni, he needed regular session work and would not give his whole-hearted support, so the discussion went on slowly, and there were a lot of delays in getting things finalised. Neither Harry nor Toni – nor Danny, too, when he eventually returned for a short while to see what was happening – were happy with the company arrangement being pressed on them, but Toni had some muscle and insisted. He finally got his way, although the talk had taken so long that by the time he won it was around teatime.

The music people were miffed at losing the argument, and instead of backing off gracefully soon began insisting on some other changes. There were more discussions, with Toni and Harry again disagreeing with the executives, and there seemed to be stalemate. But it was getting late, and as the studio people began to go off for the night one by one, the two of them were promised: "Don't worry – we've done it all before. It'll be OK on the day."

But Harry was not satisfied, he couldn't wait, and as a result he agreed to stay on working on the number – the way he and Toni wanted it. They agreed to do things their way, knowing that next morning it would be too late to change things. Between them they ended up giggling over their 'conspiracy' like schoolboys on a naughty adventure.

Harry worked out a final arrangement with Toni and Danny, then adapted his own piano arrangement to map out a full orchestration outline giving Norman directions for everything that was to take place with the song during the recording – the introduction, modulations, interludes and coda.

Harry's arrangement provided a simple backing with banks of strings and brass, and as it was getting quite late by then he sent Toni off to get some rest. Eventually Danny also drifted away, leaving Harry working on his own to complete the final individual scores. He stayed up all night preparing the full lead sheet for Norman and a complete set of individual music sheets for each instrument to make sure each would play the right notes and fit in – playing with or against each other in the sequences he had worked them out.

It was sheer hard grind, but Harry was determined to get things right for 'his' song, and by morning it was all ready. Harry was exhausted, but it all helped make the song into something rather special, and he was pleased with the result.

With everything ready, and by the time everyone else had returned – apart from the company men and Danny, who was late as usual – Harry had shaved, washed and had a bite to eat in the canteen. He was full of life, alert and raring to go – and it was easy to persuade Norman that things were just fine.

Finally it was time to record, and Danny and Harry went upstairs into the control room, where they could see Toni and the musicians through a half-wall glass above a huge banked 'desk' of controls. Danny sat excitedly alongside Harry as Toni Benito and the orchestra recorded 'Cold Streets'. As they watched, dozens of dials round the control room danced to the music as technicians slid stops up and down and tweaked mysterious little knobs to balance the sound. It was all very confusing to both of them – but show-biz'y and in its own way glitzy.

Toni had a wide vocal range and a pleasing tonal quality. His pitch and diction were just right for the song, and his relative, rather than perfect, pitch allowed him to sing Danny's words perfectly within the overall arrangement that Harry had prepared. As he sang, using his hands expressively to help the melodic chant of the tune, the words fell clear and pure onto the recording track.

It was very exciting – and magical.

When the song was done and the orchestra took a break before getting on with another recording, both Danny and Harry felt the final recording of 'Cold Streets' did justice to all their hard work – especially Harry's all-night stint. It turned out that the two writers and Toni were right all along – their version was good…and even acceptable to the bosses when they heard it.

The recording was completed in just two takes – well within the time limit that had worried the studio heads – and ended up as the tender, poignant, bitter-sweet tale of disappointed love that Danny had originally envisaged. When it was done and played back, everyone in the studio, Norman, session musicians and technicians included, applauded a good song well prepared, sung and played. "Beautiful song – it's got everything," said Norman. "And you put it over well, Toni, got the meaning and the feel just right."

The bandsmen agreed, standing and clapping – in the case of the violinists, by tapping their bows on the strings of their instruments. It was a rare tribute.

Next day, Harry and Danny took Lex along with them when they returned to the studio to sign the contracts for the previous-day's recording. The industrial estate didn't seem anywhere near as awe-inspiring as the day before, although they were all still on a high.

They were quickly ushered into an imposing office on the first floor, papers were produced and – without a word about the 'tinkering' with the official policy and their use of their own arrangement – Harry and Danny both signed a formal contract. The agreed fee might not have been as much as an established pair had hoped for, but they were both more than happy.

After the signing, the record company's PR girl, Sam Ross, a standard plastic blonde, invited the two men and Lex to join her over a long, lingering, expense account lunch – 'so we can get to know each other real well'. They willingly agreed, and Sam drove them to a very expensive restaurant nearby.

The restaurant had a very long bar along one entire mirrored wall, and tables carefully laid with pristine white clothes, glittering silverware and with three highly polished glasses by each placing reflecting the mock daylight from the chandeliers above. Although it was crowded, the maître d' obviously knew Sam – short for Samantha – very well and somehow found them a good table about two thirds of the way through the room. "I'm afraid it's not Number One today, but…" he purred.

He led them to the table, with Sam following but pausing ostentatiously every few steps to nod to almost everyone else, saying 'hello's' and 'nice-to-see-yous' to everyone – then pointing out to Danny, Harry and Lex who they were.

"He's the chair of the Rock Eye Music company," she said of one opulent looking diner, sitting with a napkin tucked in his shirt front.

"Chairman," muttered Danny automatically.

When they were finally seated, a waiter appeared almost as if by magic and without looking at his proffered wine list or asking the others what they wanted Sam instinctively ordered an expensive bottle of white wine. Danny used his old journalistic training to read the upside-down menu, and noted that it was marked down at £750.

"Er, I'll just have a glass of house plonk red," he said, while Harry simply asked the waiter for 'a schooner of blonde'. Lex politely said she'd drink Sam's wine, and then as they waited for the drinks Sam turned to Danny.

"You don't remember me, do you?" she asked.

"No, should I?"

Sam giggled. "I was a very young girl in the PR department of the film studios when you started," she said. "I had a terrible crush on you in those days, a teenage crush, but you never seemed to notice me. I always wished you'd ask me out one day."

Danny didn't know what to say, but luckily the waiter came back to the table with the wine. He offered the bottle to Sam, but she waved him away and he poured two glasses. Another waiter bought the other drinks, then offered menus, and after they ordered Lex and Harry were able to divert the conversation by talking about the recording.

During the meal, Sam talked seemingly without stop about the big stars she had handled, pausing only when someone passed the table for a quick 'hello'. She picked at her food, and spoke incessantly about her job, telling them of the successful discs she had worked on almost as if she had sung them herself. Lex listened, occasionally muttering a "Ooh, he's nice" or "What was she like?" – but neither Danny nor Harry offered much in the way of the conversation. They were enjoying the meal and the semi-adulation they had received from being seen in Sam's presence during her 'royal' tour of the restaurant, and when they did speak it was to each other to say something about their own music.

After a lengthening hour-and-a-quarter the meal came to an end. Sam signed the bill with a flamboyant flourish, and they all stood, with Harry holding Sam's chair for her. They began the slow walk to the front of the emptying restaurant, and on the way Danny asked the PR girl if she would like to meet up for a drink.

"Oh, I don't think so," said Sam curtly. "You've changed. You don't seem nearly as much fun as you used to be in the studios – you and your friends are so tied up with your music now…"

They said their goodbyes outside the restaurant, and Danny, Harry and Lex walked towards Hyde Park. They strolled casually through the park – Harry hooking his right arm into Lex's the way Danny used to when he walked there with Ady. Danny didn't notice the similarity, he was too busy noticing everything around him as they strolled in the sunshine. He took it all in.

The park looked good – the trees were green (a myriad variety of different greens), and the bedding flowers were a blaze of colour setting off the almost regimented lines of yellow daffodils sprouting among the lush recently-watered grass. As they walked, slowly, leisurely, Danny wiped Sam's final words from his mind – words similar in their way to Annie's farewell comment – and the beauty of nature set off great peals of music in his mind, and a lyric came to the front…

Blue lavender
Gives me the lavender blues.'

It was back to work.

The recording was the big breakthrough they had both been seeking so desperately. As they sat down to celebrate signing the contract, Danny and Harry both reflected on the path they had followed – the church choir in Notting Hill, the nights in Satch's, the first sales to Brent Saxon's professional band, the television butter commercial, the fiasco with Apache, and selling 'The Girl With The Silent Violin'. Harry thought of the journey from Australia, the flats at Notting Hill and Camden Town, the endless piano lessons for talentless kids with unseeing, uncaring mothers…and Danny, the sour editors and no-talent subs, the pompous PR directors and the clients without taste.

It had seemed a long, long journey, and it was only really just starting.

It took time for the various processes of getting Toni's album complete, of course. As well as 'Cold Streets' there were another dozen or so songs to finalise to perfection, and while they were waiting for the release Harry and Danny saw the singer frequently and the three of them became quite good friends.

Harry saw to it that they also kept working – working hard. He and Danny continued throwing song ideas and words at each other, and while waiting for the release of the disc, too, they decided to spend more time directly trying to sell their songs.

With the recording behind them, it was easier to get into the offices of musical agents and publishers' offices around the West End to show an early rough copy of Toni's 'Cold Streets' and their original demo discs to agents and publishers alike. But with nothing really big to show them – the album was not yet officially out, and no one took too much notice of it – they still hit the same brick wall.

Their attempts at selling meant the two men were spending less time actually writing – no longer spending every hour of every day throwing out ideas and lyrics to each other – but as they already had a decent-sized portfolio Harry was not unduly worried, although he still did write quite a lot.

Danny was still coming up with dozens of random lyrics he liked, often working in a frenzy. Late one night he was struck with a song that came into his mind while he was in the bath. He leaped out, and still dripping sudsy water on the carpet rang Harry to pass them on.

'You're essential.
Like champagne corks,
And strawberry stalks.

Like the breath that we take,
And the moon on the lake.
You're essential.'

"Let's have a song in the morning," he said full of natural enthusiasm.

"Goodnight Danny mate," replied Harry, his tone resigned.

Danny hardly ever thought of Ady now – it was as though she had never existed. But one day when he and Harry were talking about music styles, he suddenly – and for no apparent reason – mentioned her.

"What on earth made you think of her?" asked Harry.

"I dunno. A few words that just came into my head."

'There's a girl called Adela(h),
Had a fella(h),
But she dumped him'.

Harry listened, his face a blank. "Funny!" he said.

Danny nodded. "She was right, you know," he said softly. "Ady – she was right. She always told me that everything I ever said about show music and the Big Bands was wrong. I'd keep trying to tell her that real show music came from the 20s and early 30s. That that was our music – Hart, Rodgers, Porter, Kern…not Goodman, Dorsey or Artie Shaw. The Big Bands were just a style of playing the songs. Shows were the music.

"But she kept telling me I'd never write a show – just out-of-date band music."

Harry nodded, not certain what to do or say. "Perhaps she was right," said Danny. "Perhaps I have been talking rubbish all my life."

He never mentioned Ady again.

Eventually, several weeks later, the 'Toni Benito Big Band Bash' album was released, and both Danny and Harry were enthusiastically jubilant when they saw their first copy. On the front cover, naturally, there was a huge picture of Toni dressed like a 1940s Hollywood star in white tie, top hat and tails in front of some kind of huge orchestra in a misty background, but on the reverse their names were displayed quite prominently in a write-up calling them 'a great new pair of talented writers in the footsteps of Rodgers and Hart'.

It was impossible to tell which of the two men was more exuberant. They fizzed, bubbled, laughed a lot about nothing – and kept looking at the words. Lex watched them, equally delighted, but all she could tell them was… "Fair dinkum mates."

Danny laughed yet again. "Fair dinkum indeed, lass," he said. "We're going to make a pile of money out of this…it's going to be a hit. I feel it."

Harry nodded. "I heard somewhere that you have to be ruthless to make a lot of money, though. Who wants to be ruthless?"

"Writing a song like this isn't ruthless. It'll make us rich…"

"And if it doesn't – well, we'll stay poor."

'Cold Streets', of course, proved to be the huge success of the album, being picked out and played by almost every top DJ on radio, featured on 'Top Of The Pops', and becoming such a cult in clubs around the country that the album soon rose to Number One in the charts. The record company was delighted, and quickly cashed in by releasing the song as a separate single.

Toni appeared everywhere – in the papers, on the radio and on TV chat shows – plugging 'Cold Streets' and frequently giving praise to Danny and Harry not only for writing it but for their 'illicit' part in getting it ready for recording. Interviewers loved it as a favourite PR story, fully encouraged by Sam Ross and the record company, and as a result, quite apart from the catchy beauty of the song, the extra plugging soon helped it rise to Number One in the singles charts as well.

'Cold Streets' seemed to be playing all the time, and it seemed that just like the big solo numbers of the 20s, 30s and 40s records, everyone was singing it. On his way to work in Harry's flat, particularly, Danny had trouble not stopping people on the street or train to tell them he was the co-writer.

It was about a month after the song hit the top spot that Harry got a surprise letter from Australia. It arrived as he, Danny and Lex were having coffee in his apartment, and he looked at the flimsy pale blue airmail envelope for a long time before opening it. He took the letter out, turned it over to glance at the signature, and without reading any more crumpled the single page and threw it into a wastepaper basket. The others looked at each other but didn't say a word, although when Harry went to the toilet later on Lex had a quick look and told Danny the letter had come from Harry's mother asking for money.

Harry never, ever, said a word about the strange unsolicited letter, but for days after its arrival he very obviously went out of his way to look after both Lex and Danny – almost 'mothering' them as though they were his children.

Shortly after, a minor, but moderately well known, theatrical producer called Aaron Blomfield sent a note through the record company inviting Danny and Harry to meet him over dinner. "I'll take you to a high-class nosherie I know," he told Harry when they rang to fix a date. "Great food. Not quite Michelin yet, but all in good time. The manager's a good friend of mine, he'll look after us – give us a price. Meet me there, it's called Giuseppe's on Bow Street, right by Long Acre. I'll reserve a good table where we can talk – but better make it early so we can get the best spot. Say 6.30'ish tomorrow."

Both Harry and Danny were excited at the prospect. "Hey," said Danny when Harry gave him the details, "this could be the big-time old buddy."

"Too true mate," replies Harry. "A business dinner with a show producer. Wow."

The anticipation lasted into the next morning, and both men were still so keyed up that after a couple of hours trying to work in the morning they agreed to take the rest of the day off. Harry spent the afternoon with Lex, allowing Danny to go to an afternoon film.

They met up afterwards in front of the National Gallery in Trafalgar Square, and as they had plenty of time walked slowly together across to Charing Cross station and along The Strand chatting enthusiastically about the forthcoming meeting.

Harry wore a smart dark grey suit with a light blue shirt and matching tie – chosen for him by Lex – but Danny arrived wearing a vivid red shirt, a grey sweater and jeans. Harry was glad to see it was not the sweater with holes in the arms that he still wore on most days.

As they turned into Wellington Street, both looked up at the notices of the big, big musical running at the Theatre Royal, and as they moved on both of them had dreamlike thoughts that the busy throng of Londoners ending their working day could one day be the audience for one of their shows at the theatre.

There was a typical London early evening scene around them. A pale summer sun sat low over the buildings and there was a slight breeze blowing dust all round them. "It's a keening wind," observed Danny as they walked up to the restaurant, opposite the Bow Street Magistrates' Court. He wondered what on earth a keening wind was – but he knew it sounded right.

Dead on the dot of 6.30 the two writers turned into Giuseppe's.

The restaurant was a small, typical Italian restaurant, neat and tidy and a complete throw-back to the London of the 1950s/60s. Its decoration was minimalist to say the least, with wooden tables covered in crisp white paper clothes and what seemed to be wooden garden chairs. Lots of Chianti bottles hung on the walls and there was a vague overall smell of garlic – and with seemingly dozens of waiters and waitresses scurrying backwards and forward knocking into each other, there was a tremendous impression of hustle and bustle.

Although Aaron's table was ready, the two men waited by the cash desk for the producer to arrive. Danny looked round, taking in the other diners, and was amused at the way almost all of them tried to see the plates being taken to other tables, trying to see what was on each plate and wondering if it was the same dish they had ordered themselves. He also noticed that where there were big groups – several company meals were taking place – all conversation stopped when the food was put down at the table and artistically arranged by the waiters, with everyone watching everyone else's plate. The food, although simple, looked to be good and plentiful.

As they waited, Danny listened to the waiters 'prego'ing' and 'graci'ing' almost by instinct, then almost automatically started jotting down some words on a card laying on the desk:

'My Italian girlfriend
Has another boyfriend.
Prego Hugo.
Pray go. '

Blomfield arrived about fifteen minutes late, and the proprietor greeted him warmly and showed them to their seats.

Despite the sunshine, Aaron wore a thick winter coat draped obviously, fashionable and ostentatiously over his shoulders. As they got to the table, a hovering waiter took the coat, and under it the writers saw Aaron was wearing a blue suit that was obviously old, although it was well pressed and along with his highly polished shoes gave the producer an expensive look. But when he took the jacket off to hang it over the back of his chair, Danny noticed it came from Marks and Spencer.

Aaron picked up one of the huge menus left on the table. "Sorry I was late," he told the two writers. "I had to drop in to a pharmacy for a prescription…"

"Oh, you buy farms as well," joked a nervous Danny, but Harry gave him a look – 'behave'.

Aaron was surprisingly short and slight – a dapper man, slim, short, balding with grey hair at the sides, and with a heavy brown moustache and world-weary blue eyes.

"You found the place OK then?" he asked with a refined American intonation.

"Well, we nearly went in next door by mistake – the Greek place. That looked good, too – moussaka…" More nervousness.

"Oh yes, I like a good red moussaka," said Blomfield. Harry and Danny tried not to giggle, but looking at each other they find it difficult.

"Anyway, I got a terrible tum there once. I think it was an over-cooked steak tartare."

This time, the two writers were not certain if he was joking or not.

They all looked at the menus. The food was also early London – saltimbocca, veal a la Marsala and a 110% sinful tiramisu – while the wine menu listed 'superalcolici' alongside the usual range of Italian-only wines. But when a waiter came over he suggested the specials on a board he held up for them to see. Danny particularly liked 'Stuffed hare thig with speck' and 'Cozze alla marinara – mussle to pickle'. His mouth twitched as he noted the spelling, along with another of the other dishes listed as 'Brest of duck'

"I'll have the French duck. Very Italian," he said, and amid the mini-confusion Harry tried to explain – breast, Brest. He was very embarrassed by Danny's initial approach to what he considered could by such an important meal. Blomfield, though, laughed. "French duck. Brest," he repeated.

They finally ordered, and Aaron sighed. "I often bring the big stars here, Kylie, Beyonce…"

"Oh, eat drink and make Mary?" asked Danny.

Aaron laughed – "Make Mary, yeh, he he. Make Mary."

As they chatted, trying each other out, Danny began talking of the film he had seen earlier in the afternoon. "There was this huge production number," he started, and Aaron was instantly interested. "The song was the main theme in the background all the way through, then suddenly it was being played in a small club – about ten people in it, but it had the biggest stage you ever saw. There must have been around 900 chorus girls at least, and a 100-piece orchestra playing as the star sang to his girl. When he finished, everyone stood up to dance – and the band played the same song again."

"They must have done it to save cash," said Harry.

"Yes, to save cash," repeated Aaron. The two men noticed that he usually repeated the last line of things he was told.

While they waited for the food, they chatted about old films and shows and Aaron quickly let on that he loved old 1940s Hollywood musicals. He also loved the old stars – Gable, Bogart, John Wayne – and films like 'Casablanca'. "'You Must Remember This' is one of the all-time great film songs," he said, and immediately Danny teased him and got him to sing it to them out loud.

By the end, Aaron was gazing deeply, theatrically, into Danny's eyes. They both loved it, but Harry was acutely aware that others in the restaurant were watching them.

Aaron finished singing and looked over his shoulder. "Where's that food? I gotta eat, gotta keep up my strength…" he said.

The food arrived. It was almost home cooked, piled on the plate and it tasted good. Aaron ordered some water – "tap water will do," he said – but the waiter brought a bottle of mineral water and put it on the table with the top unopened. When the producer absent-mindedly opened it and poured some into his glass, the waiter instantly produced a second bottle, but this time twisted the top open so someone would have to pay for it. Danny wondered why 'a top theatrical producer' didn't order wine.

Aaron didn't need, and probably couldn't afford, wine. He ate quickly, holding his knife like a pen and pushing his food onto an upturned fork before shovelling it into his mouth. Harry watched him with amusement, because whereas he ate in his usual methodical way, a little bit of this a little bit of that combined, he noted that Aaron, like Danny, ate his food like a little boy, separating each item.

Danny had always eaten all the things he liked least to begin with, saving the best bits until last – first the veg, then the meat, then finally the potatoes. Harry had often noticed it, and usually mentioned it.

"Can't you do anything conventionally, mate?" he would ask.

Danny always smiled back at him, his cheeky, disarming smile. "Why?" he would reply. "Can't you do anything that isn't conventional?"

This time, though, Harry kept quiet because Aaron ate the same way. He and Danny kept up quite a dialogue while eating, speaking about shows and films and songs, and Harry was pleased that Danny and the producer were getting on so well.

During the meal, Aaron spoke of the way he had grown up wanting to be like the old theatre producers of the 20s…George Abbott or Moss Hart. "Or maybe like Flo Ziegfield," he said.

Danny was quick to pick up on the theme. "For me, well if I couldn't have been Larry Hart or Ira Gershwin, I'd have loved to have been Busby Berkley or Arthur Freed."

"Who?"

"Arthur Freed – he wrote a few little ditties like 'Broadway Melody' and 'Singin' In The Rain', then went on to produce all the big Hollywood musicals. 'Meet Me In St. Louis', 'An American In Paris', 'Gigi – not forgetting to mention 'The Wizard Of Oz' of course."

"Was he the guy who wanted to cut out 'Over The Rainbow'?" asked Harry. Danny shrugged.

"Let's be like those guys in the show heh?" said Aaron with a sigh, and both the boys readily agreed – especially Harry, who picked up the inference that Aaron wanted them involved in a show.

Later it was Danny's turn. "You can't ruin a good song," he told the producer – his usual theme. "Take Astaire's treatment of 'Night and Day'…not good technically…"

"Hey, hang on a moment son. That's sacrilege."

"Yeah, no – what I mean is that his version of it has rhythm and lilt, all you'd expect from a dancer…but he doesn't really get over the meaning of the lyric."

"He's still great. I'll send him a note to see if I can get him for a show, he'd fill the house."

He spoke straight faced, and neither Danny nor Harry was sure whether or not he was joking. "Yeah, he's great," added Danny simply. "But his version is pure Astaire – not Cole Porter. As I said, it shows you can't ruin a good song."

Later, while talking of Astaire, Danny said something about 'the faded elegance of the past', and Aaron agreed with him – "Yes, elegance has gone," he said, shovelling in another mouthful.

Finally the meal ended, and the proprietor personally put small glasses of green liquid in front of everyone. "For the big man, eh?" he said. It was iced limoncello, a green Italian after-dinner liqueur, and the proprietor urged Danny and Harry to sip it slowly. Danny did so and smiled; Harry sipped and grimaced; Aaron gulped his down in one go.

Soon after, they all stood to leave, and Aaron said he had been impressed by the two writers, and asked them to 'make an appointment with my lovely secretary' for the following week. "I'm hardly ever in the office," he said. "Deals to make and all that."

Although Aaron was obviously a rogue, both Harry and Danny had taken an immediate liking to him – especially Danny, who could picture him in the same guise he saw himself, as a traditional Hollywood mogul, and in his mind's eye could see them all working together on a series of old-fashioned MGM-style musicals.

As they made their way home after the meal, Harry agreed. "Yeah, he's OK. But what he was saying – it's a load of old Optrex," he told Danny.

"Optrex?"

"Yeah – a load of old eyewash."

Harry laughed. "He's hardly the greatest brain in the business is he, mate?"

"No – the sort of nouveau-riche punter who'd go to a Shakespeare play, and at the end stand up applauding and calling for the author."

"Y'know, you say that about all agents and music publishers, mate," said Harry.

"Yeah, but that man proves once again that if you can fake sincerity you've cracked it."

Next day, Harry rang Aaron's office with Danny standing impatiently by his side. They made an appointment for the following Monday, and on the day turned up at the office – a diminutive back room above some shops in Shaftesbury Avenue. There were two desks, one occupied by Aaron's 'lovely secretary' – a stern-faced woman about 70 years old.

Within minutes of their arrival, Aaron asked them if they could write the book and music for a big show he was planning. He said he wanted ideas – and he wanted 'Cold Streets' included. He did not say that was so he could cash in on its proven success.

"You've got to have something like that today," he told them. "Putting on a show here in London or in New York has now reached a ridiculous cost. You can have your 'King and I's', 'Les Mis's' and 'Phantom' – but mark my words, the day of the big extravagant musical is over. It's a pity, but that's the way things are going."

Harry and Danny were delighted. "If you could come up with something that even looks like one of those old-style shows, well that would be marvellous. Marvellous," went on Aaron.

"But keep it cut-price. What I want you to come up with is a – well, just an old-fashioned feel-good musical that's not expensive to put on. Something with some good songs people can hum as they leave the theatre."

As he spoke, Danny – his thoughts wandering along the same lines – jotted down some notes on a paper napkin he had left in his pocket after the initial meal with Aaron.

Where has class gone?
Where is elegance and her sister
Sophisticat-i-on?
Please come back to me…
I long to find you once more.'

"Heh, the creative spirit. Always there, hey," said Aaron, looking at the words. "Elegance. Sophistication. That's right – but keep it cheap."

The boys quickly agreed to see what they could come up with. Danny was all for getting right down to work, but Harry stayed cool enough to ask about money – and Aaron promised a small, a very small, retainer.

Danny and Harry left the office blissfully ecstatic, and not even Aaron's secretary could check the euphoria. "OK guys, you think you're on your way. But remember, now you're on the ladder don't forget to look at the view," she cynically warned them. "You may get to the top, but if you do they won't give you time to look – and you certainly won't have time on the way down."

Act 10: Writing the Musical

Danny and Harry were, naturally, excitedly happy at the way things seemed to be starting to turn in their favour, but they soon began to get suspicions about Aaron.

A few days after meeting him, Harry rang his office to check how the producer wanted their idea presented, to be told by his sour-faced secretary – who, they later discovered, was his wife – that the original idea they had sent in the week before was 'being considered'.

"But we haven't put in an idea," said Harry. "We weren't even involved a week ago."

There was a cough over the phone. "Oh, did you say that was Mr van Mitchell?" asked the secretary.

"No. Harry McIntyre."

"Oh sorry, I'm so sorry. I seem to have got you mixed up with another of the teams Mr Blomfield has working on the project."

"Other teams?"

There was a muffled noise over the phone, then the line went dead. When Harry rang back there was no answer.

That evening Harry told Danny about his doubts, and Danny determined to try and find out what was going on. He made several phone calls without any luck, then he and Harry went along to the office while Aaron was out and finally find out that there were seven other teams working on ideas for the producer.

They left, feeling like fools. "If that's the way show business is, I'm not sure I want to be part of it," said Harry, not realising it made sense for a producer to make soundings in several places at once.

The two men, though, had made an appointment to see Aaron, and when they met him he told them quite openly that he had been working on the idea of a big show for some 18 months – trying to raise funds by selling the idea that he had a couple of big 'household name' writers lined up. "You've heard of them –

Chaplin and Hopcroft," he said, throwing out the names of possibly the biggest-name song writers in London.

"They've told me they'll only come in when the cash becomes available, no more. I'm just trying to get an idea, then I'll use their names to sell it to the banks and the backers. But if the money men like it – well, I'm afraid Chaplin and Hopcroft will be out on their necks 'cause they haven't helped me."

Aaron smiled at Danny and Harry. "Yes, I know you're just one of several groups I've called in," he added. "But I particularly like you way you two work. You're favourites for the whole job – come up with an idea, and Chaplin and Hopcroft and the others won't know what's hit them."

What he didn't say was that he had so far had no success in raising the funds – and as most backers obviously wanted to know details of the show he was planning, he was just looking for new writers to provide them. Nor did he mention that all the writers he had approached were, like Danny and Harry themselves, more or less unknowns – and cheap. He had promised them all months of work – although he had never quite getting round to signing any contracts – but no one had as yet come up with any kind of an idea.

A couple of weeks later, Danny and Harry heard that the two big name writers had discovered what was going on, and with dodgy promises about backers, theatres and the like and no money to pay out, they had decided to pull out. But although hearing of the other teams involved was disappointing, it only made Danny and Harry more determined to be THE writers that Aaron would finally choose.

They put their disappointments behind them, with Harry and Lex, especially, insisting that it was still a big opportunity, and the two writers got work immediately.

Things did not go well at first – they just could not find any kind of hook for the show. They continually discussed ideas, but no matter what they came up with nothing seemed suitable – they couldn't find any real peg to hang the show on. "It should be dead easy – all you need is glamour and glitz for a musical," insisted Danny. "You don't need a fancy build up, a story-line that's out of Proust or Chekov. All you need is boy meets girl, boy loses girl, boy finds girl again, and a happy ending. You want escapism. That's all. Escapism, passion – and some good songs."

No matter how many times they discussed it, neither of the two men could think of a subject that might fit. And as time went on, Danny would invariably break up their discussions with memories of 'the daft stories' that were used by the famous song writing teams to stage 'the good old 20s and 30s' musicals.

"It was the music that mattered, the singing and dancing," he insisted. "I mean, take shows like 'Lady Be Good', 'Ziegfeld Follies', 'Anything Goes', 'On Your Toes', 'Girl Crazy', 'Babes In Arms' – anything by Cole Porter, Rodgers and Hart, Jerome Kern or Irving Berlin. Their stories were just something to hang the songs on."

Harry agreed – to a point. "It's different today, though," he maintained. "These days you need a good story line."

"Why?" asked Danny. "What's so different today? It's just that fashion dictates……"

"Yeah, mate, a fashion set by your mates Rodgers and Hammerstein," threw in Harry.

"Forget all that," went on Danny. "All you still really need are good tunes – like the old shows. I reckon the story can still be rubbish – it's the music that counts. Give 'em something they can hum on the way out."

"Sorry, an' all that, but you just wouldn't get away with it these days, y'know," replied Harry. "You need a strong story line to hold the audience attention – something like 'The King & I', 'South Pacific', 'Chicago' –"

"No," interrupted Danny yet again. "It's just good music you need. I mean, if you want to quote modern shows, just think of something like 'Mamma Mia'," he said. "That didn't have too much of a book – but everyone was up and singing and clapping. Proves you don't need any story really. People who go to see a musical don't want Shakespeare, they just want fun. Good music, good dancing…fun."

It became an almost daily argument, amusing for Lex when she listened in but hardly constructive. Eventually, Harry and Danny agreed to differ – although they did finally agree to try for a mid-point…a reasonable story linked with the good songs.

"We don't want messages – people are too tied up with their own problems for that," insisted Danny, and for once Harry agreed with him. "So OK, let's just give 'em a release from everyday life, some relaxation if you like," he replied. "But we've still got to have some kind of a story."

As they tried to work things out, Danny said that rather than trying to fix 'their' show in the more usual musical style, he felt they should try an old-fashioned musical comedy, linking revue numbers in a loosely constructed plot. "It's unfashionable – but we could set a trend," he insisted.

Goodness knows how long it might have gone on for, until one night Danny took a TV dancer he had once worked with – one of a succession he had dated both at the time and ever since – to a club for a meal. They were shown to a seat, and after ordering a bottle of red wine – Danny didn't ask the girl what she wanted – he looked round.

On the other side of the dimly lit room, he spotted an elderly couple he thought he recognised. He left the girl, walked across, and breezily and brashly began chatting. "Didn't you used to… I mean, aren't you Greta Faulkes and Joe Gibbon?" he asked, giving the names of a one-time famous musical show singer and a well-known musician.

Irritably, the man said a brusque, bad tempered 'no' – but the woman, who was old, near blind and arthritic, just laughed. "Why hide it?" she asked. The voice retained the deep, husky timbre it had when she was top of the pile on stage in London and New York.

Danny sat down without invitation and started chatting, asking Greta about her time as a star. She was amused by the interruption – although Joe was still rudely irritable about it – and began recalling how she started. She told Danny that as a young child she had been forced to stand on a table and sing for the other guests when her parents held a party for their adult friends on her birthday, and said she had felt humiliated as she protested before being forced to perform. "I was shy when it all started, but eventually I began to love the attention…and then the applause," she told him.

Danny was intrigued, and when she replied with questions of her own began to tell her about the songs he and Harry had written. They conversed happily for a while, but then the crotchety Joe started to get annoyed. Greta explained that Joe had been her pianist all the way through her top days – she smiled as she explained that he had been a rising writer-lyricist who had heard her and given up his own career to write exclusively for her. "He began playing piano for me, but I guess he never reconciled himself to seeing me have all those affairs with all those big-name stars," she said.

"You never did know I was just in love…hell, it was a long time ago," said Joe.

"Not that long – we all remember her," replied Danny.

Greta smiled, a long-remembered enigmatic smile. "Maybe," she said. "I wonder. Remember that line in, oh what was it? 'Only the parts got smaller'! Well, maybe I could still be a star – the parts may be small, but I'm not…"

Greta started to sing one of her famous songs. Her voice was still youthful and silky, still melodious and powerful. It was soft at first, but slowly it began to get louder and a couple of waiters started to move towards the table to shut her off – but the maître d' put up a hand to hold them back.

As the voice filled the restaurant, all the other diners stop to listen, and when she had finished, there was a smattering of applause. Greta looked round and nodded appreciation. "Trouble is, I can't reach the higher notes anymore." she said, mopping her mouth with a napkin.

Danny was enthralled, but then Joe pointed out that his date was getting ready to leave. Danny said his goodbyes, and darted back across the room to apologise. "Just watch that lady – once a star, always a star," he told the girl.

Harry and Danny continued to discuss ideas after that, but though they worked hard at it they still couldn't find a 'real' peg, the hook, to hang the show on.

Harry still talked frequently about the theories of writing show music. "Even when we get a basic idea, there's still a long way to go," he insisted from the start. "We've got to write and work the music and words around so they fit into the plot – so they don't stand in the way of the story – they have to become part of it. Dances, too."

Danny would try to look interested. He just wanted to get on with the writing. "I remember reading something Richard Stilgoe said once," added Harry. "He said that show songs have to take the story from A to Z rather than just A to B – there has to be a reason for them to be sung."

Despite all the work and thought, the idea just wouldn't come. But the meeting with Greta stuck in Danny's mind, and several days later when he and Harry were sitting together watching a video of an old Busby Berkeley movie in an attempt to find inspiration for their show, a vague idea that had crossed his mind after meeting the singer came back to him. He told Harry about it.

"Are you suggesting putting an aging star and her long-time lover together?" asked Harry. "It's been done before, y'know."

"No, not the old idea, even I'd think that too hackneyed," replied Danny. "But…" – he began thinking aloud – "…well, it doesn't have to be about Greta and Joe – just think of all the old chorus dancers and all the other acts who must have backed them. Any of them that are still alive must be well into their 90s by now – just like Greta."

"Yeah, OK – so? What's the hook?"

"Well, I reckon we could set it in an old people's home – a home for retired show biz people, like a resting place for old time variety people. Then suddenly their young characters come out of it and put on their act as they used to be."

Harry had worried from the beginning about finding reasons to fit in Danny's dream of including what were in essence a series of variety acts. "We've got to have a motive to bring them in," Harry had insisted on the first day.

"Why?" Danny replied, unconcerned.

"Because there has to be. Simple as that mate," insisted Harry. "A dance or a song has to be like dialogue – it has to take the show forward. There has to be a reason for it."

Danny now knew the solution. "It's dead easy really," he said. "The members of the home are talking about their pasts, and that leads them into memories and then we've got the reason for the re-creation of the song. It'd all be based round the old 'uns remembering their days as youngsters when they could dance and sing…when they were alive, on stage. Their talk could lead to a mix of hard hoofing or romantic ballroom dances, singing, whatever we want. Where's the problem?"

"We'll have the modern acts moving in and out of the story of the old folk's home – with the old timers taking the story forward from there. We could make it almost like a concert, where you don't have to put up with the boring bits in between but just get the best songs and the best entertainment. It's a great idea."

The thought began to spark off ideas in both their minds, with Danny leading the way and suggesting that they could start each act in the home and then go into 'flash-backs' of each resident's previous stage life.

Harry nodded. "Yeah," he said, starting to capture a flicker of enthusiasm from Danny. "Sounds good. You could fade in and out of the home almost like a film, putting the acts on front stage," he mused.

"Maybe we could even resurrect Greta Faulkes and Joe Gibbon – well, maybe their look-alikes, I don't reckon she could stand up on a stage without falling flat on her face," said Danny, passion running on overtime. "But someone like that – old face, young voice…we could have her sitting in the home and then get some dolly in front dancing while she sang over."

Harry listened carefully without saying anything as the words came tumbling enthusiastically out of Danny. "We'd just base it round all the old 'un's memories," went on Danny. "They'd lead us into the songs, then we could have all the young singers and dancers representing them as they were in their youth, in their hey-day!"

Harry nodded his head in agreement, now becoming as keen on the idea as his partner.

"We could make it an old-fashioned show just like they used to have," went on Danny, hardly pausing for breath. "Cabaret girls, high kicking chorus lines, comedy, and lots of dancing. Lots and lots of dancing. Tap, romance, the lot. Boys and girls together. Songs with rhythm and words that tell a love story. I'm sure it could be a whiz –"

"There'd be lots of movement…" interjected Harry.

"Of course, lots of movement, lots of colourful costumes, long-legged girls, guys in top hats and tails. We could make it like an old Hollywood movie – Fred and Cyd Charisse, Gene Kelly swinging on a lamppost in the rain, that kind of thing. Music and lots of rhythm to tap you feet to, that's what people need these days – let's give it back to 'em. No messages, just lots of fun and…well, above all let's have lots of sheer entertainment and glitz."

His eyes were almost ablaze with fervour. "Start with a big opening. Two rows of dancers high kicking – one male, one female – and after their big opening production number we'd settle into the home and then pick out a few of the oldies for their individual stories."

The words were literally pouring out of Danny's mouth. Harry was listening carefully, taking it all in and starting to get as excited as Danny himself.

"Yeah, mate, fine. But how are you going to get all that movement into an old people's home? I mean, if you want a high-kick chorus opening…how could you connect it back to the old 'uns?" he asked. "How could you link it all up – switching from the old people's home to all the acts in between? How d'you plan to do that mate?"

Danny thought for a moment. "Easy," he said. "At the end of the opening, use lighting to fade into the home and have a couple of the old biddies talking of their days as chorus girls. Then some of the others throw in their recollections…and we kind of fade back to front stage and away we go."

Harry clapped his hands. "Y'know, mate – I think you're on to something here," he said eagerly. "I don't think you've quite got the link, but we've got something to work on. We'd better get down to it and try and map out an idea we can give to Aaron. I think we've got something here that he could definitely turn into a show."

The pair set to work immediately, trying to work out details of how they could make the basic idea work as an old-fashioned musical with lots of elegance, dancing and singing woven into it. Between them they started dreaming up different stories for the 'old' characters to re-live, and they quickly realised that they had to try for the kind of dialogue of a 1930s musical – although Harry insisted that they had to be careful not to make it sound too dated.

"Don't you dare put in that big line from 42nd Street," joked Harry. "Busby Berkeley did that – you couldn't hope to beat it."

"Maybe, but it's the kind of thing we've got to get into it. Remember, although the old timers will be living in the present, all the acts would have to be from their youth, back in the 20' or 30s," replied Danny.

The two men quickly settled into a pattern, working flat out to complete the basic treatment of their idea, throwing out more and more ideas – in Danny's case, some much too far-fetched to succeed – and getting things down on paper, although not yet in actual script form. They cut out everything else – even Lex was ignored, and was reduced to providing coffee and snacks as they worked in a hurry to beat the other teams trying for Aaron's contract. Getting things right became a way of life – it was life for both of them.

Soon, they had a rough draft and began to fill in the detail. Both were tired by the long, hard hours they were putting in together, but both worked with a zeal, passion and dedication that rode above the tiredness.

The big issue that still bothered them both was how to mix from the old people's home that was to provide the background and continuing story lines to the modern acts showing the old-timers when they were young. Neither could sleep – their heads were too full of ideas and characters and situations…and the missing link.

Then one night, Danny suddenly hit on the solution to their main problem, and although it was barely dawn called his pal.

"Got it," he said when Harry answered the phone after just three rings. "Use a revolve – split down the centre, with the home on one side and a theatre stage on the other. Use the lights dimming and brightening up as it turns…just like you once said, like a film fading from one scene to another."

"Yeah, mate, I think that's it," replied Harry, his mind picturing it all. "We could make it more like an old film musical, too, if we could somehow get in a background theme linking it all." He yawned. "Look mate, I'm knackered. We'll work out the final details in the morning – then we're almost there. Now for God's sake, go back to sleep."

With the conundrum solved, the two were able to concentrate on the detail – it became largely a matter of sorting out the kind of acts they would need in the 'flash-forward' sequences. They continued to work hard trying to fix in their minds what would be needed.

Getting to the bottom of the switch from old to new and back again settled Harry down quite a lot, and as he and Danny continued trying to iron out the details he composed a rough theme for their 'background music' and would often play it on his baby grand to help them concentrate on the theme of the show.

With the basic pattern fixed, completing the treatment became simpler and the outline was quickly turned into a complete, finished treatment of the whole idea. When the two men were satisfied with it, Harry rang up to fix an appointment to see Aaron and the sour-voiced secretary told him she could fit the two writers in the next morning – but said Aaron would be in a hurry as he had 'an important business meeting with some interested financiers'.

Next morning, dead on time, Harry and Danny took their idea to Aaron. "Nice to see you see you again," said the producer. "But you'll have to be quick – I've got a funeral to go to."

"I thought you had a meeting," replied Harry, looking across at the secretary. "Was he a friend?"

"It is a business meeting. I want to make sure he gets on his way," laughed Aaron. "And yeah, he was a real friend – he once rooked me for £4K, I'm just 'dying' to see his funeral!!!"

"Hey, that's my kind-a line," said Danny joining in the laughter.

"Yeah, well," replied the producer. "At least it's not my funeral. Mind you – at my age..."

"Don't worry about old age," said Danny. "It's better than the alternative. At least, I think it is."

"Age is all in the mind," said the secretary across the office. "As long as you're fit..."

"Me? You think I look fit?" asked Aaron.

"Well you look fit."

"Yeah, fit shmit," said Aaron. "But I suppose I do have the fit figure of an athlete…a Russian woman discus thrower! He, he." He laughed at his own joke. "I'm so fit I should get a medal. A medal."

His secretary looked across the room at him. "A meddle would be better," she said straight-faced, meaning it.

They all laughed and the mood was relaxed as they went into talk of the show.

Harry took the lead, describing his and Danny's idea to Aaron with Danny eagerly butting in now and then to put across some special point. Harry was eager to give Danny praise for his original idea.

From the start, Aaron seemed keen on the concept, nodding his head and muttering 'yes, yes' every now and then. When Harry and Danny had finished, he put his hands on the desk. "Well boys, I think you've got something there," he told them. "I've been given a couple of other ideas, but I think this is the one – it seems to have…I don't know, some class. And I know about class.

"Leave the treatment with me for a couple of days – I want to get an idea of how much it would cost. But if that's OK, I think you've got yourselves a show."

Harry was still not done, though. He went on to tell Aaron that he and Danny could write the whole book – and Danny, who had not even thought there was any doubt on that line, agreed. Aaron nodded yet again. "OK, if the finance works, the job's yours."

Harry looked across at Danny. Danny looked back at Harry. They both had infantile grins of happiness on their faces.

The writers were in a bit of an agitated state for the next four days until Aaron contacted them to say he wanted them to start work on the book of the show immediately. They went to his office again to sign a formal contract, and once again departed in a state of high euphoria.

When they left, they went for a coffee nearby and as they sat contemplatively watching the world go by both had the same thought. Up to now they had been incredibly lucky. They had 'happened to' meet the church choir; they had 'happened to' meet the musicians looking for songs in Satch's; they had 'happened to' meet the butter agency advertising rep; they had 'happened to' see the girl with the silent violin and the upright lady; they had 'happened to' get good advice about a demo disc; they had 'happened to' meet Toni Benito just when he was looking for a song for his album.

If you like, Danny had just 'happened to' lose Ady at the right time and was able to come up with 'Cold Streets'.

It had all 'just happened'. Now they were to work on something special for Aaron – a job they had worked to win against opposition and probably against all odds.

The two were determined their show was going to be a success. "We'd better get a title," said Harry, coming out of his reverie. He looked across at Danny, and while the lyricist was sipping his coffee came up with a name – 'The Age Of Romance'. "I was just going to say the same," said Danny as he put his cup back down on the table ignoring the saucer.

They began work on the book almost immediately they got back to Harry's flat. Because they had a specific objective in mind, the show, Danny and Harry now spent less time aimlessly playing notes, writing jingles, preparing half-formed songs. They concentrated fully on sorting out some actual songs from their collection that could be used in the show, and although not everything they wrote fitted, of course, their one aim was the show. It was the only thing.

Over the next couple of weeks, Danny, rather naturally, did most of the writing and coped surprisingly well with it – hardly realising it was almost, almost, what Ady had wanted him to do. Harry gave him encouragement, ideas, and lots of help – but they were largely Danny's words that went down on paper.

By taking the lead, Danny became even more forceful than before, and Harry was content to let him work that way – just putting his own point of view quietly, and guiding rather than instructing Danny.

Harry was far more relaxed now because he felt satisfied that things were well on course and that the final idea was workable, but Danny could still not settle – although the book was not yet complete and agreed, he wanted to get on organising singers and songs; dancers and dance routines; settings, staging and spectacle.

He began visiting clubs, cafés, pubs – any place where he could see live acts – in the hope of picking up inspiration. And that's how he came to visit a small club in Soho late one night shortly after he and Harry had worked out their so-called master treatment. The club was past its sell-by date, but the management was trying hard to keep things alive there by putting on some good quality acts. Judging by the crowd when Danny arrived soon after midnight, it was a policy that was working.

He was sitting on a high stool at the bar, a glass of neat whisky on the counter in front of him, when the lights suddenly went down and he heard soft music from somewhere backstage – apparently a string orchestra, although Danny suspected a tape recording. He looked across as a single bright spotlight picked out the face of a man. His body was in darkness – there was just the face in a veritable sea of darkness.

A man's voice began singing – also from behind the scenes.it crooned in a pleasant voice, and then slowly a second spot flicked on to pick out a beautiful girl across the room on the other side of the stage.

The girl gradually began to move across to the man…

A girl's voice picked up the refrain.

The two figures closed together. The two spotlights pulled out, widening to show both dancers were dressed in dark costumes – he in an evening dress and she in a spangled, glittering full-length dress. The still-unseen violins start to swell, and the two fell into each other's arms and began to dance in an old-fashioned way.

They swayed and swirled, flounced and flowed. It was smooth and romantic. Very romantic and loving, and it seemed that all too soon the dance was over.

Finally, there were just the voices off-stage, singing together as the two spotlights closed down on the dancers' faces again and then faded away one by one.

The house lights came up on an empty stage and the applause was terrific, and the crowds at the tables stood as it erupted and broke over the room. Danny watched, entranced, as the two dancers re-appeared, bowing and each graciously offering the limelight to the other.

Dance music grew, the applause died down, and the mood calmed. Not too long after, the male dancer came up to the bar. He had changed into street clothes, and as he ordered a drink Danny moved across to him. "I'll get it," he said.

"Thank you. Bourbon." The voice had an accent. Spanish, Mexican?

Danny nodded to the barman and held out his own glass for a refill. "The number was great," he told the dancer. "One of my favourite songs, and you did it beautifully."

The dancer bowed his head slightly in acknowledgement. "I'm Danny."

"Carlos. Carlos Loueen," replied the dancer.

"Do you always get that kind of reaction to the number?"

"Usually," says Carlos casually, looking round the room.

An idea was beginning to build up in Danny's mind, and as they drank he questioned Carlos about the old-fashioned dancing that had earned such huge acclaim. "It's like Astaire and Ginger Rogers," said Carlos. "People still seem to like that kind of old music and presentation – but it has to be lyrical and romantic. Loving."

"Hey, that's right," replied Danny. "You've got to have romance. Love."

"Yeah, well any old crap will do really," went on Carlos cynically. "Make it schmaltzy enough and you've got the audience hooked. I mean......take any couple who come here for their only night out of the year. They leave their drab two-bedroomed semi to find something special. Give 'em something that seems like the romance that's missing from their drab little lives and they love it. It's crap, but it makes them happy – and that makes me a living."

Danny had been listening intently, realising that it was almost what he had been preaching to anyone who would listen – especially unappreciative song publishers. Romance, love, a bit of glitz and glamour.

He carried on, drinking rather heavily, talking at Carlos and telling him how he felt music should be presented as sentimental, starry-eyed, passionate. Carlos did not say anything, and then after about half an hour Danny asked him if he wanted one more for the road. "Oh, no. Sorry," replied Carlos. "I think my partner's here. Got to go." He stood, and Danny watched him walk to the main door of the bar, the street door from the club. He saw him go up to another man, put his arm round his shoulder, and kiss him on the cheek before they left arm in arm.

Romance, love, sentiment, thought Danny, turning back to the bar. He reached in his pocket for a pen, then began scribbling on a beer mat on the counter.

'He'ing and a-he'ing,
Is better than a-me'ing and a-me'ing,
But not half as a-feeling,
And a-he'ing and a-she'ing.'

He quickly finished his drink, reached in his pocket, and tossed a handful of notes on the counter before turning and also going to the door, leaving the beer mat and his words on the counter.

Although by then it was four in the morning, he dashed round to Camden Hill Road and twenty minutes after leaving the bar he was at Harry's apartment, ringing the doorbell incessantly until Harry finally answered it. "D'you know what time it is?" asked Harry, yawning and trying to focus on his watch.

Danny pushed past his partner and into Harry's living room. "Hell, it's nearly half past four," said Harry sourly.

Danny ignored him and went straight to a drinks table on the far side and helped himself. "Christ man, you're always doing this to me in the middle of the night," spluttered Harry.

Danny turned round, an enormous whisky in an elegant tumbler in his hand. "I've got a great idea for the show," he replied simply, walking across to the baby grand on the other side of the room. He sat down and opened the lid, putting the whisky on top of the piano. Then he stood again and began to tell Harry the story of the two dancers and the reaction to their antiquated dancing.

"We need a couple of speciality acts," he said. "I reckon we could get Carlos and his girl – they're the couple of dancers I saw tonight. We'll need speciality numbers, and they could do their duet and then a couple of solos. They're good." He took a sip of his whisky and replaced the glass on top of the piano.

"As I was walking across here I got this song in my head where we could use 'em," he started, but Harry just looked at him without a word.

There was a long pause, then Harry walked slowly to the kitchen, put water in an electric kettle and switched it on. As he prepared two mugs of instant coffee, Danny followed him into the kitchen, watching – silent now – as Harry poured boiling water into the mugs, added milk and sugar, then stirred them.

Without a word, Harry picked up one of the mugs and handed it over to Danny, then he took his own coffee and led the way back to the living room. Danny followed, and puts his undrunk coffee on a side table.

"It was dark out there, and I saw all sorts of shadows," he finally explained. "Shadows – silhouettes…"

He picked up his coffee mug and took it back across to the piano, leaving the saucer where it was and putting the cup on the piano lid beside his whisky glass. It left a small ring mark on the piano. Danny sat at the piano, and looked across at his partner, who was sipping his own coffee. "I know there was a song 'Two Silhouettes', but I can hear this one with a different mood…" said Danny limply. He started humming assorted notes.

It sounded rough and the melody was raw and moody, but there was a certain air of romanticism that flowed. Harry listened for a moment more, nodding as usual, then he walked over to the piano and indicated that Danny should move across to make room on the seat for him.

Instead, Danny stood and went to get another whisky, using a fresh glass. Harry watched him, knowing that at the same time he was thinking lyrics, a storyline for the new song. When Danny got back to the piano, it was in his mind.

"Shadows and silhouettes. That's good," said Harry.

Danny nodded. "It could be the big love song – the two leads singing on either side of the stage as Carlos and the girl dance it," he mused softly. "The boy walks onto what he thinks is an empty stage for an audition, and sees the girl coming from the other side. Then we fade the lights down, and Carlos and the girl take centre stage to dance out their romance…".

"A dream within a flashback – sounds great," said Harry. "But man, how the hell are we going to fit it into the theme of old stars?"

"I dunno," replied Danny happily, "but we'll manage it somehow. It'll be a great scene."

There were, inevitably, many other challenges, and trying to provide a suitable background for the 'show' part was a big one. Although neither had any theatre experience, both realised instinctively that there would not really be enough space on the revolve to build big glamour Hollywood-style sets for the dancing or singing acts. But Danny – as so often – finally found the answer. "In the old days, the real old days, mediaeval times, they didn't build sets – they just used the audiences' imagination," he said one day. "They told 'em something, and they imagined it was there. Well, why don't we do that – the old folk tell them what the scene is meant to be, then when we revolve we'll only need a minimum setting hinting at it, possibly only a painted backdrop, and the audience will imagine the rest."

Aaron, surprisingly, kept out of the way, busying himself, he said, arranging the financial side and leaving Danny and Harry to get on with the book. But while Danny concentrated on setting the story out in the right way, Harry kept in close, constant touch with the producer – either phoning him with news or taking individual scenes or song ideas to his office for a brief discussion.

One day, when Harry went to see Aaron for a chat – and possibly a bit of an advance, as no money had as yet been offered – Danny put his mind to getting things down in script form.

ACT 1

Scene 1

*Open on two rows of dancers. Chorus girls in
front, spangly, tights etc; row of top hat/white tie
& tailed boys behind with canes. Curtain rises on
girls high kicking, boys swaying in rhythm. After
opening dance, girls slide back and the boys go
into a slow tap routine.*
*At end of the high-kicking routine, the revolve starts and
as the dancers snake off stage left, on the reverse the
home is revealed – the old folk moving into the room
sluggishly on zimmer frames, sticks etc., 'following' the
dancers and singing their special intro song in a similar
(but slower) way. They sit and start to ad-lib.*

*The nurse enters left. She listens for a moment, then
starts singing:*

SONG: 'Gossip, gossip, gossip'

The song ends.

OLD WOMAN
She's a lovely-looking girl, eh Fred?

OLD MAN
Yes, lovely. Reminds me of that girl in The Follies, of course. She was your girl, wasn't she, Billy?

*Old Man and Old Woman look across at Billy,
sitting in a corner wearing a woolly cardigan
and scarf, his head slumped on his chest.*

OLD WOMAN

You were a good-looking lad, Billy...
Billy wheezes – loudly.

OLD MAN

In those days.

OLD WOMAN

They were a lovely couple.

OLD MAN

I remember...her.

NURSE

What was their big song called?

A couple of the residents start tapping out a rhythm
with their teaspoons against the side of their cups.

ANOTHER OLD WOMAN

Wasn't it something about Clacton-on-Sea......?

As she speaks, the lights start to dim in the home,
and the stage begins to revolve. The orchestra
picks up the teaspoon rhythm and goes into the
song: 'My Home Town'.
Front house lights begin to fade up to show young
Billy and partner...

It didn't take too much longer to draft out the actual detail of the book, and when it was done Danny started putting it into script form while Harry set to work organising the extra songs they both felt were needed – a big establishing number, segues, bits of underscoring to go under dialogue as they prepared for the links between the old and the new sequences.

They already had the ballads, romantic songs, and some up-tunes to raise the mood where they felt the action might drag a bit – they were largely from their existing collection. But they wanted some special material tailored to the character's specialist needs, and although both knew things were likely to

189

change, Harry started to concentrate on writing these new songs especially for the show.

As the book itself had reached a stage where it simply needed a bit of tweaking and nudging to get it in final shape, Danny, who had been concentrating on writing the script, joined in. Fired with enthusiasm for the show, he was by now also writing some extra-specially good lyrics, with subtle internal rhymes and clever lines that slotted into place within the show. "You have to act the words as well as sing them – dance your voice to the rhythm and meaning of the song," he told Harry, unnecessarily.

Between them, the two men produced two songs in particular that they felt were as good as anything they had ever written – '*Parents hold your hands for a short while – but your hearts forever*' and '*God collects your tears and dries them to turn into sunshine*'.

Then Danny came up with one song with a 12-note range, a whole octave and a half, and was quite upset when Harry reckoned they wouldn't be able to find a modern singer able to carry it. Harry suggested a 10-note range, and one evening asked Toni Benito – still a friend – what he thought. Toni said he preferred it better with 12-bars.

The song worked – but perhaps more important, Toni became interested in the show and wanted to know more about it. "If there's a part for me, let me know," he told his two friends.

Danny and Harry thought that was a good idea, and instantly set to work to try to find a role for the singer. But how to fit him in? It was Danny, inevitably, who thought he could play the twin roles of the old folks' home warden – himself an old music hall star – in both old and new stages of the show. It would be a starring character role involving a bit of acting and some singing, and it would make the warden the central linking personality.

"He'll give us a star name, at least," said Harry in his matter-of-fact way.

"And while we're about it, why not give him some sort of love interest?" suggested Danny.

He was joking, but Harry took it seriously. "What, as the warden – or in the flash back?" he asked.

"Both," said Danny with his big schoolboy grin.

"Well how the hell are you going to fit that in?"

"Oh I dunno – perhaps one of the old dears could have a secret pash on him. Or one of the nurses – a carer…"

"Y'know, that's not a bad idea, mate," mused Harry. "Toni and a nurse. Nurses always look good in uniform…we could give them a big, big duet to sing. It could be a show stopper…" His mind was already thinking of a possible song.

It was agreed, and 'The Age Of Romance' was re-scripted to include the new angle.

Harry knew Aaron wanted 'Cold Streets' for the show, but he still felt they needed to produce another song for Toni's character and suggested a melody that had been in his mind for some time. Danny liked the tune, and soon drafted out some lyrics for Harry's beautiful little song.

'I'm so down I want the sun to set.
I've lost the best girl I ever met.
I want the rain to fall,
The snow to cool,
On passion only she could get.
It's been a bitter blow.
I want the sun down low.
I'll never love again,
Can't stand the pain,
That follows that warm, warm glow.
But time now flies.
And with a big surprise
I see a girl with a grin
Welcoming me in.
And I want the sun to rise'

Although they agreed on the song, they saw it differently – Harry pictured the singer's voice carrying the main melody, with the whole orchestra, particularly the strings, providing a separate counterpoint below it in big echoing crescendos. Danny, on the other hand, pictured the music – and lyrics – as soft rippling waves romantically breaking over a sunset beach.

Eventually they arranged both ways, with Danny's words like a deep gorge flowing smoothly through the savage, swirling mountain ranges of Harry's music. That way, it would nonetheless rely on Toni to get the song across.

They were both pleased with the final result. "But don't forget old man Aaron still wants 'Cold Streets' to feature," said Danny suddenly.

"I know. But I think we'll try and forget that mate. This new song will give him a new Number One to enjoy…"

Act 11: Preparing the Show

When Danny and Harry felt they had done everything possible to get the book and main songs of 'The Age Of Romance' completed, they took them along to Aaron. He was delighted when they outlined the romantic 'old-fashioned' song-and-dance idea set against the old theatricals' home, then he quickly skim read through Danny's script, chuckling at the funny lines, nodding his head wisely, and repeating several of the jokes out loud.

It didn't take him long, then Harry hummed some of the songs – with Danny occasionally croaking his lyrics to them – and although it sounded quite peculiar presenting a musical show through two untrained out-of-tune voices, Aaron seemed to like the music ideas as much if not more than the story line.

When they had finished, Aaron told them he would have a final read through the script that night.

Neither Danny nor Harry felt as exhilarated as they felt they should be, but they listened attentively as the producer optimistically went on to tell them that while they were writing the book he had been busy finding sponsors and fixing some of the money, getting a provisional theatre booking, arranging details for a tour and the like. When he had finished, the two writers were amazed at how busy he must have been – it seemed quite out of character – and their natural excitement began to regroup.

By now the three of them were more or less in full agreement on the basic outline for the show, "providing the script feels right when I read it tonight," said Aaron – and for a while they carried on discussing some of the slightly finer detail.

Aaron said he had already started thinking about getting a cast together, then Harry, supported fully by Danny, told him of their idea of having Toni Benito for the lead. Harry told the producer that not only was the singer interested in trying to break into the theatre, he had also expressed interest in the show idea itself – and more importantly, perhaps, he reckoned they could get him fairly cheaply. "Perhaps it might be possibly for him to bring 'Cold Streets' to the show," repeated Aaron.

Harry was still not too sure about that, but before he said anything Danny came up with a suggestion that they have a chorus of twenty or thirty lively boy and girl dancers. Aaron liked the idea, and they switched to talk about old shows and old musical films.

Next morning, as promised, Aaron contacted the two writers and told them he liked the finished script. He asked them to call in to the office again, and when they did later that afternoon he already had contracts prepared for them to sign. They did so without a murmur – it was a dream starting to come true.

"Reading your script, I've got no doubt it's going to work," said Aaron. "Better than any of the other rubbish I've seen – yeah, it's going to work."

Aaron said he had also been thinking of a director, and showed them a list of names for them to look at. None were really topflight men, and although they had vaguely heard of one or two neither Danny nor Harry had any particular ideas on which to choose. They decided to let Aaron get on with it.

Eventually, Aaron called the two writers to his office to introduce them to Matty Peters – real name Matthew Pederson – who was quite well established after a few small runs in London and some outstanding hits in the provinces. When they turned up at the office, Matty was casually dressed with a rather dated roll-necked sweater and a brown sports jacket. They shook hands all round, then after a few moments embarrassed pause while they sat looking at each other, Aaron explained that Danny and Harry had written 'Cold Streets'.

"So that was your 'and then' time," said the director, brusquely.

"And then?"

"Yep, look at any star's biog. 'I went to school, Mum pushed me, tried hard, worked the halls, got nowhere…and then…"

"Yeah, well," said Aaron. "And then these two met me. And I'm going to make them all big names…all three of you really."

He smiled at them all. "Now Harry, I've tried to tell Matty about your songs – but my voice isn't as good as it used t'be when I was a dashing young beau. Maybe you could tinkle the ivories to let him hear the music…"

Harry was glad to oblige. He went to the piano in the corner of the shabby office and began playing. Danny sat listening for a while, then stood up and went to stand by the side of the piano singing the words softly. Aaron joined in – missing out the higher notes.

When he had finished, Harry went back to his chair, and a few moments later Danny followed him. There was a short pause while Aaron's secretary bought coffees in cracked mugs, then they got down to talking about the show.

From the outset, Matty started laying down the law – he was grumpy, argumentative, and disagreed with a lot of the ideas Harry and Danny had laid out in their script, insisting that somewhere they had to make a distinct moral point about something, anything.

It was pompous, and both Harry and Danny thought it ridiculous. "We don't want messages – people are too tied up with their own problems for that," said Danny. "Let's just give 'em a release from every day, some relaxation if you like."

"Yeah, that's OK. They'll get that release from the songs – but don't forget it's the dialogue in between that makes the drama," said Matty.

"Drama? Hell, man, this is just a sophisticated revue remember?" replied Harry.

"Look, you're new to this business. I've been around a while, and I'm telling you people want drama. Those songs – they're great – but where's all that drama in them?"

Harry pursed his lips. "I think Aaron likes the songs well enough the way they are," he said after a pause. "In any case, I think and Danny and me are the best people to know how our music should be played."

"Yeah, and if it's some kind of exciting palaver you want, surely that will come with your staging," added Danny, going on to carefully explain how they had scripted the dances and transitions in 'film style', with the fades in and out of the revolve providing all the possible drama that could be needed – emphasising the use of special spotlights like the 'Long Ago' routine to highlight pieces of action in much the same way as close-ups or mid-shots do in film.

It quickly became clear that Matty had only skimmed through the script, and that he had ideas of his own he wanted to introduce that were nothing at all to do with the OAP home background. As he spluttered and tried to get his way, Aaron sided with the two writers, and when the meeting broke up after a couple of hours Matty had backed down and agreed that the script was just fine.

Before they left the office, Aaron arranged to meet all three again. As he liked holding his meetings at Giuseppe's, they fixed up to meet up there in a couple of days, and when the time arrived Danny and Harry turned up eagerly on time. Aaron was about ten minutes late, and as he sat he took off his jacket as before – turning awkwardly in his chair to do so and wincing as he twisted his back.

"Are you comfortable?" asked Harry considerately.

"Thank God – I've got a little bit of money in the bank, a pension, and a friendly bank manager," Aaron wisecracked back to him, beaming at the writer.

While they waited for Matty, the producer and Danny continued to bad-joke to each other. Harry was delighted to let his partner get on with things that way.

"Maybe we should've met in the Greek place next door for a change," said Danny.

"Why the Greek place? Don't you like Italian…?" asked Aaron.

"Well, perhaps if we'd changed we'd have been able to find out what a Grecian urn is," replied Danny straight-faced, knowing how the conversation would continue.

"A Grecian urn? What's a Grecian urn?"

"Twelve-pounds fifty an hour…plus residuals."

"Plus residuals…he, he," said Aaron.

Luckily for Harry, Matty turned up seconds later, perspiring and calling to a waiter for a beer. After it arrived, they ordered food, and while waiting for it began talking about the show and how it was to be presented. It quickly became apparent that although he had indicated that it was all fixed when they first signed contracts for the show, Aaron's financing deals were far from arranged – he had only held some preliminary talks with a few sponsors who now needed 'selling' the idea, something the producer wanted the two writers and the director involved with.

But while Matty Peters said he didn't have time 'for that kind of thing', both Harry and Danny agreed to help. They could afford not to work because by now they had a good portfolio of songs to hand, and the money from 'Cold Streets' had given them both more independence, although the only real difference it made to either of them was they tended to ride in taxis more often than going by Underground.

With the extra time on their hands, they were able to attend several meetings with potential angels, backers, and with music publishers, theatre people and the like. Throughout all the discussions, Harry tried to dress smartly in suits and tie, tried to look business-like, but Danny continued to be almost deliberately untidy – casual even for the most important meetings.

It was like that when Aaron called them both in to join him at a presentation for some potential backers at the Savoy Hotel the next day. Aaron had arranged a private room with a piano, and Harry arrived and sat playing a few songs while he waited. Aaron followed soon after with a group of aging, suited, businessmen, and as Harry rose to greet them he noted that they all looked rather hard-nosed and suspicious. He had an automatic feeling that they wouldn't be forthcoming in any way.

Danny was late turning up. Harry realised he had been drinking, although he was not slurring his words, and listened with a kind of horror as his partner launched into his usual drunken bad-taste frivolous patter. He shuddered, but couldn't stop the flow – instead, he just started playing the first few bars of one of the songs from the show. Danny interrupted quickly – was late turning up. Harry realised he had been drinking, although he was not slurring his words, and listened with a kind of horror as his partner launched into his usual drunken bad-taste frivolous.

> '*If Don Juan was*
> *The reign in Spain...*'
> he ad-libbed...
> '*was Don Wan really –*
> *The pale lover?*'

Aaron laughed. "He he. The pale lover. What a writer." None of the businessmen said a word, and Harry just sighed and started playing the opening song for the presentation.

When they got home, Harry, as so often, berated Danny for his behaviour, and the wordsmith promised to do better once again. And that promise was still in his mind about a week later when Aaron arranged another sponsors' meeting, this time at the Ritz, where he planned a formal tea. "They're American – they'll love all that. The formality. Tea at the Ritz," he said.

The Ritz tea was something else – but it turned out to be successful. For once Danny realised the conventional values of the place and wore a suit. He was on his best behaviour, and turned up at the mannered Piccadilly hotel with Aaron and Harry in plenty of time to meet their guests. Apart from a slight hiccup when the head waiter ignored them while they waited to be seated – "we're not quite ready, just walk around for a while," he told Aaron when he queried the wait – they were in place at their reserved table in plenty of time.

As they waited, Harry had a few words with the aging pianist sitting just in the entrance, and he was given permission to take over for a short while during the tea. Somehow, Harry realised instinctively that this was to be a kind of final audition for the songs – a chance to interest backers and persuade them to give their money to the show.

When the sponsors arrived, there were five of them and they were all young men, all smartly, fashionably dressed in suits, all American and all wearing fashionable ties, apart from the sole Englishman in the group who wore an open-necked shirt with his dark grey suit. They fussed their way to the table where Aaron and the other two waited, and sat down after drawing a lot of attention from the true-Brits around the dining rooms because of their group look-alike Americanism. It took only a few moments for both Harry and Danny to catch their bright-eyed look and to realise they were all eager to be involved.

The five men looked around the dining room. Lots of fading gilt; lots of fading elegance; lots of fading, aging people who looked as if they belonged to another era; a few brighter young things having the experience of a lifetime. Danny, particularly, realised they were impressed, and in a way he, too, was caught up in the glitzy, ritzy atmosphere of the Ritz.

As tea was served by the mainly foreign waiters in the Ritz's inimitable way – real tea in a silver tea pot with a strainer, in cups and saucers, and with a plate of ultra-fresh cucumber sandwiches cut into quarters – they all chatted amiably. There was a tiered tray of scones (the Americans pronounced them 'scoanes') with butter and thick cream and jam. It was all terribly British – and the five young men loved it.

The Americans were a willing audience as the conversation flowed, with Aaron careful, at this point, not to mention the show, exchanging his usual mickey-taking chit-chat with Danny in a way that amused the young men. Danny was in good form, and was able to ostentatiously greet a couple of aging TV 'celebrities' he was able to point out across the room and whom he knew from his old PR days. He told stories about them and some of the other stars he had met.

When a couple of characters – one in a wide brimmed hat, twirling an old-fashioned-villain-style moustache and with a cape, the other a woman of about

90 made-up like a twenty-year-old – sat at the next table, Danny made up stories about them to help make the tea go well, and they all fell about laughing at a Japanese couple sitting a couple of tables away being very formal over the tea ceremony, then acting like tourists when they began taking snaps of each other grinning childishly.

After the food had gone, Harry excused himself and went to the piano. The pianist, who had been playing some old-fashioned waltzes in very slow time, was delighted to give up his seat so he could take a break and go to the loo, and Harry sat down and began playing some of the songs he and Danny had written for the show. At the table, Aaron explained how they would fit into the show, while Danny made notes on a paper napkin…

> *'Sand grains on a beach,*
> *Pebbles on the shore…'*

He knew they would come in handy one day.

As Harry finished, there was applause from around the room, particularly from the five potential sponsors Aaron had brought along. They seemed very pleased, and when they eventually said their goodbyes, Aaron wiped his brow theatrically. "Thanks boys. I think it went well – let me buy you a real drink, you've earned it," he said leading the way from the tearoom to the bar.

Tea at the Ritz turned out better than anyone could have imagined.

The five men Aaron had hosted had decided to back the show through their company DuVal Enterprises of New Jersey and had taken a majority shareholding – 56 per cent – and with that promise in place, Aaron was able to use it to get more corporate funding and the backing of literally dozens of small investors. In what seemed to both Harry and Danny an incredibly short time, he had pledges of between three-quarters and a million pounds – including the DuVal money. None of it was his own cash.

With the financing virtually set up, Aaron was immediately able to get down to working out the final details of staging 'The Age Of Romance'. All his apparent vagueness disappeared, and apart from being an equivocal wheeler-dealer he soon proved he was a sharp, adept theatre man with the ability to get things done – in a hurry.

While waiting for a first instalment from DuVal, Aaron told everyone he had a theatre booked in Shaftesbury Avenue, and with Matty Peters help set about trying to organise a list of people for crew and cast. They also settled on a probable opening date, and Aaron and his secretary got down to fixing the start of rehearsals. "Might do a pre-opening tour – just like they did in the old Broadway days, hey boys?" Aaron told Danny and Harry. "Just like old Broadway."

What Aaron didn't tell anyone was that the theatre booking was still very provisional, and would not be made definite until a huge cash deposit was laid – and the only date he could get for it was for mid-summer, the worst time for a new show. It was, however, the only theatre that was 'dark' – a theatrical term for empty – and had the added advantage of having a ready-installed full-stage revolve. After redecoration, said Aaron, it would be available for the later run throughs, with a consequent saving on rehearsal room costs.

At another meeting at Giuseppe's, Danny and Harry listened as Aaron and Matty listed the crew they wanted, almost awe-struck at the way they threw out big names without a thought. For a start, there had to be a choreographer, music director, set and costume designers, a lighting designer and a stage manager – and having got the list sorted, Aaron asked Matty to get on with fixing up meetings with each to get them on board.

Harry suggested getting a set designer and lighting man appointed early to help establish the filmic style, and immediately Aaron asked Danny and Harry if they would like to sit in on all the interviews – to be a bigger part of the team.

With the names at least lined up for the crew, the next step was thinking about the actors, singers and dancers. Aaron had several promises to fill so most of the cast fell straight into place, but it was not quite as easy – largely because Matty insisted that they had to have a big-name lead.

Danny and Harry once more put forward Toni Benito's name as they had discussed with Aaron, but Matty did not want to know. He said Toni was 'just a pop music guy' with no stage experience and not used to acting. He said he'd rather Marlon Dyson, a TV soap star, took the lead, and although Danny and Harry didn't like the idea, Matty was adamant.

"But what about 'Cold Streets'?" asked Harry. "You said you wanted it for the show."

"We-e-e-ll," Aaron drew the word out. "I've been in touch with the record company, and they told me I couldn't have it."

Harry looked across at Danny. "And as you've written that other song for the main character, what was it – oh yeah, '*I want the sun to rise*' – well, we don't really need it anymore."

"In any case," added Matty Peters, "I've spoken to DuVal about Dyson, and they want him. They've almost insisted."

"Why the hell didn't you just say…" started Danny, but Harry silenced him. He knew they had no argument, and with Aaron going along with the idea of having the television star, they had to agree. Dyson was signed up, and from the outset got along well with Matty – virtually ignoring Danny and Harry during their various brief meetings.

Things were starting to move. The show seemed to be taking on a life of its own, and was becoming a living, breathing life form with Aaron definitely at its heart.

Matty was kept busy helping Aaron sign up the creative crew, and although they did not know the people involved Danny and Harry were kept in on the meetings because the producer knew he had something good with them and wanted to keep them happy. He agreed, for instance, when they disputed the need for an orchestral arranger as Harry wanted to keep control of that side of things.

Gradually the backstage team built up.

First on the scene was the musical director, the orchestra conductor. He had the unlikely name of Mario da Cosi – but it was genuine, because although he had a strong Cockney accent his father was an Italian born in England and his mother a Londoner. Mario himself was born in the East End, and was short and rotund. Everything about him was round – face, eyes, body, and even his ears seemed circular.

"You've put on weight since the last time we met," Aaron greeted him when he came to the office to join up.

"Too true. It's cost a lot of producers an awful lot of money," said Mario, patting his corpulent stomach. "But I'm not really fat – like some other people have barrel chests, I've got a barrel tum."

"Just a waistline starting at the neck," interrupted Danny. "A sunken chest really."

"A sunken chest," repeated Aaron. "He, he."

The others came in. Matty wanted a drama director to deal specifically with the old folks' home scenes, and Andy Mallett was brought in – quickly proving that he just wanted an easy life looking at the show girls.

Choreographer Eddie Martin was next. He was a rather elderly man with skin wrinkled under his chin and around the neck, and although he had once been quite a dancer himself he was now flabby all over. "I've got the muscles of a glass eye now," he joked.

Danny thought Eddie 'looks like a grandfather', but despite his slight grossness and the fact that his hands, which he used a lot to describe dance routines, were also podgy, his fingers were remarkably slender. He was squat, and looked as if he should always have a cigar between his teeth.

'The Age Of Romance' was to be Eddie's first-time working on a stage show, because in the past he had only worked on TV commercials and in film, where he had fancied himself as the new Busby Berkeley. Aaron had taken him on after Harry's request for people who could give a filmic look to the show, and both Danny and Harry took to him immediately because he agreed with all their thoughts on the style of the show. From the outset, he began working out ways of staging them in the kind of filmic way they wanted.

"In films and TV, I can use editing to get the movement – the camera does it all for you and you can use all the angles," he said. "Seems like I've got to get the dancers to do it themselves here."

"Yes," agreed Harry and Danny, "with the lighting and all the other business."

"It going to be different to anything else I've done."

Next in was the vividly-red-haired set designer Anne-Marie Besser, later to take on extra work designing the costumes as well – one of Aaron's ideas to save money – followed quickly, by lighting designer Freddie Excell (the lighting gaffer or sparks) and company stage manager Rob (Robbie) Cadell, another who was once a big name actor himself but was now past his good-looks prime.

Aaron himself decided to look after the PR, with a bit of help from Danny, and for starters invited all the top show biz writers to join the entire backstage crew at a getting-to-know-you party. Giuseppe's normally closed on a Monday, but Aaron persuaded the manager to open up for the crew get-together, and they all turned up ready for a party.

Danny and Harry were there from the start, waiting with Aaron to greet the others as they arrived.

Music director Mario was the first, and he came bounding in full of good humour. "Any way we can fit in a can-can?" he asked.

"Why?" asked Harry.

"No reason – just that I like the can-can," said Mario, grinning widely.

Matty Peters came in next. "Hey Mario, you're getting a little thinner on top, eh?" he called to the conductor.

"Well, grass don' grow on a busy street."

Danny, standing nearby, heard that and started singing loudly…

'Two bald men who accidentally meet,
Tell each other 'Grass don't grow on a busy street'
So why, asks one, in a whining bleat…
Don't I have a beard on my busy, busy feet?'

Aaron heard him. "Hey, hairy feet, he he. Di'n' I tell you he was a genius? A genius," he said out loud to no one in particular.

Eddie Martin joined the two writers, and Mario went off to talk to some of the others. It was a good party, and the crew seemed to gel fairly quickly. Aaron insisted it augured well for the show.

The show was still evolving from the original idea, now with its own life. Aaron had got all the others to give him suggestions for the various acts he was pencilling in, and soon he had a long list of possible solo dancers and singers, sophisticated duets, an urbane stand-up comedian, a jazz quartet, a magician with an unusual sleight-of-hand act, and a seven-strong ensemble of dancers with a highly structured and colourful routine. He wasn't certain which of them he really wanted.

At Danny's insistence, Aaron went along to see Carlos Loueen and his partner dancing their intriguing version of *'Long Ago And Far Away'* and agreed they would fit in well. He had words with the dancers and made a provisional booking for them to join the show as well.

Over the next few weeks, Danny and Harry were kept in a maelstrom of re-writing along with Aaron and Matty. Danny decided to have several of the old people in the home as former chorus girls or choir singers so they could put on some spectacular production numbers – but that idea was all too frequently counter-balanced by Aaron, who kept coming up with a succession of good ideas for big, expensive scenes although he always insisted everyone else save money.

Aaron did decide, however, that he had to cut the pre-opening tour to save costs.

Danny and Harry soon got used to the idea that they had to continually re-write the book as new characters had to be dreamed up for the old people's home to fit in with the new acts that became available according to the theatre bible, 'The Stage'. There were so many that Danny, who had always kept a pad and pen by his bed to jot down ideas, woke up so often during the night to make notes that he learned to write in the dark without turning on the bedside light – and found he could still read the scrawled notes in the morning!

Where the music was concerned, Aaron would always side with him and Harry because he liked their easy-on-the-ear melodic style for the show, the style of Broadway in the 30s. When Matty frequently suggested reprising more songs to save time writing new ones, Aaron backed Harry and Danny's arguments – they wanted to write more. "Leave 'em to it," he told Matty. "They're good songs, ain't that the truth?"

Danny listened, and idly scribbled some words.

'Veracity,
Mendacity,
Audacity,
Superciliacity'

It was a flying melee of excitement and fervour for everyone now concerned with the show. Danny and Harry were going along with the flow, polishing the script and their songs all the while and blissfully unaware whether or not things were proceeding as normal. They were both working hard in a tight cocoon of enthusiastic optimism, and as Danny said one evening in awe – "Hey, we're actually working on a big musical show. What we've wanted."

Lex heard him and smiled at Harry. "A dream coming true," she told him.

Lex was also happy to go with the swing. She had given up her job on Harry's insistence when he got the recording money, and was, these days, more or less an encouraging housewife passing comment on the songs only occasionally when asked. She was quite happy at the way things were going for Harry and concentrated on keeping in the background, benignly and happily giving assistance and encouragement where she could.

At work, Aaron was in complete control. Having signed up the technical crew, more or less got the full financing, and got theatre and pre-opening try-outs more or less fixed, he was not only helping finalise the script but planning for the final casting – and the auditions. He had always been careful not to upset any of the theatre unions, and he also found time to see their officials to make sure he had cleared all their various regulations.

The one area he refused to get involved in was in the formation of the orchestra – that was to be Mario's job. Mario had almost immediately got to work thinking of the musicians he wanted for his orchestra, although he knew they would not be wanted until well into the final rehearsal period. He knew the theatre, so he knew how many would fit into the orchestra pit, and he had checked with Aaron to find how many musicians he could afford.

The others has been busy, too, and the crew seemed to grow larger day by day as they enlisted lighting operators, follow-spot operators, electricians, sound engineers, a wardrobe mistress and two assistants, scenery builders and riggers, and a four-man stage crew.

Finally it was all set up. All that was needed was a cast.

Aaron had already made preliminary contact with a number of the speciality variety acts, but he wanted to see what others were available and he needed actors to play them as old folk. There was also a need to sign up the ensemble chorus and the various backing singers and dancers.

This time he advertised in the trade papers and magazines, and booked a fairly large audition room in South London for a week – cheaper than the West End – and arranged that on the day before he would entertain the full backstage crew and Marlon Dyson at Giuseppe's.

The second party was another success and helped everyone start to integrate as a team, but from the outset, Marlon Dyson turned out to be a pain. Harry played the songs he and Danny had prepared for the show, but Dyson continually tried to adapt many of those allocated to other characters for his own use. He complained bitterly about all kinds of things, and was generally disruptive. "Hell, I'm the star of this show," he said over and over again.

At one stage during the gathering he even began insisting that one of his own songs should be included. But he got very irritable when he sang it to Aaron and heard Danny summing it up.

"Makes me think of an NHS doctor who's signed on for a job at a funeral parlour while his patient's on the operating theatre table," said Danny.

The next day was boiling hot. When Danny and Harry walked up to the rehearsal hall for the start of the open call auditions they were perspiring, and they found a queue of athletic young men and woman standing outside not only sticky and covered with sweat but grimly determined to put up with anything for the chance of auditioning for a part in the show.

The adverts had worked, and word of mouth had spread like wildfire – and well before the ten o'clock start time there were over 150 people waiting outside the hall. The two writers made their way past them and were admitted, to find Aaron and Matty Peters inside with the rest of the technical crew.

The hall itself was nothing special, not exactly where you might expect to see the birth pangs of a glamorous, glittering, vibrant, musical extravaganza. It was, in fact, a church hall – large, high, and echoing. It was dusty, and although there were half a dozen or so bare bulbs hanging from the ceiling, they were unlit and the room was badly served by windows high up in the ceiling. The hall was more or less empty apart from an ancient-looking upright piano against one wall. There was a long bare-wood table with metal legs folded leaning against a wall at the rear, and a few wooden folding chairs lined up alongside it.

Matty was busy reading the script, and as they walked in Harry and Danny were greeted by Mario, the conductor. "I'm going to play the Joanna today – but if you want to take over at any time feel free," he told Harry.

They all chatted for a while, still sweating profusely, and while they did so the table was set up at one end of the room with half a dozen of the chairs behind . it, and the piano was moved closer in to be near the table. Just before the due start time, Aaron indicated they should all sit – but himself stood on the other side, facing the team and talking to them.

He explained that they were looking for the lower ranks – he had the star in Marlon Dyson and was lining up a well-known singer for the female lead, but he wanted everyone to have a say in the final choice of the singers, dancers and smaller character actors. By the time Aaron had finished it was almost ten o'clock, and he finally suggested they get the hopefuls in ten at a time.

Aaron walked slowly round to take his place in the centre of the seated line up. "OK, let's get the cattle call started," he said, and stage manager Robbie Cadell opened the doors.

Aaron had organised the auditions so the dancers came in the mornings and the singers went through their paces in the afternoons. One day mid-week was reserved for the actors wanted to play the straight roles of the old people in the home.

At the start of that first day, therefore, it was a variety of dancers – the gypsies – who turned up. Danny and Harry sat behind the now unfolded long table with

Aaron, Matty Peters and choreographer Eddie Martin watching the succession of hopefuls come in full of enthusiasm and hope. They formed a hard-faced panel, sitting without emotion as the various acts appeared before them, only occasionally did one or another make a note no matter how good or how bad the performer.

Both Danny and Harry found it harder to stay detached, and as the heat got more and more oppressive they both wondered how the dancers managed to put so much energy into their work. But they did. Many were desperate, and that overcame everything else.

They came in all shapes and sizes. Long legs, short legs, wide hips, narrow hips, big busted, petite, brunette, bottle blonde, natural blonde, extrovert, introvert, talented and the others.

Eddie Martin would watch with his head on one side to see how they walked in and approached the table, telling the two writers it gave him a general idea of their movement. He was watching for poise and grace and bearing, and only then did he look at the body, then the face and only then at the dance ability. He also gently asked each candidate if he or she could sing and act.

"They need more than just latent talent as dancers – they have to be all-rounders, and they have to have patience, determination, artistic appreciation…and sheer bloody-mindedness to succeed as well," he said.

It had been decided that the show needed a 24-strong chorus line – half male, half female – but on the first morning alone there were more than 90 hopefuls. "But George White once auditioned 4,000 people – and he only called four hundred of them back for a second look," said Aaron when Danny queried the numbers during a pause. "He finally chose just sixty of them."

"There was another case – 500 girls came in – and only eight of them got jobs," added Eddie, with a yawn and a stretch.

All the dancers came in, approached the table, answered questions, then did a few carefully rehearsed 'impromptu' steps to show off their talents. When Eddie asked them to do something specific, they did so, then stood anxiously waiting for some sort of comment. Most had received formal ballet training before specialising in jazz, tap, modern, ethnic or ballroom dancing, and almost all knew the routine. They used their whole bodies artistically, and neither of the two writers could tell which were the best. But they listened as Eddie muttered and made notes – "He looks good, he's got quick feet."

No audition lasted longer than ten minutes, and after each gruelling trial every dancer rushed to bags left by the side of the door to get their publicity photos – glossy 10x8 star-like head shots with their CV's on the back. Some were told instantly that Eddie would like a second look and went away delighted, most were simply told – "We'll let you know." Anyone who was anywhere near 30 years old was in the second group – they were 'too old'.

But still they came, in their dozens. Despite his record, Danny was remarkably tolerant and patient, and only let things slip once. That was when one girl dancer came to the front. "Name?" asked Eddie.

"Teresa."

"Teresa Green," muttered Danny.

The girl looked bewildered. "Er, no – Teresa Burnett," she said.

"Just dance," said Eddie.

After a lunchtime break for coffee and sandwiches, the cattle call continued. It was still boiling hot in the room, but now came the singers. Mario took over from Eddie Martin to listen to sopranos, lyric sopranos, mezzo sopranos, baritones and lyric baritones, tenors, contraltos, soubrettes and comedy ingénues. There were people who had played leading roles, soloists, small groups, larger groups, and choir singers – once more, all kinds, all hopeful.

The day was long, arduous and very hot – far worse than anything either Harry or Danny had ever envisaged. They sat in with the others watching the seemingly never-ending procession of singers and dancers, and at the end of the day staggered back to Harry's apartment for a final nightcap. They had only sat and watched, but they were exhausted – and they knew there were another four days to go.

The auditions went on throughout the week and Danny and Harry found them hard, demanding oppressive work. They went home every evening as shattered as they had been on the first day, their minds in a whirl of dancers, singers and repeated choruses of the same old rehearsal songs, relieved only when Aaron called in some music hall acts for a change.

Some of the dancers came back for a second chance, and a few – a very few – were called back for a third or, in one case, a fourth audition. To most, rejection was its usual disappointment, but as Danny said: "It's a no-talent competition really."

Although Danny and Harry sat in for all the sessions, the actual selection was mainly done by the experts – Aaron, Eddie and director Matty Peters. "I love auditions – it's the hindsight," said Mario on the second day.

"Hindsight? Don't you mean forethought?" asked Harry.

"No, hindsight," replied Mario. "I just love looking at the girl's asses."

Later that day, Aaron announced that he had signed up Julia Ross, a well-known West End singer, as the female lead, but still the search for talent went on.

One very large, lumbering black man turned up dressed immaculately in a dark lounge suit and sober tie. Called forward, he carefully took off his jacket, meticulously laid it on a chair in front of the table, and before anyone could speak began a slow tap dance. Harry was at the piano, and almost as he started picked up his rhythm and followed him the dance slowly began to speed up. Despite his size, the dancer was very delicate and stylishly out of character on his feet, and everyone in the room stopped to watch him as he ended up with a series of entrechat that saw (and heard) him tap at least twice on every landing.

"OK Joe. You're in," said Eddie.

As on the first day, a funny collection of individuals turned up – some gifted, many not, but all hopeful. There was one little old lady – literally little, standing about four foot seven inches tall and wearing an ankle-length black dress, a multi-coloured woolly jumper, and Doc Martens boots. Matty asked her what she did, and after she had told him she was a dancer she proceeded to massacre a kind of heavy, unrhythmical clog dance.

"Sorry, try again next time," said Aaron kindly.

"Well, I only came for the free coffee anyway," she replied as she shuffled away. As she left the hall, Aaron told the others he had known 'Old Kate' for years. "She's been along to every audition I've ever held," he added.

On the afternoon of the third day, a young singer arrived with his own song. Harry was again at the piano, and the singer handed over his music. Harry gave the song a quick look through, then played for the audition. The singer did not realise that Harry had written the score of the show, and at the end of his own song told Aaron that if he wanted, he could produce any extra songs they might need.

Marlon, who has dropped in to watch, got quite rude. "Why would we need you?" he asked. "I can do it if necessary." Aaron calmed him, and placated the singer. "Come back tomorrow and try some of the show songs," he told him.

Luckily, Danny had gone to the loo and didn't hear anything, but Harry listened to it all knowing how desperate the singer must be to get a break. He'd been there, and he muttered some soothing words to the baffled singer.

Harry told Danny about it later, and that night they stopped off at a nearby pub before going home to try and get rid of the bitter taste Marlon's action had left. The pub was putting on a showcase for entertainers, and while they were at the bar Harry's eye was taken by a very pretty girl on the other side of the room. She was very drunk, but as she stood with a group of friends he could see her feet were beating time expertly to the music. Harry watched her, and while she was at the bar she moved into an outrageous tap dance that attracted some musicians in a corner to follow her lead.

Still remorseful at the treatment of the afternoon's singer, Harry wrote a note inviting her to contact him at the audition next day and handed it to her as he and Danny left.

When they got back to Harry's flat, they found Lex had filled her time while they were working by tidying up. "Look," she told them brightly as they came in, "there's a lot more space now."

"That's the trouble with women – the love creating space," said Danny almost by habit. "Just means they can go out and buy more things to fill it with." He shrugged. "Goodnight folks, I'm dead beat. See you in the morning."

He went off, and Lex made two coffees. She snuggled down on a couch next to Harry. "It's been a helluva day. I'm bushwhacked," Harry told her.

"But happy?"

"U-huh," said Harry, relaxing. "But I'll be happier when…if…we could get married. D'you want to?"

"You know I do," said Lex perkily, full of life. "But now you're in show business, isn't marriage a risky thing? So many show biz'y people seem to get divorced…"

"We won't," yawned Harry. "We won't become show biz'y."

Next day started just as busily as the others, with the queues still there. Harry did not expect to see the girl from the night before, but surprisingly she did turn up – and he was just as surprised when Eddie invited her to come back for a second audition.

She was one of the few being invited back. Quite unlike another man with obvious experience, who showed he had a good voice and was a competent dancer. He was very British, but he had a slow drawl that he had cultivated to try and give the impression that he's from across the Atlantic. Harry had noticed him waiting his turn, and had seen that when he took a mug of coffee that someone brought him his fingers seemed to dance expressively into a grip. His eyes were grey and cloudy, but generally he had an appearance of toughness – and he insisted on telling the panel he really wanted to be a big dramatic actor.

"Cagney did it," he insisted before he was told like so many others – "We'll let you know."

Then finally the audition week was over – the technical team was in place and casting was now complete. But before the show could really get going, there was to be a major drama backstage that in Harry and Danny's eyes – and Aaron's if it came to that – was much more dramatic than anything they planned on stage.

Act 12: Into Rehearsal

Casting was complete. Most of the business talks, technical discussions and general get-togethers had been finished, the crew was in position, the theatre booked, some of the actual cash was in the bank and the rest tied up in promissory notes. The show was on its way.

A rather extended twelve weeks of rehearsals had been planned and budgeted for, and now everyone was committed to up to twelve hours a day hard work, six days a week, before the West End opening.

Rehearsals were held in a dance studio in west London – a barn of a room, draughty, dusty, windows high up on the wall – unglamorous. There were a couple of chairs littered around – with the regulation barre facing a long mirror along the whole length of one wall, a tall, broad mirror opposite, a single radiator that hissed slightly when the heating came on, a coffee machine – and off to one end two or three small dressing rooms. A couple of small theatrical lights were littered around, the cables snaking untidily and in the way across the floor.

Rehearsals were a whole new world for both Danny and Harry, but they quickly realised how good the professional crew was. They had selected the right people from the mass who had attended the auditions, and come up with a good, workable cast.

They also began to realise how much hard work Aaron was putting in. He was everywhere – still working on extra financing and budgets, helping the crew, talking contracts to actors, singers and dancers, dealing with problems from designers and set builders, helping with the theatre arrangements, fixing ticket agency sales, replying to letters, handling the hundred and one other matters that arose, and generally running things and making certain everyone else was doing their job.

He booked practise rooms for the singers, dancers and dialogue scenes, and with rehearsals ready and everything seeming to be going well began to devote most of his time to working out things like the anticipating bar takings, programme sales, souvenir books, clothing sales and the like. He looked at advertising, began sorting out press arrangements – and he even worked out how much chocolate and ice cream to order for each performance. He was a real bundle of energy.

Matty had worked out a routine for his weeks of rehearsals – the dancers, singers and two speciality acts for the first two weeks, the principals and their backing groups joining in for a further two weeks, the 'old people' straight actors and actresses for a week on their own, the next two weeks set aside for the six big production numbers, and finally the entire company for the last five weeks, during which time he hoped to be able to go into the theatre itself.

Rehearsals started at the end of March – the onset of spring, thought Harry – and Aaron planned to open in the West End around the start of June.

With Aaron busy, Matty was in charge of the rehearsals. And the result was that although for the first week everything was fine, small niggles began to creep in. Matty wanted to change things round, and Marlon Dyson began to pick holes in his part of the script. The inexperienced Harry and Danny were caught between the two, and an atmosphere soon began to build up.

On the very first day, Matty had the dancers in on their own, putting them through their paces with choreographer Eddie Martin to a piano played throughout the day by Mario. From the start, Eddie wanted more time than Matty would allow him to work out routines with the dancers, and by lunchtime the two men were hardly talking. In an effort to calm things down, Danny singled out Eddie for a chat and got him talking about dancing.

Eddie was something of a history buff where dance was concerned, and he and Danny got on well talking – as Danny so often did – about 'the good old days'.

Danny proved a good listener as Eddie explained that in those by-gone days, dance directors like Balanchine, Busby Berkeley, Jerome Robbins, Bob Fosse, Gower Champion, Tommy Tune and Michael Kidd worked with legendary producers like George White, George Abbott and Florenz Ziegfeld to work out the precision routines made up of simple steps in a variety of fixed patterns that their chorus girls could perform like machines.

"It was all regimented – like an Army parade," said Eddie. "But it was simple and entertaining. And it worked. Eventually, of course, Busby Berkeley made himself quite a big hit doing the same thing on film."

While they were talking, Mario and Harry joined them. The four told each other stories they had read or heard about old musical shows, especially the legendary old shows from Broadway.

Soon after, Robbie Cadell also joined in, and during a slight pause asked Danny how he got his ideas. "I mean, how could anyone take a story about old pros and start off with a line of chorus girls?" he asked.

Danny smiled. "It's the old story, but with a slight twist – I put the end at the beginning," he said. "Remember, they always used to say that if there was a lull in the show you had to bring on the dancing girls. Well, I thought – why wait for a lull? Start it off with the dancing girls."

"But why did they always say that?" asked Robbie.

Danny laughed. "I read that it dates back to ancient Egypt," he explained. "Apparently, when any of the Pharaohs died, they had to make sure he was a real goner." He started acting out the scene. "They laid him out, put the finest wine and the richest food beside him – and waited. If he still didn't move, they'd bring on the dancing girls in their veils and see-through whatnots…and if ol' Pharaoh still move a muscle…why, he sure was dead."

The others laughed, then Matty called them for them all to watch 'a little bit of business' he had worked out.

It wasn't always that friendly. Marlon's little niggles were like a stone thrown into a pond – the ripples began spreading wider and wider, and a general air of meanness and disquiet began diffusing through the whole cast.

He would always act the big star, and on occasion would try to belittle Danny's lyrics. "All the books say you should always write your words in square blocks, not like these," he said in a loud voice in front of the whole cast during one afternoon session.

"What does that mean?" asked Danny?

"Hell, how the hell should I know? You're the writer."

Almost from the start, Marlon claimed he didn't really like musicals. "I know I became famous on TV for singing and dancing, but I really want to do real theatre, straight acting," he proclaimed. "Standing on a stage, waiting to be dramatic, waiting for things to go wrong and knowing it's up to you to ad lib your way to safety, Thrilling. That's what we really need – not all this romantic pap."

"So why did you take this job?" asked Danny.

"Money," replied Marlon disdainfully.

Marlon was a continual nuisance. He insisted they rewrite some of the script dialogue so that instead of an 'old folks' home' the others spoke of 'sheltered accommodation', with him as the chief executive rather than a warden. "I don't really want to be associated with old people or their homes," he said.

He also refused to have the girl lead as a girlfriend – either as nurse or carer – because he felt that might take the attention away from himself.

Even Danny got caught up, and towards the end of the first week when he presented a new song, '*Thanks For Having Me*', and was told he couldn't use it because it was too suggestive the way he'd written it – he argued that it was just what kids say when they leave a party. But Matty wouldn't have it, and Danny sulked.

Harry seemed to let the bad mood ride over him, and soon after the principles had begun their stint he sat at the piano during a lull and began idly plotting out a new song – nothing to do with the show. He soon got into the swing of it, and then played it right through in an almost-complete way. "Hey mate, what d'you think of that?" he called out to Danny, who had been sitting opposite him. When there was no answer, he looked up to finds that Danny had fallen asleep!

"Hey Danny, you wuss…"

Danny woke with a start, shook his head, and listened to the new song. Pushing himself off the floor, he walked over to the piano and instantly gave Harry a lyric that fitted perfectly. '*It's Time To Say Goodbye*'

"Now can I go back to kip?" he asked.

Even Marlon was impressed, and a few days afterwards, when Aaron, Matty, Danny and Harry were lounging against a wall discussing things, he moved across and began bending their ears. "We really need some new words to this song – these don't fit my image," he insisted. "You've got nothing else to do – can't you write something for me off the cuff, like you did the other day? Maybe something I can record…it'll, er, be good publicity if it's a hit."

Danny and Harry looked at each other, their expressions letting on that they didn't like the idea. "But hey, if you can't do anything – maybe I could give you something of mine," went on Marlon. "How about…"

He started to sing one of his old TV numbers, and after a moment Danny felt he had to interrupt. "Well, it started horrendously – then slowly began to get worse," he commented, loudly. "Perhaps you should have used a Hammerstein line – 'The corn is as high as an elephant's arse'!"

Marlon scowled, but didn't let it deter him. He continued being stroppy, and a couple of days later he again started insisting that a special song should be written for him in his own well-known TV style – out of keeping with the character of the show. Matty agreed, and said that cashing in on Marlon's TV celebrity would be good for business. This time, though, the two writers insisted they would not compromise the show – both Danny (in particular) and Harry refusing to produce anything new.

Over the next couple of days things got quite nasty, and Aaron was eventually called in as an arbitrator. He listened to everyone, and eventually agreed with the writers. Marlon was not to be given an out-of-character song.

Marlon was furious, and walked out in a huff. The next thing anyone knew, his agent had contacted Aaron to say he was pulling out of the show altogether. Aaron straight away got in touch with his solicitor, but there was nothing he could really do. "Good riddance," summed up Danny.

It was not quite so simple, though, and the next day Aaron got a call from firm of solicitors saying DuVal was claiming a legal get-out loophole involving Marlon in its contract and was also planning to pull the plug on its financing. It turned out that from the start Marlon had been currying favour with the DuVal people, who had backed him after attending some of the auditions and felt that their best chance of getting a return on their investment was to give him the full star treatment. When rehearsals started, he had persuaded them that as the 'big star' he should have the extra songs he felt he deserved.

A shocked Aaron told Matty and the two writers about it. "The mongrel," said Harry. For once, Danny was more practical and suggested going back to Toni Benito.

Toni's album and the single of 'Cold Streets' had both hit the million sales mark in Britain and was by now taking America by storm, and he was possibly the biggest singer of his kind in Britain. Despite his rapidly growing fame he had stayed friendly with the two still-unknown writers, and when Harry contacted him, he said he was still interested in taking part in a musical.

Toni's touring pop show had seen him develop as a dancer as well, so Aaron agreed to take him on, and while a formal contract was being drawn up for him Toni went to his recording and music publishing companies and got their offers of financial support. They already knew of the success of Harry and Danny's songs, which was a help, and after getting a promise that they would have first rights to all the songs from the show (especially Toni's) they agreed to underwrite all the DuVal promises on funding, guaranteeing the entire cost of the show.

It was only a matter of days after he signed on as a substitute for Dyson that the replacement financing – several hundreds of thousands of pounds – was in place.

Because of Toni's good looks and popularity with women, Aaron now agreed to put back the romantic interest Marlon had insisted be chopped out, and Danny re-wrote the script overnight to include one of the nurses in the home as his former partner and lover.

Despite the quick re-writing, Toni was not available for a few weeks, so the rehearsal time was extended – and a new opening date provisionally arranged for the end of June or beginning of July. Meanwhile, the other rehearsals went on and the crew began working on their final plans. Aaron was bombarded with plans of sets, costings, lighting patterns and the like.

Because there were now virtually two shows – one in the home and the other 'on stage' – Matty got down to deep discussions that gave Andy Mallett, his second director, responsibility for the straight scenes, saying it would leave him free to concentrate on the musical side.

It would call for perfect timing between the two – for instance, in one scene Danny had a group of dancers swaying off stage and stopping in a frozen frieze with arms and legs positioned in mid-dance as the revolving stage started to turn, to be replaced by their older characters positioned in the same way ready to move and then walking on in a similar line from the opposite side.

Andy was delighted with the extra responsibilities, but he had just been promoted from his former stage manager position and insisted on a title. After a long meeting that held up rehearsals, Aaron diplomatically decided to call Matty the dance and music director and Ken the drama director.

"Time wasting," said Danny, and Aaron agreed.

Soon after, Matty – in an attempt to maintain his authority – decided to change the name of show from 'The Age Of Romance' to 'Ages Of Romance'.

It was all time consuming and unnecessary, but Aaron cautioned Danny and Harry to bear with it because of the people concerned – he had to play to what he called their 'artistic egos'.

Because of the delicate state the rehearsals had reached before Marlon's departure, Aaron decided he had better stay closer to the rehearsals and set up an 'office' in a corner of the room. And with other things also hotting up, he also abandoned his original plan to do his own public relations and brought in a man called Austin Irving from the office next to his own in Shaftesbury Avenue.

Austin, a well-dressed young-looking man in his early forties, immediately got to work on his mobile phone, standing next to Aaron's desk in the rehearsal room as he contacted his friends in the press and TV. He chatted to the cast and crew easily, and soon figured out who he should promote and who could be ignored.

It all filled time until Toni came in, however, but when the singer did arrive things settled down again and the artistic side took over once more. Toni slotted in seamlessly, his good humour and cheerful nature pleasing everyone. Matty did try and put him down a bit over his inexperience in what he called 'real theatrical work', and would often make a point to him unnecessarily loud and in front of everyone else.

"Always play to the gallery – don't just sing to the stage struck teeny-boppers standing as close to you as they can get," he shouted out one day. "Otherwise, it's just the front ten rows of the stalls that get to hear the words…" Toni smiled and got on with things.

It was decided that Toni needed a song he could sing with the nurse in the home. *'It's Time To Say Goodbye'*, the tune Harry had idly knocked out in an earlier rehearsal was resurrected, and Danny stood by the piano – its top removed, and the insides exposed so you could see the keys hitting the wires – and re-wrote the lyrics to fit. Within half an hour or so, the 'hangover' (the name usually given to a song previously written and moved into a new show) was re-named *'Now We Can Say Hello Again'*.

Rehearsals continued well, and both Harry and Danny were surprised as the show, due to be seen within the limitations of a stage, slowly came alive in the vast rehearsal room, without sets, proper lighting or sound equipment. The actors had to work out their moves with tables, chairs and other props simply marked out by chalk lines on the floor. Despite that, with bits of acts and scenes being tried out in various corners, it slowly began to take shape.

The amount of hard work was amazing. In some ways it was almost like a Hollywood film of a Broadway show – the girls in leotards and tights, many with thick woollen socks around their ankles, the boys in tights with body-hugging lycra tops. The room was littered with coffee cups filled with cold, stale, undrunk liquid, there were paper plates, uneaten sandwiches and the debris of the hurried take-away meals delivered far too early to be eaten and left to stand around.

It was utterly enthralling for both Danny and Harry, and every day they both enjoyed the experience of seeing 'their show' take shape. In particular, Harry enjoyed technical talk with Mario and the musicians, while Danny liked chatting up the show girls.

Occasionally the writer would wander over to the other musicians. "…I felt a Diminished Fifth in the twelfth bar…" Danny would listen for a moment. Technical stuff! Boring!!! He would turn away and go back to the girls.

They would watch entranced as Eddie Martin stood in one corner of the rehearsal room, taking a group of dancers through a routine. They heard the sound of their tap steps echoing around the room – *rat-a-tat-a, rat-a-tat-a'*.

Opposite, some singers rehearsed their numbers to Mario's piano. *Rat-a-tat-a, rat-a-tat-a.*

Other dancers limbered up in another corner waiting their turn. *Rat-a-tat-a, rat-a-tat-a.* "Give me some action," cried Matty.

The opening chorus lines were rehearsing over on the left. They could hear the Dance Captain, the head girl, calling out the steps as the girls kicked…two left, two right, two left, two right, one left, one right…two…

A comedian was going through his old-time stand-up routine… "My parents were in the iron and steel business – mother ironed and father stole!"

"Why not try the other old one?" asked Danny. "'Dad's in a mental hospital, mum a sanatorium, and sister Jane has epilepsy and thinks she's a washing machine. But brother Bill is at Oxford…in a jar!'"

Danny and Harry were spellbound as the dancers ended their individual bits – then carried on in the far reaches of the rehearsal room, repeating their series of bumps, grinds, hulas and cooch dancing as they waited for their next turn to audition.

Rat-a-tat-a, rat-a-tat-a. The sheer energy of the dancers amazed Danny and Harry.

The singers were given new lead sheets virtually every day, and sometimes had to rehearse them with the dancers. They came in from their own rehearsal room to join in the hubbub. It was noisy, confused, chaotic – but slowly the various scenes started to come together.

Harry often subbed for Mario as the rehearsal pianist, and Danny was frequently asked for new script re-write lines as well. While watching everything that was going on in a bewildered world of wonderment, they both adjusted, amended, re-wrote scores, interpolated numbers and underscored a theme for the general switch-over music between the home and the stage. There was a lot to keep them busy, and during the early rehearsals after Toni had come in they also became deeply involved in re-writing songs and lyrics to fit in with either the story line, the changing characters or simply for reasons of practicality. Then Andy Mallett decided he didn't like the link music behind the home and the stage scenes, and asked for a lively, recognisable, 24-bar establishing number that would always be played during the revolve switching between the two.

Luckily, both Harry and Danny were willing workhorses and apart from their natural enthusiasm for the show got on well with Aaron and Mario. Once, after they had re-worked an old song from their early days and given it some new lyrics that fitted in better with the show, and while Harry was busy orchestrating the various band parts, Danny chatted to Mario. "Funny how the new lyrics seem to have given it a new life," said Danny.

"It's always like that," replied Mario. "I remember a story about Irving Berlin – 'e wrote a tune called, believe it or not, *'Smile And Show Your Dimple'*. It just didn't catch on, so – well, when 'e wanted another song years later 'e only re-wrote the lyric…"

"And?" asked Danny.

"It was just *'Easter Parade'*, that's all," laughed Mario.

Rehearsals were starting to pull everything together again. They were all meeting up more and more in just the one rehearsal room, and Matty was able to put various complete scenes together, although without a revolve it was obvious he could not get a complete run through. It had got to the stage where everything that could be done had been done, and it was just a case of waiting for the theatre to become available.

Mario had been busy organising his orchestra, and most of the musicians had been signed up and were due to join the company about a month before opening night. He had selected a brass section with five trumpets, five trombones, and five saxophones; four clarinets; a string section with eight violins, four cellos and a double bass; a piano – another could be used on stage if required – a harp for one particular number that was planned, and drums.

Danny and Harry went along for the first gathering of the orchestra in a room near the Globe theatre in south London, and as the musicians began to assemble they both recognised several of them from old sessions at Satch's. They chatted to the musicians as they tuned up, and as a double bassist arrived and began taking the bulky instrument out of its case Danny stood with Mario and wondered why anyone would want to play anything that big.

"Fancy having to lug one of those around," he wondered. Then pulling a pen from his pocket, he told the conductor: "This is all I've ever needed – it doesn't weigh anywhere near as much and it's easier to take on the train." Mario nodded. "If you think about it, I don't really need to have it with me all the time either," added Danny.

Later Harry joined in a conversation with one of the old Satch's gang. Somehow the subject of Harry's childhood in Sydney came up.

"Funny, I never realised before that you were an Oz," said the musician. "You don't sound like an Australian."

"That's 'cause he always tried to speak like an Englishman – thinks it'll make him a gentleman," said Danny, happy in a familiar environment. "But, y'know, you're right. I don't think I've ever heard him speak Strine either."

"Strine?"

"Yep, Australian slang."

Harry butted in. "D'you mind, mates? It's me you're talking about," he said. "Thing is, it was something I was never allowed to do at home. My parents were always over-strict – I think they thought they were posher than they were. They'd never allow that sort of slang – I always had to be careful of what I said, especially if we had people call round."

Mario called the bandsman over, and Danny put an arm round Harry's shoulder. "I always knew there was something unnatural about you," he joked. "Never realised it was because you didn't speak properly – no wonder you always needed my words......"

They wandered over to join the orchestra. Mario had seated them, and had handed out band parts for them to look over. Now they were to play together for the first time – sight reading the overture of the show. Danny and Harry listened in raptures as their music was finally played by a full theatre orchestra for the first time.

The arrangements were fine, and the musicians played professionally and with instant understanding of the harmonies. Mario wanted a full run-through of all the show's music, and from the first bars things went well considering the bandsmen had never seen or heard the songs before.

They played the songs without words, and when they got to Toni's big romantic number they quickly picked up the right mood and feel. There was a single violin swaying, with a persistent deep drum beat below it, and it captured the essence completely. Danny and Harry were both entranced, and although it was their own melody caught the emotion without knowing why. Then suddenly the full panorama of the orchestra exploded – the violinists bouncing their bows insistently on their strings, the brass blaring out, the percussionist drumming under it insistently.

It was far, far better than hearing a church choir – or even hearing a recording studio's session musicians' playing their version.

Discussions continued all the time as Matty, Eddie Martin, Danny, Harry and Aaron came up with suggestions. Sometimes they improved things – other times they were tried and didn't work.

Mostly they all agreed, but there was one time when they didn't. Matty had got the singers going through a series of routines with microphones strapped round their heads, and Danny, who had been watching some dancers – lasciviously – left the leering to go to him. He was vehement in his demand that he didn't want anyone singing HIS lyrics with any artificial aid, and said he wanted the actors and singers to be able to project their voices, to use their own abilities to carry a simple harmony with the right tones. "They must have the right theatrical technique," he insisted. "I won't have 'em miked up."

Harry had joined them, and agreed. "Technology is now running things completely," he said. "We're back to the old days of Marlon – he needed 'foldback' to make himself heard. If you go along that route, you'll soon have whole musicals done by talentless people who can't sing miming away to electronics like disc stars."

"Surely that's the way they do it in the movies," replied Matty.

"Maybe," said Danny. "And I know we're trying to get an old cinema effect here – but this isn't a film. This is theatre – the singers should be able to do things properly. We want a big orchestra, real voices, music and lyrics you can hear."

Eventually, they called Aaron over again as arbiter, and he agreed with the writers. Microphones were banished.

A few days later, Danny was busy, happily, relating the story to a show girl called Bettye while Harry and the Mario were trying to re-organise an arrangement of one of the songs. They were standing fairly close, and were having trouble with one of the sections – a trumpet solo. After they had been at it for about ten minutes, Danny looked over to them.

"Try it with a bugle instead, like the Boy's Brigade. That should do it," he joked. Bettye laughed, but the other two men stopped to think about it. "Yeah, I think that's it mate," said Harry.

Generally, though, things were moving along nicely, and – to Danny and Harry's minds – at a quite alarmingly quick rate. It did mean, however, that they now had more time to study the things that were going on. Danny took full advantage, and spent quite a lot of time chatting to the girls.

He would spend most afternoons watching the dancers warming up – performing their individual plies, practising their turned out and turned in positions, side bends and contractions. He enjoyed seeing the girls go through their floor exercises, sometimes doing impossible splits or bending double, lifting and lowering shoulders while holding the head and torso as still as possible. He often laughed out loud as they wiggled their hips back and forth and up and down, lifting up on tiptoes.

One dancer in particular always attracted him. She invariably wore a see-through white blouse with a black athlete's bra under it, and her skimpy white skirt was held in place with an old school tie round her waist. Danny found it fascinating, but the girl wouldn't talk to him.

He watched with interest as Eddie Martin put the chorus line through its paces. "*Turn, turn, toe down, back step, brush, brush.*" Eddie would check things against a stopwatch he wore on a silver chain round his neck, timing the steps, kicks, backbends, measuring how long it took the line to turn, counting seconds for a ballet combination. "I don't expect you to get it perfect from the start – I just want to see that you know what I'm talking about," he called over and over. In reality, at the beginning he wanted to see how fast they could take in details of new dance steps.

"*…five, six, seven, eight…shake one shoulder, now the other…head to the left, head to the right…pivot and move back…now straighten the torso, keep the pelvis going.*" A quick clap of his hands would stop the dance and the music. Then he'd called for a new rhythm from Mario, playing the upright piano in a far corner…

Eddie was continually talking to the dancers in the strange choreographic slang of their own. "It needs to be danced in 4/4 tempo," he'd say. "*Left foot in, count one, drag right foot in air behind it to left oblique and slap your right heel.*"

It was meaningless to all but the dancers, but they responded to the coaxing tones of the choreographer and produced the routines he wanted. *"Right foot to back, small step on and left foot to front. Face the front on a count of four. Then repeat all."*

At various times the dancers would perform whole series of different steps – jigs, toe and heels, cakewalks, buck and wings – a solo tap dance with springs, leg flings and heel clicks, the buck being a stamp of the foot and the wing being simple hop with one foot flung out to the side. They would perform kicks, jumps, and turns, pumps, bumps, grinds, drags, camels, flicks, shimmies and crossovers. They rehearsed so hard that sometimes one or two of them rested with bleeding feet.

"You can't teach someone to dance – they have to feel it for themselves," insisted Eddie.

The magic was there day by day as Danny and Harry tried to take it all in. By now, the writing was more or less set – it was pretty static, as much had been re-written and only minor modifications were needed in dialogue or lyrics. Most of the changes were for the six, extravagant production numbers featuring banks of chorus, individual dancers and singers, either Danny or Harry having to shorten or lengthen a song to fit in exactly to Eddie Martin's routines, or else re-writing lyrics or changing things to fit a particular voice. Occasionally, minor alterations still needed to be made to the book to fit in with a particular characteristic someone, often the actor, wanted to put in.

It got to the stage where Matty called a slow-down to rehearsals so the cast wouldn't get stale. Rehearsals were limited to mornings only, but all that meant was that because they had more time to fill, Matty insisted that Danny and Harry now write in 'proper' show language when adjustments were needed, although he had accepted their work exactly as they presented it before.

"You've got to write in the stage markings," he insisted. "Use the directions – from front, the footlights and the curtain line, and up-stage at the back." Although he was making his own decisions, he wanted the writers to actually script the dancers' entrance points – first, second, third or upper parts of the stage, and the actors' positions marked as front, right oblique, right, right oblique back, back, left oblique back, left and left oblique.

Although Danny and Harry had heard the words before, neither really understood them – although Danny professed that he did. Luckily, Eddie Martin understood their reticence in telling Matty, and explained what was wanted in simple language when the writers needed to know something for a change in a particular number.

And so the rehearsals and final re-writes went on. And on.

As they did so, Aaron became busier than ever looking at the various designs brought in by the set and dress designers almost daily as they started to prepare the costumes themselves and got things ready for the builders, who needed to know the final requirements for the sets. They rustled bits of papers, cards with sketches on, and Matty got annoyed at the continual noise and disruption from Aaron's corner of the rehearsal room as they did so. He argued with Aaron, and a bad aura began to creep back among the cast.

By now, Danny had read up about all the stage phrases and had diligently begun re-writing the book with the correct stage directions in mind. Now he knew all about the technical terms of 'stage right or left', 'downstage', and the historic 'cyc' – the cyclorama – he was able to make it look far more professional, and these days he could think in terms of actors 'doing the scene in one right' – working at the front of the stage on the right hand side – although he still had trouble understanding what Matty meant when he insisted that he 'write for scenery'. Harry and Aaron noted the changes, and although the original had been right enough, they let him get on with it because it made him feel good.

There were still a few re-writes to fit the actors and singers – and Matty and Aaron's sudden quirks – but most times these were soon put back into their original shape. Danny began to get bored with the constant unnecessary alterations, and reckoned he had already done his bit – although he was always available to whip off new lyrics as and when they were really required and for the reprises.

He spent most of his time looking and chatting with the chorus girls. Sometimes, too, he got involved and sat in with Matty and Harry when one of the smaller members of the cast had to drop out and extra auditions were needed as a replacement.

It was during one of those auditions that Matty blew his top. "What's this terrible caterwauling I can hear?" he asked as he listened to yet another aspiring nobody. "Is it a bird? Is it a dog caught up in a mousetrap? Is it just a load of rubbish? No wonder we win 'nul-points' in the Eurovision Song Contest…although you've got to say that's at least better than the minus points we deserve.

"Why do you people these days sing unnaturally. Why does 'morning' always come out like 'maw-awning' – and why do people end every line with 'wo-oh-oh'? They whine, they don't sing. Listen to Sinatra, Fitzgerald, Garland…now THEY sing and you hear and feel every word. But today, all you hear is a nasal…well, something coming through the nose. It's terrible. It's not singing."

The young singer looked suddenly afraid, and Danny walked over to him. "Look son, don't take too much notice," he said softly, although he was barely older than the singer. "It's just not the style we're looking for."

"Go on – get out," said Matty brusquely to the young vocalist.

Harry went over to Danny. "Calm down, mate," he said rather sadly, and took his irritated partner out of the room to go for a quiet drink at the pub next door. "The trouble is, I agree with Matty," said Danny as they went through the bar door. "It's discourteous to us writers – not only messing about with the words, but distorting the song to cover their own inadequacies."

"You always say that," replied Harry.

Danny calmed down. "Yeah, maybe. There are plenty of bad singers – but no matter how bad they sing, they just can't ruin a good song," he said.

The atmosphere at rehearsals was still deteriorating, because for some reason or other Matty was being even more objectionable than ever. Toni and the other leads just got on with things, but some of the senior members of the crew and several of the dancers were finding it hard going. Danny and Harry, too, often became the butt of Matty's moods mainly through their lack of theatrical experience – it was, as Aaron told them, a case of 'Marlon déjà vu again'.

After one particularly bad outburst, Matty dismissed the cast and stormed off early, leaving Mario to put the orchestra through a full run-through of some of the songs. When it was over, Danny stayed behind drinking tepid coffee with Mario and some of the orchestra. "'e's comin' it a bit ping pong these days," said Mario. "Bloody poof."

To try and relieve things, one of the orchestra sideman, a trumpeter, offered to take Danny to a new jazz club, and Danny called Harry's mobile to get him back to the rehearsal room. When he arrived, they went off to the club.

It was on the South Bank, and it looked just like Satch's in the early days. It was dark, with coloured strobe lights flashing on and off in every direction, and as the evening wore on it became very hot and sweaty. The three of them had a few drinks, listening casually as a group of young musicians played off the cuff before Harry and the trumpeter eventually joined in a few sets – swinging with the rest of them and spending several hours jamming it up. Danny carried on drinking alone, and was quite drunk when Harry and the bandsman called it a day. They finally pulled out at around three in the morning.

The two writers had a great time, relaxing completely after all their hard work. And Harry was so impressed that next day he got to the rehearsal room early and began working on a new introduction to the second act that included a lot of cadenzas designed to show off the individual solo talents of the orchestra. Mario realised what had happened and was delighted.

He had the same feelings for his bandsmen, and soon he got back into the usual chat with Danny about 'the good old days', both of them throwing out stories they had heard over the years. After a while, Harry came back into the room and listened to them, sitting quietly by their side as they spoke.

"…then of course, there was that old Gershwin show, 'Girl Crazy'," Mario was saying. "You'll never believe who was in the orchestra…"

"No. Who?" Danny was deeply involved and didn't notice Harry.

"Well, it was a Red Nicols combo," went on Mario. "The geezer played himself, of course – along with……wait for it…Benny Goodman, Jimmy and Tommy Dorsey, Gene Krupa, Jack Teagarden, Glenn Miller and Harry James."

"What, all together in the pit?"

"Yep, amazin' isn't it."

"I'll say. Amazing," said Danny. He reflected for a moment. "But it was a small world in those days. I mean, my favourite story is about Ira Gershwin going to school with Yip Harburg – and then brother George going to high school with Howard Dietz and being pals with Larry Hart and Oscar Hammerstein at college at the same time. Yeah – it really was a small world, eh…"

Harry spoke up – Danny turning with surprise at his voice. "Y'know, I can't really imagine that," he said. "Just think, mate – all of them sitting side by side. What must the English teacher have thought?"

They all laughed, then carried on talking about the 'elegance and tradition' of those old songsters before saying their farewells and going home. "You only seem to get it with the Last Night of the Proms these days," summed up Mario.

"Now that's a night," added Danny. "And that song they end with, '*Land of Hope And Crosby*' – my God, I wish I could write a hit like that."

By now, Aaron was starting to get letters from B-list celebrities touting for seats at the opening night, and as the spring weather began to cool sales of tickets to the public started to grow in noticeable numbers. Danny was chatting to one of the singers when Aaron called everyone together to tell them of his latest, revised plans for the opening.

Danny noticed that he has missed a small tuft on the side of his chin when he shaved that morning, and couldn't take his eyes off it. But the message came through – the pre-opening tour has already been cancelled to save costs, and Aaron now said that instead of having a whole series of previews there would be just one big final public dress rehearsal for an invited audience of critics, friends and celebrities on the night before the opening.

"The wrecking crew," he described them.

The news gave Austin the chance to press for a big press photo call, which went ahead a week before the dress rehearsal.

It took place in front of the theatre, and Austen had managed to get an area roped off so those involved were free of traffic. Despite that, the snappers insisted on moving into the centre of the road to get the dance girls – many in scanty, glitzy costumes – and the theatre in shot. When an irascible traffic warden (prodded on by Austen himself) tried to shoo them all back onto the pavement, there was a bit of a kerfuffle, and more pictures were taken – many of which won the show a couple of extra lines on the front pages of the next day's tabloids.

The whole cast and many of the backers turned up, and as things went on Austin unashamedly handed out free gifts to the press people that included tickets for two to the final run-through. Everything went well. Austin did his job superbly, much to the relief of Aaron and Danny, as an ex-PR man himself.

When the formal part of the call was over, the reporters got busy. Some rang their offices from their mobiles, others sat in corners tapping into their laptops – one even using the kerb edge as his 'office'. Eventually, all of them moved inside the theatre foyer – the photographers flirting with the showgirls and the reporters simply getting at the free drinks and nibbles.

On a whim, Danny had invited Greta Faulks and Joe Gibbon along because, as he explained, she was the one who had originally inspired the show. Greta had said she didn't want to take anything away from the main purpose of the call, so she waited until the main business was over before turning up with the pianist. When they did arrive, Danny was a bit concerned that her appearance might take the limelight away from Toni and Julia Ross, but he needn't have worried because few of the young journalists remembered her.

Greta, in any case, was very good about it all. She listened as the cast sang some of the songs from the show – loving it, in particular, when Julia Ross took over to sing her big love song to Toni, slow, haunting, romantic, a bit moody even without the banks of strings that would be behind her in the show. "It sounds great," said Greta, leading the applause when it was over. Later, she told Danny that she saw Julia as a much younger version of herself.

Mario was playing the piano, and Danny was once more making up his instant rhymes:

> 'My heart's a-quiver,
> Over a quaver.
> But I never shiver.
> I'm a real old raver,
> And I'd run hither-and-thither,
> If you'd do me a favour.
> And lo...ove me...ee.'

Then as the evening wore on, Danny persuaded Greta and Joe to join him at the piano singing some of their old hits. Harry listened, and it soon became clear to him how Danny's previous meeting with the singer had formed the original idea for the show.

Greta's presence helped the evening turn into a big party, with Mario eventually leading a small section of the orchestra not only playing the songs from the show but all the old favourites – Rodgers and Hart, Porter, Irving Berlin, Rodgers and Hammerstein.

As they played, Danny was back to his old self, laughing, cracking corny jokes, ad-libbing stupid lyrics, the life-and-soul. Harry could hear him over the noise – "The Third Man, that was Orson Kart wasn't it?" and "You've got acute appendicitis – and the rest of you ain't so bad either."

Although Danny was getting drunker by the minute, Harry let him get on with it – the party seemed to be his partner's natural environment, and it just made him realise how dedicated Danny had become since selling their first song, and especially since starting work on the show. Danny's voice boomed out as Harry left for home.

Next morning Danny was back to his sober, professional, modern self. Thinking back to the night before, he, too, realised how much more committed he had become. Sub-consciously, like Harry, he realised that show writing was the only place to be – and that it was worth making sacrifices to be there.

And so rehearsals began to move into their final stages.

Act 13: Rehearsals End

With the decision made to cancel a pre-West End tour to save money, the team was now building up to one single final dress rehearsal for an invited audience of friends and critics the day before the opening night itself.

And with just three weeks to go, they were able to move into the theatre itself for the final rehearsals.

The move was planned for a Tuesday morning – and the day before, everyone was given an extra day off. Toni and Julia Ross were both caught up with a series of press and TV interviews, mostly based around the idea of a possible real-life romance between the two – a notion floated by Austin Irving, and not too far off reality.

For Aaron, though, there was still work to do, and he invited Danny and Harry to join him for a look round the newly redecorated theatre. It was another new experience for both.

Backstage hadn't been used for a while, and although decorators had been in to clean up the front of house, there was the usual musty smell of a 'dark' theatre – a bare stage, an open proscenium arch looking out on a forlorn auditorium – a palace whose transient beauty needed the buzz of human impact to fuel it into life.

The footlights were dusty, and the apron stage, too, was in need of a good sweep. With the curtain up and no stage lights or front-of-house lighting, there was just one solitary naked pilot light – the Ghost Light – glowing on a stand on stage because of theatrical superstition. Although there was a long line of unlit footlights and banks of other lighting on hinged stands, the theatre was dark and cavernous, the shelves – the dress circle and upper tiers – forlorn. The single bulb on stage did, indeed, make it a ghostly looking place.

Backstage, there was a tangle of ropes, wires, cables, props – quite different to the view from front of house. A huge electrical switchboard was off to one side of the wings, and behind that again were the fly loft and scenery dock. A tatty dirty green temporary backcloth hung at the rear, although that would obviously be replaced by the show's own backdrop when it was completed.

At the back of the stage, too, Danny and Harry saw the racks holding the fly system – large poles on which the various larger bits of painted scenery and pieces of set would hang, all the ropes controlling them numbered so the right one could be raised or lowered into place at the right time. There were more than forty in all.

Neither of the writers said a word as they looked around them, taking in the maze of footlights and battens, the spots and floats and the lighting board bristling with switches from which detailed lighting plots had to be carefully followed to get the required stage effects.

To the side, as well, there were more banks of amplifiers and the like, and tucked away at the sides the scene docks and props room.

The three men looked at it all, then went back on stage to look over the front into the orchestra pit – enclosed, but with a few now-blank TV screens so the musicians themselves would be able to see what was happening on the stage. The conductor, standing in front of them facing the actors, had his own monitor to see the audience and anyone else who might need to send him signals from front of house.

Those signals would probably come from someone in the control room behind the last row of the stalls, inside which there were banks of racking and dimmers for the stage lighting, and a wide sound desk to help control music levels and any other noises that may be required. During performances, controllers would sit there watching things through a wide glass panel running almost the width of the theatre.

"It's awe-inspiring," said Aaron, slightly subdued although he had seen it dozens of times before. It turned out he didn't really need to be there, he had no business to carry out, but he wanted to show Danny and Harry what it was like – he wanted them to experience the same tingling feel an empty theatre always gave him.

As they stood in the eerie half-light, Danny could almost feel the hundreds of characters who had been brought to life on that stage. But that, said Aaron, was just part of the fairylike air of mystery created around the theatrical world.

"Every theatre claims its own ghosts," he explained. "That's why we leave the Ghost Light on, on stage. It's to stop the ghosts from rehearsing!"

"Ghosts?" Harry looked interested.

"Oh yes," continued Aaron. "You could have the mysterious 'Grey Lady', she's a favourite – or it could be an actor searching for his loved one." He laughed. "As a producer, I have to know all the superstitions.

"There's a lot of others – you'll probably hear the cattle asking me about them…" He mimicked a high voice… "…'what time does the ghost walk?'" He laughed again. "The ghost walk? It's what they always ask when they want to know when pay day is."

It was Harry who again asked the question. "But why not just ask it?"

"Well," said Aaron, "there's a practical reason. You see, in the old days – perhaps back to Willy Shakespeare himself – actors didn't want outsiders knowing they might have money backstage. It would be left unattended while they performed, so they used a code word only they knew, to establish the time of the pay call. 'What time does the ghost walk?'"

He led them on a further exploration of the backstage area. Their footsteps echoed on the bare boards of the stage as they crossed to some steps off-stage, steps up and down leading away from what would be the hustle and bustle of the stage area during a performance.

They went down first of all to see the dressing rooms, varying in size from the large, almost plush, rooms for the stars to the two communal rooms for the 'also rans' of the chorus and choir.

Then it was up again, and to the area high above the stage. A gallery faced on to the various racks and backdrop hangings, with hefty counterweights dropping down out of sight, and Aaron led the way across a walkway bridging one side to the other out of view by the audience.

On the far side, there was an administrative area with a couple of offices, unnaturally tidy as the theatre had not been in use for some time, and there was the green room – the actors' rest room – and some more small dressing rooms.

There was a fair-sized rehearsal room, with a new-looking sprung wood floor to help the dancers and with the inevitable barre bars and mirrors lining three walls. A few chairs were littered around.

But it was back on stage that the 'glamour' hit home. Both Danny and Harry felt at ease there – suddenly their hopes were being realised. This was truly their theatre of dreams.

Next day was more of a dream. The cast and crew moved in, and this time it was the actors' footsteps that echoed on the bare boards as they made their entrances. As each new member of the cast arrived, everyone else turned to look round at them. Most of them were nervous, but with stage hands and various set-building technicians running around there was an air of restless tension in the air.

The dancers, the chorus girls, arrived first, immediately making themselves at home in their communal dressing rooms and laying out their basic make-up paraphernalia, their Leichner sticks – the light ivory coloured No 5, the brick ref No 9 and the like. The put down their pancake bases, creams and other grease sticks alongside their face paints, sponges, brushes, and cleansing lotions, cold creams and make-up remover oils.

Some of the girls had brand new make-up sticks for use on opening night – for fear of falling foul of the ancient 'tradition' whereby you could get revenge on an enemy by leaving a half-used stick with a needle stuck in the centre that he (or she) might steal then rip their face to pieces. The experienced girls, while refusing to admit to the dozens of old theatrical superstitions like that, usually refused to unpack their make-up kit until the first night was over for fear of putting a hoodoo on a long run, leaving it all in old cigar boxes to show they were not newcomers – not amateurs, the worst insult that could be paid to anyone in the professional theatre.

Soon after, Toni Benito, Julia Ross and the other principals turned up, making their way to their allotted solo dressing rooms and putting out their personal dressing gowns, lucky charms and toys. Strangely, Julia also gave credence to the old superstitions, and she bought in two bars of soap knowing that some people claimed that if you leave your soap in the dressing room you will return to the theatre, although others declared that you should take it away with you if you want those good notices and a return engagement.

"If I have two bars, I can't go wrong," she smiled. "I'll take one away and leave the other when the show is over!" Toni, as a comparative newcomer to the theatre, didn't bother with any of the hoodoo ideas.

It was stage manager Robbie Cadell, who was busy organising things, who summed it up. "Gypsies and hoofers are goofy people," he told everyone as he watched the various strange rigmaroles being carried out by the actors and dancers as they installed themselves.

Robbie had installed a desk far over to one side of the stage, with a single dim light – yesterday's ghost light – shining down on it so he could call out any instructions from Matty or Aaron. He had a headset and microphones leading to the various dressing rooms and technicians, and would be sitting there during shows calling the cues as required.

Slowly the rehearsals started up again, but now there was a different feel to them. The show was no longer being tried out bit by bit in a gloomy rehearsal room – strangely, considering it was all make-believe, there was more of an air of reality about it. At last the optimism of the early rehearsals had the added excitement of the actors at getting onto a (bare) stage at last. And now, they at least had the advantage of having some real props to rehearse with.

Things were still being done a little at a time without scenery, but as the actors, dancers and singers went through their various routines yet again it was on a stage – and instead of being stuck in the middle of them, Matty, Danny and Harry and other leading members of the crew sat in the gloomy theatre, watching from seats half way back in the stalls. In essence the scenes were being performed to audience – an audience remote from the action.

Quite often, however, Eddie Martin would climb onto the stage to sit with Robbie and his harried assistant to be closer to the action while the dancers were doing their thing. "Come on," he'd urge, "You're dancing as if this was a telly commercial – this is gymnastics, not dancing…"

Often he would gather the whole troupe together centre stage while he demonstrated a new move, a new way of doing things. Often he would literally 'dance' with himself, playing both boy and girl parts to a background of muted trumpets or swaying violins.

But everyone quickly settled down to the new way of things – they were, after all, professionals. But now, watching from a distance, Danny and Harry could see better how things were shaping up, and they could see that there were still gaps in the story, parts that needed speeding up, or explaining, or cutting. With a stage, it became more apparent that too often, intricate scenes or dance sequences would have to be abandoned or songs added or removed.

They realised there was still work to do – and there were other occasions such as when the comedian asked if he could be given more time for his usual stand-up routine, and when a lower-ranked singer said he felt there was room (and a need) for his baritone solo. With the show starting to take its final shape, Aaron was proving invaluable – giving Harry and, especially, Danny good, sound advice on tunes, lyrics and the book.

All the time the scenery and sets were being built and slowly installed, but even though only a few of had been completed and tried out, it became obvious that Danny's original plan for 'imagined' scenery didn't really work. The idea of letting the audience use its imagination to picture the sets would have to be changed.

As a result, one day set designer Anne-Marie Besser approached the two writers with a bundle of plans and sketches, explaining that because she needed to build larger sets and there was limited space due to the central division in the revolve separating the old people's home from the old stage, she and Aaron had decided that a lot of the introductory talk in the home would need re-writing to set the scene.

Anne-Marie explained that she had modified the set plans so that the home would fit into quite a small section, allowing by far the greater part of the stage to be used for some of the elaborate sets they wanted for the big dance routines that were planned, and she also showed how re-writing in a certain way would give time for the scene hands to put up parts of the highly ornate sets outside the revolve.

Instead of the audience's imagination, she explained that Aaron had hit on the idea of using some BP – back projection – which would give even more space and help provide 'the Hollywood look' they wanted. He had spoken to Matty, and the Gaffer – Freddie Excel – was organising the tricky lighting changes that would be needed during most of the moves into and out of the revue numbers, each of which would be a separate scene in itself.

Danny and Harry immediately went to one of the dressing rooms to begin re-writing.

On stage, though, the rehearsals were getting increasingly tense, nervy, and strained. Matty didn't help – in fact, he was largely the cause because he was over demanding, pernickety, and generally letting the tension get to him. Aaron frequently tried calming him down, but got nowhere.

There was an instance where Mario was rehearsing a duet – two men singing in turn, their voices merging in and taking over one from the other – and as they began, Matty shouted an interruption. "Crap," he said. "Try it in tune." Mario looked at the singers and the orchestra and shrugged. "Let's take it from the top," he said calmly, and they proceeded as before.

The next morning, they held another complete run-through using the new scripting Danny and Harry had miraculously provided in double quick time. It was the first time they had tried everything in continuous order on stage, and sitting in the third row of the stalls Danny was amused when he saw one old actor waited his turn in the wings – as soon as his cue arrived, he superstitiously tapped the prompt book gently three times. "It means I won't dry on stage," he explained, almost embarrassed.

Later on in the day, Mario was once more taking the orchestra through its paces. This time, Danny was sitting in the front row of the stalls listening to the music when one of the backstage helpers walked across the stage singing along to one of the songs. He had a deep, pleasant voice, but nobody took much notice until Matty – who was sitting a few rows behind Danny – called the young man back.

"Just what the hell are you doing?" he asked.

"Only…only my job," said the stagehand.

"No – you were singing, that's what you were doing. Singing on my stage…"

"I'm sorry Mr Pederson. I thought it was a band-only rehearsal. I didn't realise…"

"Well you should have. Band-only means band-only – not some nobody singing to himself. I don't want wanna-be singers interrupting. You won't do it again – you're fired."

The young man looked startled, but there was little he could do. He walked, shoulders slumping slightly, off stage again.

Danny was incensed. He jumped up and quickly made his way backstage to find the young man packing a small holdall. "Look…"

"Ben, sir. Ben Welles."

"OK Ben – I'm sorry about that. Matty had no right. I'll talk to Aaron about it," said Danny.

"Thanks." The young man had an American accent that seemed to go with his fresh, young-looking face.

"You've got a nice voice."

"Thanks again. I just wish I could get a chance to use it," said Ben. "I'd give anything to get into show business. All I want to do is sing in a musical, sir. It's my dream."

Danny told him to wait and went back front of house to try and get the sacking rescinded. But Matty stuck his heels in and Ben had to leave the theatre.

There was now a definite clash of personalities during rehearsals. Robbie Cadell, sitting at his desk on stage, tried to keep things calm. But like Aaron, he seemed to have no influence on Matty.

Matty himself was getting increasingly nerve-wracked, the tension getting to him more and more as various members of the cast kept asking for better dressing rooms, pay rises, tickets for their friends, more personal publicity, and the like. "None of that's anything to do with me," he would growl, going off to snap at somebody or something else.

But no matter how Matty reacted to people and the crew reacted to him, the intense concentration of rehearsals pushed everything out of the minds of the seasoned actors – everything else in their lives was thrust to the background.

Yet it was a fact that things had generally started to go wrong. Mistakes were made – accidents began to happen. Someone was hit by a flying prop, pieces of scenery being built fell over in the middle of a big rehearsal, an electrician switched off a light at the wrong time, a chippie started hammering away at the back of the stage as Matty and Eddie Martin tried to arrange a line of girls to a slightly tinny CD amplifier. The dancers ignored the technicians and carried on their dance routine, but Matty again blew his top.

Many of the straight actors and actresses had been tending to mumble their way through the early rehearsals, letting their characters develop slowly as time went on. But from the start, Matty hadn't accepted that from Toni, who seemed, in particular, to be the frequent butt of his vindictiveness. And this time Toni took the full brunt of the director's anger.

"Look, I know you're only a pop singer really – but at least try to be an actor in this show," Matty told him, although the interruptions had been nothing to do with Toni. "At least try and get some emotional response from the scene. Remember, you're supposed to be having an affair with this bimbo –"

Danny jumped in. "The song is meant to be about love – a romance, not a sordid affair," he interjected.

"Whatever," continued Matty, ignoring the writer. "But don't just have your character come in, speak his lines and exit – have him do a bit of business, do something interesting."

"I just follow the script," Toni replied icily. "And the direction......"

It did not appear as if he had been hurt – but he had. And when rehearsals finished for the day he made a point of sitting down with Danny, Harry, Eddie and Mario in the third row of the stalls, just to the right of the aisle. The main stage curtains were drawn, the house lights were down, the flies up and no scenery – but the stage was still lit by a couple of floodlights from the side. It looked a bit weird – stage lighting and bare boards and a brick wall adorned by the clutter of backstage.

The conversation turned, as ever, to light-hearted talk about old-style musicals, elegance, good music, big production numbers. They all loved that.

"In the old days, you'd just have the piano leading the melody, with violins filling in – then the brass sections took over in the Big Bands. The dancing was different – from spectacular production numbers to smoother Astaire and Rogers," Eddie was saying.

"Agreed, it was not quite so spectacular," Mario replied.

"Look, I think we've all been influenced by the old Busby Berkeley musicals," said Harry. "I mean – this is reality, it's not Hollywood, y'know."

"But this show would make a good Hollywood film," interrupted Toni. "You two have virtually written it as a film –"

"Oh yeah," interrupted Danny. "But it's not like the movies, where they don't puff and blow even after a high speed tap routine. You should have realised that by now Toni."

They all laughed, and a bit more of the tension of the day relaxed.

Next day, Toni got a phone call that also helped lighten things up when he passed on its message at rehearsals. His record company, which was largely backing the show, wanted to rush through a single of his duet with Julia Ross – '*I Want The Sun To Set – I Want The Sun To Rise*' – to be released to coincide with the opening night of the show.

"Great news," said Aaron.

"Great publicity," said Austin.

"Great song," said Mario.

Danny and Harry were delighted – although they couldn't help wondering why they hadn't been asked before a decision was taken. But they said nothing, and for a while the mood at rehearsals improved. Things were lighter and more fun again.

A few days later Matty was taking some of the actors through their old people routines, and Danny sat in the stalls again with Eddie, Harry and Mario carelessly watching them. Eddie had a pad on his lap with a pile of notes and some diagrams with lots of squiggles and arrows. Every now and then he redirected an arrow to another position.

"It's called the labanotation system," explained Eddie when Danny asked him what the notes represented. "A way of recording dances using a written system."

Danny looked at the scribbles and tried to make sense of them. "It all looks too complicated," he said. "Can't you just tell 'em what you want?"

"Can't you or Harry just tell a trumpeter what you want?" replied Eddie. "Don't you have to write it down for them? It's the same here…" he turned a page of the pad to show Danny another diagram… "using these notes, I can get the dancers exactly where I want them at any given time – every time."

Harry was about to ask a question, but before he had a chance Matty called a halt to the actors' rehearsal and called for Eddie. The dance director eased himself out of his seat. "Time to get the gypsies back to work," he said as he left to go back on stage.

Mario followed him, going to a piano in a corner of the stage to help with his rehearsal, and after a few moments Harry joined him. Danny stayed where he was – he was comfortable, and he loved eyeing the dancers preparing for their workouts, moving easily from the tedium of hanging around drinking innumerable cups of coffee and eating badly to warming up thoroughly and getting ready to dance.

The dancers, hoofers, were clannish and didn't mix too readily with the straight actors, although they did have a certain affinity with singers and accepted Danny – he made them laugh. They were dedicated to their job, most of them living only to dance – and Danny had often noticed that even when they danced off stage and out of the audience's sight they kept dancing behind the scenes and well into the wings. They loved it: it was their life.

A single spotlight beamed down on Toni, who was running through a number centre stage. Its arc of blinding white light slowly widened from its original pinpoint as Freddie Excell tried different things, his electricians standing on huge ladders reaching almost to the ultra-high roof almost 60 feet above the stage to move lights and baffles. The coloured gelatines on the huge banks of lights to one side began to flash over Toni's face in a rainbow of changing colours.

Rehearsals usually took place with the house lights down – but Matty was out for the day, and Freddie the Gaffer and his crew were taking advantage of his absence by experimenting with their lighting, trying blackout techniques, extinguishing all lights suddenly, dimming out or fading up, with Freddie often calling out loud over Toni's singing voice to ask if he needed to be slow, medium or fast with his lighting moves. The problem was the need for constant need for cross fading between scenes on either side of the revolve.

Toni just ignored it all and carried on with his singing, a couple of girls standing behind him harmonising '*Love, love, love*' over and over to his romantic ballad – bored with the endless repetition.

He was getting used to the turmoil and commotion around him by now, because quite apart from the never-ending lighting experiments most of the bits of set had been delivered from the scenery builders and stagehands were busily working on installed the scenery – building up their scene changes with split-second timing among the daily rehearsals.

Some costumes had been delivered as well, and rehearsals were now being sporadically broken up as costume designer Betsi Walsh and her wardrobe girls handed them out for fittings or for the cast to try the quick changes they would need to make in the wings.

But although it all seemed quite bizarre to Danny and Harry – particularly Harry – everyone else accepted the chaos. They could put up with things such as when the orchestra played one number in the pit while Eddie Martin had a group of dancers on the stage above them going through a routine to another song. The dancers simply ignored the music as Eddie called the timing – "one – two – three – four......five – six – seven – eight," he cajoled as they danced at complete odds to the music and the rhythm of the orchestra.

So rehearsals went on in a pandemonium of confusion. Every day seemed more shambolic than the one before – with Matty at the heart continuing to spread discontent.

It became apparent during a run-through of one scene set in the home that there was a badly sagging section, and Danny and Harry started writing a new song to boost it. As the residents were supposed to be old music hall stars, they came up with a lively jingle called '*I've Never Got Bored With The Boards*'.

As they worked on the new song, Harry realised that when Danny was working under pressure he immediately reverted to his old vague, careless, unaware attitude to life around him. As he scribbled lyrics for 'Bored', he would leave half-filled coffee cups wherever he put them down, would scatter bits of paper to concentrate on the words he had to fit to the music, would ignore almost everything.

The cast – especially the dancers – were untidy like that, but with Danny it was somehow different. He just put himself into a different world, where the song was all important. He had always been like that, but now, working against a deadline, he became more so – the work over-rode everything else. It occurred

241

to Harry, probably for the first time consciously, that his partner's mind simply switched off all the things that were of no consequence for the immediate moment, and that made him seem irresponsible or just plain forgetful. As it had when Ady left him and he wrote 'Cold Streets'!

Matty was being his usual objectionable self. One of the singers had phoned in sick, and the director was cursing and shouting that he was surrounded by amateurs – the worst thing he could have said to the professionals of the cast.

"Don't worry," said Danny, taunting him. "I could pick any unknown to sing that bit for you."

"Oh yeah?" growled Matty. "Go on then."

By chance, earlier that day Danny had spotted Ben Welles, the cleaner who had been sacked a couple of weeks before. He was now working for the theatre itself as an usher, and Danny went to the front of the stage and called out for him.

Ben was in the royal circle tidying up and answered. "Come to the front of the circle and sing us something from the show," called out Danny – and Ben did so, singing one of Toni's songs unaccompanied but magnificently, impressively. When he finished, Aaron and Harry lead the applause from the near-empty auditorium as Danny stepped forward again.

"OK Ben, come down here," he called into the near darkness of the auditorium. "Let's see you…"

Ben made his way down to the stalls and jumped onto the stage just in time to hear Aaron talking. "He's good – good. We've got to find him a small spot in the show," said the producer.

"How about that bit just at the end of Act One?" said Danny, a smile in his eyes.

"Yeah, yeah. End of Act One. Do you want the job kid?"

Danny studied the young usher's face. It was long, with a pointed chin and a small triangle of beard – and his lazy blue eyes were unnaturally wide as he listened to the exchange between the people on stage. When he heard Aaron offering him a part, his whole face took on the look of a young child suddenly given the biggest present he could imagine at Christmas.

Matty was still angrily sullen, though. "Look, we can't just take a kid……"

But Aaron was adamant. He loved the idea. "A new discovery," he said. "An unknown…I've discovered him…"

Austin Irving, the PR man who was in the theatre, saw it as a great 'theatrical rags-to-riches' story and said he would arrange immediate interviews.

"It's his 'and-then' time," muttered Harry.

Danny just smiled, on a high having been proved right although he knew it would only make Matty worse.

And it did, indeed, create a bit of a brouhaha, although Matty's temperamental moods made most of the cast and crew side with Danny. During the rest of the day Matty tried to re-establish his authority, with Harry and Aaron working to smooth things over until rehearsals slowly got back to their normal professional way.

The next day started with one of those dull, nothing, autumnal mornings when the leaves on the trees in the park looked wet and there was a smell as if someone had a smoking bonfire hanging over everything. Danny and Harry made their way to the theatre solemnly to find everyone there feeling utterly miserable. Then rehearsals started, and the music, dancing, singing and general action soon made most people lighten up and feel better. All except Matty.

He was still incensed at the previous day's debacle, which he had seen as a personal slight to his authority. His increasing moodiness had been dividing the whole team for weeks, especially the cast, and where they had all started to integrate, they were now drifting into fragments – dancers, singers, actors. After the previous day's dispute, Matty continued to be argumentative and divisive.

As he worked on stage, he could hear Aaron talking quite loudly to Austin in the front row of the stalls, and it was just another notch in the troubles that were making him so irritable. But it wasn't until a stagehand walked across the stage whistling one of the show's songs that he finally flipped. As the hand disappeared off stage, Matty suddenly stopped talking to the chorus girls and rounded on him with a fury. It was Ben Welles all over again.

"Don't you know it's unlucky to whistle backstage," he shouted. He rushed towards the wings to give the technician a verbal going-over.

"Don't know about that sort of thing, guv," said the hand. "I only do the light and dark side of things. I don't want to know about actors and that lot."

Matty was almost incandescent with rage. "Get this man out of here," he screamed, eyes bulging. "I don't want people around me who don't know the basics of theatrical tradition…"

"What the hell is that all about?" asked Harry.

"Another old superstition," replied Aaron, who had watched without saying a word. "In the old days, a lot of sailors got jobs hoisting the flies – they were used to it with the rigging on their ships and they knew the best knots to hold 'em in place. They used whistles to pass instructions on ship – so anyone whistling could cause one of the sailors to untie a rope and maybe drop something on somebody."

He giggled. "Some actors think whistling in the dressing room brings on bad luck, too," he added. "If anyone does it – well, he has to go outside, turn round three times and knock for re-admittance."

Toni had listened to what was going on, and now he joined Aaron in trying to detract attention away from the fuss. But Matty was not having any of it. "I've had enough," he suddenly shouted, turning away from the stage hand to look down at Aaron in the stalls.

"I quit."

There was a moment of silence. For a about a week Matty had been talking to some favoured members of the cast about his preference for another show he'd been offered that would have given him a lot more money. Most of them thought it was just bravado because he wasn't getting his own way – but now it suddenly seemed a reality.

"OK," said Aaron quietly. "What will you do instead? You do know that other job you've been talking about has been given to someone else?"

Matty didn't know. "Well, I could do the Scottish play at the National. That's been offered, too," he said.

"Yeah," replied Aaron. "You'd make a fortune out of that."

The two men looked at each other for a moment. "Just let me think about it for a while," said Matty, and he turned and walked out.

The theatre was completely silent for a few moments more. Then Mario broke in. "Well, what do you make of that then?" he asked out loud.

"A right pain in the arse," replied Harry – pronouncing it in Mario's own deep Cockney as 'a right pine in the arze'.

"Let's call it a day now and start over tomorrow, eh?" said Aaron. "But first I want a coffee – someone get coffees all round."

Everyone stood around muttering in groups until after a while someone produced the drinks in plastic cups brought in from the café next door, and one of the dancers came up and gave Aaron and the two writers a Danish pastry each. Danny nibbled a corner of his, then put it down on a chair and promptly forgot about it; Harry carefully broke his in half and shared it with Mario; but Aaron wolfed through his voraciously.

"Why did he speak of the Scottish play?" asked Harry.

"Mentioning 'Macbeth' by name – whoops – is supposed to call up the curse of the Scottish Play," Andy Mallett explained. "The only way to break the curse is for the offender to spin on the spot and then spit." He laughed. "It's supposed to be a purification ritual. The spin turns back time, and the spit expels the corrupting poison." He carried out the traditional rite and the mood lightened a little.

Then Martin Eddie piped up. "You know, some of the great choreographers and directors have dreamt up all kinds of funny things for musicals – but I've never heard of any routine like that one," he said. "Maybe we could use it in a dance."

Before Matty's outburst, members of the orchestra had been wandering in and taking their places in the pit ready for their turn. They had sat there while the argument went on, but now, sensing the mood on the stage above him, the drummer's foot began to beat out an insistent death-march throb on his bass drum.

A dancer – one of the girls Danny had noticed in particular, Suzi something – jumped in. "Hey, come on you guys. There's no funeral – put some life into it drummin' man."

Danny started when he heard the last words. The name.

The girl started shaking her body, her brown curly hair bobbing as she spoke, and after a moment and without any notice, she started singing a version of the latest moody song Danny and Harry had written – changing the words slightly to fit the situation…'*I Wish I'd Cuddled My Mother*' became '*I Wish I'd Cuddled Matty*'! As the drummer picked up her rhythm she turned it into a sexy number in the jazzy style of 'Chicago', and a muted trumpet quickly joined in, ad-libbing. The rest of the brass section followed, lifting the beat up another notch, and then came the strings, the violinists fingering their instruments together like fury to get the required vibrato.

Using a chair she picked up from the back of the stage as her partner, the girl began to boogie while continuing to sing. When Harry joined in at the piano, she picked up the tempo once more and turned it into a most provocative dance – wrapping her long legs round the chair in an erotic way. The other girls around the stage sang along with her, clapping their hands in a wild beat. It was an impromptu moment that lifted everyone's spirits – performers relieving the tension in the only way they knew…by performing.

Aaron watched it all, a huge smile growing on his face. When the dance ended, he called Andy Mallett across. "Andy – you've got the job now," he said simply.

While everything had been going on, Mario had jumped down in front of the bandsmen. He let them play themselves out, then called on the orchestra to calm down. "Great," he called. "But we don't want to go home, yet do we? Let's get on with some work – the overture to start with."

As the orchestra settled, Aaron went over to Suzi and muttered quietly to her. "I'll have a word with Danny and Harry to see if we can write a bit more in for you, eh?" he said. "More lines. More money. Good, uh?" Suzi kissed him on the cheek.

In the pit, Mario – who normally used a silver biro during rehearsals in place of a baton, which he was saving for the actual performances show during itself – now tapped the pen on his music stand. "OK – from the top…one, two…"

Standing in front of the orchestra, he began waving his arms. Danny watched, and as usual thought that Mario was as useless as most conductors, brandishing his arms round a lot with no one appearing to be following him. "He's got the beat all wrong…" he thought, "…the rhythm isn't there." But it sounded right – something was making it cohesive.

Although none of the musicians seeming to look at the conductor directly at any time, they professionally noted the movements of the biro and of the empty fingers of his left-hand wheedling and cajoling the lilt of the music and turning the individual sections of the orchestra into one entity.

Despite Danny's misgivings, the two rows of violinists, the girls all with long dark hair or shorter brown bobs, lifted their bows as one and then moved them backwards and forward in complete unison as if tied with an invisible string.

Opposite them were the double basses, and the players there held their bows high in right hands which balanced their bulky instruments as they plucked the strings with one finger of their left hand – the 'spare' fingers of the right hand almost dancing on the top of the strings to shorten or length them in time.

At the back of the orchestra, an oboist rested his bulky brass instrument either on a chair behind him or on his lap when he was not playing, chatting relentlessly to a trombonist next to him trying to make him laugh.

Mario began to sweat. "Piano – piano," he called. "No-o-o-o-w……glissando. Yeah…Robin 'ood, Robin 'ood."

Next morning, Matty turned up at the theatre as normal. Everyone was embarrassed as he said he wanted to see Aaron, but as the producer hadn't yet arrived he waited – despite the extreme discomfiture of everyone else because of the situation. Andy Mallett called on his mobile to tell Aaron what was happening, then made himself scarce.

Eventually, after half an hour or so, Aaron turned up. "What do you want?" he asked Matty brusquely.

"Well I was a bit hasty yesterday. A bad day. Maybe… maybe we could just forget what happened."

"And do what?"

Matty gave a nervous little laugh. "Carry on as normal?"

"With you directing?"

"Yes."

"There'll be a chill wind in hell before I give you another job," said Aaron. He turned to Danny, who was standing nearby. "A chill wind in hell – he he."

"Sounds good. Maybe we can use it in the script, eh……"

"No, no," said Aaron, laughing. "I've already plagiarised it – I heard it in a film somewhere!"

Aaron confessed a few days later that he was glad Matty had left because, he said, he had noticed how unsettling he had been and had wanted to get rid of him anyway. "I didn't like him as a fella – and it was an easy way out of the contract," he told the two writers. "A cheap way out."

With Andy in charge, anyway, things bucked up all round. He made few, if any, changes, but there was a much happier mood around the rehearsals as he told everyone that his job was really just a case of fine tuning. "You all know what you're doing anyway," he told the whole crew on his first day in charge. "All we've got to do now is keep at it until opening."

The immediate target was the full dress rehearsal, which Aaron planned for the day before the official opening night., He told the cast and crew to invite their friends and relatives to the run through – 'for free yet', he joked – and everyone now got on happily with the task of readying not only themselves but the whole ensemble for that night.

The major change now was to get some new lines for Suzi. It was easy, and Danny's fertile – and quick – imagination soon knocked out a 'romance' for her with one of the male dancers in one of the old music hall scenes. He and Harry wrote a special song for her as well – '*A Melody Is Just A Memory*'. "It's a nice song, easy to sing – but remember, every song in the show has to be a show on its own. Think of Abba – each song is a little musical on its own," said Danny.

Suzi and one of the dancers rehearsed her number on their own for a while, then slotted in effortlessly with the rest – although Suzi laughingly 'complained' to Aaron and Danny that her partner 'kisses as though he's practising the trumpet'!

Things went with a smile these days, as when one of the 'old-time acts', just an old song-and-dance man really, moved from the wings and slipped going front of stage, knocking over a chair. "Great," he muttered, jumping to his feet. He put the chair back upright, jumped over it, and looked out over the stalls. "That means I'll get to play this place again sometime," he said, self-consciously. Everyone laughed – another superstition.

By now, the excitement of a new musical opening had become tangible – both within the theatre world and among the public at large. But all too soon, it seemed to the two writers, it was the day before the night-before-opening dress rehearsal. Despite Aaron's encouraging remarks, both of them were going through the normal writers' agony of wondering whether their creation was any good – wondering whether others would like it as much as they did – could they have done better?

Danny and Harry arrived at the theatre early for what was virtually the last day of full rehearsal. Andy had called for one final complete run through, and the glittering backdrop and early scenery were already in place, – although they were now dark and drab without the stage lights to bring out the glitter. While waiting for the performers, Danny and Harry went on stage.

"How d'you think it'll go, old buddy?" asked Harry, his voice quiet.

"Yeah, no – it'll be alright," replied Danny. But inside, he was not quite so confident.

Soon, the actors, singers and dancers began drifting in, two or three at a time, stage hands and electricians busied themselves, setting up the lights and finally lowering the front curtains. At 7.45pm – the time planned for the real opening – Andy called for a start.

In many ways, although it's a cliché, it was just like all those scenes in films or plays about the theatre. Everyone backstage was flustered and nervous, Andy was tight-lipped, and Aaron tried to appear optimistic. It was a cliché coming true.

Then finally the run-through was over. All was now ready for the full-dress rehearsal in front of an audience the following night.

Act 14: The Dress Rehearsal

It was the day of the final dress rehearsal – the final run through before the opening night.

It was a brilliantly sunny day, and although they had the windows of Harry's flat wide open, admitting the noise and the fumes of nearby heavy traffic, it was still far too hot to really do anything. Danny and Harry lolled around drinking cold drinks, frequent cups of tea made by Lex, chatting aimlessly, and generally wasting time. Harry looked at his watch about every fifteen minutes.

Austin Irving had done a good job, and interest was high. Ticket sales were more than promising, and although a few ticket agencies called the theatre to say they couldn't fill their full quota, most others said they had sold out and needed more. There was an air of expectancy in the theatrical world, and newspapermen were still calling for interviews (and free drinks at the reception after the show), while out of work actors, actresses and their agents kept a continual flow of telephone calls to Aaron's office asking for freebie seats.

Late in the afternoon, Danny and Harry made their way to the theatre, to find Aaron waiting for them with Andy Mallett and Eddie Martin. Mario was unnecessarily busying himself in the pit with pieces of music, Freddie the Gaffer was moving lighting fractionally, and the rest of the crew and cast slowly came in.

There was a surreal air to everything. All the writing, the planning, the days of rehearsal were over – now it was almost time for the real thing.

As the performers were getting ready, Eddie and Andy stood quietly chatting next to the desk that stage manager Robbie Cadell had installed over to one side of the stage. There was a single dim light – yesterday's ghost light – shining down on the desk, and Robbie wore a headset and had microphones leading to the various dressing rooms and technical areas back stage so he could quietly call the cues as required or pass on any instructions or messages from the director, choreographer or producer during the show.

It was still very hot, but despite that a small crowd had gathered by the stage door in the alleyway at the rear. Toni Benito was the main reason for their being there, and most of those waiting were not theatre addicts but fans of his very popular (although not pop) music. Unlike many performers, Toni was in no way precious – as with almost all the others in the cast, you never heard him being overly show-biz'y. It showed how well Aaron had selected them all from the early days. He really was a good producer.

Toni had actually entered the theatre through the front foyer, but when he heard there were people waiting, he went back to the stage door and went into the passageway to speak to them. They loved it.

As Toni chatted, Julia joined him – and the crowd enjoyed it even more when some of the unknowns in the cast also stopped to talk to them, even asking them for autographs although they did not know who was who.

Inside, a few of the crew were chatting to wives or partners. The dress rehearsal was to be watched by friends and relatives, and as they started to enter the theatre Aaron waited in the foyer listening to the talk. A few knew him and nodded, for some reason, probably because they were on free tickets, unwilling to make direct eye contact, but most just thought he was someone connected with the theatre itself and ignored him. Aaron listened to them, taking it all in with an experienced attitude.

Everyone seemed to have exceedingly high expectations – but Aaron, like all those connected with the show, knew that their final comments would be tainted, possibly with faint praise.

This was almost the real thing. Almost, but not quite.

Although there was plenty of time before the start, the theatre began to fill early. Aaron moved from the foyer to stand at the back of the stalls, still trying to gauge the mood of the invited audience, while Harry joined Danny in the wings watching the dancers and others busy making their final preparations.

At one stage, Danny had nipped along to the general dressing room to watch the girls putting on their theatrical slap – their stage make-up. It was something that had fascinated him from the start of the theatre rehearsals, and he chatted easily to them – and they to him. They were quite happy to have him in the room with them as they began to apply the greasepaint and powder.

Most of them started with a base about one shade deeper than their natural skin tone, following that with grease sticks providing a heavier makeup. The most popular, he knew by now, were the light creamy ivory Leichner No 5 or peach rouge for the girls, while the boys usually opted for the brick red No 9 – something the girls found most unnatural for some reason.

They would start at the highest part of the cheekbone, shading with a darker colour or highlighting with a lighter one – blending it all in, then gently powder over the make-up, thickening the eyebrows if necessary, then carefully applying eye shadow – medium blue for the girls and brown for boys.

Many of the dancers had their own hand mirrors because they subconsciously believed in the old idea that it is bad luck to look over someone else's shoulder into the dressing room's own mirror as it linked them to the evil eye!

When they had finished, they turned on Danny and almost as one told him to leave the dressing room – it was time for them to change into their costumes. Danny protested, but it was no use – he had to leave!

Finally the dancers were ready, the girls enticingly, but skimpily, dressed in the tempting opening number spangles and tights that were at the same time alluring, entrancing, and somehow seedy. It was all part of the reality non-magic of backstage, but although he had seen the costumes so many times before Danny was fascinated as he watched them assemble in the wings, many holding well-used high wigs on heavily stained wig stands.

In many ways, although it is a cliché, the final hours were just like scenes from old films or plays about the theatre. Everyone backstage was flustered and nervous, Andy was tight-lipped, and Aaron was trying to appear optimistic. It was a cliché coming true.

They could hear the audience moving down the aisles and shuffling their way to their seats, and one of the young male dancers tried to take a look through a gap in the front curtains. "Don't do that," shouted Robbie as loudly as he dared, "It means curtains for the show."

"Overture and beginners…"

Soon they heard the instructions to cut the house lights, and the various performers already on stage for the opening number gave each other the traditional greetings – break a leg; be brilliant; enjoy yourself, have a marvellous time. None of them ever wished each other good luck – in theatrical terms that means you give your own luck away and shows the Gods you need intervention to get good fortune!

The old comedian, standing in place well before he was wanted, turned to one of the actresses. "Skin off your nose," he said. "Break a leg old timer," she grinned back.

Soon, the opening bars of the orchestra's introduction could be heard playing the various themes of the main show songs, interweaving them as a tapestry of sounds, sewing them together like a giant musical embroidery. The curtain rose slowly, almost majestically to reveal the black cavern of front of house. The show was under way.

As the run-through developed, both Danny and Harry's feelings of catastrophic deficiencies in their work grew – as song followed song, scene followed scene, neither could see why they had written the piece in the first place. After all the weeks of rehearsal, the whole presentation seemed not dream-like but nightmarish.

Carlos and his partner danced *'Long Ago And Far Away'* in silence, the comedian won a few laughs, the chorus girls got a smattering of applause – and even a few laughs when some of them missed steps.

It was a bad performance all round, and several things went wrong – far too many really. Despite the perfections of all the rehearsals, cues were missed by the stage hands, actors appeared – or did not appear – at the wrong moment to the consternation of Robbie sitting just off stage with his cue script, they stumbled over lines, lighting changes did not quite match the movement of the revolve, the dancers were not always exactly together in line. Only Toni and Julia Ross were completely right with the duet they had recorded. It won the biggest applause of the whole dress rehearsal –

> *'I'm so down I want the sun to set.*
> *I've lost the best girl I have ever met.*
> *I want the rain to fall,*
> *The snow to cool,*
> *On passion only she could get.*
> *It's been a bitter blow.*
> *I want the sun down low'.*

The final curtain eventually dropped and there was an almost audible sigh from everyone. "Hey, they missed a line," exclaimed Danny. It was all he could think of to say.

"No, they never say the last line of the script at the final dress rehearsal. It's unlucky," muttered Robbie.

"Yet another damned bit of mumbo jumbo," muttered Harry.

Aaron came backstage and joined the others. He had four bottles of champagne in his hands, and as he called for some plastic cups he also asked everyone to gather round – cast, crew and musicians. He was trying to smile, but his lips were pursed as his mind went over it all. "Remember, they always say that a bad dress rehearsal means a good opening night," he said as he poured the champers and began handing the cups out. "A good opening night."

"Maybe, but have you ever known a first night that's come up to expectations?" asked Eddie Martin. "Isn't it always a let-down?"

Aaron smiled at him, but his apparent optimism fooled no one. "Well, I'm taking this as our dress rehearsal," he added. "That means tomorrow's opening is going to be just fine. Just fine."

All the seniors started discussing what had gone wrong. "Carlos and the girl don't come over, do they?" said Danny. "The dance just doesn't work – it's too remote. It seemed so...so...right when I saw it in the club – but it's just too intimate for a big stage. I was wrong." The dance had been part of his initial inspiration for the show.

They decided to cut that scene and make a few more slight adjustments the next day. Finally, the curtain was raised up again, the stage lights went down, and as the house lights came on the stage hands got things ready for the opening of the following night's opening night. As they worked, the musicians turned their attention to their families and home life while backstage, the actors, singers and dancers – unnaturally quiet after the bad performance – cleaned the make-up from their faces and changed into their usual untidy street clothing.

In the old phrase, they were 'leaving their glamour hanging in the dressing room'.

Before too long, Robbie Cadell went round hurrying the stragglers along, the stage doorman locked up and pulled a switch, all that remained was the dark theatre – dark except for the little ghost light moved back from Robbie's desk at the side to centre stage.

Danny and Harry picked up Lex, and although she tried to cheer them both the two writers were still restrained and withdrawn, knowing that ahead of them, the next day, they both had to face up to the ultimate results of their ideas and efforts. It was to be the day of the opening.

Everyone said their despondent goodbyes, and Harry, Danny and Lex went to a late-night bar for a conciliatory drink. "Anyway, we're nearly there now," said Danny. "Nothing we can do right now – tomorrow's another day. The opening of the show – hey, come on you guys it's our show."

"Sure it is," replied Harry.

"It's been a long road. I can't believe we're nearly there."

"I've still got that queasy feeling," said Harry. "I was so sure, but now…well, now there're more doubts than ever."

"But it's a show. Our show," repeated Danny, revealing more confidence by the moment, although he probably didn't feel it as much as he showed it. "Y'know, I'm getting this feeling that maybe Aaron was right. I felt lousy before, but now…well, I think, hope, it's going to work."

"And it's going on in just a few hours. Just what we always planned……"

Harry nodded. "Yeah. But mate, it'll never be the same again no matter what happens," he said after a long pause. "We won't just be able to just write songs like we used to – because we wanted to – after this we're going to have to write songs to order – for shows."

"But that's what we always wanted to do."

"I know, but it'll be different."

"But better."

Harry took it as a question. "Will it be better?" he asked. "I dunno."

"Sure it will," said Lex.

Danny pursed his lips in his typical way. "Yeah. It's all going to take off. What we've worked for…"

He pulled nervously at a piece of hard skin in the corner of the nail of his right thumb, and small pieces of white dropped onto the table. He grinned suddenly. "Ye-eah – it's our show, and it's about to take off," he said.

Harry and Lex finished their drinks and said their goodbyes. Danny watched them make for the street, then turned back to the barman and ordered another drink.

It had been a long day. A very long day. He knew, as did Harry although neither had said anything to the other, that the show was no longer theirs – it would soon belong to the public. It was like giving up a child.

Act 15: Opening Night

Danny had gone on from the bar to a small jazz club he knew in south London, and had met up with a group of musicians and stayed out drinking with them until the early hours. He hadn't got home until around four in the morning – well, to Harry's home in fact, because in his drunken state he had given the taxi driver Harry's address, and had used his own key to let himself in quietly when he got there.

Lex found him flat out on the couch when she got up at eight o'clock, but it was not until Harry woke up at around half past nine that she actually roused Danny. While she made coffee, Danny tried to recall the events of the night before for his partner.

When Lex brought in the three mugs they all sat around chatting, trying hard to skirt round the whole idea of the show. Lex began teasing Danny for sleeping in Harry's apartment when his own was so close.

"Can't you two ever make a move without the other one being there?" she asked.

"No, we're joined at the hip," retorted Danny with a smile. He playfully put his arm around Harry's shoulders. "We just...like...each...other," he said, obviously.

In due course, Danny went off to his own flat to change into something a little less dishevelled than the clothes he had slept in. When he returned about an hour later, he and Harry went to the theatre to make the adjustments from the night before. Aaron was waiting for them, and the work was soon completed – just writing around the removal of the Carlos dance and cutting a few choruses of some of the other songs. It would not take much to implement them, and they did not feel it necessary to call anyone else in early.

Danny and Harry returned to Camden Hill Road, where Lex prepared a hefty snack for them. Harry was not hungry, he still had fears and reservations underneath it all, but while Lex urged him to eat Danny tackled his food with gusto. He seemed far more bubbly, far more his usual self.

Harry managed to hide his feelings for a while, until after the meal he could not hold on. "I just wish I could get rid of this feeling that we could have done more," he said, solemnly.

"What – you mean after last night?" asked Danny.

"It's not only that, mate. It's just a feeling…"

"About what?"

"About the whole show. There's something – well, I've got a nagging feeling that maybe the whole thing is wrong."

"What d'you mean? The basic idea?"

"No, it's not that." Harry struggled with words. "I know there's a place for an old-fashioned musical like ours – but… but, well you know what it's like. There's always that flat feeling when you've finished, and you can't do any more."

"You always say that."

"Yeah – I'm just a creature of habit. But I always have this feeling when I've finished writing something. I just can't put it in perspective."

"Look, let me put you right old matey," said Danny. "We've got to be optimistic – we've written a good show, good music…and in any case, it's too late to change anything now. Maybe we'll have to do some work if it doesn't gel with an outside audience…"

"Yeah, but…"

"No buts," went on Danny. "Aaron's got some good acts and some elegant dance numbers –"

"Boys, boys," interrupted Lex. "The show's fine. It's got that feel-good factor."

"Even after last night?" Harry persisted.

"That was just a funny old audience," said Danny. "It wasn't Joe Public. Ordinary people always love good music, good singing, good dancing."

"You really think so?" asked Harry. Danny nodded. "Sure," he said.

Later in the afternoon, Danny went back to his own flat to collect his clothes for the dress rehearsal, taking them back to Harry's to change – he had surprisingly allowed himself to be persuaded to wear a formal dinner jacket, and when Lex came out of the bedroom she found him standing there with his dress shirt on, his black tie in place, and in his underpants. He had bright yellow socks, one pulled up and the other rumpled around his ankle. His hair was unruly.

Lex herself was wearing a shimmering, eye-catching, figure-hugging light blue gown that complemented her long honey blonde hair and looked superb. Danny commented on it, noting that she had slimmed back to her former self, and Harry looked on proudly as he stood in the bedroom doorway watching her silky movements in the tight-fitting dress. "Come on, Danny," she said, smiling, handing Danny his trousers. "Put these on. And don't forget – black socks. Black."

Danny did as he was told, and quickly finished dressing, brushing his hair just as the hire car Aaron had arranged to take them to the theatre arrived. He wore his dress suit well, and looked quite at ease with a bow tie.

They arrived at the theatre almost two hours before the show was due to start. As the car drew up outside, there was no hint of what lay ahead – the building was just waiting for the opening, the show's beginning. For now, it was empty – no lights outside, and inside just the usual single lamp on stage and a couple of safety lights in the auditorium.

Andy Mallett and Eddie Martin were already backstage, but the three of them were only outside the locked front doors for a few minutes before Aaron arrived with his wife. They stayed in the foyer chatting somewhat anxiously about the evening ahead.

Toni arrived with Julia Ross on his arm about an hour before the show, entering through the foyer rather than the stage door because that as where the photographers were waiting. Julia looked even better than Lex – she was also dressed stunningly for the occasion in a glamorous vivid red off-the-shoulder designer gown that showed a lot of flesh, and both she and Toni knew the snappers would take full advantage of it all.

A tabloid paper reporter standing close by noticed. "Is this A ROMANCE?" he asked. "He actually said the word in capitals – headline capitals."

Both the stars just smiled – knowing smiles.

By now, Danny had disappeared backstage. Harry told Lex he had probably gone to chat up the girls, but they found him shortly afterwards, fast asleep on a prop sofa in the wings as the pre-show hustle and bustle continued around him. The mix of nerves, excitement and the exertions of the previous night had caught up with him.

Harry woke him as Mario and the orchestra slowly started to move into the pit. It was quite different to all the rehearsals and run-throughs, this time they were all uniformly dressed – the men in dinner jackets, the women in dark skirts and white blouses. It was a Mario rule.

There was the usual cacophony of sound as the various instruments were tuned. The musicians blew and twanged, banged and blew – chatting lightly to each other between times. Unlike the mood behind the plush stage curtains, they were all very relaxed – just another night playing music.

Backstage it was different. Nervous performers and stagehands were running around in a seemingly haphazard way, Andy and Eddie tried to look as if they were not there, and Robbie Cadell was trying to coordinate things but apparently being overwhelmed by all that was happening. It seemed chaotic, but there was a certain realistic inevitability about it all.

Aaron just drifted around among the pandemonium, soothing, calming, smiling like a grandfather. "Remember – I've never erred…except on the side of expensive," he joked.

Despite it all, there was a general air of buoyancy regardless of the previous day's disastrous dress rehearsal performance – an optimism as in the early rehearsals and when the actors finally got into the theatre itself.

From the stage, they could all hear the dulled sound of the audience chattering coming through the curtain as they took their seats, a curtain lush and velvety from the front but with a ragged, torn lining stage-side.

With ten minutes to curtain up, Aaron left to take up his usual position at the back of the stalls to listen to the audience. He gave everyone a final encouraging smile.

The dancers for the opening sequence waited in the corridor outside their dressing rooms – the girls highly made up and in their scanty costumes, all spangles, sequins, sparkle and fishnet stockings; the boys in top hat, white tie and tails – all looking very different to the people who had turned up for the weeks of rehearsals in jeans and sloppy tops.

***

Every one of them was a stunning-looking girl or an Adonis, but as the cluster of chorus girls and boys walked calmly onto the stage behind the drawn curtain most of them had a hard line of anxiety sketched on their beautiful features.

Opening night of a new show. Their living, their rent, their immediate future depended on how they were received.

As they slowly lined up, fiddling with shoulder straps, adjusting fishnet stocking seams, patting hair into place, wiping the odd corner of lipstick smooth, adjusting white tie and tails, and generally getting themselves prepared, they could hear the audience shuffling, coughing, and chattering softly through the closed heavy theatrical curtains.

Heavy stage lights flashed on, and as they checked the line and linked arms some of the girls looked down and made sure their stomachs were drawn in. One or two coughed lightly showing more nervous tension, but in the main they were silent. Front of house, the audience was almost in place. The photographers had snapped irreverently at any of the big-bosomed minor starlets who had turned up to pose, bigger name actors and actresses who had tried – not very hard – to slip by unnoticed, but turned on the smiles when the cameras focussed, and people who were famous for being famous tried to attract attention.

A new show. A big, glamorous musical.

On the other side, front of house, the orchestra was already in place, and as the house lights dimmed only the illuminations above the musicians' stands broke the dark around the closed stage. The audience quietened down, and as the conductor slipped onto his stand in front of them there was a smattering of half-hearted applause. He raised his baton, and the first notes of the overture began to fill the giant auditorium. The audience quietened down.

The music the dancers had drilled to so well during rehearsals came through the curtain – soft at first, then growing loud, strident, blaring, but always tuneful. "Magic, those first notes of a new show," muttered the producer to himself.

In the wings, Danny Grover and Harry McIntyre watched and waited even more fearfully than the girls. It was their music. Their songs. Their first show.

After years of dreaming, years of working to find a way of bringing back the elegance and sounds of the great days of the big stage musical, this was their night. A packed audience was waiting with anticipation – would they like this rummage into stylish nostalgia?

Danny looked at the girls – winking at the nearest, trying not to show the tension he felt. "After the show," he mouthed at her. The girl frowned, and ignored him, turning to look the other way along the long line of other chorus girls. Danny shrugged. After a moment, the girl glanced back at him. "See you later?" he whispered again.

The girl shook her head slightly. She looked away again, down the line of other girls, still frowning but smiling inside.

There was an almost physical feeling of excitement. Tension. Edginess. Anxiety. Everyone waiting for curtain up felt they could touch it.

Danny himself picked at a loose piece of fading gilt from the side of the proscenium arch. Both he and Harry were also nervously expectant... Harry obviously edgy, but Danny trying hard to be his usual flippant self.

He carried on absent-mindedly picking at the gilt, all the time looking out almost vacantly across the stage.

The stage manager, sitting at a table just off stage in the wings on the opposite side of the stage to Danny and Harry, waited for an instruction through a set of earphones.

A props man ran across in front of the chorus line to pick up some small object he had spotted on stage, as the overture switched to the dulcet tones of the big romantic number.

The dancers settled down, the girls leaning their chins on their right shoulders as the stage manager gave the nod to get them ready to dance. With the music picking up speed again on the other side of the still-lowered drape, they got a second nod, then a thumbs up – and as they started to kick their legs up in unison, the boys behind them began swaying from side to side in rhythm.

By now, Danny was picking at a loose bit of skin on his right thumb. Then he rubbed an itch behind his left ear, wrinkling his forehead.

Then, slowly, the curtain began to rise, and the audience got its first glimpse of the dancers. A smooth, regimented, sexy, high-kicking line of girls, their traditional show costumes swirling up and gyrating sexily as they tapped and high kicked for all they were worth. The second row looking like a line of Fred Astaires. A spontaneous burst of applause greeted the long-forgotten sight of an old-fashioned chorus line in full swing.

"Hey, they're playing OUR song," said Danny...